MEL HARRISON

The Ambassador is Missing

An Alex Boyd Thriller

HALLARD
PRESS

THE AMBASSADOR IS MISSING Copyright © 2020   Mel Harrison
All rights reserved.

Editor: Hallard Press LLC/Paula F. Howard
Cover Design by Hallard Press LLC/John W Prince
Page Design, Typography & Production by Hallard Press LLC/John W Prince

Published by Hallard Press LLC.
www.HallardPress.com   Info@HallardPress.com   352-775-1143

Bulk copies of this book can be ordered at Info@HallardPress.com

Printed in the United States of America   .

ISBN: 978-1-951188-07-8

TESTIMONIALS

It is a pleasure to add my endorsement for the second book featuring the exploits of Diplomatic Security Regional Security Officer, Alex Boyd.

Mel Harrison, author, has produced another enjoyable read based on his own extensive knowledge of the embassy security environment. Being set in Rome, which was my first overseas post, made this story that much more fun to read. I am happy to say my time in Rome was much less traumatic than Alex Boyd's trials and challenges.

While this is a work of fiction, the situations brought to life in the book are based on the exciting world of embassy security and will keep your interest to the end.

Well done, Mel.

—*Greg Bujac, former Director of the Diplomatic Security Service and Principal Deputy Assistant Secretary of State for Diplomatic Security*

"*The Ambassador is Missing* is told from the eyes of a man who has been in the trenches of protecting American diplomats for decades. You won't be disappointed."

—*Fred Burton, former State Department special agent and New York Times best-selling author*

DEDICATION

This novel is dedicated to the brave and talented men and women of the Diplomatic Security Service who routinely put themselves in harm's way to keep those who carry out America's foreign policy safe from harm or injury.

Whether protecting dignitaries, conducting criminal investigations, ensuring our embassies are safe from espionage and other threats, or leading US Marines in battle against terrorist attacks on our facilities, they serve so that others may remain safe.

Personnel and Acronyms

THE AMERICANS

At The Embassy

Ambassador
Anthony Scarmatti
* Top authority at any embassy worldwide
* All civilian and military agencies within the embassy report to Ambassador

---

Deputy Chief of Mission (DCM)
Alden Chandler
* Ambassador's deputy
* All agencies report through the DCM to the Ambassador

Regional Security Officer (RSO)
Alex Boyd, Senior RSO
Joe Roberts, Deputy RSO
George Cefalu, Assistant RSO
* Special Agents with the Diplomatic Security Service
* Responsible for Embassy Security
* Skilled in VIP Protection, physical security, criminal investigations, and they lead the Marine Security Guards

---

Security Engineering Officer (SEO)
Samantha (Sam) Carson
* Responsible for electronic Countermeasures
* Installation of electronic security equipment and repair of same

---

Embassy Press Affairs Officer
Rachel Smith
* Follows US and Italian media
* Explains US policies to local media and crafts the US image to the Italian public
*Acts as Embassy spokeswoman

Management Counselor
Charlotte Eaton
* Senior State Department administrative officer in the embassy

FBI Legal Attache (Legatt)
Mark Terranova
* Embassy liaison position for FBI
*FBI interface with Italian legal authorities

CIA Station Chief
Carter Ambrose
*Responsible for covert intelligence collection and liaison with Italian intelligence service
* Supported by other CIA case officers

Political Counselor
Ames Burnham
* Responsible for embassy political reporting and analysis

Incident Response Team (IRT)

Washington based support team to help Embassies resolve crises
Head of the IRT and Coordinator for Counter-Terrorism in the State Department
Ambassador Charles Van Camp
* Usually a career State Department political officer

Senior FBI Agent on the IRT
John Reynolds

Assistant Secretary of State for European Affairs,
Department of State, Washington, DC
Ambassador Archibald Watson
* Responsible for European political policy for the US Government

Director of Diplomatic Security,
Washington, DC
Jim Riley
Career Diplomatic Security Special Agent

The titles of Italian police ranks have been "Americanized" for ease of understanding.

THE ITALIANS

Italian Minister of Foreign Affairs
Foreign Minister (no name given)
Head of the Ministry of Foreign Affairs
and part of the Italian Government Cabinet

Italian Deputy Minister of the Interior
Umberto Ferrara
Oversees the *Polizia di Stato*

Polizia di Stato
General Raffaele Ghiberti
National Director who reports to the Italian Ministry of the Interior

---

Nucleo Operativo Centrale di Sicurezza (NOCS)
Police Hostage Rescue Unit
Colonel Vitttore Adriani, Commander
Captain Paolo Capelli, Squadron leader in the NOCS
Captain Nino Agostino, Squadron leader in the NOCS
Lt. Guido Campanelli, Chief of Surveillance for NOCS

Intelligence officer, Polizia di Stato
Captain Gina Bianchi
In charge of Intelligence Reporting and Crime Collection Evidence

---

Chief Investigating officer, Polizia di Stato
Colonel Carlo Vicencia
In charge of the Scarmatti Kidnapping Case

The Carabinieri
National Police, but reports to the Italian Ministry of Defense
General Romano

New Red Brigade
Terrorist Organization
Titular Head
Cosimo di Luca
Terrorist

Table of Contents

Chapter 1

KIDNAPPED

The driver took a final drag on the cigarette between his finger and thumb, then flipped the butt out the window of a white Fiat sedan. Parked down the street from the American Ambassador's residence in Rome, four of them were waiting for Ambassador Anthony Scarmatti to leave his home. It wasn't a social call.

The Ambassador, his wife Francesca, and Charlotte Eaton, embassy management counselor, were just leaving mid-morning. The men watched the heavy residence gates open and the black Ford Mondeo slowly pull out into traffic.

The four in the Fiat had pledged their loyalty to the New Red Brigade. Two more terrorists were sitting on motorcycles at each end of the block. They all saw the vehicle leaving, but, it took a brief moment for the them to realize the Scarmattis were now passengers because the woman had arrived alone.

"Red One to Red Two and Red Three, the target is onboard. Don't crowd the target," the lead terrorist in the Fiat called over his walkie-talkie.

Red Two and Red Three on motorcycles acknowledged.

Five minutes later, as Eaton pulled over to the curb in front of her apartment building, Red One said, "We will pass them by. Red Two and Three stay behind them."

"Affirmative."

All six terrorists watched and waited as Eaton got out of the car. They saw Anthony Scarmatti shake hands with her, while Francesca gave her a warm embrace. When Eaton entered her building, the Ambassador got behind the wheel and Francesca moved into the front passenger seat. Within seconds, the Ambassador merged the car into traffic.

Ambassador Scarmatti skillfully maneuvered in and out of Rome's chaotic traffic until he connected with the autostrada heading north. The Fiat and two motorcycles followed a safe distance behind. The terrorist leader in the Fiat used his mobile to call Cosimo di Luca.

"We are headed toward Orvieto as expected."

"Excellent. You know what to do. Do not leave any witnesses alive if you are seen," di Luca ordered. "I will notify the safe-house to expect you."

Communication among the terrorists was kept to a minimum. Driving for an hour, the Fiat and motorcycles took turns staying within sight of the Ambassador; alternatively falling back or passing him. Then at the Orvieto exit on the autostrada, they all followed the Ambassador's car off the main road, but not too closely.

Skillfully, the Ambassador snaked through winding streets until he found a parking space in a quiet, secluded area not far from the great cathedral. On one side was a masonry office building with few windows; being Sunday, no one was working. The other side of the street was lined with houses, each having a high wall and purple-flowering wisteria hanging vines, all blocking any view of the street.

The two motorcycles passed the Ambassador, slowing to the

side of the road ten meters in front of the Scarmattis parked car. Blocking the street directly behind the Ambassador's vehicle was the Fiat. All the men quickly put on nylon masks. As soon as the Ambassador and his wife were out of the car, the terrorists struck, rushing the pair with pistols drawn; one put the barrel of his pistol to Francesca's head.

"Cooperate or I will shoot her," he yelled at the Ambassador, pushing the gun harder against Francesca's ear, causing her to cry out.

Ambassador Scarmatti's eyes flashed back and forth among the kidnappers and his wife. For the first time in his life he was at a loss for words. One kidnapper spun him around and forced his hands behind his back; placing plastic flex-cuffs on the Ambassador's wrists and tape over his mouth. Once he was secure, they did the same thing to Francesca. Then a kidnapper pulled Scarmatti's car keys from his pocket. Mere seconds passed before they roughly shoved the husband and wife into the trunk of the Fiat, slamming it shut. Only then, did the kidnappers take off their nylon masks.

One man, who had arrived in the Fiat, got behind the wheel of the Ambassador's car and drove off, followed by a single motorcycle. The Fiat and remaining motorcycle left Orvieto via the A-1 autostrada heading north toward Bologna.

The entire snatch was accomplished in under one minute, and no one in town saw a thing.

Chapter 2

A FEW MONTHS EARLIER

Special Agent Alex Boyd thought a post in Rome would be paradise after living three years in Islamabad, Pakistan. His Diplomatic Security Service assignment there had found him thwarting an attack on the American Embassy and killing vicious terrorists at close quarters while defending the Ambassador's residence. So, he figured this new assignment in Italy should be a cakewalk.

But he was wrong, dead wrong.

Sitting in the grandest embassy office he had ever seen, Alex stared at a high ceiling decorated with colorful frescoes of Italian scenes and admiring crown molding painted in gold leaf. Two sets of tall French windows were adorned with long silk drapes of a deep royal blue. This spectacular room was just an outer office for the Deputy Chief of Mission (DCM) located in the U.S. Embassy in Rome. The building was widely known to Italians as *Palazzo Margherita*.

Now on his very first day of his new assignment, Alex was waiting to see Alden Chandler, DCM and second in command at the Embassy. He had already been sitting for fifteen minutes. Now tapping his fingers against the arm rest of a leather chair, he wondered what the hell was taking so long. The DCM's inner doors were open, so Alex knew he wasn't on the phone or with another visitor.

"How was your Italian language training in Washington?" Liz Waters, secretary to the DCM, asked while interrupting his thoughts.

"I enjoyed it. I already speak French and Spanish, so I found the grammar similar," Alex said. He also spoke decent Arabic as a result of living in Cairo for a few years as a young teenager but decided that wasn't relevant to her question.

Her phone buzzed; she answered.

"The DCM will see you now."

Alden Chandler rose from behind his uncluttered desk as Alex walked in. They grasped hands. Alex's grip was firm, but he felt Chandler's grip rather weak. At fifty-five years of age, Chandler was twenty years senior to Alex, with thinning brown and grey hair. He wore round tortoise-shell glasses, was a bit overweight, and stood some five feet-ten inches tall, four inches shorter than Alex. Chandler motioned him over to a set of sofas near the window.

"Welcome to Rome. Is this your first time here?"

"No, Sir. I've traveled here once before with the Secretary of State."

"Oh, you mean when you were on his protective detail." Chandler's tone implied such work was akin to being a knuckle-dragger.

Alex, slightly offended by the comment, remained cool.

"Yes, sir. I've heard you served in Rome previously."

"Yes, I have, twice: Once as a young officer in the Consular Section, then I returned many years later as the Political Counselor."

"What wonderful opportunities those must have been," Alex smiled cordially.

"Indeed," Chandler answered without elaboration or emotion.

Damn, this man is turning a courtesy call into an ordeal, Alex thought.

"I'm really looking forward to contributing to the Mission," Alex said, using typical Foreign Service bullshit jargon expected by all, and occasionally believed by some. He noted the DCM nervously tapping his left foot but made no comment.

"Where else have you served?" Alex asked, although he had researched Chandler in advance and knew the answer.

"Oh, the usual round of posts," feigning boredom. "I served in Madrid, Brussels, and *Vienna*," with an uncomfortable emphasis on Vienna.

Alden Chandler paused to let this sink in.

"I know you are joining us from Islamabad, and you've had assignments in Buenos Aires and Tunis as the Regional Security Officer. I think, however, you'll find Rome to be quite different."

Chandler was being pompous, but Alex wasn't averse to playing mind games, at least a little.

"Well, culturally, Italy certainly has an abundance of things to do. I hope to expand my knowledge of the Renaissance, and of the Gothic period while I'm here," giving a faint smile, seeing Chandler blink twice, as if he didn't expect a Regional Security Officer to have any interest in such things. Alex loved being a wise ass.

"But in terms of my liaison with the police and making sure the Embassy is prepared for all security contingencies, I doubt there'll be much difference between embassies in different geographic bureaus."

Alex knew full well, however, even though it was the mid-1990s, Foreign Service Officers in Europe had a different attitude from those serving in the Middle East; the former believing it a crisis when the local boutique grocery ran out of *foie gras* and vintage wine, while in the Middle East, officers knew a crisis happened when you ran out of ammunition.

Chandler's eyes focused with intensity on Alex's face. His hands gripped the arm rests tighter, and he leaned forward.

"In Europe we have a clear chain of command. This is not cowboy-land, Mr. Boyd. Let me remove any doubt you may have. I'm a friend of Winston Hargrove, who worked for me in Vienna. He was a *fine* officer, but you *destroyed* his career in Islamabad. You were under his chain of command during the attack when you disobeyed his direct order to have the Marines refrain from using deadly force."

"Hargrove might have been a good Political Officer in Europe," Alex replied, surprised by Chandler's vehemence. "But his judgment in Islamabad was dangerously flawed, and his actions were unprofessional. As you know, the Ambassador agreed with me, and sent Hargrove back to Washington prematurely, while the Accountability Review Board specifically stated Hargrove's actions were negligent, incompetent, and dangerous while the Embassy was under terrorist attack."

"That's only because you failed to follow the chain of command when Hargrove was the senior man on the scene."

"With all due respect," Alex replied, "you weren't there when five thousand demonstrators rioted at the Embassy compound, then ten highly-trained terrorists assaulted the Embassy and five more terrorists attacked the Ambassador's residence on the same compound. They'd already hit us with two rocket-propelled grenades when Hargrove tried to interfere."

"I understood he told you to retreat to a safer location in the building."

"You've been misinformed. I was in communication with the Ambassador and the DCM up until the point when the first RPG hit the Embassy. And, that so-called 'safer place' in the Embassy, had been destroyed by the first RPG."

"Listen to me Boyd," Chandler said, leaning forward in his seat and pointing a finger at him. "You report to me here in Rome. Remember, I'm watching you *very carefully*. Try anything against my wishes and I'll send your ass back to Washington. Is that clear?"

"Perfectly clear."

They both rose. It was obvious that Chandler was not going to extend his hand for Alex to shake. The meeting was definitely over, yet he was certain he hadn't heard the last from Deputy Chief of Mission Alden Chandler.

A booming voice bellowed across the reception area as Alex left the DCM's office and was about to bid the secretary goodbye.

"Alex! I'm glad to see you've finally arrived," Ambassador Anthony Scarmatti called over to Alex with warmth and surprise.

Chandler, standing next to Alex, looked as if he had just choked on a Sardinian olive pit. With somewhat awkward short, choppy steps, Chandler followed Alex's long strides across the room as Alex reached out to shake the Ambassador's hand. Chandler stood next to both men, his mouth gaping open.

"You know each other?" Chandler asked.

"You bet, Alden," Ambassador Scarmatti replied grinning. "We met in Washington, when I had my confirmation hearings. While I was waiting for the Senate to get its act together, Diplomatic Security gave me the usual dog and pony show and asked Alex to break out of language training to sit in on the briefings. He was of immense help to me."

"How fortuitous," Chandler sniped, as he adjusted the knot on his tie.

"Alex, come into my office," Scarmatti said

"Yes, sir," Alex smiled, looking back over his shoulder at Chandler who hustled behind, not wanting to be left out.

Walking over to a pair of gold-colored upholstered chairs and a sofa at one end of a long opulent room with crystal chandeliers, Ambassador Scarmatti addressed Alex.

"I thought we agreed in Washington you'd just call me Tony,

unless we're in a formal setting," Ambassador Scarmatti said.

"Yes, sir… I mean Tony." Alex maintained his even smile. Chandler seemed to be having an attack of acid reflux.

"I guess you haven't had time to settle in yet," Scarmatti stated.

"Yes, and no. My air freight should be here later this week. But Rachel and I will be living together in her apartment, so the furnishings are already in place."

"Excellent. By the way, Rachel's doing a great job here as Press Officer. Alden, did I tell you both Rachel and I went to UCLA? Of course, I'm a lot older. I was years ahead of her, but she got her undergrad degree there, and I got my MBA." Chandler managed an uncomfortable, small grin.

Alex really liked Ambassador Scarmatti. He was a fifty-year old self-made man, a real estate developer from Los Angeles, with black, thick and wavy hair. He stood around six feet tall and wore rectangular, silver-framed glasses, which complimented his trim physique. Alex knew he had contributed big bucks to the current President's election campaign.

Unlike many Italian Americans, whose Italian often had a pronounced Sicilian accent, not favored by Roman elites, Scarmatti's Italian was polished, having spent his junior college year in Florence. His frequent business dealings in Milan over the years had also helped hone his language skills.

"Rachel must be glad you're finally here," Scarmatti said.

"You're not kidding, Tony. We both missed each other terribly while I was studying Italian in Washington. She only needed a short refresher course because she already spoke the language." Alex paused briefly. "You know, Tony, we went through a lot together in Pakistan."

"I know, Alex. The Director of Diplomatic Security said you and Rachel distinguished yourselves there."

Alex glanced at Chandler, who was obviously trying to repress a

THE AMBASSADOR IS MISSING

grimace at Alex's use of the familiar 'Tony.' Scarmatti's remark about his performance in Islamabad hit home as well.

"Do you know Rachel and Francesca play tennis almost every week at the Residence?"

"Yes, I do. Rachel told me Francesca's a pretty good player and really enjoys their friendship. She said they've known each other for years having played tennis against one another in Los Angeles tournaments."

Francesca was Scarmatti's second wife and considerably younger than the Ambassador. An accomplished businesswoman, she had owned a successful catering company to the stars in Los Angeles before moving with him to Rome.

"Do you mind my asking a security question, Tony?"

"Not at all."

"In Washington, you expressed a desire to have as much freedom as possible in Rome. How's it working out with your Italian police bodyguards?"

"Well, I think they're great. They're always present wherever I go. But, maybe, they don't need to be so omnipresent."

Alden Chandler entered the conversation.

"You know, Alex, no one has ever tried to attack or kidnap an American Ambassador in Italy. Maybe you could relax his coverage from time to time," Chandler looked at the Ambassador, hoping he was pleased with this suggestion.

"Well, I'll certainly review the protection we have in place, but I don't want to make any promises. Not only are we facing a worldwide threat from our Arab and Persian friends, but the old Italian Red Brigade had a history of kidnapping VIPs. As I'm sure you'll recall, in 1982 they kidnapped the American Army commander, General Dozier. In 1984, they assassinated Leamon Hunt, an American diplomat, who was the Director General of the Sinai Multinational Force and Observers, based here in Rome. They also kidnapped, and killed, the former Italian Prime Minister, Aldo Moro, not far from here, while he was protected by the police."

"But as you said," Chandler stated, "that was the *old* Red Brigade, and they're now either in jail or dead."

"True," Alex retorted, "but there's a new organization. They call themselves The New Red Brigade, trying to emulate the older version. They've already robbed banks, set off bombs, and may be growing in strength. Their issues are the same as with the old bunch, typical left-wing extremist views on the evils of capitalism and the greatness of Marxism."

"Okay, okay, I get the message," Scarmatti said, holding up his hands as if to say, 'enough already'. "But please just look at whether I can get a little leeway, if only on the weekends."

"I'll examine it, Tony. I can assure you."

Alex knew in his heart that he wouldn't reduce the Ambassador's protection at all.

Chapter 3

THE BANK ROBBERY

Leaving the Ambassador's suite, Alex admired the gorgeous sixteenth-century paintings hanging on the corridor's marble walls. Ceilings were eighteen feet high, covered with more beautiful frescoes. All this priceless art was inherited by the Embassy when buying the building after the Second World War. He glanced at everything but was deep in thought.

Taking the elevator to the ground floor, he walked down the hallway to his new office. Upon opening the door, he saw the familiar and smiling face of Nancy Williams, his secretary who had been stationed with him in Islamabad during the terrorist attacks.

"Alex, so good to see you again! How did the meeting go?" she asked.

"Incredibly bad. Turns out Chandler is a close friend of Winston Hargrove."

"That same jerk in Pakistan, who almost got us killed?" Nancy groaned when he nodded.

"I'll tell you about the meeting after I go across the street to the BNL bank. I want to open a checking account; should take about thirty minutes. Let the rest of the team know we'll have a staff meeting when I get back."

"You got it. But I think you better count on the bank taking at least an hour. This is Italy, after all."

He smiled and waved as he left.

Nancy was probably right. In fact, she was always right.

Sliding on his heavy Barbour against the January cold and rain, Alex headed across the street to the imposing marbled entrance of the BNL. Motorcycles and little Fiats whizzed passed him as he deftly navigated the crossing. Car horns blew, although not necessarily at him. The cacophony of sounds on a typical Roman street was staggering.

The enormous bank lobby was perhaps fifty meters long by fifty meters wide. Because the bank was accustomed to opening accounts for American diplomats, they finished Alex's paperwork in a record-setting forty-five minutes. He was very pleased.

Leaving the private cubicle of the account manager, Alex noticed an exceptionally well-dressed, silver-haired older gentleman, chatting amicably in the lobby with someone Alex presumed to be the bank manager. Standing next to the older gentleman was a rather large young man dressed in a dark suit. He had a bulge under his jacket and was wearing an earpiece; Alex immediately identified him as a bodyguard.

"*Buon giorno,*" Alex said, nodding at the bodyguard as he passed.

"*Buon giorno e lei,*" the bodyguard responded amicably, yet stayed serious.

Five meters further on was an overweight, uniformed bank guard observing the lobby and some twenty customers waiting in lines to see the tellers.

Just as Alex passed the bodyguard, the tranquil scene suddenly turned into complete chaos. Three men entered the bank lobby with two of them pulling double-barreled, sawed-off shotguns from inside their long trench coats. The third man pulled a pistol and began yelling.

"Everyone raise your hands and stand still," he yelled in Italian while waving his gun. The first man ran to the banker windows, pointing his shotgun at the tellers.

"Give me all the money behind the counter," he screamed at one employee.

The second robber covered the bank guard with his shotgun, while the third man swiftly moved in Alex's direction next to the silver-haired older gentleman, and his bodyguard. He pointed his pistol at Alex, perhaps instinctively recognizing him as a potential threat.

But Alex was unarmed, not having had time to retrieve his own pistol from the office safe on his first morning in the Embassy. Now he could only hope the hold-up might end without violence as tellers filled a large bag with money.

Foolishly, the uniformed guard tried to draw his gun. The second robber blasted him point blank, sending the guard sprawling to the floor. The noise from the shotgun roared and reverberated throughout the lobby. Several female customers screamed and dropped to their knees. Alex looked at the dead guard, fighting back nausea as he saw the man's intestines had spilled onto the floor with blood and flesh splattered everywhere.

Then the bodyguard made his move. Crouching and brushing back his coat, he drew what Alex thought was a Beretta 9mm pistol. He raised an arm to fire, but the third robber was quicker on the trigger, firing a bullet directly into the bodyguard's face.

"Oh, *Dio mio!*" the older silver-haired gentleman cried out, putting a hand to his mouth.

The bodyguard fell to the floor mortally wounded, blood oozing out the back of his head where the bullet had exited. With the shooter totally fixated on the fallen man, Alex took two quick steps forward, and in one clean motion, snatched the gun out of his hands, positioned it and rapidly fired two shots into his chest. The man collapsed to the floor. Now Alex had a clear line of sight to the second assailant who had killed the uniformed bank guard. As the man spun to face him, Alex fired two more shots, hitting him directly in the face and chest. The assailant fell backwards, his shotgun clattering loudly as it hit the marble floor.

Before Alex could take aim at the final robber at the teller's window, the robber grabbed an elderly customer and held his sawed-off shotgun against her head. Everyone began screaming.

"Drop your gun!" the robber yelled in Italian to Alex.

They were about thirty meters apart. Even if Alex had his own 9mm Sig-Sauer pistol, a head shot would have been extremely difficult at this range. Not using his own weapon, he wasn't sure the pistol had been sighted accurately, so Alex lowered it. He had no intention of dropping it, not after killing two of the man's partners. This remaining robber would want revenge. He was certainly desperate.

Shuffling his female hostage toward the exit, the last robber was surrounded by a squad of cops bursting through the front doors. Within seconds it was over. The holdup man gave up immediately, being faced with overwhelming force. He released his hostage, putting his hands behind his head. The police violently threw him to the ground and handcuffed him.

Placing the pistol gently on the floor, Alex stepped over to the older well-dressed gentleman, who was bent on one knee next to the bodyguard. Alex's own hands were slightly trembling from the adrenalin rush of the gun battle. He helped the older gentleman to his feet.

"Are you alright, *Senore?*"

"*Si*, you are most kind....?"

"Alex... Alex Boyd." He grasped the man's hand firmly.

Paramedics raced into the bank, attempting to give first aid, but all who had been shot were dead. The beautiful Carrara marble floor had pools of bright-red blood where the bodies had fallen.

The man who Alex had assumed to be the bank manager was speaking rapidly to the police and pointing at Alex, which made him feel uncomfortable. He could only make out a few phrases since there was a lot of background noise from yelling customers, not to mention his own hearing having been impaired by the gunfire.

Another police officer arrived, appearing to be senior man on the scene. To Alex's surprise, he approached not the bank manager, but the older well-dressed gentleman, standing next to him, and saluted. Then, with great respect, the cop escorted him out of the bank.

"*Senore*," a police officer said to Alex," I need you to accompany me to the police station to make a statement."

Showing his black Diplomatic passport, Alex, nevertheless, agreed to go to the station when the officer was not impressed. He reached for his cell phone to call Nancy, but the officer objected, then reluctantly allowed him to do so after Alex produced his Diplomatic Security Special Agent credentials and badge. The latter was a worldwide symbol of law enforcement, even if the precise nature of his badge probably wasn't understood by the Italian cop.

An hour later, Alex finished making his statement at the Central Rome Police Headquarters, known as the *questura*. It was pure luck Alex was carrying both his Diplomatic passport and his DS Special Agent credentials. The badge seemed to impress the cops far more than the passport. As he was about to leave, the senior cop, who had been at the bank, approached Alex. They spoke in Italian.

"Thank you for your statement, Mr. Boyd. Under Italian law an investigating magistrate will review this incident. For now, you are free to go. It is likely that whichever magistrate is given the case, he or she will want to speak with you." With that, the cop turned and left before Alex could ask anything about follow-on procedures.

From the *questura*, Alex hailed a taxi back to the Embassy. Once in his office, Nancy said, "I called the DCM's office an hour ago to tell him about the incident at the bank, but he was out, so I left an urgent message with his secretary for him to call you back. I also tried to speak to the Ambassador, but he was out as well. Finally, I called the Diplomatic Security Command Center in Washington and gave them the basic facts. They want you to call them with details."

He was impressed with Nancy's actions and thanked her. Just as when they were in Islamabad, he could always count on her to run the office in his absence.

"I think we better have that staff meeting after I call Rachel and the Command Center. Please let the staff know."

He entered the inner office and sat behind his new desk.

This may be my first and last staff meeting before DCM Chandler kicks me out of Rome.

Chapter 4

TELLING RACHEL

It was late in the morning and Alex felt he needed to call Rachel before she heard about the shootout from someone else. He dialed her office number on his cell phone.

"*Pronto, oficina di Rachel Smith.*"

"*Buon giorno. Mi chiamo Alex Boyd. Posso parlare con Rachel?*"

"Ah, Alex. Welcome to Roma. I hope to meet you in person soon." Chiara said "*Un momento, per favore,* I'll transfer you."

Chiara had worked in the Press Office for twenty years and her English was excellent, although she still had a charming Italian accent. Now, serving as Rachel's secretary, Alex had been told that Chiara was a gem.

"Alex, how did the meeting go?" Rachel asked enthusiastically.

"As we guessed, he *does* know Winston Hargrove from their time in Vienna, and he thinks the guy's terrific. More importantly, he holds me responsible for Hargrove's career crash."

"Oh, that's not good. How are you going to handle this?"

"I'll fill you in later; first, I have something really important to tell you."

He detailed the entire morning's event at the bank and at the police *questura*. There was a long silence at the end of the line. He couldn't tell if she was furious, in shock, or just amazed.

"What's going to happen now?" Rachel asked in an even tone. He imagined the chill in her voice came from thinking about political repercussions from such an incident involving a foreign diplomat killing two Italian citizens in a bank robbery, even if it was self-defense. He was right.

"I'm not sure," Alex replied. "This is going to be front page stuff and I don't know how the Italians will handle it."

"Will Diplomatic Security back you? I mean, you did kill two guys on your first day here, for God's sake."

"I think they'll defend my actions, but that doesn't mean they'll fight to keep me at post if the Embassy and the European Bureau make a big stink about it."

"Oh shit, Alex." There was a long pause. "I want to see you so much, but sorry, I really have to run. I have a meeting with the newspaper *La Repubblica* in ten minutes. Did you talk to the DCM or Ambassador yet about the bank incident?"

"No, they're both out, but Nancy left messages."

"Damn, Alex, this is bad. Really bad. Call me as soon as you speak with them, okay? I have to go. Thank God you're safe. I just hope *La Repubblica* reporters don't ask me any questions about it. See ya later," she said, blowing a kiss into the phone, then hanging up.

Staring at the wall for a few moments, Alex tried to work out the consequences of his actions at the bank. Then he called Washington, speaking to the Diplomatic Security Command Center, which afterward patched him through to the Director of Diplomatic Service, Jim Riley, his former boss in Islamabad. Riley assured him that he would do battle with the European Bureau if they disagreed with Alex's actions.

"I have your back," Riley said. "Just watch yours for a little while."

Alex felt some comfort from his remark, but if they complained to the Secretary of State, Riley might be powerless to save him. Moreover, Jim and Alex agreed the wild card in all this was whether the Italian Government would decide to do something about the incident and exactly what. They might even want to prosecute Alex, depending on how the issue was spun in the press.

Alex ended his call to Washington and asked Nancy if the DCM or Ambassador had called yet. She told him "No".

Things were starting to gnaw at him.

I should have heard something by now.

He looked at his watch. It was hours since Nancy had called the Front Office. Worry was setting in, but he was trying not to let his face show it.

Alex looked around his plain off-white office. Not a fresco in sight.

Apparently, serfs aren't entitled to great office art, he thought, somewhat in amusement, while waiting for his staff's arrival. Otherwise, his new office was of good size with a high ceiling. Two well-used leather chairs were placed in front of his desk. In the corner of the room was a small conference table and six folding chairs.

Nothing fancy; that's for sure.

Tall windows were bordered by white sheer curtains. The view outside overlooked the front of the Embassy, through which the never-ending traffic of Rome was visible, moving up and down the now rain-drenched Via Veneto.

Alex leaned back in his chair and contemplated that in spite of this morning's incident at the bank, life seemed good to him. He and Rachel had clicked from the start a year ago, and their passionate feelings had now deepened into love.

Maybe I should marry her.

Alex glanced out the window again, enjoying the thought of exploring the city with her. He leaned against the front of his desk and waited for the staff to arrive.

First in was his Deputy, Joe Roberts; next, came the Assistant RSO, George Cefalu. The three of them had already met on Sunday for a planned lunch at a restaurant near Rachel's apartment.

Joe Roberts, a former U.S. Marine Corps First Lieutenant, was a thirty-two-year-old African American, married, just under six-feet tall, and very fit looking. Since joining the State Department, he'd served in Bogota and Kinshasa.

"Thanks for meeting Rachel and me yesterday."

"No problem. It was my pleasure," Joe replied. "What the hell happened this morning at the bank?"

Alex briefly explained the details to him and George, mentioning he wasn't sure who all the participants were.

"Are you all right?" Joe asked.

"Yeah, I'm fine. Why wouldn't I be fine?" Alex replied, perhaps too defensively.

"Well, it's not every day there's a shootout in the middle of Rome."

"I know. But it's over now, except for the political fallout. I spoke with Director Riley and I'm waiting to talk to the DCM or the Ambassador. There's nothing more I can do at this point."

Joe and George stared at him; he guessed they wondered if he was in denial.

"Look, it was a traumatic incident, I'll grant you that. But I have to wait for the matter to play out. In the meantime, let's just continue with our duties as normal."

They each nodded.

"What do you think of the front office? Pretty amazing looking, isn't it?" George Cefalu asked, trying to regain a neutral atmosphere.

His family originated from Sicily, but George and his parents had been born and raised in New York City, where George had been a NYPD patrolman for four years. He was twenty-nine years old, single, and six feet tall with longish, slicked-back, black hair. Rome was his first overseas assignment.

"Amazing isn't the half of it," Alex responded. "Most museums in the States would kill for that artwork."

Samantha Carson arrived next. Preferring to be called 'Sam", she was the Security Engineering Officer, or SEO, for short. Based in Rome, she also covered Malta, Portugal, and Spain. At forty-years old, with an electrical engineering degree, Sam had worked at AT&T for several years before joining DS. Alex had heard that she had very high-energy and was a work-alcoholic.

"First, let me say I'm delighted to be here," Alex opened the meeting. "Secondly, all of you received a lot of praise in Washington when I made the rounds of the offices. I hope I can come up to speed as quickly as possible. I'll ask a lot of questions to make sure I understand what's going on.

"My style is to give advice and guidance when I think it will be useful or requested, but I like to let each person assume responsibility when given a project. Don't hesitate to talk to me about what you're working on. If you have a concern, then I want to hear about it. You know that old saying, the only bad question is the one never asked."

Alex felt his message got a favorable reaction.

"How are relations with the rest of the Embassy?"

"They're pretty good, with a few exceptions," Joe Roberts said. "The CIA is supportive; the State Department rank and file doesn't cause any real problems, although they don't seem to think about security much. Most of the other law enforcement agencies have good relations with us."

"But?" Alex said. "I sense there's an issue somewhere?"

"The DCM ignores us," Joe continued. "He doesn't seem to care about anything other than political events. His major concern is the care and feeding of the Ambassador."

"In this case, that may not be a bad thing," Alex stated, thinking the less he saw of Alden Chandler, the better it would be.

"Does the DCM at least support security in general?" Alex asked.

"Not really," Joe replied. "George, why don't you tell Alex about your case?"

"Yeah, I was working on a visa fraud case involving allegations against an American officer at the Consulate General in Naples. Your predecessor and I tried to arrange a briefing with the DCM, but he kept blowing us off. We wanted to bring him up to speed. Twice he told us to just brief Admin."

"You mean he only wanted you to brief the Management Counselor, Charlotte Eaton?" Alex asked, incredulous at the lack of Chandler's interest in his own job responsibilities.

"Yeah. She did a good job listening to us, and supported us when we nailed the guy, but I thought DCMs were supposed to take an interest in felonies committed by Embassy staff."

"They usually do. Are there any other problems?" Alex asked.

"It hasn't exactly been a problem, because your predecessor backed off, but the FBI Legal Attaché, Mark Terranova, is very touchy about police relations," Joe said.

"How so?"

"For some reason, Terranova thinks the FBI is first among equals, and whenever another Embassy law enforcement agency talks to really senior Italian cops, he wants to be there."

"How do other agencies feel about that?"

"They think Terranova's a jerk," George chimed in. "You can ask any of them, Immigration, Customs, Secret Service, or DEA. All Terranova wants is to have the FBI take credit for the work of others and appear to be in charge."

Mark Terranova's reputation in Washington had already reached Alex. The word was that while personable, he was too slick by half and a total snake. He'd been in Rome for five or six years as the senior Legal Attaché, known as the Legatt, which gave him a huge advantage over other US law enforcement types usually only serving three years in Rome. More to his advantage, he had good contacts and spoke excellent Italian.

"Well, I guess Mr. Terranova and I will have to work this out," Alex said. "Just so you know where I stand, I intend to expand our contacts, and we'll talk to whomever we need too. But we'll try to cooperate with Terranova in other regards."

"Sam, how about you?"

"I don't have any problems with the other agencies."

"Is the CIA Station cooperative?"

"Yes. They even ask for my help when some of their equipment breaks down."

"What about when their own electronic whiz kids come to town? Do they touch base with you?"

"They do. We share info all the time. By the way, should I ask for a job title change to 'whiz kid?' They all laughed.

"You've just witnessed the extent of my technical expertise."

Turning to Joe Roberts, Alex said, "In a moment, if you have time, Joe, I'd like to walk around the compound with you. Also, this afternoon, either you or George can brief me on the Ambassador's protective detail.

"But first, I want to mention one liaison opportunity coming up: When I was in Washington, the DS Anti-Terrorism Assistance Program, or ATA for short, was hosting four members of the Italian *Nucleo Operativo Centrale di Sicurezza,* also known as "NOCS", for a show and tell. You may know that's the hostage rescue unit for the National Police, the *Polizia di Stato.*

"Well, ATA invited me to meet the NOCS guys so I sat in on some of their briefings. A few of us had drinks later that night. They've invited me to watch their annual exercise in Abruzzi coming up in a few weeks. That's a big competition with some other European police hostage-rescue forces. I think the Israelis may also be there. So, I'll be gone for a long weekend, unless the DCM has a problem with the plan. I think this will be an important connection for us. You never know if we'll need them in an emergency."

"Okay, thanks everyone, that's it for now. Joe, are you ready for that walk around the compound?" Joe nodded.

As they left the office together, George nodded towards Alex and whispered to Joe: "This is going to be fucking great!"

Chapter 5

MAN WITH THE CAMERA

It was raining lightly outside. Alex grabbed his waxed Barbour jacket while waiting for Joe.

"Why don't we stop in the Marine office first before walking around?" Alex suggested when he arrived.

"Excellent idea."

As they moved toward the door, Alex asked Nancy Williams to call the Ambassador and DCM again, waiting as she did so. No luck: they were still out.

The men walked down the hall to Master Sergeant Pete Clarke's office area. Clarke was the Embassy's Marine Corps Detachment Commander. Because there were twenty-five Marines in the detachment, the Marines Corps required a very senior Noncommissioned Officer in Charge, and Clarke fit the bill perfectly.

"Sir, it's good to have you on board," Clarke said, firmly shaking hands with both men. "Come on in and pull up a chair."

The walls were decorated with a typical assortment of Marine Corps paraphernalia: photos of Marine infantry in combat, a drawing of two Harriers rolling in on a target to make a bombing run, and a landing craft dropping Marines on a beach. Alex liked this Marine Corps stuff. It reminded him of his Naval Intelligence days. Looking at the photos, his thoughts raced.

If the State Department tried to emulate such public relations photos, at best they could have a 'dramatic' shot of an officer sitting at his desk typing a political message to Washington, or perhaps, an action photo of an Ambassador eating a canapé at a cocktail reception. Macho shit, indeed. He smiled at his imaginings.

"I spoke with Gunny Rodriguez a month ago," Clarke said, referring to Alex's former Detachment Commander in Islamabad, Pakistan. "He sends his regards, and said he'd follow you into battle any day."

Alex smiled at the unexpected comment.

"Rodriguez is a good man and a good leader. How's he's doing since his transfer to Mexico City?"

"He loves Mexico but misses the action in the Middle East."

"I'll bet he does. I'd like to set up a longer meeting with you to discuss everything about the Detachment. Why don't you call Nancy and pick a time this week?"

"Yes, Sir. And feel free to call me 'Top,'" he said, referring to his own informal title as Master Sergeant. Their meeting continued, then concluded with a promise to talk more later.

Leaving Top's office, they exited the front door of the Embassy. Outside, about 15 meters away, were three Italian cops at the front gate. Each one was armed with a Beretta submachine gun and pistol. Nearby was a parked police SUV with two cops inside, both smoking leisurely. Alex wondered if any of those cops had responded to the robbery at the bank.

"Is this the normal cadre of cops in front of the Embassy?" Alex asked. Joe nodded.

Approaching the three cops, Alex introduced himself in Italian, shook hands, and asked some questions. Then he and Joe walked on.

It was drizzling by the time they reached the Via Veneto, and cold enough for Alex to still see his breath. The US Consular building was twenty-five meters up on the right. Inside the entrance was another screening operation and a Marine Security Guard Post.

"Do you want the full tour inside?" Joe asked.

"Not yet. After I meet the Consul General, in a day or so, he can show me around." They turned to walk around the side of the compound on Via Boncompagni. At the corner of Via Veneto and Via Boncompagni was the enormous Hotel Westin Excelsior, one of the best hotels in Italy. There were always VIPs staying there, which accounted for cops stationed outside. Several black Mercedes were parked in front of the hotel entrance for guests, as well as unmarked police cars, all dark blue Alfa Romeo sedans.

"I stayed at the Excelsior once while protecting the Secretary of State," he told Joe. Alex recalled the lobby as huge and perfect for casual conversations. He thought, perhaps, he and Rachel would go there this evening for a drink, even if it did cost a small fortune.

As they were about to leave the Via Veneto and turn right onto Via Boncompagni, Alex noted a newspaper and magazine kiosk across the way.

"Hold on a second, Joe. I want to see if the kiosk has today's *International Herald Tribune*."

Waiting for the light, Alex crossed the street crowded with pedestrians, most of whom appeared to be tourists. Nevertheless, he spied one man, next to the kiosk, taking pictures in the direction of the Embassy, and indeed, of Alex himself. By the time he reached the area, however, the man was gone.

Well, Alex thought, it's probably another American tourist. After-all, the Embassy is an historic building on one of the world's most famous streets. But he made a mental note that the man wore a grey wool coat, flat dark cap, brown corduroy pants, and was carrying a canvas shoulder bag.

He found the day's edition of the paper and waited for the traffic light to change as he flipped to the sports section.

Hot damn, he thought. *On Saturday, my University of Virginia Cavaliers beat Duke 92-88.* The basketball gods once again determined that justice was to be served. When Alex had played point guard for UVA, they rarely beat Duke. He folded the paper and stuffed it into the pocket of his coat while rejoining Joe.

Now they were walking down Via Boncompagni. Alex recognized it because that morning he and Rachel had taken the public bus for a ten-minute ride from their apartment on Via Tagliamento in the Parioli District nearby. He and Joe walked the long block until they reached the Embassy compound's rear entrance.

"Here's where most of our cars enter," Joe said. They flashed their Embassy ID badges and entered through the gate. Walking a short distance to the parking area, they now had a view of the other villa on the compound. It was occupied by the Public Affairs Office, where Rachel worked.

"Do you want to go inside?" Joe asked.

"Yeah, I'd like to see Rachel's office." The villa's ornate exterior was light-colored cream stucco with three floors and tall windows on all floors.

"Let's see if Rachel's back from her meeting with the *La Repubblica* guys," Alex said. They walked up the stairs and into Rachel's suite of offices. Chiara greeted them.

"Oh, hello Mr. Roberts, can I help you?"

"I'd like to introduce Alex Boyd. He's..." Joe's introduction was cut off.

"Yes, Alex, at last we meet." She rose quickly from her chair, smiled and shook his hand. "I'm sorry to say Rachel is still in the conference room with the journalists. But you can wait in her office if you'd like."

"No, thank you, Chiara. We're just walking around the compound. But please tell her I was here."

"*Certo*. I will do that," she replied with a broad smile.

"Okay then. I'll see you later. *Ciao*," Alex said.

Joe suggested they snake their way through the Embassy compound to return to the main building, but Alex said he'd like to return the same way they came, describing the man he had seen taking photos by the kiosk.

On their return trip, the rain had stopped, and the streets glistened with a thin layer of water. The man was nowhere to be seen. But Alex's sixth sense left him feeling uneasy. He now had doubts the man was really a tourist after all.

Chapter 6

RACHEL REMEMBERS PAKISTAN

Thirty minutes after Alex left her office, Rachel returned from her meeting.

"*Signorina* Rachel, Alex was here with Joe Roberts," Chiara explained.

Rachel showed disappointment at missing his visit, then smiled at the thought he had wanted to see her.

"Thanks, Chiara." Rachel looked at her watch and saw it was already one o'clock; she needed some lunch.

"I'm going to the Embassy cafeteria for a Panini and bottle of water."

"*Va bene, Ciao Rachel.*"

She hoped to run into Alex but knew it was unlikely since he liked to eat early. Sitting in the small cafeteria, with two Italian newspapers while eating the sandwich, her mind drifted.

Leaving Alex in Washington to complete his Italian language studies had been hard for them both. After the attack on the Embassy in Islamabad, and during the next year together at post, their relationship had evolved from incredible sex into deep emotional love. When things settled down in Pakistan, and the State Department psychiatrists descended upon the Embassy to judge the mental condition of all remaining staff, Rachel had lied when questioned, saying she felt fine. In truth, she had recurring nightmares about her battle with the terrorist at the Ambassador's residence. On occasion, she still woke in the middle of the night thinking she was covered in blood from her fight. Her only comfort, however, was knowing that her physical prowess and martial arts training had saved her from death that day. Still, it was hard coming to terms with the sheer viciousness of the assault.

How could people be such animals, she wondered. *How could they want to behead another human being?*

She put her panini down as tears formed in her eyes; she wiped them away. In doing so she felt the scars on both her cheeks, inflicted by the terrorist who had punched her repeatedly. But she had given as good as she got, inflicting severe damage to the terrorist using her hands, elbows, and legs before killing him.

Nevertheless, she had been a bloody mess at the end of the fight. Back then, when Alex had finished his battle in the main Embassy building against the larger group of terrorists, he had joined her at the Ambassador's residence. He had also been covered in blood and dirt, but it was terrorist's blood from killing several attackers, including two in hand-to-hand combat.

Maybe one day, she thought, *I'll have the scars removed with plastic surgery, but for now it's not a top priority. Besides, my makeup does a pretty good job of hiding them.*

She paused to swallow some water and take several deep breaths. She was thrilled Alex was in Rome with her now. He was her rock and kept her emotions on an even keel. She felt safe with him nearby. When they were in Washington studying Italian together, the occasional nightmares had stopped temporarily. Still, the recent separation from

Alex, between late November and early January, had been emotionally trying, besides, it was never good to be alone during Thanksgiving and Christmas. She and Alex had spoken often on the phone, but it wasn't the same as having him physically beside her.

On the positive side, in his absence, she had bonded with the Ambassador's wife, Francesca Scarmatti. By coincidence, they had been friends—not close, but more than acquaintances—in Los Angeles years before.

Now in Rome, where Francesca was totally new to the diplomatic world, she relied on Rachel to give her advice. Rachel knew the ropes of living abroad and was delighted to guide Francesca through her new world. Her own past included serving in Hong Kong, Beijing, Islamabad, and once briefly in Rome until the Secretary of State asked her to return to Washington to be the Department's Deputy Press spokeswoman,

Rachel liked Francesca a lot. She was genuine in her feelings and refused to put on airs just because she was the Ambassador's wife. Playing tennis with her every week had been a wonderful outlet and allowed Rachel to burn off some calories, not to mention easing the frustration at not being with Alex.

She smiled at the thought that Francesca was a better tennis player than Alex, who had too much testosterone and not enough subtle skill. Of course, he was great when it counted, like wrestling in bed... really great! A grin spread across her face thinking about this past weekend with him. She would be even happier with her thoughts of him, except for today's shooting incident at the bank. Now, what might happen to Alex as a result of his actions was casting a pall over her attitude. She collected her unread newspapers.

Enough lunch. Time to get back to work.

Chapter 7

BIG TROUBLE

Alden Chandler was in a rage when he called Alex at 3:00 pm. He could hardly contain his fury and demanded Alex come to his office immediately. Alex steeled himself for the tongue-lashing, knowing he might even be kicked out of his post.

As he walked out the door of his office, Nancy called out "good luck", her eyes moist with tears knowing how dire the situation.

Entering the DCM's office, he saw Ambassador Scarmatti was already present. Chandler, his face red with anger, yelled out the first words.

"I can't *believe* you've *already* caused an incident. I *warned* you about this type of behavior!"

"Alex, it's serious," Ambassador Scarmatti interjected. "I received a call from the Foreign Minister about the shootings at the bank. He personally wants to see us now. Why didn't you notify us when it happened?"

"Exactly!" Chandler's voice blasted out. "You should have gotten to us immediately!"

"I called both of you, twice, with urgent messages. Both your secretaries said you were tied up in meetings, out of the building, and couldn't be disturbed," Alex replied. "What else was I to do?" He knew he was in deep shit.

"Listen, Alex, I spoke with the Assistant Secretary of the European Bureau in Washington," Scarmatti said. "He wants a full investigation into the incident." Alex judged that Scarmatti, though pissed off, looked a little uncertain as to what State Department protocol should be followed in this circumstance.

"I hope you haven't unpacked your bags yet, *Boyd*," Chandler piped in, "because I want you relieved *immediately*. For now, we're all going to see the Foreign Minister. Let's *go*."

The three of them took the elevator down to the Ambassador's waiting Cadillac. Although the journey took only twenty minutes. It was the longest ride in Alex's life.

* * *

At the Foreign Office building, they were escorted up the Minister's office. When they entered the large, ornate room, the silver-haired older gentleman who had been in the bank that morning, was also present, which puzzled Alex.

Scarmatti and Chandler shook hands with the Foreign Minister. Then, to Alex's surprise, they greeted the older gentleman warmly as well. No one offered their hand to Alex. The Foreign Minster suggested they all take seats around a richly-hued mahogany coffee table. A large, ornate silver pot of coffee was surrounded by exquisite lapis lazuli-colored china cups and saucers, with gold trim.

If I'm to be executed, or thrown into jail, Alex thought, at least the Italians do it in style. The Foreign Minister offered them coffee, but all declined.

The Ambassador opened the conversation by apologizing for Alex's actions at the bank. Chandler piled it on, fully acknowledging that Alex's actions were unprecedented and would never happen again by anyone in the Embassy. Alex watched the expressions of the Foreign Minister and the older gentleman. The Foreign Minister held up his hand to interrupt and both Italian dignitaries smiled.

"Ambassador Scarmatti, Mr. Chandler, I believe you have misunderstood the reason why I called you here."

Alex's heart skipped a beat. He focused his attention on the Foreign Minister's next words.

"Mr. Boyd, let me introduce Mr. Umberto Ferrara, our Deputy Interior Minister." The silver-haired gentleman stood and extended his hand to greet Alex, who also stood and warmly shook it.

"I want to *thank you* for saving my life this morning," Ferrara said, speaking in upper class, sophisticated Italian. "The ill-advised, but well-meaning actions of the bank guard and my own police bodyguard jeopardized all of us. Had you not interceded, I think I, and many others in the bank, would certainly have been killed. *Senore* Caputo, the Bank Manager, also wishes to extend his thanks for your actions."

There was complete silence in the room. The Deputy Minister sat down and a relieved Alex followed suit. He was dying to jokingly ask if this meant the bank would give him free checking, but thought better of it and remained silent.

This was incredible. The number two man at the Ministry of the Interior, the man who oversaw the National Police, and a potential primary contact of Alex's, had just *thanked* him for saving his life. He glanced at the Ambassador, who was smiling broadly, but noticed that Chandler could hardly hold his anger in.

"Mr. Minister," Alden Chandler said, "what about the press coverage of the incident? Surely you won't want it known that a representative of the American Embassy killed two Italians in the bank."

"Oh, I quite agree, Mr. Chandler," the Foreign Minister responded. "That is why we have released information that it was an undercover police officer who killed the robbers. The bank personnel have agreed to support this statement." He faced Alex.

"Mr. Boyd, were it not for this necessary subterfuge, I would recommend to the Prime Minister that we grant you an honorary medal. But I am sure under the circumstances, you will understand this is not possible."

"I completely understand, Sir," Alex replied in his best Italian. "Such an award isn't necessary. I'm sorry the situation required the use of force to save lives, and I am completely grateful for your support of my actions."

The Foreign Minister and Deputy Minister Ferrara beamed their appreciation for Alex's statement. Scarmatti gave him a discreet thumbs-up. The DCM, however, remained silent and had apparently misplaced his smile.

"You know Mr. Minister, I believe I would like some coffee after all," Scaramtti said. The Foreign Minister summoned an assistant from another room, who entered and poured coffee for all as the five of them chatted for another fifteen minutes.

With the meeting over, the Foreign Minister escorted them to his outer office. Deputy Interior Minister Ferrara made a point of warmly putting his hand on Alex's shoulder, and giving him a business card.

"Alex, please feel free to call me any time you have an issue of importance," Ferrara said. "You saved my life and I will never forget it. My private cell phone number is on the card."

On the ride back to the Embassy, it was agreed that Alex would draft a secret detailed telegram to Washington, telling them everything that had transpired at both the bank and the Foreign Ministry.

He finished the message and sent it before the close of business, taking great delight in watching Chandler put his initials on the outgoing telegram, indicating his endorsement of the message.

All's fair in love and war, Alex thought on his way out the door.

Chapter 8

NEW RED BRIGADE

Cosimo di Luca looked out the window of the second-floor apartment on Via Principe Amedeo. The afternoon light was slowly turning to dusk as he stroked his neatly trimmed dark beard. Watching for the arrival of the last of his group, Tufo and Valeri, he glanced at his watch. It was six in the evening. He made a mental note they were late.

A patient man, he had spent thirty-five years of his life waiting for something. As a freeance journalist, he had waited for interviews, waited for phone calls from sources, waited for approval of his quickly crafted stories, and waited for his wife to return from her university classes most evenings. Across the room Carlo Mancini and Giovanni Fenzi had already arrived and were reading today's newspapers. Everyone was waiting for Tufo and Valeri.

Di Luca had rented this sparsely furnished one-bedroom apartment some time ago. It was two blocks from Rome's Termini Central Train Station. The immediate neighborhood was lower-middle class at best, with lots of transitory people of various nationalities. Some were Italians, but mostly Bangladeshis, Indians, Pakistanis, students from the nearby University, or people who needed to stay one or two nights at an inexpensive hotel before catching an early morning train out of Rome.

Ethnic south-Asian restaurants dotted the area and pungent cooking aromas of curry filled the air. Many buildings were covered in graffiti on the ground level; street gutters needed a good cleaning. All of this was exactly what Cosimo di Luca wanted for his safe house. He needed anonymity and ease of access. The train station provided excellent links to every city in Italy. Moreover, Termini was a hub for Rome's bus service, as well as the intersection for the city's two subway lines.

Finally, Tufo's black VW Golf pulled into a parking space. Moments later, Agosto Tufo and Antonio Valeri knocked on the door. Di Luca opened it casually and invited them in. The others put down their newspapers, focusing attention on Cosimo. Valeri dropped his canvas shoulder bag on the floor, put his grey wool jacket on a chair, and tossed his flat cap on top of the jacket. Tufo simply took a seat at the table.

"So, I think we'll begin with Carlo and Giovanni telling us about their observations," di Luca said. Carlo Mancini, a tall, slender twenty-nine-year-old political science student at the local university, took a long drag on his cigarette and began his report.

"Giovanni and I tried to do surveillance on the British Ambassador for several days. This was not easy because his residence, the Villa Wolkansky, is adjacent to their Embassy. He can go to work without really leaving the combined residence and Embassy grounds, which are enormous."

Carlo spread out a city map and pointed to the Villa Wolkansky near the Basilica San Giovanni in Laterno. Cosimo took off his long-distance lenses to see better close.

"From here to his residence, it is not a long walk through the Esquilino area. In any event, when we were able to follow him, he always had a bodyguard, even on weekends. We think he might be a more difficult target than the others."

"Thank you, Carlo," di Luca said.

"Tufo, Valeri, what have you got for me?" di Luca queried. He liked both men. They were skilled at surveillance, cautious, and worked well as a team. Both had graduated from university, and like many Italian youth, had found only part-time employment, relying upon the welfare state to supplement their income.

"We've been watching the American Ambassador for a week," Agosto Tufo began. "Like the British Ambassador, he also has a large house with extensive gardens. It is called the Villa Taverna and is about a mile and a half from the American Embassy. His villa has a high wall running around it and residential guards that control access, plus there is a police car with two cops stationed right next to the entrance gate most of the time. More importantly, he has police bodyguards when he travels. One bodyguard rides inside the Ambassador's car and three are in a follow car. They operate very professionally."

"What type of car is the Ambassador in?" di Luca asked.

"It is usually a black Cadillac. We cannot be sure but judging from the body language of the driver or the bodyguard when they open the car doors, we believe the car is armored."

"This doesn't look very promising," di Luca frowned. "Should we forget him?"

"No, not at all, Cosimo. Here is the interesting thing: Last weekend he drove out of his residence without bodyguards. Unusual, yes; but he did so. He was driving himself in a Ford Mondeo with American Embassy license plates, not the Cadillac. His wife was with him. The police at the gate didn't even notice when he left."

"Really!" di Luca raised his eyebrows in shock. "Where did he go?"

"We don't know," Antonio Valeri, broke into the conversation for the first time. "We didn't want to be in front of the villa for too long, so we left our car and walked to a nearby café. Returning from a cappuccino, around ten in the morning, we saw them drive out of the villa. It was too late to follow without drawing attention to ourselves."

"That was a good decision to stay where you were," said di Luca. "Did you see them return?"

"No, but we weren't there all the time. Shall I mention our surveillance of the Embassy now?"

"Yes, please," di Luca said. He was ecstatic with this latest bit of information.

Tufo spoke again. "I've been using the video camera to watch whatever I can see. One day, I will position myself on the Via Veneto, slightly downhill from the Embassy. Occasionally, I will sit in the enclosed glass part of the Hard Rock Café. Other times, I park my car on the Via Veneto and just sit there filming. Antonio has been more mobile. He uses his 35mm camera with a powerful lens."

"Yes, sometimes I am across the street by the Banco BNL," Antonio explained. "Other times I can stand by the newspaper kiosk on the Via Veneto, or just wait at one of the bus stops. The security at the Embassy is much too impressive to even consider kidnapping the Ambassador there, or immediately nearby. His driver drops him off inside the perimeter gate, and not only are his bodyguards there, but there are always police in front."

"Speaking of the Banco BNL, did you see what happened this morning?" di Luca asked.

"I did," Tufo responded. "I was standing next to the outdoor Café, across the street, when I heard shots coming from inside the bank. Then police were running from every direction toward the bank, and cars with sirens, headed there as well. I was worried about being seen, but I discreetly filmed the front of the bank. I guessed it was a robbery. Did our people have anything to do with this?"

"No, we didn't," di Luca clarified. "But the idiots who attempted the robbery almost blew our surveillance operation. Now, we will have to be more careful."

"Getting back to the American Ambassador, it sounds like we may have a chance to capture him on weekends, yes?" di Luca asked.

"Perhaps," Tufo said. "But we'll need more surveillance to find out if he has a pattern of driving himself without his bodyguards. It is hard to imagine that the Americans are so stupid as to permit that."

"I agree. Soon we will have to decide. If we are to successfully release our New Red Brigade comrades from that stinking Italian prison, not to mention getting a ransom, then we must act sooner than later. Of course, we need to grab the most impressive target possible to ensure it will make headlines," di Luca said.

"Here's what we'll do: I'll get more of our comrades from Bologna to help with the surveillance of Ambassador Scarmatti, especially on the weekends. He looked at his watch and saw it was almost seven o'clock.

"That is enough for today. You have done well," di Luca said. "Let's go home, *Ciao*."

Chapter 9

THE HUMAN SIDE

Cosimo di Luca left the safe house and walked two blocks to his parked Piaggio motor scooter. He unlocked the chain linking to an adjacent fence, put on his helmet, and drove off toward the suburb south of the city, called EUR.

It was dark now and temperatures had dropped another ten degrees into the high forties. Over his sports coat, he wore a down-filled black parka for the 40-minute ride home having foreseen the cold weather.

Weaving among the flow of traffic, he began roaming through his thoughts: One potential target, the British Ambassador, was now removed from consideration; another, the American, held great promise. Still, he considered, they couldn't be sure, and needed their plan to work while escaping safely in the end.

As leader of the New Red Brigade, he felt a deep responsibility to make the right decisions. At present, his group was only a mild irritant to Berlusconi's government which was already on the ropes because of impending fraud charges. The government had much bigger problems than a small terrorist group, even if it did bear the name of the once feared Red Brigade from the 1980s.

If Cosimo and his comrades could successfully pull off a high-profile kidnapping, then he might be able to raise more money from left-wing sympathizers, as well as recruit a new group of activists to their cause of bringing down capitalism. The goal was easily defined: to create the first Marxist state in Western Europe. It wouldn't be easy. However, a strong Communist following already existed. Cosimo believed if he could push the government into retaliatory excesses to counter his actions—kidnapping, bank robberies, and murder—then hopefully, the people in the middle, the Socialists, would join the Communists in defeating what he thought was the modern-day incarnation of Fascism.

Forty minutes later he arrived at his apartment. The Via Montagne Rocciose in EUR was a lovely area full of pleasant apartment buildings, small food markets, adequate restaurants, and decent transportation into the center of Rome. He found a parking spot on the street, walked into his building, and took the elevator up to the fourth floor. To his amazement and delight, his wife, Antonietta, was already home and cooking dinner.

"*Ciao, amore mio.* Why are you home so early?"

"University classes were canceled after I arranged a strike to protest the government's plan to charge a small tuition fee for students," she said with a smile.

"Excellent... keep putting the screws to Berlusconi. He can't hang in much longer."

He kissed the back of her neck while taking in the amazing aromas.

"Whatever you are cooking smells wonderful. What are we having?"

"I picked up some veal on the way home and decided to make *involtini*. But first we'll start with *pasta alla siciliana*," she answered with her back towards him, tending to the cooking.

"What a treat! I love that," Cosimo said enthusiastically, sliding his arms around her waist and nuzzling the back of her neck which he knew she loved.

In return, he loved her stuffed veal rolls, but her *pasta alla siciliana* with eggplant, anchovies, olives, capers, tomato, and garlic was truly special.

"What about the children? Where are they?" He asked.

"Oh, they've been invited to dinner with the Di Bello family in the next building. The Di Bello's kids are in school with ours, and one of them is having a birthday party."

"Even better." He opened a bottle of red wine from Emilia Romagna.

"So, other than organizing a strike, did you have an interesting day?"

Although Antonietta did teach a few classes in Sociology at Sapienza University of Rome, professors did very little actual teaching. Antonietta spent most of her time organizing Italian Communist Party events and propaganda. Sapienza was the biggest university in Rome, founded in 1303. Her father who had been a professor there, and her grandfather, who had also been a professor, had taught in Bologna until he was arrested and killed by the fascists in the 1930s.

After pouring wine for them both, Cosimo looked at Antoinetta and marveled at her beautiful features so familiar to him. Her long black, wavy hair had several distinguished strands of grey, premature since she was only in her late thirties. They made her look mature, experienced, and very much the woman that he loved.

"I taught one course in the morning on the evolution of corporate control of the state media. I tell you, Cosimo, these students are unconcerned when it comes to what's happening in our culture. All they want to do is party and use drugs."

"Is that any different than in our student days?"

"I suppose not, but at least we were socially aware."

Cosimo smiled as Antonietta looked at him for agreement. Although he always voted for the Communist Party, he remembered while at university, just how much time he spent trying to get laid. As much, maybe more, than he did studying Marxism.

"*Va bene*, it's ready," she said.

Antonietta filled two plates which they carried into the dining room. Their apartment was large with three bedrooms. The living room and dining room would have appeared more spacious had the rooms not been filled with bookcases. Both Antonietta and Cosimo were voracious readers and saved every tome they read. The best part of the apartment, however, was the terrace, with its mock Etruscan wall fountain pouring water into a large basin. The terrace floor was covered with rustic looking terracotta tile.

"So, what about your day?" Antonietta asked.

"Oh, my usual attempts to interest editors in accepting a new article."

"Any luck?"

"A little."

He hadn't told her about his leadership of the New Red Brigade. He knew she shared his extreme left-wing views on politics in Italy but didn't want to put her in danger by concerning her with his criminal activities. He was afraid she might want to participate.

Then, what would happen to our children if we were both either caught or killed?

"I was reading an article today in an American magazine," she said.

"An American magazine? Don't tell me your politics are changing?" Cosimo laughed.

"No, no, that's not the point. The article was about how American politics and business must adapt to the increasing strength of the European Union. I thought maybe you could do a story for the Italian press from the American perspective. Perhaps even cover what it is like to be an expatriate living in Italy. You can spin it any way you like."

Cosimo was speechless. Not only was Antonietta's idea brilliant from a journalistic perspective, but perhaps he could gain access to the American Embassy, or even to the Ambassador's residence by requesting an interview.

"Antonietta, I love your idea nearly as much as I love you!" He leaned toward her as she reciprocated.

With the children gone for a while he had an idea of what to have for dessert as he walked her to their bedroom.

Chapter 10

RACHEL, MY LOVE

"Fifteen more minutes? Do you really have to stay at the office?" Alex asked Rachel on the phone. His battered dive watch read 7:00 p.m. He was anxious to see Rachel, and damn hungry, too.

"Yeah, sorry. I need to finish notes on my meeting with the *La Repubblica* journalists today, before I forget the small details. But, for God sakes, Alex, what did the Ambassador and DCM say about the shooting at the bank? You only left me a message saying everything was all right."

Alex described Alden Chandler's initial anger, the Ambassador's guarded irritation, and their subsequent happy meeting with the Foreign Minister and Deputy Interior Minister.

"Oh Alex, I've been so worried all day. I thought..." she was suddenly silent, then Alex heard her sob once or twice. The ritual nose blowing followed, before she continued. "We have to celebrate."

"Okay, why don't we meet in the lobby bar at the Excelsior Hotel in half an hour?"

"Wow, how chic! I didn't know you had that much class."

"Yeah, yeah, very funny. Or, we could always meet at McDonalds for a shake if you prefer."

Laughing heartily, Rachel said, "No, the Excelsior sounds great. I'll meet you there."

He easily walked the block to the Excelsior and entered the hotel. To his right, was the rich mahogany reception desk. He continued walking up a few stairs into the enormous lobby with its magnificent high ceiling. The large area was tastefully decorated in soft colors; clusters of sofas and chairs created intimate nooks and nearly private areas.

Picking an empty sofa in the middle of the room, he removed his overcoat and sat, relaxing and beginning to people-watch as they came and went. Within five minutes, a waiter approached him, taking his order for a scotch and water. Alex pulled the *International Herald Tribune* out of his coat pocket and read, while looking up every few seconds to spot Rachel.

Twenty minutes later, he saw her arrive. She lit up the lobby, as if a supermodel had just arrived... a well-built supermodel. Her long, wavy brown hair now hung gracefully over her shoulders; it had lengthened since their days in Pakistan. She removed a long dark blue coat as she scanned the room for Alex. Underneath, she wore a knee-length red dress, cinched at the waist with a wide black belt. Her high heels made her even taller than her five-feet, ten-inches. If anyone doubted her athletic prowess or power, they needed only to look at her perfectly shaped and muscled calves as she glided toward Alex.

He stood, and they embraced next to the sofa as he put his arms around her and whispered in her ear: "God, you're amazingly beautiful." He loved the feel of her sensually firm body.

She gave him a longish kiss on the lips, which Alex imagined caused envy from every male in the room. With heels on, they practically looked at each other eye to eye. Finally, they sat down and Alex caught the waiter's attention. She ordered her usual vodka on ice.

"So, how was your meeting with the Italian journalists?"

"It went well," she sounded upbeat, he thought. "Their questions were good and not unexpected. I believe I answered everything to their satisfaction.

"How were the journalists personally?"

"They were pretty nice. Even though both were married guys in their thirties, one of them tried to hit on me. He gave me way too many compliments for a professional meeting."

"But this is Italy, doesn't that come with the turf?" Alex asked.

"That's no excuse."

"Did you punch him?"

"Of course not." Rachel chuckled. "I save that treatment for you."

"I bet he stared at your legs," egging her on.

"He did. Are you jealous?"

"Not unless he touched them."

"Okay, this is getting silly" But she was still smiling, so Alex knew he'd kept her in a good humor. They continued making small talk while finishing their drinks.

"I'd like to take you to my favorite restaurant," she finally said. "It's called Otello alla Concordia and is off Via della Croce near the Spanish Steps. We should take a taxi."

Walking out of the hotel, they found a line of cabs waiting on the corner. After a five-minute drive, they arrived at the Piazza di Spagna, at the base of the Spanish Steps. They exited the cab next to its large, imposing fountain. Alex looked around in wonder at the beauty of the area. At the top of the Spanish Steps, technically known as the Scalinata Della Trinita dei Monti, was a large and beautiful 16th century church. The piazza where Alex and Rachel stood, was surrounded by elegant buildings.

Despite the cold weather, people were milling around, hanging out on the Spanish Steps or clustered around the fountain. They walked two blocks to Via della Croce. The area, Alex knew, had a reputation for high end shopping.

About one hundred meters further on, they came to the alleyway leading to the restaurant. Alex looked down the dark, narrow path and saw parked motorcycles and bicycles.

"Are you sure this is the right place?" he asked.

"Don't worry, this place is great."

The narrow walkway down the alley was short before opening up twenty meters further on which surprised Alex. Although straight ahead was the main restaurant, on the left was a glass enclosed terrace with many tables. There were modern frescoes on the back wall of the terrace, plants strategically placed here and there, but most importantly, Alex saw tall space heaters glowing warmly. Rachel said a few words in Italian to the waiter, who ushered them inside and sat them at a small table near the frescoed wall. Another attentive waiter arrived and spoke to them. In response to the waiter's question, Alex asked Rachel, "red or white?"

"I'd like red."

"Signore, vorrei una caraffa di vino rosso della casa, per favore" Alex asked the waiter using the polite form, 'I would like,' to order a carafe of the house red wine.

"Si, signore," the waiter responded, leaving them to get the carafe.

When he returned with the wine, he spoke in English.

"Your Italian accent is pretty good Signore, but I do speak English if you would like."

Rachel looked at Alex and chuckled. Alex had to admit it was funny.

"Okay, we'll order in English," Alex said. "Rachel, you've eaten here before. What do you recommend?"

"Why don't I just order for both of us and we can share?" Alex nodded.

"We'll start with an order of *Zucchini fritti,* and a bottle of sparkling water, please."

"Next, I'd like one plate of *Spaghetti Otello*." She explained to Alex, "It's not on the menu, but it's one the restaurant's specialties and it's delicious."

"Finally, we'll have two orders of *Saltimbocca alla Romana*." Looking at Alex, she said, "That's prosciutto and sage on top of veal scaloppini. It's a classic Roman dish."

The waiter finished making them comfortable and receded to the kitchen. They began a long talk about how exciting it was going to be living in Italy. She had researched plans for traveling around the countryside with him on weekends. She had just purchased a two-door red Alfa Romeo convertible for those occasions and now she was ready to fulfill her desires with Alex.

"I can't wait for the warm weather so we can put the top down and hit the back roads in Tuscany and Umbria," she said.

They held hands until the waiter brought their food. Afterward, Alex told Rachel it was the best meal he had eaten in a long time, then paid the check by doling out a gazillion lira.

The need to walk off the substantial meal found them walking over to the Via Condotti to look in store windows. The street was a who's who of Italian labels.

"Rachel, look at this; there's Gucci, Pucci, Brioni, Ferragamo, Dolce & Gabbana, and Fendi. I also see a Burberry's store, Cartier, Prada, Bulargi, and Armani. Jesus, even the people walking down the street are elegantly dressed."

He stopped to look inside the Brioni window at a handsome men's suit.

"Oh my God. Rachel, look at the price. That's a lot of money."

"But you're worth it," she purred softly.

"That's supposed to be my line for you," he smiled at her.

"Of course, I'm worth it. That goes without saying," she batted her eyelashes at him.

"I see," Alex said. "So, exactly when are we going to return here to buy some things for you?"

"For a hunky jock, you're not so dumb after all."

They hugged each other and kissed in front of both the passersby and the mannequins in the window.

"Let's get a taxi home," Rachel said with a mischievous grin. "I think its playtime."

Chapter 11

MEETING CHARLOTTE AND CARTER

"Good morning, Nancy," Alex greeted his secretary as he entered the office the next day. He actually felt refreshed and ready to dig-in to his new position.

"Good morning to you. I hope you're ready for a busy day, Alex. The Management Counselor, Charlotte Eaton, just called. She's looking forward to meeting you and wonders if you'll be free this morning. Shall I call her back and say it's okay, perhaps in about fifteen minutes?"

"That'll be fine. How is she, by the way? She has to be better than the clown we had in Islamabad."

"She's a lot better. She doesn't have it in for Security and is well-connected to the European Bureau in Washington." Alex grunted his approval.

"I heard in DC she's lucky to be here," Alex said.

"Yeah, I understand Central Personnel wanted to send her off to the Third World, apparently, only because she'd had too many European assignments lately. In the end, DCM Chandler made a strong pitch for Charlotte because of her connections and competence. I heard he even went all the way to the Director General of the Foreign Service to get the assignment approved. So, she owes him big time for getting the job."

"You bet she does."

Nancy continued, "Also, don't forget you have a meeting with the CIA Station Chief, Carter Ambrose, at ten o'clock."

"What can you tell me about him?"

"He's been here about four years and he once served in Milan."

"Okay. Does he treat us well?"

"We haven't had any problems with the Station."

"Excellent. Anything else on the agenda?"

"Yep. At eleven you've got a meeting with Top Clarke."

Twenty minutes later, after reading overnight classified telegrams for his office, Alex was ready to meet the regular characters in his new assignment. He walked down the hall and entered the Management office suite where Charlotte Eaton was in charge. It was abuzz with activity. Eaton had a Foreign Service secretary, as well as a receptionist who was a part-time local hire.

"You must be Alex Boyd," a pleasant female voice said from the adjacent inside office. Alex turned and saw a smiling, tall, trim woman with short brown hair striding confidently toward him. She appeared to be in her early fifties.

"And you must be Charlotte Eaton."

"I am. Welcome to Rome, Alex" she answered, extending her hand. Her handshake was actually firmer than the DCM's. "Come into my office."

He quickly viewed the memorabilia around her room. Two State Department Superior Honor Awards were mounted on the wall behind her desk, and another Meritorious Award on a second wall. On a third wall was a certificate indicating she'd received a master's degree from the National War College in Washington, DC.

All right, Alex thought, *Charlotte clearly wants visitors to know she is a woman of accomplishment. Actually, all anyone needs to know to figure that out is that she is the Management Counselor in Rome, one of the State Department's most prestigious assignments.* He also knew she'd been the Deputy Executive Director of the European Bureau, and before that, she had served as the Management Counselor at the U.S. embassies in Stockholm, Brasilia, and Prague. He'd done his homework on her and felt, in all, she had a very impressive resume.

"I can't tell you how much I'm looking forward to working in Rome," he said.

"We're delighted to have you here," Eaton replied, still smiling as she spoke. Alex wondered if Eaton was sincere or just spouting the usual bullshit.

"I'm sure we'll be working closely together," Alex said, with a hint of a smile.

"I understand you and Rachel Smith are living together in Parioli. If you need anything for the apartment, just let me know."

"Thanks, that's very considerate of you to offer." *Maybe I underestimated her willingness to be supportive,* he thought.

"How are things on the budget front? Does Washington give us most of what we need?" Alex asked, intentionally exploring her relationship to the power brokers back home.

"We fare very well, overall. In fact, I usually speak with the European Bureau every day."

This told him a lot. If Charlotte really did speak to the Executive Office of the European Bureau every day, then she probably was one of the inner circle of senior management officers universally known by Diplomatic Security Agents as, "The Black Dragon Society." Of course, the group didn't really exist as such, they weren't *dragons* obviously, rather mostly white guys. But the name humorously implied a secret society of master bureaucrats who controlled resources and programs. And, that's exactly what they were.

"How long have you been at post?" he asked.

"It's been two years now. My husband and I are enjoying every minute."

Alex glanced at his watch, seeing it was nearly ten o'clock.

"Charlotte, it's been really a pleasure meeting you, but sorry to say, I have to run. There is a meeting with Carter Ambrose I must get to in a few moments. You and your husband should join us for dinner or drinks so we can get to know one another better."

"We'd like that. Thank you, Alex, it was nice meeting you."

He sort of liked Charlotte Eaton. After Islamabad, he swore he'd never trust another Management Officer, but perhaps he'd become overly critical. So, he would give her a chance. Still, he realized she was beholden to Alden Chandler for her assignment; that would make her an ally of his in any potential battles he might have with the DCM.

They both rose, shook hands, and Alex returned to his office to prepare for meeting Ambrose.

Ten minutes later Alex was at the entrance to one of the Embassy's controlled access floors. He punched in the code for the lock, then walked down the corridor to Carter Ambrose's office. As he rang the doorbell, Ambrose's door buzzed, releasing the electronic lock. He pushed it open.

"Alex?" Ambrose's secretary asked.

"Yes, that's me."

"Hi, I'm Courtney. Mr. Ambrose is expecting you.

She got up, peered into Ambrose's office and said, "Alex Boyd is here."

Ambrose was a very big man, standing at least six-feet four-inches tall and weighing perhaps two-hundred-and-fifty pounds. He wore a double-breasted dark-blue suit that appeared very expensive. While shaking hands, Alex realized the dimensions of Ambrose's hands were huge. His full head of straight hair was a tad long, and mostly grey. Alex guessed Ambrose was probably in his mid-fifties.

"Alex, let's sit over here," Ambrose said, directing him to a leather sofa with two matching chairs.

"By the way, just call me Carter. We don't need any formality between us."

"That works for me, Carter"

There was nothing personal on his walls: no awards, no certificates, only a few attractive prints of ancient Rome. This was no surprise as CIA officers never had personal awards in their offices. Those types of things were reserved for their secret files in Langley.

"Jim Riley sends his regards," Alex said.

"Ah, how's he doing since his promotion to Director of Diplomatic Security?"

"He's doing great. I think the job suits him; we couldn't have a better Director."

Riley had finished his tour in Pakistan a year before Alex left, and was then promoted to Director of DS. Alex had been promoted to Riley's Senior Regional Security Officer slot in Islamabad.

"Jim told me you served in Moscow together," Alex stated.

"Indeed, we did. Jim was a great RSO. We worked together for two years. He was knowledgeable about Soviet espionage tactics, and very discreet. I'm glad to see he's risen so high at State."

"Jim also told me your Russian is pretty good."

"It's okay. I minored in Russian in college, and the Agency gave me a lot more training since then."

"How's your Italian?" Alex asked.

"I think it's not bad," he said modestly. Alex had heard it was excellent.

"It's a language I really enjoy speaking," Ambrose said. "You probably don't know I served in Rome twenty-five years ago. Later, I also had a four-year tour in Milan. So, those years in Italy, plus the last five here as Station Chief, have given me an opportunity to improve my Italian. I've taken full advantage of all those years."

"Tell me about threats here in Italy? First, do you get good cooperation from the Italian intelligence agencies?" Alex asked.

"Our relationship is excellent. Our agencies have worked together for fifty years."

"You don't have to comment if you don't want to, but do you have significant unilateral operations in Italy, or is it all liaison?"

Carter smiled.

"Langley told me you were smart, and you'd ask a lot of questions." Alex returned the smile but didn't comment; he waited for Carter to answer.

"The answer is, yes, we do conduct some unilateral operations. But we don't operate against the Italians. We target the usual third country suspects. However, our joint work with the Italians is a big part of our program."

"While I was in Washington, I asked for a CIA briefing on active terrorist groups operating in Italy," Alex stated. "The briefing was pretty good, but I'd like to hear your views on what's happening here."

"Okay. All the Middle East terrorist groups have offices in Italy, but normally they focus on fundraising, logistical support for terrorists outside of Italy, and propaganda. That's not to say they couldn't operate violently here. As for Italian groups, the old Red Brigade folded in 1984 and was then replaced by splinter groups, who still do the occasional assassination, kidnapping, etc."

"How big are the new Italian groups, and are they well-funded?"

"That's the good news. We estimate there are only around fifty hardcore members. But they do have additional sympathizers. As for funding, it seems to be enough for what they want to do, with their limited numbers."

"How good is the Italian intelligence service?"

"Well, prior to 1970 there was only one service, other than the police. Afterward, two organizations were created. One is the domestic agency and its run by the Interior Ministry. The other is the military secret service and its run by the Defense Ministry."

"So, how does all this work from the CIA's perspective."

"It functions," Carter replied sarcastically.

"Does the FBI Legatt get involved with these agencies?"

"Not very much, Alex. We control the relationship for the Embassy. Besides, the FBI is more focused on criminal activities involving potential cases in the United States, Mafia type activity. All this cloak and dagger stuff isn't what they like doing. There isn't much of a public relations benefit for them."

"Hmm, did I just detect a little cynicism?" Alex asked with a smile on his face.

Carter smiled and shrugged.

"How do you view our front office?" Alex asked.

Carter paused for a moment.

"That's also complicated. I like the Ambassador. He's personable and smart. But like many political appointees, what the CIA does is new territory for him. He's supportive, but sometimes it takes a little more explaining for him to see why we approach certain issues the way we do.

"Chandler, on the other hand, is just the opposite. He's served in Europe for so long he's seen a lot of our intelligence operations, for better or worse. I remember briefing him years ago when we were both serving in Washington, and the guy wanted to micromanage one of our operations. Naturally, that wasn't going to happen. But he's obsessed over details. The good side is at least he's smart, and he knows Italy. The bad side is he's full of himself and doesn't care if he insults you.

"But, here's a word of warning, Alex. He didn't treat your predecessor very well. Frankly, the last RSO didn't have many contacts. We got along fine, but I never felt he even wanted to be a player at post. By the way, Chandler once told me that he hated to see the rise of Diplomatic Security in the State Department. I think he's more comfortable in the 1939 Foreign Service—all Ivy League types plus one or two code clerks. But, let me caution you that while he stays on top of everything in the Embassy, it's clear his only passion is Italian politics.

They chatted for another ten minutes. Then, Alex felt the need to close the meeting.

"If there's anything I can do for you, please let me know. You can count on me to protect your information."

"I heard that I can," Carter replied.

Alex left feeling he really liked Ambrose Carter, hoping his instincts were right.

Chapter 12

MEETING THE NOCS AND GHIBERTI

A few days later, Rachel was in Milan with the Ambassador providing press support for his visit to promote US textile exports to Italy. A resident RSO in the Milan Consulate General made Alex's presence unnecessary. Instead, he decided to pay his first visit to the famous Italian hostage rescue team, the *Nucleo Operativo Centrale di Sicurezza,* known by their initials, the "NOCS".

Shortly before coming to Rome, Alex had met the unit Commander and two of his officers in Washington. The Commander, Colonel Vittore Adriani, had invited him to visit their Rome facility once Alex settled into his new job. Now, he decided to have his deputies, Joe Roberts and George Cefalu, accompany him so they could all build relationships with the NOCS.

Shortly before eleven in the morning, an Embassy car and driver dropped all three off in front of a nondescript building in central Rome. There was no unit emblem on the building, nor sign of any kind. First, looking up at the security camera, Alex then pressed the wall buzzer; the door opened electronically from within. He immediately recognized the two men greeting them at the door as people he had met in Washington.

"Alex! It's good to see you again," Captain Nino Agostino spoke in Italian while giving him a friendly hug. Joe and George watched in amazement. They were aware Alex had met the men in DC, but the warmth of the greeting was unexpected.

"Welcome to our home," Captain Paolo Capelli said, also greeting Alex with an embrace.

Quickly introducing Joe and George, Alex saw them stand firm, not leaning forward for the European-style hug. They simply shook hands all around.

"Please come with us to see Colonel Adriani," Nino said. "He is waiting to see you again, and to thank you for taking care of us in Washington."

As they walked up two flights of stairs, Joe quietly asked Alex, "Tell us again why you know these guys so well?"

"Diplomatic Security broke me out of language training to meet them when they were visiting the Anti-Terrorism Assistance Program."

"There must be more to the story than that," George queried.

"Well, we did have a few drinks at the end of the day."

"Only a few?" George asked.

"Okay, you guys are too sharp for me," Alex laughed. "If you must know, we closed a bar in Georgetown at about two in the morning. As you can imagine, we covered a lot of ground that night."

Colonel Adriani was waiting, smiling broadly. Again, more embraces. "I want to practice my English, so, no Italian until lunch," Adriani announced.

The Colonel was wearing a casual, well-tailored sports coat and turtleneck sweater. His uniform hung from a coat rack in the corner of his office. Both Nino and Paolo wore leather jackets and blue jeans.

Clearly, Alex thought, *this is a unit that emphasizes the ability to deploy discreetly and quickly, rather than worrying about formal attire.*

They took seats around the conference table at one end of the Colonel's spacious office. On the table in front of them were two pieces of paper for each of the Americans. The first page was a schematic, in English, of the NOCS organization, and where it fit into the hierarchy of the *Polizia di Stato,* or State Police, sometimes called the National Police. The second page was a phone list for emergency contact within the NOCS. It included office telephone numbers, home numbers, and mobiles. The list was pure gold as far as Alex was concerned, and he thanked Colonel Adriani.

"As you are aware, gentlemen," Adriani began the briefing, "that NOCS is well-known for its hostage rescue capabilities? We have safely rescued numerous kidnap victims. But we have also been extremely active in supporting other police units combating various types of violent crime, such as ending sieges resulting from bank robberies or other armed holdups." He went on to detail some of the NOCS' exceptional work.

"I have a question for you Colonel," Joe Roberts said. "I know the Carabinieri also have a special unit for hostage rescue. How are its responsibilities different from yours?"

"An excellent question," Adriani replied. "The *Carabinieri* do have a good hostage rescue unit. Although they have a big presence throughout the country, as we do, technically the *Carabinieri* are the military police or *gendarmerie.* In practice, however, there is not much difference between us. It is one of the anomalies of Italy that two organizations can do the same thing. I believe you also have overlapping capabilities in the US, no?

For example, you have the FBI, state police, and city police. Also, you have both Diplomatic Security and the Secret Service that do VIP protection with assistance from various police departments. So, in truth, if you want to know in advance who will handle a specific hostage rescue crisis within Italy, I can't tell you. It depends on who assumes responsibility first, and what the politics are for each event."

Joe acknowledged the answer with a tip of his head in assent.

"Now, let's take a walk around my headquarters. I'll introduce you to our section chiefs and we'll visit the armory."

Thirty minutes later, after chatting with section chiefs for intelligence, logistics, technical support, and assault teams, they arrived at the armory in the basement. The NOCS had an impressive array of weapons. Everything from assault rifles and machine guns to pistols, smoke grenades, and tear gas.

"Would you like to see some of our men shoot," Colonel Adriani inquired

"Absolutely, Colonel," Alex replied.

"Please, you must call me Vittore! Okay, come with me."

A large indoor shooting range was located inside the door they pushed open. No doubt the Colonel had planned this exhibition in advance. Each one put on ear protection, then Adriani asked two officers, who Alex had not met, go to the firing line. On command, they each fired two shots from their pistols within two seconds at silhouette paper targets, which were perhaps five meters away.

"Good shooting," George commented first, noting all four shots were placed in the target's chest. Next, the Italians switched to submachine guns, each firing a burst into the same targets, but this time from 25 meters.

"Maybe you would like a turn?" Adriani asked.

"With pleasure," Alex smiled. "Since there are only two targets set up, I think Joe and George should fire first."

The Italian's 9mm Beretta model 92 pistols were selected. Both men scored center mass target hits from five meters. Then, it was Alex's turn.

"Let us give you a new, clean target," Adriani stated.

"Thanks, but it won't be necessary," Alex replied.

"With all of the holes already made, how will we know if you even hit the target?" Adriani asked.

"That won't be a problem, Vittore," Alex said, matter-of-factly, and smiled. He had a plan.

Because the target's chest areas were indeed riddled with bullet holes, Alex decided to shoot at the target's heads. On command, he drew the pistol they had given him, and fired a total of four shots, two at each target, all under three seconds.

A moment of complete silence.

"Bravo! Alex, Bravo!" Colonel Adriani erupted.

Two shots were cleanly visible in the center of each target's forehead. Alex smiled, again, and returned the gun to one of the Italian police officers.

"Perhaps I should ask your Embassy to transfer you to my unit in order to become one of my assault leaders," Vittore said.

"Well, if the food in your canteen is better than in the Embassy cafeteria, you have a deal," Alex grinned in response.

"Speaking of food, this has all made me hungry," Adriani declared. "Ready for lunch?"

Colonel Adriani had made reservations for five people at Ristorante da Fortunato, one of the best restaurants in Rome. Located one block from the Pantheon on a narrow, mostly pedestrian street, it wasn't far from the Parliament. Adriani had arranged for a police SUV to take them. He, Alex, Joe, and George went to lunch while Nino and Paolo stayed behind.

Walking through the front entrance, Alex immediately noted photos along the walls of famous politicians, actors, and other celebrities. The lunch crowd, they were informed, always included a host of politicians or important movers and shakers.

"Ah, Vittore, good to see you again," welcomed the *maitre d'*, warmly shaking Adriani's hand. "I have you seated at the General's usual table."

"General?" George quietly queried Alex. Hearing the question, Adriani explained in English.

"We are being joined by Police General Raffaele Ghiberti. His actual title is *Dirigente Superiore Questore,* but everyone just uses the term 'General'. He's in charge of the State Police throughout all of Italy." Joe Roberts caught Alex's eye, silently mouthing the word, "Wow!"

As the *maitre d'* escorted them through the dining room to a round table in the far corner, Alex saw how elegantly everyone was dressed. Men in well-cut, dark blue suits dominated the room. Several women in very fashionable attire were wearing colorful silk scarves around their necks. Colonel Adriani's group was seated and made small talk until the General arrived.

Within moments, a distinguished looking grey-haired man of average height, wearing a dark civilian suit, entered the room and was escorted to their table by the *maître d'*. Alex noted two men, who had arrived with the General, positioning themselves by the front door, obviously the General's bodyguards.

"Gentlemen, I am sorry to keep you waiting," General Raffaele Ghiberti said as they all shook hands.

"We have only just arrived," Alex replied in Italian. "It is an honor to meet you, General. We could not have had a better interim host than Colonel Adriani."

The General beamed. "Vittore," he said, "coming here was a good choice because I see Mr. Boyd is quite a politician, or should I say diplomat?"

"I only speak the truth," Alex replied with a grin.

"Your Italian accent is excellent, Mr. Boyd. But I think we can use a mixture of English and Italian, if that helps the conversation."

Joe Roberts showed a sign of relief, and everyone agreed to using first names for the rest of their lunch.

Ghiberti then began describing the broad nature of Italian police cooperation with American law enforcement. He also mentioned that he had attended some training in the States, funded by the FBI.

While enjoying his *Spaghetti alla Amatriciana*, Alex started getting the impression his new best friend, Raffaele, was a fan of the Embassy's Legal Attache, Mark Terranova. Then, thought maybe he was reading too much into what Ghiberti just said and steered the conversation elsewhere.

"Please give our best to Danny Aaron," Raffaele continued. Danny was a Senior Program Officer in the Diplomatic Security Anti-Terrorism Assistance Program and Alex knew him well.

"I know Vittore met Danny during his visit to Washington, but how do you know him?"

"Ah, Danny was here maybe two years ago to discuss training we give to other countries. He is a nice man, a smart man. Speaking of training, Alex, I hope you will be able to attend our annual two-day hostage rescue exercise. Naturally, Danny is also invited. We'll hold it in Abruzzi. There will be SWAT teams from many European countries and some observers from America."

"I've been counting on it, Raffaele. Thank you, again, for the invitation. I also want to extend an opportunity for some of Vittore's officers to visit our Embassy and look at its security. I think we should have them familiar with the inside of the Embassy just in case they would ever need to come to our aid for an incident. They should do it ahead of time and understand how we use our armed Marine Guards."

"Thank you, Alex," General Ghiberti responded. "Thank you, very much, indeed. I really appreciate your cooperation. None of your predecessors have offered such an opportunity in the past."

Two hours later the lunch was over. In the cab ride back to the

Embassy, Joe spoke up.

"I can't tell you how refreshing it is to make these new senior contacts. It won't come as a surprise to you that, previously, we only had some low-level connections."

"I gathered as much from Nancy," Alex replied. He deliberately didn't mention that Carter Ambrose had said the same thing.

"I don't understand it," Alex said. "Why join Diplomatic Security and serve overseas if you don't want to maximize every opportunity to make foreign contacts? You just don't know when they'll come in handy. After all, how many emergencies occur between nine-to-five, and then only during the workweek?"

"George, this is perhaps the most important lesson you'll learn during your first tour. Make as many contacts as possible, cultivate them, show respect, and get to know them as friends. Knowing guys like General Ghiberti and Colonel Adriani can let you bypass all the bullshit and bureaucracy."

"I'm with you, boss," George replied.

* * *

Back at the office, Alex called Danny Aaron in Washington. "Hey Danny, its Alex Boyd. How's it going?"

"Good to hear from you. You know, same old bureaucratic bullshit here in DC. The new Assistant Secretary is trying to downsize Diplomatic Security into oblivion, and Jim Riley has his hands full fending him off."

"I'm sorry to hear that. Just goes to show you can't trust the Foreign Service to support its own security program. Listen, Danny, I just had lunch with General Ghiberti and Colonel Adriani. They send their best and have extended an invitation for both of us to attend their upcoming hostage rescue exercise."

76

"Fabulous! I'm coming. They're good guys. Email me the details."

"They told me which foreign SWAT teams will be there, but I actually forgot to ask if the *Carabinieri* will also participate. What do you think?"

Danny laughed loudly.

"You must be kidding! The cops and the *Carabinieri* hardly speak with each other, and then only because they have too. I seriously doubt the *Carabinieri* will be present."

"I guess you're right. I'm looking forward to seeing you here. Come a few days early and we can drive to Abruzzi together."

"Looking forward to it, Alex."

Chapter 13

AMBASSADOR ON THE LOOSE

Saturday turned out to be sunny and cloudless, the air crisp and chilly. Ambassador Scarmatti and Francesca sat in their sunroom drinking coffee and reviewing guide books on Umbria in general, and Orvieto specifically. Both were dressed casually in comfortable walking shoes since today was going to be a personal outing without the trappings of his office.

He had given his bodyguards the day off by telling them that he was tired and just wanted to rest at home. The police made him promise to call their special police number should he change his mind. Scarmatti had agreed. But in truth, he had no intention of calling them today.

"Tony," Francesca said, "the guide-book says Orvieto's main street is loaded with ceramic shops. We have to buy some colorful bowls or vases there."

"Anything you like, Francesca. Let's go directly to the shops when we arrive, then have lunch. Perhaps, we will look at more shops afterwards. I also want to see the famous 14th-century cathedral.

Did you know Orvieto is linked to several Popes responsible for having the cathedral built?"

A car made noise on the gravel pulling in front of the house.

"That must be Charlotte," the Ambassador said. He rose and went to the front door, opening it and greeting her.

"Good morning, Charlotte! Please come in; would you like some coffee?"

"No thanks, Tony. I just ate a late breakfast with lots of caffeine, so I'm wired for the day."

"Hi Charlotte," Francesca said, rising from her chair and joining them. She gave her a kiss on the cheek.

"I'm bringing you the same car as last time," Charlotte said. "The motor pool filled the tank, so you'll have plenty of gas for the trip. You're taking your mobile phone, right?"

"Yes, it's in my pocket already," Scarmatti replied. "I spoke with Alden earlier, so he knows we're going to Orvieto, though I am not sure where else we may go. I really appreciate you arranging an Embassy car on short notice."

"Thanks, it was easy. But, I must ask if Alex Boyd knows about your trip?"

Ambassador Scarmatti frowned, looked sheepish, and rubbed his chin as he spoke.

"No. I decided not to mention it to him. He wouldn't allow it without my bodyguards. I know he's right, but damn it, we need a little time strictly to ourselves. The cops are with us ninety-nine percent of the time. That's enough!"

"Okay," Charlotte said, "just as long as you considered telling him."

"I have. Do you need a ride home?"

"No thanks, I'll walk over to the Villa Borghese and look at the museum there. Have a nice trip and be very careful."

Loading maps and bottles of water into the car, the Ambassador and Francesca then seated themselves into the black Ford Mondeo and drove out the Residence grounds. As they passed the front gate, they noticed Charlotte talking with the uniformed policemen on duty, conveniently distracting them.

What they didn't notice were two motorcyclists down the street from the residence. Cosimo di Luca had paid two student extremists from Bologna to watch Scarmatti's residence on weekends, hoping Scarmatti would repeat his earlier foolishness of driving without bodyguards. Had he bet on it, he would have won.

As soon as the gates had opened, they spotted him and his wife leaving. Just the two. Slowly pulling into traffic a block behind their car, the two motorcyclists maintained a discreet distance. Traveling north, the Ambassador left Rome, catching the autostrada, and eventually merging into the A-1 highway until the exit for Orvieto. The journey took about an hour.

"Tony, let's try to park near the cathedral in case we buy some ceramics; then we won't have to carry them too far back to the car."

Scarmatti negotiated the winding, narrow streets of the medieval town center until he spied a rare parking spot and pulled into it. Both were delighted with their good fortune.

The two riders, wearing helmets with dark visors, passed the Ambassador and Francesca getting out of the car. Francesca noticed the riders, but only because they seemed to be looking at her.

At least they are not paparazzi, she thought.

The riders drove another block, parked, and followed the Scarmattis on foot.

As the couple entered the cathedral, the two cyclists, Bruno and Silvia, decided to stay in front of the cathedral. No point in exposing themselves by entering the church. Bruno had his digital camera inside his jacket. Now, posing Silvia in front of the cathedral's steps, he waited, then snapped the Scarmatti's photos as they exited the church and passed behind Silvia.

"Bruno, let them walk on," Sylvia said. "We don't want to be too close."

"Agreed."

Scarmatti and Francesca left the square, walking along a pedestrian street that ran the length of the town center. Stopping in various shops, they talked with owners about their wares, then continued to the next store enjoying a leisurely pace.

When they seemed to have spent an inordinate amount of time in one shop, Bruno suggested to Silvia they have a look. She objected at first, but finally relented. Walking by the shop, they saw Scarmatti buying an old print of what looked to be a typical Italian village. Silvia led Bruno further on past the store.

Five minutes, Scarmatti and his wife emerged, print rolled up under his arm. They next entered a ceramic shop across the street called Belloci.

"Look, Tony, this place has exactly what I want," Francesca said, thrilled with her exploratory success.

"What are you looking for, *exactly?*" the Ambassador said playfully.

"Different things, my sweet. I want a pair of really big vases, like four feet high that we can put small bushes in. I also want some serving trays, pots for flowers, and little knickknacks. And, I'm looking for some ceramics by Innocenti. He's a famous Italian pottery maker."

Scarmatti knew his wife well. When she called him "sweetie" or "my sweet", he knew Francesca was signaling she seriously wanted to buy something. He didn't mind. After all, if it made her happy, then he was happy.

The store owner was reasonably fluent in English, and the conversation flowed back and forth from English to Italian. Outside the shop and across the street, Silvia observed Francesca picking out several items and talking to the owner about large vases. She told Bruno to take pictures of the shop as it might prove useful in the future. Twenty minutes later, it appeared Scarmatti and Francesca were ready to leave. Silvia saw Scarmatti pay with a credit card.

"Bruno, listen, I think one of us should find out whatever we can from the owner about the Scarmatti's visit. Why don't you follow them? I will pretend to want some vases. When I'm finished, I'll call you on the mobile to find you."

"All right" Bruno replied, turning in the direction the Scarmattis had taken.

Carrying a medium sized bag of new treasures, the Scarmattis walked another ten minutes, then discovered an attractive looking restaurant. Meanwhile, Silvia entered the shop and began looking around.

"Can I help you?" the owner asked Silvia.

"Your ceramics are so beautiful. I am interested in vases."

"What size?"

"Oh, I think large ones, like those over there," Silvia said, pointing to the same ones Mrs. Scarmatti had been admiring.

"Ah, an excellent choice. These are our last two in stock, but we'll have a new shipment coming from the factory in a few weeks."

"I see. I was looking for colors different from those two, though they are very pretty. Do you ship out of the country?"

"We do. In fact, another couple was just here minutes ago who also asked me about shipping."

"Really? Where did they want to ship to?" Silvia asked.

"To the United States. I probably shouldn't tell you, but when I saw his credit card, I recognized his name. He's the American Ambassador."

"You must be kidding!" Silvia exclaimed with contrived wonder. "Is he a regular customer?"

"This was his first time here. You should have seen his wife. She is so beautiful."

"Yes. It seems beautiful people like beautiful things, don't they? Well, thank you, I'll come back when your new shipment arrives," Silvia said.

"I hope you will." She gave Silvia a card with the shop name and phone number on it. "Who knows, you may meet the Ambassador and his wife next time since they also want to inspect my new shipment."

"Great. Did you say your shipment would arrive in a few weeks, yes?"

"That's right, well, maybe even sooner. There is no fixed schedule," the owner affirmed.

Leaving the shop, Silvia called Bruno to get his location and joined him near the restaurant. She excitingly told him everything she'd learned.

"Let's grab a panini across the street in that snack bar," Bruno suggested. "We can keep an eye on the restaurant and follow the Scarmattis when they leave."

An hour later the Scarmattis left the restaurant, walked around town, and finally drove back to Rome. Silvia and Bruno followed at a safe distance to be sure they were returning home. After seeing the Scarmattis through the residence gates, Bruno called Cosimo di Luca, happy to tell him they had information he would want to hear.

Chapter 14

PLAYTIME AND FLORENCE

Alex was the first to wake up. He watched Rachel's face as she lay sleeping, a lock of hair laying carelessly over her left eye. He moved to brush it back, his touch arousing her from sleep. She opened her eyes and smiled. That, in turn, aroused him. Reaching under the light covers he felt her soft skin, smooth curves. They began lovemaking again until about ten in the morning.

Satisfied for the moment, they were lying in bed, bodies entwined. Alex was running his hand through Rachel's long wavy locks. He moved to kiss her full lips, the ones he loved to watch whenever she spoke to him. Her hand was a bit further down on his body. She smiled.

"You always feel so good,"

That's all he needed to begin again.

When they finally stopped to breathe, Rachel asked an unexpected question.

"Do you think I'm too heavy?"

"What? No! Where did you get that idea?" Alex scrunched his face, truly perplexed at Rachel's concern.

"I mean, I know I'm fairly well muscled, and you like that, but maybe I should lose some weight." She was serious.

"You don't have to lose an ounce! You're a hundred-and-sixty pounds., but you're five-foot-ten and you've been a jock your whole life. You're still a jock, in fact. Why do you think you have to lose weight all of a sudden?"

"Well, two days ago in Milan, when the Ambassador was helping promote our textile exports to the Italians, I saw all of those runway models in the office. They were so gorgeous and thin, I felt fat."

Alex wanted to laugh but knew he dared not make fun of Rachel's perception of her body.

"Look, those girls are paid to be emaciated. It goes with their profession. They have no strength, no endurance, and they never eat anything of substance. Don't compare yourself to them. Believe me, most men think runway models are much too skinny."

"But maybe I should lose just ten or fifteen pounds," Rachel insisted.

"You're not listening to me. You look amazing. You have firm abs, a nice chest, a great ass, and the best legs in Italy."

She smiled and rolled closer to connect with his lips. He liked that; he always did.

"Besides, if you get too skinny, how are you going to hold up your side of our wild fun times? If one of those supermodels wrapped her legs around me, I wouldn't even know she was there."

Rachel exploded with laughter and slid her muscular thighs around his waist, squeezing him with just enough power calculated to make him hard. It worked, and they spent another thirty minutes enjoying each other in bed.

* * *

Lunch was at the restaurant La Carbornara in Campo de Fiore. Afterwards, Alex and Rachel walked through the outdoor market in the square and headed toward Piazza Navona. While Rachel was in a great mood, Alex realized she had only eaten the marinated zucchini, mushroom, and olive antipasto for lunch.

So maybe she is trying to drop a few pounds from her muscular frame after all, he thought.

First stop was the Pantheon where they delighted in its extraordinary architecture and beauty, one of the first temples made for everyman. Its dome was truly a world changing concept. Then, they walked to several small shops nearby and entered an antique store specializing in old fountain pens.

"I want to buy one of these for you," she told him.

"I appreciate the thought, but I don't really use fountain pens. Now, a baseball glove or a bowling ball would be really useful."

"Very funny. Seriously, it makes an elegant statement. Now that you're more senior in rank, and almost ready to leave adolescence, you should use a proper fountain pen."

Alex laughed. "Now who's being silly?"

"Here," Rachel said, "look at this one." She handed him a black pen made by the Italian company Aurora. A salesman took special interest in her selection.

"It has been adapted to take replacement ink cartridges, so you don't have to use an ink bottle even though it looks as if you should," he noted. "See how sharp the stylus is? One would think you need to dip it in an ink, but no, the ink just flows."

"I don't know," Alex said. "How old is it?"

"It is probably sixty years old, but completely refurbished," he replied.

"Did Mussolini use it?" Alex asked.

"I don't understand, *Senore.*" There was a long pause, then he said, "Ah, you are making a joke," the salesman grinned.

"I want to give you a gift," Rachel insisted. Turning to the salesman, she said, "We'll take it." And that was that.

"I want to see you carrying it at all times," she told Alex on the way out of the store.

"Even in bed?"

With mock exasperation, Rachel said, "See, I told you, you were almost out of adolescence. No, not in bed. You already have one great pointed tool for that."

They walked hand-in hand toward the Spanish Steps. It would take another fifteen minutes to get there, plenty of time for Alex to think of what he should purchase for Rachel.

When am I ever going to use a fountain pen?

* * *

A week later, Alex was on the 'Rapido' train from Rome to Florence, escaping the day-to-day drudgery of his job. Seated next to him was his local investigator, Tomas Longo, and across the fold-up table was Rachel, who would be reviewing press coverage set up by the Consulate for tomorrow's event.

The Ambassador would be arriving by train for a speech to the Tuscany Chamber of Commerce. He would spend the night at the palatial house of an old friend in the city. Since the speech would attract a lot of media attention, it was open to a cross section of the population. Alex wanted to personally review the security arrangements in advance. Just being cautious.

"Tomas let's go over our itinerary again," Alex said. "When we arrive at the train station by ten o'clock, we'll take a taxi to the hotel to drop our bags, then all three of us will go to the American Consulate. Following the meeting with the Consul General, you and I will see the Chief of the *Polizia di Stato* for Florence. Rachel stays at the Consulate and meets some journalists. Then, with a senior policeman accompanying us, we'll all visit the Chamber of Commerce together."

"Sounds good, Alex," Tomas replied. "Here's a list of police officers we'll see." Alex examined the typed list and memorized their names and ranks.

"Rachel, do you have anything to add?" Alex asked.

"It's pretty straight forward from my end: The press will be at the Chamber of Commerce for the speech and can ask questions afterwards, or during the lunch that follows. The Chamber has graciously set up a side room where the Ambassador and journalists will meet exclusively after lunch. This should take us to about three in the afternoon.

The Ambassador then departs for his friend's house, which we'll see in advance this afternoon. His friend and overnight host, the Conte di Tomasella, is a wealthy Florentine, with money both from his inherited fortune and through his business acumen. Friday evening, Conte di Tomasella is having a private dinner for the Ambassador with Tuscan businessmen, financiers, and some cultural big-wigs."

"Is he really a conte?" Alex asked.

"He would be, if they still used titles officially in Italy. He can trace his title back to the Middle-Ages."

Satisfied, Alex turned his attention to the view outside the train's window. The Italian countryside was a mixture of cultivated farmland, vineyards, and ancient hilltop villages. He imagined the farms and stone houses were all owned by the same families for generations. Relationships between friends here were formed by families who knew one another for centuries. Part of Alex was envious of this stability, knowing their future was connected to their past, yet another part of him rebelled at the notion that life was set, inalterably based upon family lineage and location. Upon deeper reflection, Alex knew he needed adventure in his life, variety, and even risk.

* * *

The Florence advance visit for security and press arrangements went smoothly, in large part because the American Consul General had done an excellent job with preparations. Alex and Tomas met the Chief of Police and his team and were delighted with the protection set up for the Ambassador. Security at the Conte di Tomasella's house in central Florence, where Tony and Francesca Scarmatti would be spending the night was superb and secure.

That evening, he and Rachel's schedules were free. Rachel, who'd been to Florence before, took him to eat at Osteria Del Cinghiale Bianco, an excellent restaurant across the Arno that specialized in wild boar dishes. The two rooms for dinner were packed with tables close together. The emphasis was on coziness and friendly décor, rather than grand elegance. The owner remembered Rachel from her last visit and came to the table twice to chat. Alex figured he had a crush on her; who wouldn't?

"Rachel, this *pappardelle* with wild boar sauce is superb," Alex said, then sipped an amazing Tuscan red called *Brunello di Montalcino*.

"I'm glad; what's appealing to you?"

"It hard to put my finger on it. It tastes a lot like regular meat sauce, but with more pizazz. I guess that it's just a tad stronger, which I like." They also shared some zucchini *fritti* with the main course, and a *tiramisu* for dessert.

Afterward, they walked back together across the bridge over the Arno, called the *Ponte Vecchio*, toward their hotel. It was a beautiful night with full moon and light soft breeze. The bridge was full of couples, some kissing, some just embracing, and others enthralled with the view along the Arno river, surrounded on both sides with wonderful Florentine architecture. Halfway across the bridge, Alex pulled Rachel close to him, wrapping his arms around her, and kissed her passionately.

"Wow, what was that all about?" she asked with a grin.

"I'm just thinking how lucky we are to be together." Then, looking deep into her eyes, he said, "I love you so much," kissing her, again, more gently this time.

Rachel was momentarily choked up. She squeezed Alex tightly, then relaxed her embrace. Her eyes were moist.

"Let's window shop," she said, taking out a tissue and wiping her eyes.

The bridge was unique with shops on the ground level with a second level containing storage areas. Inside the many windows were displays of glittering gold jewelry. Even in the moonlight, it was dazzling: necklaces, rings, and watches in abundance.

Rachel said most items were probably handcrafted in Florence since the city was famous for its artisans. She seemed to look with special interest in two specific shop windows, focusing on various wedding rings.

He started to say something clever about romance, love and weddings, but decided on discretion instead. He did, however, file the names of two of the jewelry shops on the bridge for future reference.

Chapter 15

MISSED OPPORTUNITY

The following morning, Bruno and Silvia were sitting across the street at a café as Ambassador Scarmatti and Francesca were driven out of the Villa Tarverna in Rome. They were now a normal complement of Cosimo di Luca's rotation of surveillance teams.

Spotting the Ambassador's limo, they immediately jumped on their motorcycles and followed a half-block behind the police follow-car. Surprisingly, the limo did not go to the Embassy, but instead went to the central Termini train station. They watched as Scarmatti and his wife entered the station along with two bodyguards, all carrying modest-sized pieces of luggage.

"You stay here with the motorcycles," Silvia told Bruno and ran into the station building intending to find where the group was going. Once inside, she slowed to a casual walk and managed to spot the Ambassador's group. As she passed, she heard one bodyguard tell the Ambassador they had twenty minutes before the train to Florence would be leaving and they needed to board immediately. Quickly, Silvia approached an electronic ticket machine and purchased a one-way ticket for herself on the next train to Florence. She assumed the Ambassador and his wife would be traveling first-class, so bought a first-class ticket for herself. Then she made a quick phone call.

"Bruno, they are going to Florence. I bought a ticket and will try to stay near them. Call Cosimo and ask if he can give me support in Florence. Call me back if he can find someone to meet me at the train station at ten o'clock. I need him to arrange for two men with motorcycles to help with surveillance."

"All right Silvia, I'll be in touch."

All first-class tickets had a specific seat assignment in a particular carriage. Silvia was happy to see the Ambassador, his wife, and the two plainclothes police bodyguards all in the same carriage as she entered. The Ambassador's entourage was seated in a grouping of four. He and his wife sat in window seats facing each other, the two bodyguards had the aisle seats.

To Silvia's delight, she had a seat in the adjacent grouping of four seats directly behind them. She grabbed the window seat behind the Ambassador, their backs toward one another. For the next two hours Silvia strained to overhear their conversation. Although her English skills were only average, and the train noise made it difficult to hear clearly, she did pick up some vital information.

"Oh, Tony, I am so looking forward to our visit. I really like the Tomasellas," Francesca Scarmatti said.

"Yeah, this should be great fun," he responded. "You know, I owe them a huge debt of gratitude. When I was a student spending a year in Italy, they took me under their wings. At that time, they weren't even married yet, just students like me. Well, not exactly like me; they each were loaded, as in truly wealthy. They introduced me to a world most of us only read about in history books. It was a most memorable time."

"I think it's marvelous you've stayed friends over all these years," Francesca said. "And he's been a good business partner on your joint ventures, hasn't he?"

"Absolutely wonderful, Francesca. I really feel fortunate we are still close to this day."

"Oh, Tony, I forgot to mention, the ceramic shop in Orvieto called. They expect their new shipment to arrive in a week. Let's make plans to go back there."

"Fine. We'll make another day of it; have lunch after we shop, maybe see some other villages." The Ambassador pulled out his pocket calendar, perused his schedule, and asked Francesca if a particular date would work for her. She said, yes, and repeated the date.

Silvia couldn't make out every word, but did pick up the words "Orvieto", "ceramics", and the date.

Sometimes luck is better than skill or careful planning, she thought.

As they approached the Santa Maria Novella train station in Florence, Silvia got up and walked to the carriage door. She wanted to be off the train before the Ambassador's group and have time to look for the two men Cosimo di Luca was sending to meet her. They would be waiting for her.

Everything seemed normal at the station awaiting the arrival of Ambassador Scarmatti and his wife. Alex, the Consul General, and Rachel were waiting as the train rolled to a stop. Also present were two plainclothes *Polizia di Stato* bodyguards from Florence and two more policemen nearby in their vehicles.

The Consulate would be their first stop. One of the Florence-based cops would ride with the Ambassador and Mrs. Scarmatti in a police-provided dark blue Alfa Romeo sedan. The other officer would get into a follow car along with Scarmatti's two bodyguards from Rome. Alex, Rachel, and the Consul General would ride back to the Consulate in her car.

Armed with his SIG Sauer 9mm pistol, Alex could have insisted he ride with the Ambassador as his prime bodyguard, but he thought, 'What would be the point?' The police were with him every day and did an excellent job.

While on the platform, Alex noticed two young men, perhaps mid-twenties, standing some twenty meters away from him, nervously talking to each other. They were also apparently looking for someone to disembark from the train. He continued watching them until all three made eye contact. When that happened, the two men spoke briefly to each other and slowly walked in the direction of the station exit. Alex's experience told him that behavior anomalies were significant. In his mind, the two guys had just behaved oddly.

Just then the Ambassador and his group stepped off the train. On alert by the actions of the two young men, Alex stayed close to the Ambassador. Everyone shook hands, chatted for a moment, then followed one of the policemen toward the exit leading to the parking lot.

As they were about to leave the station, Alex, again, saw the two young men, this time talking with a university-aged female. It might have all seemed natural except the three briefly glanced toward the Ambassador's group. Alex quickly turned to the nearest bodyguard in the entourage, pointing toward the three who were now aware of Alex's interest and separating, leaving via different exits.

"Those three have been observing us," Alex told the cop. "I want you to question them."

"Which three, *Senore?*" The bodyguard tried to understand who Alex was pointing to in the crowded station. He scanned the large area, but hesitated, uncertain who to follow or what was going on. The opportunity to detain anyone was lost.

Damn it, Alex thought.

He didn't blame the bodyguard, but had he asked either Joe Roberts or George Cefalu to accompany the Ambassador from Rome, perhaps, either would have been quicker to act and detain at least one of the three for questioning.

The rest of the Ambassador's visit to Florence went without incident. At the Chamber of Commerce for the Ambassador's speech, Alex scanned the crowd, both outside the Chamber and within the hall, to see if he could spot any of the three from the train station. Nothing.

Maybe the incident is just my imagination working overtime.

Returning to the hotel, but before bed, Alex called Joe Roberts to brief him on the trip so far, and request that he and George meet him the next day at the Termini train station in Rome. After explaining the strange behavior of all three young people, he described what they were wearing.

He asked Joe to conduct counter-surveillance with George at the train station in Rome, looking for anyone fitting the descriptions, or any others seeming to observe the Ambassador on the arrival platform. Alex felt better prepared with his own men on watch.

The next day, Joe and George posed as passengers awaiting the arrival of the Ambassador's train. Joe stood near the arrival platform and George hung out at a nearby coffee bar. Both were in cell phone contact with Alex as he and the Ambassador's entourage disembarked from the train. Though they kept close vigilance, no one seemed suspicious.

Better safe than sorry, Alex thought.

* * *

When Silvia called from Florence, Cosimo Di Luca agreed to meet with her and Bruno immediately upon her return.

While guarded on the phone, Silvia had referred to important information she described as "game changing". Cosimo thought it best to have Agosto Tufo and Antonio Valerie also present since they were part of the Ambassador's original surveillance team. He was a man who liked everyone on the same page. It saved time and avoided confusion.

"So, Silvia, tell us what happened yesterday," Cosimo asked while leaning forward from his chair. They were all now gathered in his safe house near the Termini train station. Silvia lit a cigarette and described how she had followed the Scarmattis to Florence.

"Excellent initiative, Silvia," di Luca was impressed. "What else?"

"By pure luck, I was seated within hearing range, and overheard them talking. I heard the Ambassador was staying at the Conte di Tomasella's villa. They also talked about returning to Orvieto when the new ceramic shipment arrived. I have the date the Ambassador mentioned. This is our opportunity. The last time they went to Orvieto, it was without bodyguards. They simply drove themselves."

Cosimo considered this amazing development. Until now, his teams had merely been following the Ambassador. Moreover, they were exposing themselves to the danger of being spotted. But now, they could prepare in advance, knowing a location of the Ambassador's unguarded movements.

"Are you certain about this, Silvia?"

"I am certain what was said." She shrugged and blew smoke into the air. "Who can be sure they will go on that exact date?"

"Okay," Cosimo responded. "Tell me what happened once you arrived in Florence. You said you decided to break off surveillance."

"I had to. Those two boys you sent to the station to meet me were spotted by one of the Ambassador's security men. I think he's American."

"Why do you think so?" Cosimo asked. Silvia dropped her cigarette on the floor, crushing it with her foot.

"I am not sure. With his looks, he could be European, and he was well-dressed in a dark blue suit like a Roman businessman. But maybe it was the way he carried himself. He seemed self-assured, physically fit, very alert. In any event, I snapped a photo of him with my mobile."

Pulling her phone from her jacket pocket, Silvia showed the photo to Cosimo who passed it to Tufo and Valerie.

"Ah, this is the American from the Embassy," Tufo exclaimed. "I took his picture weeks ago on the Via Veneto. I also think he was involved in the bank holdup."

"He robbed a bank?" Silvia said, throwing her hands open wide in a gesture of disbelief.

"No!" Tufo laughed and shook his head. "He was in the BNL bank when it was robbed. One newspaper report said an undercover cop killed two of the robbers. Afterwards, that story was kept under wraps, but rumors say it was a foreigner who did the shooting."

"I see," Cosimo said. "In that case, this American may be very dangerous to us. All right, let's finish talking about your trip to Florence. So, you broke off surveillance because the boys were spotted."

"Yes. Besides, there was too much security around him to stay any longer. I saw at least four cops on the train platform, five, if you include the American. I did understand he was going to give a speech somewhere, but it seemed fruitless and dangerous to continue surveillance. I tell you, Cosimo, those two boys you sent are morons. They waited for me right on the platform for everyone to see them."

"I know. I am sorry, Silvia, but they were the only ones available at the last minute. It just goes to show, to be successful, we must plan well in advance."

"Now, let me sum up where we are," Cosimo continued. "We have already decided against kidnapping the British Ambassador.

That leaves the American Ambassador, who we believe will return to Orvieto in the very near future, probably without security, if he runs true to form. Therefore, I am advancing our plans to kidnap him. I will notify the armed team who will snatch him and tell them to be on high alert.

"Silvia, you said it would be a weekend trip, so we can maintain the normal level of surveillance during the work week and ramp up next Saturday and Sunday. Tufo, ensure the other safe houses will be ready should we need to move the Ambassador there on short notice.

"By this time next week, I expect we will have Ambassador Scarmatti begging us to take money for a safe return."

Chapter 16

THE NOCS EXERCISE

The day after returning from Florence, Alex was still suspicious about the Ambassador being watched at the train station. He met jointly with Scarmatti and Chandler and emphasized, again, the need for the Ambassador to take bodyguards with him at all times. Looking Alex straight in the eyes, Scarmatti promised he would. Alden Chandler, however, looked away and remained silent.

Alex wasn't deceived in the least. He hated being a cover-your-ass type of guy, but wrote a memo documenting this latest conversation, and sent copies to the Ambassador and DCM along with copies to Diplomatic Security Director Jim Riley in Washington. Then separately, he met with his police bodyguards to discuss his suspicions.

His next task was to fulfill the promise he made to *Polizia di Stato* General Ghiberti of attending the annual Italian hostage rescue exercise in Abruzzi.

Danny Aaron of the Diplomatic Security's Anti-Terrorism Assistance program in Washington had arrived in Rome the day before. Alex had invited him over to the apartment for dinner so he could meet Rachel. Now, Alex and Danny were driving to Abruzzi in Rachel's bright red Alpha Romeo convertible for the SWAT team exercise hosted by the *Polizia di Stato* unit, the NOCS.

"Glad you're driving, Alex, instead of the Italian cops," Danny said. "The last time I was here for this exercise I rode in a police car. That damn guy drove over one-hundred miles an hour on these winding country roads. We rocketed through a small town until he slammed on his brakes, calmly looked over at me, and asked if I wanted to stop for a cappuccino. Jesus! He seemed plenty wired to me already; I said no. What I needed was a valium and a change of underpants."

Alex laughed. Although Danny was a civil service employee, not foreign service, Alex thought he had a better feel for security and international affairs than most RSOs, or Foreign Service Officers. Moreover, he liked that Danny was a straight shooter when addressing problems to senior management in the State Department, a characteristic not appreciated by the politically correct crowd.

"Danny, I owe you a great debt for introducing me to Colonel Adriani in Washington. I think we'll have a terrific relationship. Both he and General Ghiberti are wonderful guys."

"Believe me," Danny replied, "I was delighted to make the introduction. Honestly, you seem to be among a small group of RSOs who truly value their police contacts."

Alex downshifted on a tight turn. The scenery was breathtaking at this point.

"By the way, how is your relationship with the FBI Legatt, Terranova? He has a history of running over RSOs."

"Still have to see how it develops."

"What about the Ambassador and the DCM?"

"The Ambassador's a nice guy," Alex responded. "The DCM is a dickhead."

It was Danny's turn to laugh. "Well, what can you expect from that type of Foreign Service Officer in Europe? Remember last night, I said the new Assistant Secretary for Diplomatic Security is trying to gut DS and shift money to other parts of State? Your DCM sounds like the same type of guy."

They drove in silence for another ten kilometers just enjoying the sun, the breeze and being out of an office.

Hopefully the Secretary of State will put a stop to this ridiculousness about destroying Diplomatic Security. But it's a broad problem within State. I've personally heard several senior Foreign Service Officers calling DS the 'tail wagging the dog.' Alex thought.

The sign for Aquila and other destinations was up ahead. He took the Aquila turn, shifting smoothly through gears while increasing his speed. He'd been driving about twenty kilometers an hour over the speed limit the entire time. From here, it would be another fifteen kilometers to the exercise location. Just as they entered a small village, Alex slammed on his brakes, coming to an abrupt halt.

"What the shit!" Danny looked as if he was about to have a heart attack.

"Do you want a cappuccino?" Alex calmly asked.

Danny, completely red-faced, laughed and yelled, "You prick. You goddamn prick." Alex chuckled, and put the car in gear again.

* * *

Arriving at the sprawling facility of the *Polizia di Stato* by midmorning, they dropped their bags at assigned billets and walked to the main office to find their handler.

"Glad you could make it," Captain Nino Agostino of NOCS greeted them with warm handshakes and offers of cappuccino, which made Alex smile at Danny.

The three of them piled into a Land Rover Defender and drove to the firing ranges. The entire area was hilly and fairly barren. Arriving, they saw several units with snipers zeroing in their rifles. Nino took them around to "meet the boys".

Alex and Danny were introduced to the French police counter-terrorism unit with the initials RAID, as well as the German GSG-9 Border Police assault team. To his surprise, they also met some observers from the US Navy SEALS and the British SAS.

Alex thought only police units participated in this exercise, but clearly these military observers were here for liaison. Although Alex, as a former Naval Intelligence Officer, had been assigned years ago to support a SEAL Team, these US Navy guys at the exercise were unknown to him, except for one chief petty officer whom he recognized. Finally, there were police units from Spain, Portugal, Greece, and, of course, the NOCS from Italy.

Other than snipers shooting at long range, most of the units had their men firing weapons at both stationery and pop-up targets at shorter distances. This would be a prep day only to ensure that all equipment was functioning properly following travel from home countries.

Alex was informed by Nino that tomorrow was the big event. Each team would conduct several mock hostage rescues in a series of shoot houses; each house was lined with material to absorb live fire. Artificially constructed life-size targets would be placed throughout these shoot-houses and the national teams would have to enter the rooms, killing mock "bad guys" to save cardboard "good hostages." Each assault would be timed, accuracy of shooting measured, and everything recorded on video.

With the introductory phase over, Alex and Danny returned to the main office. While they'd been out at the ranges, General Ghiberti and Colonel Adriani had arrived with a small entourage of other senior Italian police officers.

Maximizing the opportunity to make new contacts, Alex and

Danny picked their brains on crime in Italy, cooperation among various regions, and the terrorist threat. He offered support from the American Embassy for their programs. Seeds of camaraderie were planted everywhere.

After two hours of chatting, Alex and Danny returned to their billets for a quick shower before dinner where they would talk to other national units.

"Dinnertime. That's when I'll have a cappuccino," Danny said. Alex didn't say anything, but he chuckled a little, because he knew that Italians never drank cappuccino at night. Danny had a few things still to learn.

Chapter 17

LIVE FIRE

Saturday morning, before sunrise, Alex and Danny were seated in the middle of a long table in the mess hall finishing breakfast of scrambled eggs, melon, and prosciutto. Across the table was Sgt. Bill Turpin of the British Army's 22 SAS and on either side were Captain Paolo Capelli of the NOCS, and Chief Petty Officer Jim Horton of the US Navy SEALS. Everyone was engaged in conversation.

"I'm glad to meet you, mate," Sgt. Turpin was saying to Alex. "I was part of a British training team that visited Islamabad about six months after you left there. Our remit was to train the Pakistani Special Forces. We heard all about you from our spook, Geoff Ainsworth, and from Ambassador Farnsworth-Smythe. To be honest, at the time I thought they were bullshitting me because I'd never heard of a civilian kicking ass like you did when the rag heads attacked your Embassy."

"He's a former Navy man," Chief Petty Officer Jim Horton exclaimed, giving Alex a wink. "I wouldn't have expected less."

"So, you really did grease six of the terrorists, then?" Turpin asked.

"Yeah, I did. Four with my Uzi, one with a terrorist's AK-47, and one with a terrorist's own knife in hand-to-hand fighting," Alex replied. A brief memory washed through his mind. He didn't like thinking back to then. Rachel had come too close to being dead.

Turpin stared at Alex and shook his head, a look of admiration on his face. Alex would have preferred to stay modest, but it wasn't possible since Turpin asked for every detail in the battle that occurred nearly two years ago.

Hopefully, I won't have to repeat the story again this weekend.

He had never felt his actions were any different nor more heroic than the Embassy Marines he had led in battle that afternoon, nor of the other DS officers in the fight. Everyone had done what they were trained to do, and had done it well. In Alex's mind, Rachel's injuries placed her in an even higher category of valor since she was not a trained Special Agent and hadn't been expected to fight a vicious terrorist one-on-one.

Sgt. Turpin again pressed for information.

"You said your girlfriend also jumped one of the terrorists at the Ambassador's residence and killed him?"

"Yep, but Rachel gets pissed off easily." Everyone laughed.

"Fuckin' amazing," Turpin replied.

When Horton, Capelli, and Turpin left the table, Danny turned to Alex and said, "Talking with General Ghiberti, Colonel Adriani, and the others at dinner last night really solidified my office's ties with the Italians."

"They're good people should you ever need them," Alex said, "I think it's time we grabbed our stuff and headed to the exercise."

* * *

As special guests of General Ghiberti, Alex and Danny were given seats next to him in a control room to observe the assaults. There were numerous CCTV monitors and they could see every room in all three of the large shoot houses, some two-hundred meters away. Each house represented an Embassy, government facility, or a commercial office building. One national team at a time would assault a shoot house while the other teams waited their turn in a holding area adjacent to the control room.

"First, we'll see the Spanish assault team," Ghiberti explained to Danny. "Then, we'll have the Italian NOCS team, and so on. Each team will make three assaults during the day. We should finish up around six o'clock this evening. Oh, and inside each shoot house it's totally dark, no lights, other than what comes in through a few windows. So, the teams will have to use their night-vision goggles or flashlights attached to their weapons."

They watched the Spanish team assault on the CCTV monitors perform with impressive precision. When finished, Alex and Danny walked out of the control room to observe the other teams preparing for their turns.

While watching, Capt. Nino Agostino, one of the Italian team leaders, approached the men. He was dressed in black with a tear gas mask pushed up on his head. All members of his team were standing behind him dressed the same. Their load-bearing vests held a massive assortment of items. Each carried a radio, extra magazines, a combat knife, and flash-bang grenades. Agostino held a submachine gun across his chest and wore a pistol in a holster on his leg.

"Danny, how do I look?" Nino asked with a grin on his face.

"You look fearsome! Very machismo, Nino."

"*Va Bene*, we go now," he said, still grinning. With that, he ordered his men into their vehicles for the assault.

Walking back into the control room, Alex laughed. "Nino is so Italian, Danny. *La Bella Figura*. Not only do they have to be good at their jobs, but they have to look good doing it."

* * *

As the afternoon ended, Alex realized it had been a long day, broken only by a quick lunch of sandwiches and bottles of water. He waited for the Italian team to finish their third and final assault of the day which would end the exercise. Colonel Adriani and Capt. Nino Agostino walked toward him.

"Alex, may I ask a favor?" Adriani said in Italian. "You see, one of our men sprained his ankle on the second assault. He is no good to us now. Would you care to replace him?"

"What? Really, I didn't bring any of my equipment," Alex sputtered, his heart racing with anticipation.

"Don't worry, you can borrow ours. It's only the bulletproof vest, a radio, the guns, some equipment, and the gas mask. I think you are proficient with our Beretta pistol and the H & K submachine gun, yes?"

"Yes, I am. Okay, I'm honored that you asked me." He looked at Danny and raised his eyebrows in sort of a salute meaning, "Well, here goes."

Fifteen minutes later, after speaking with the other NOCS members and learning what his role would be in the assault, Alex felt ready. Before he and the NOCS got into their vehicles, he turned to Danny.

"Well, how do I look?"

Danny laughed. *"La Bella Figura."*

"Va Bene," Alex smiled and ran to his team's vehicle.

Standing on one of the special outside runners of the heavily modified Land Rover, his hands grasped the purposely-designed handrail. The driver accelerated toward the shoot house, covering 200 meters of bumpy road in seconds, as did a second Land Rover carrying an additional assault squad. When it stopped, Alex jumped from the vehicle and stacked behind three of the NOCS on the left side of the front door. Two other NOCS placed an explosive frame charge on the door and quickly moved to the right side.

Immediately the frame charge exploded, and the door was blown inward. Alex's stack moved through the opening. Entering, he caught sight of the other squad putting ladders up against the house to enter through second floor windows.

As planned, Alex went left after he threw a flash-bang into a large darkened room. The bright flashlight on Alex's submachine gun illuminated the gas and debris hanging in the air. His own breathing was heavy as he glanced through his gas mask.

Spotting two "terrorist" targets standing behind a sofa, he fired short bursts with his submachine gun, hitting both targets in the chest. He quickly swung around, the attached light on the submachine gun showed no terrorists behind him or elsewhere in the room. Then, he entered the next room as two pop-up targets jumped up in front of him from behind tables. He fired once, but his machine-gun jammed. He let it dangle on its lanyard and quickly drew his pistol, double taping each target in the head. He made Swiss cheese out of one more target in the kitchen area with his pistol. The area now clear, he called over his radio.

"Americano One to Control, five tangos killed; area now secure."

Once back at the control room, Colonel Adriani smiled at him.

"How did you like it, Alex?"

"It was great. I can't thank you enough for the opportunity, Vittore."

"Did you also enjoy my surprise?"

"Surprise, what do you mean," Alex asked?

"You don't think the gun malfunctioned by accident, do you?"

"You mean you put a dud round in my submachine gun magazine?"

"Yes, we wanted to see how you would handle it. You were splendid!"

Alex gave the Colonel a solid pat on the shoulder then nodded toward General Ghiberti who was nearby listening. He walked over to where Danny was standing.

"I can't believe they let you join their team," Danny said. "Normally, that's a no-no since accidents can happen."

"I know." Alex was still pumped from the experience. "I was lucky one of their guys sprained his ankle."

"Bullshit," Danny said. "Look over there," pointing to the rest of the Italian team. Alex saw the guy who had given him gear walking away without a limp. He shook his head in admiration for the thoughtful consideration of Ghiberti and Adriani. They were still standing nearby, looking at him, so he pointed to the team member walking without a limp, and saluted the two senior officers. Nothing more need be said.

That night after a final dinner for all the teams, Alex, Danny, General Ghiberti, and Colonel Adriani stayed behind in the mess bar, getting a little drunk and swapping war stories—some of them were even true.

How could he know this weekend of bonding with the NOCS and General Ghiberti would be crucial for his own survival, and for the Ambassador's life, in the future. That future was very near.

Chapter 18

THE FBI VS. ALEX

Alex was sorry to see Danny depart from Rome on Monday morning for Washington, DC He felt a real friendship had begun to form.

Then, shortly before attending the Ambassador's Country Team meeting, Alex received a call on his secure phone line from Diplomatic Security with important news. He was advised that Ramzi Yousef, the mastermind of the 1993 World Trade Center bombing in New York, had been captured in Islamabad by the RSO who replaced Alex.

The RSO had gotten support from DEA agents assigned to the Embassy, and from a special Pakistani Police unit Alex and Jim Riley had initially funded through the Anti-Terrorism Assistance program. Alex was elated.

The caller, then, gave him full details of the event. But he also relayed disturbing news that the State Department's Coordinator for Counter-Terrorism, a typical senior State Department Political Officer with no background in counterterrorism or law enforcement, had actually blocked a routine request by DS to have their Press Spokesman announce Yousef had been captured by DS agents with the help of others.

Why had that happened? Because the FBI had threatened the coordinator with "obstruction of justice" if the Department dared to "spill the beans" on Ramzi Yousef's arrest. Apparently, the FBI intended to take full credit, even though their agents were never even present for the arrest, or for the development of the intelligence leading to his capture.

Rachel walked into Alex's office, briefly overhearing the second half of his call with Washington. She handed him a press release from the FBI reporting Yousef's capture. Alex read it, shaking his head in disbelief.

And they wonder why there's friction between departments, he thought.

"What are you going to say about that release in today's country team meeting?" Rachel asked after she waited for his call to end.

"I'll let Terranova speak first, then think of something."

"Play nice."

"Rachel, whenever have I not played nice?"

"Yeah, as if," she rolled her eyes and smiled.

"Well, you realize, I will have to set the record straight, if the issue is raised."

They left Alex's office and headed toward the conference room. Alex took a seat, positioning himself next to where the FBI rep usually sat. Sure enough, Mark Terranova entered the room and sat next to him. He would likely be called upon before Alex if the Ambassador followed his usual routine of a clockwise rotation.

As usual, the meeting was semi-useless, with various section heads talking about issues of little interest to the broader group.

Finally, it was Terranova's turn to speak, a moment Alex awaited with relish.

"I want to report that the FBI has brought Ramzi Yousef back to the United States. Yousef is wanted for the 1993 World Trade Center Bombing. He's been on our most wanted list for several years. Our agents landed with him in New York a few hours ago, and he's being held pending full charges for his trial in Federal Court."

"Excellent work," the Alden Chandler, declared. "It just goes to show what hard work and dedication can do."

Terranova had nothing else to say. Now, it was Alex's turn, and first, he reported on his weekend exercise with the Italian police, then closed with a statement.

"Not only did the exercise give me a chance to evaluate the hostage rescue capabilities of the *Polizia di Stato,* but I also was able to chat with General Ghiberti, the national commander of the police, and with Colonel Adriani, the head of the NOCS."

Alex noticed Terranova taking detailed notes during his presentation.

"Very good," Ambassador Scarmatti said. "Do you have anything else for us?"

Alex saw the DEA Attaché was looking intently at him, as was Rachel, who had two of her fingers discreetly crossed and resting on the conference table.

Alex turned to Terranova and smiled.

"I'd like to congratulate the FBI for successfully bringing Ramzi Yousef back. I've heard the hand over from the RSO to the FBI went very smoothly in Islamabad."

Terranova's own smile slowly became a trifle smaller, while he tried to maintain his composure.

"Oh, I'm sorry," Alex continued. "The group probably doesn't know yet. In fact, I only received a secure call this morning. Based upon the Diplomatic Security 'Rewards for Justice Program,' a Pakistani informant contacted the RSO about Ramzi Yousef's presence in Islamabad, and following confirmation that the information was true, the RSO, accompanied by DEA agents and the Pakistani Police, raided his safe house. Yousef was there, he was arrested, then held by the police in a secure jail, and finally turned over to an FBI team that flew in a few days later. Until the FBI presents all of its terrorism charges against Yousef, he's being held on DS charges of passport and visa fraud. I think it was a splendid job of cooperation between three federal law enforcement agencies."

Alex smiled as if he meant it, and extended his hand toward Terranova, who had no choice but to shake it.

The DEA Attaché was grinning broadly. Rachel was resting her chin on her hands, her smile partially obscured. Alex saw the bright twinkle in her green eyes.

"Yes, good work to be sure," Chandler stated flatly, "perhaps we should move on.

An hour after the Country Team meeting ended, the DCM called Alex to his office.

"I just received a complaint from Mark Terranova that he wasn't invited to the NOCS exercise in Abruzzi. I know you cleared your travel with me a few weeks ago, and I should have thought about it at the time, despite my busy workload, but Terranova has a good point. We can't have just one officer meeting with the most senior Italian police official in the country without coordination among the other agencies."

What a prick, Alex thought. Both Chandler and Terranova were pricks. He felt strongly that Chandler should be delighted the State Department RSO had such great contacts. After all, that was a critical part of an RSO's job. As he stood in front of Chandler's desk listening to this bullshit, he decided not to tackle the matter head-on.

"I quite agree."

"Then, why did you do it?" Chandler looked steamed.

"First, Alden," Alex saw the DCM bristle at the use of his first name, "I didn't know General Ghiberti would be there."

This was a total lie on Alex's part, but he was prepared to stick to his story.

"Attendance at the exercise was a personal invitation to me and was supposed to be merely a chance to see the Italian shooters in action. Pretty low-level stuff, actually. Secondly, since it was a personal invitation, how could I have taken along others who weren't invited?"

"But the FBI would have been useful," the DCM declared.

"Perhaps not, Alden. After all, none of the Legal Attaches here are former SWAT team members, and none of them are responsible for the security of the Embassy."

"But Terranova missed a chance to talk to General Ghiberti," Chandler insisted sternly.

"As I said, no one mentioned Ghiberti was going to be there. Besides, how could I ask Terranova to come along, but not the Secret Service, Customs, Immigration, or DEA? They all have a vested interest in a liaison with the Italian police."

Alex knew he was winning the argument on its merits, but Chandler wasn't about to give in.

"Look, Boyd, as I've said, you need to think of the broader picture. You can't think only of benefiting the concerns of just your office. Coordination among agencies is key, and always will be key."

"So, does this mean whenever Terranova visits General Ghiberti, or other high-ranking cops, he will coordinate with me? Even invite me to go along?"

Now, he was pissing off Chandler and held his hand up to delay Chandler's response.

"Actually, I agree with you," he said, trying to sound sincere.

"Let me suggest that I chair an inter-agency law enforcement working group. We can all discuss our issues and develop a strategy to coordinate with the Italian government."

The DCM blinked rapidly, his brow furrowed, his hands fumbling with his pen. Then he cleared his throat, but didn't say anything for several seconds, only staring back at Alex.

"Let me think about that. I'll get back to you," he finally said.

Chandler picked up some documents on his desk, pretending to read them. The meeting was clearly over, and Alex knew he was being dismissed.

A chuckle escaped him as he walked down the hall to the elevator, knowing full well the DCM would never ask him to chair a working group. Most certainly, if he did, he would never acknowledge it was Alex's idea.

Chapter 19

FOR HIS OWN PROTECTION

It wasn't often that Alex took a dislike to a foreign guest with whom he was dining. But this evening was the exception.

He and Rachel had joined the Embassy Secret Service agent, Chuck Nelsen, and his wife for dinner. Two other guests were also attending: Captain Sergio Bucato, from the *Polizia di Stato*, and his wife, Sophia. Bucato was in charge of VIP protection. Alex and Chuck worked with him whenever the President or the Secretary of State visited Italy. Moreover, Bucato's unit was in charge of Ambassador Scarmatti's protection detail, making him a vital contact.

Nelsen had picked the venue for this evening's dinner—La Tana De Noantri, an interesting restaurant on Via delle Paglia in Trastevere. Since spring had finally arrived and the weather was mild, they sat at an outdoor table surrounded by ancient Roman walls. They could feel history surrounding them with the gentle breeze.

Thirty minutes into the dinner conversation, Alex took a dislike to Captain Bucato. He sensed Bucato felt it unnecessary to have so many officers assigned to the Ambassador's protection.

"Do you have specific threat information indicating the Ambassador is being targeted, Alex?" Bucato asked.

"No, Sergio, I don't. But targeting may have been deterred because of the excellent protection given by your officers. I think it's important we consider the capabilities of both Italian and Arab terrorist groups, even if we don't know of specific plans."

"I understand," Bucato replied, while finishing his pasta. "It just seems odd we protect him during the week with armed officers, but while he is doing nothing on the weekend, he dismisses his protection team entirely."

"What?" Alex was shaken by surprise. Rachel had told him that Francesca Scarmatti mentioned they traveled into the countryside on occasion. But, he had naturally assumed the Italian police were always with him. Until now, Bucato had never mentioned the Ambassador traveling into the countryside. Perhaps, he was referring to other weekends?

"Sergio, I promise to look into this matter of weekend protection. Have your officers gone with the Ambassador on any weekend trips outside of Rome?"

"Yes, we have gone with him to Milan, Florence, and Naples." Captain Bucato said, realizing he may have just shot himself in the foot and now would need to provide coverage on all weekends.

"I'm sensitive to your manpower problems," Alex said, recognizing the look on Bucato's face. "But, let me assure you, we need to have the Ambassador protected at *all* times."

The rest of the evening was not as pleasant as it could have been since Alex kept thinking about this news. He resolved to talk with the Ambassador and DCM about the Scarmatti's weekend activities immediately.

At nine o'clock the next morning Alex was in the Ambassador's office. He had already spoken to Scarmatti's secretary who told him that if the Ambassador didn't have anything on his schedule for a particular weekend, she wasn't sure what he did with the bodyguards.

When he finally saw the Ambassador, he got right to the point.

"Tony, I understand from the police you sometimes dismiss your protection officers on weekends," He watched as Scarmatti raised his eyebrows in a surprised gesture.

"Just when I have no plans and we stay home, maybe play tennis, just read, or host some casual friends at the house. Of course, the police posted out front are always outside of my residence. Why? Is that a problem?" Alex sensed Scarmatti wasn't being completely truthful. He decided it was better to do more research before challenging him.

"Okay, but I just want to emphasize again, should you go into the countryside, you need protection. Do you agree?"

"I'm not sure I always need it, but I'll agree for now."

Alex next went into the DCM's office, and basically got the same party line. No, Chandler was not aware of the Ambassador going out without his protection. Yes, he certainly would mention to Scarmatti the importance of working with the police at all times.

If they were lying, Alex felt this could lead to disaster.

* * *

Alex's next stop was the Embassy motor pool to talk with the Ambassador's driver. Alex knew it was not unusual for Ambassador Scarmatti to give him the weekend off occasionally.

"On Friday afternoons, I always receive a call from the Ambassador's secretary, Julie Crandall. She tells me sometimes the Ambassador has nothing on his schedule for the weekend."

"And you're certain no one else substitutes for you."

"Only when I take my annual holiday. Otherwise, there is a duty driver on call who can be used in an emergency, but he's rarely called upon."

"Okay, thanks," Alex said. He next planned to see the Management Counselor, Charlotte Eaton.

"Good morning Charlotte," Alex said, entering her well-appointed office overlooking lovely gardens.

"I was wondering, the Ambassador sometimes dismisses his driver on the weekends, isn't that right?" Without waiting for a reply, he continued, "Well, Francesca mentioned to Rachel that she and Tony, on occasion, go to the countryside on a Saturday or Sunday. Have you had any requests for an alternative driver to take them around?"

"Why? Are you investigating misuse of overtime?" she replied with a laugh. Alex figured either she had a sense of humor or she was trying to deflect the conversation.

"No, not at all. It just seems inconsistent for the driver to be off duty, and yet for the Scarmattis to see the countryside unless they have another means of transport. Moreover, the police tell me that, occasionally, Tony gives them the day off on the weekend, saying he won't be doing anything. So, I really need an answer: Have the Scarmattis been given another driver on the weekends?"

"Alex, I can assure you that I have not authorized such a thing." Alex crossed his arms and leaned back in his chair. They stared at each other, neither saying anything for a few moments. Finally, Charlotte broke the silence.

"Would you like me to have the motor pool dispatcher bring up his logbook for your inspection?" She picked up the phone, waiting for his answer.

Alex relaxed a little, smiled, and said, "No, thank you, Charlotte. It was nice of you to offer, but that won't be necessary." He didn't want to insult her, but also knew she was smart enough to have doctored the books in advance if she was lying.

"I guess this anomaly will just have to remain a mystery," He smiled, made small talk, and then said he needed to return to his office.

As soon as Alex left, Charlotte Eaton called the DCM.

"Alden, we have a problem. Alex Boyd is asking questions about the Ambassador using a different driver on the weekends to travel outside Rome. Of course, I truthfully denied authorizing another driver to take him, but he's suspicious."

"So, he didn't suspect Tony driving himself?"

"No, he didn't."

"All right, I'll mention it to Tony. Just make sure there are no written records. I don't want to give Boyd the upper hand on *anything* in this Embassy."

"Understood."

Hanging up, she had a nauseous feeling. She never liked lying to anyone, not to Alex or to Diplomatic Security in general. But she'd served under enough Ambassadors and DCMs to know the score. Supporting the chain of command was how you got along and prospered in the Foreign Service, even though most senior officers drew the line at outright lying. Furthermore, she wouldn't be in Rome if it wasn't for Alden Chandler. As part of his team, Alden expected her loyalty.

In her experience, rules and regulations were mere suggestions and could be pushed aside when they interfered with desires of people like Chandler in the Foreign Service. At least, if you could get away with it. Otherwise, you found someone else to take the blame and be held responsible. She knew Chandler was a master at this and didn't want to be made responsible for his sins.

After his chat with Charlotte Eaton, Alex called an office meeting. Now, seated around his conference table were Joe, George, Nancy, and Sam. He opened the meeting by reviewing what Captain Bucato had mentioned at dinner. Then revealed what Francesca had told

Rachel about their weekend visits. Finally, he concluded with his conversations with Charlotte Eaton and the Ambassador's driver.

"So, you think he and Mrs. Scarmatti are sneaking out by themselves?" Joe asked.

"Yes, I do. He's already asked me to review his bodyguard coverage to give him more freedom. So, it's plausible."

"But that would mean the DCM is probably lying as well," Joe said.

"I wish I knew that for sure, but at this stage I don't," Alex replied.

"Too bad he isn't using his official car," stated Sam matter-of-factly. "We could put a tracker on it. But I guess he wouldn't be driving his own armored limo."

"Not hardly," Alex said. "But here's what we'll do."

"George, I want you to speak to the bodyguards. See if you can get specifics on when they've been given the weekend off by the Ambassador. Also, talk to the cops assigned to the residence and see if they know anything about the Ambassador leaving by himself. Nancy, ask Top Clarke to come in here."

They stalled the meeting for five minutes until Marine Master Sgt. Clarke arrived.

"Top, please have a seat. I need to coordinate something with you." Alex then turned to Sam.

"Sam, if I'm right, our CCTV coverage of the Ambassador's residence is recorded and stays in the residence guard house. Is that correct?"

"Yes. It's kept for thirty days, then recorded over on the same disk."

"Can you run a feed or send a signal to the Embassy and have it recorded at Marine Post One?"

"It's possible, but I'll have to look at the equipment to see if it has the capability. What do you want covered?"

"I want to see the driveway and parking area at the Ambassador's residence. In fact, let's see if all the camera videos can be sent to Post One."

"Top, the issue is that I think the Ambassador is sneaking off on his own without his bodyguards, and I need proof of it. If we can send a signal back to Post One to be recorded, I can review the weekend tapes on Monday morning, or even sooner than that. Do you see any problems with this?"

"No, Boss. We'll make it happen from our end."

"Good. Sam, let me know what you find out when you look at the equipment."

The next morning, Thursday, at nine o'clock, Alex called Sam Carson to his office.

"So, Sam, how's the camera monitoring project going at the Ambassador's residence?"

"Not good, Alex. I've set up some equipment from my stock, but it was defective. So, I ordered new transmitters, receivers, and signal scramblers from DC."

"How long will that take to arrive?"

"Probably a few weeks."

"Look, Sam, we don't have weeks to wait. Try to get some gear from a nearby post. Maybe you could try the Regional Support Center in Frankfurt. If they have it, I want it, ASAP."

"Right. I'll check. It still may take a few days for them to ship it here."

"The sooner the better," Alex said, realizing they were facing another weekend without knowing what the Ambassador was up to, or how to keep him safe, despite himself.

Chapter 20

THE KIDNAP

S unday morning began with great promise. Francesca Scarmatti cooked breakfast since the servants had the day off. She excitedly reminded Tony about the call from the ceramics shop. They had confirmed the new shipment had arrived, and the large vases Francesca wanted were in the shop. Now, she was looking forward to their drive to Orvieto, again.

"This will be great, Honey," Tony Scarmatti said. "After we pick up the ceramics, let's go on to Montepulciano and Cortona. We may not have too many more chances for outings without the police bodyguards. I had to promise Alex Boyd that I would behave myself." Francesca said nothing.

She knew how important the security issue was to Alex but convinced herself that everything would be fine. After all, what would anyone want with them?

Shortly before nine o'clock, Alden Chandler arrived at the Scarmatti residence. He drove his own car, a five-year-old black Mercedes sedan. Scarmatti greeted him at the door and went into the Ambassador's study to discuss a crucial issue. The Embassy needed to downsize staff to match U.S. government–wide budget cuts.

Ten minutes later, Charlotte Eaton arrived in an Embassy motor pool black Ford Mondeo sedan, which she parked under the portico at the front entrance. She entered, greeted Francesca, and joined the conversation in the study. By half past ten, the meeting was over and the Scarmattis were ready for their weekend adventure.

"I want to thank both of you for supporting our private jaunts out of town," Tony said.

"It's the least we can do, Tony." Charlotte replied. "I can't imagine what it's like being followed everywhere."

"Thank you. I know you're aware that Alex wouldn't approve, so I appreciate your discretion."

"That's not a problem, Tony," Chandler declared. "You've been doing this for some time, now, and nothing has ever happened. Have a nice outing, and don't worry about anything. I can handle the likes of Alex Boyd."

The DCM departed first and drove out of the villa's grounds. Then Charlotte got behind the wheel of the black Ford and waited. A few minutes later, the Ambassador came out the front door and sat in the passenger seat. A moment after that, Francesca followed and joined them, taking a seat in the back-right side behind her husband. Charlotte started the car and pulled out the driveway. They passed the Embassy guard booth where the guard was on the phone, paying little attention. The gate opened, and they drove to Charlotte Eaton's apartment nearby.

"Thanks, again, Charlotte, see you in the morning," Tony said as he got behind the wheel. Francesca moved into the front passenger seat. Neither of them noticed the white Fiat sedan that had been following them, and now had pulled over to the side of the road to wait as they let Charlotte off at her apartment front door. They also didn't give second thoughts to two motorcyclists who passed them by. They simply pulled out into traffic and headed to Orvieto, one hour away from Rome.

The white Fiat sedan with four terrorists of the New Red Brigade also pulled out into traffic at a discreet distance and again followed behind. The two motorcyclists, also members of the New Red Brigade, slowed to let the Scarmattis pass them, keeping a safe distance.

* * *

All six had seen the black Ford Mondeo arrive earlier at the Ambassador's Residence with only Charlotte Eaton inside. When she had driven off later, it only took a moment for all of them to register that the Scarmattis were now inside as well.

"Red One to Red Two and Three, the target is on board. Don't crowd the target until we confirm where they're going," the lead terrorist in the Fiat said over his walkie-talkie.

Red Two and Red Three on the motorcycles acknowledged. Five minutes later, as Eaton stopped the car in front of her apartment building, Red One said, "We will pass them by. Red Two and Three stay behind them."

"Affirmative."

All six terrorists had watched and waited as Eaton got out of the car and the Scarmattis changed positions. They saw the Americans shake hands and Eaton enter her building while the Ambassador got behind the wheel and Francesca sat next to him before they drove off.

Now, Ambassador Scarmatti drove through Rome's traffic until he connected with the autostrada heading north. The Fiat and two motorcycles followed. The terrorist leader in the Fiat used his mobile to call Cosimo di Luca.

"We are headed toward Orvieto as expected."

"Excellent, you know what to do. Do not leave any witnesses if you are seen," di Luca ordered. "I will notify the safe house to expect you."

Driving for an hour, the black Mondeo kept a steady speed. The Fiat and motorcycles took turns staying within sight of the Ambassador; alternatively falling back or passing him. Then, at the Orvieto exit on the autostrada, they all followed the Ambassador's car off the main road, but not too closely. Skillfully, the Ambassador snaked through the winding streets until he found a parking space in a quiet, secluded area not far from the cathedral. On one side was a masonry office building with few windows; being Sunday, no one was working. The other side of the street was lined with houses, each with a high wall and colorful flowering purple wisteria hanging vines, all blocking any view of the street.

The two motorcycles passed the Ambassador one more time, slowing to the side of the road ten meters in front of the Scarmattis parked car. Blocking the street directly behind the Ambassador's vehicle the Fiat pulled up and stopped. All the men quickly put on nylon masks. As soon as the Ambassador and his wife exited their car, the terrorists struck, rushing the pair with pistols drawn; one put the barrel of his pistol to Francesca's head.

"Cooperate or I will shoot her!" he yelled at the Ambassador, pushing the gun harder against Francesca's ear, causing her to cry out.

Ambassador Scarmatti's eyes flashed back and forth among the kidnappers and his wife. For the first time in his life he was at a loss for words. One kidnapper spun him around and forced his hands behind his back, then placed plastic flex-cuffs on the Ambassador's wrists and tape over his mouth. Once he was secured, they did the same thing to Francesca. One kidnapper pulled Scarmatti's car keys from his pocket. Mere seconds passed before they roughly shoved both the husband and wife into the trunk of the Fiat, slamming it shut. Only then, did the kidnappers take off their masks.

One man, who had arrived in the Fiat, got behind the wheel of the Ambassador's car and drove off, followed by a single motorcycle. The Fiat and remaining motorcycle left Orvieto via the A-1 autostrada heading north toward Bologna.

The entire snatch was accomplished in under one minute, and no one in town saw a thing.

* * *

Forty minutes later, the Fiat and one motorcycle approached the Bologna outskirts, but took an exit in another direction marked Marconi. They drove to a weathered farmhouse and parked in an adjacent barn. One kidnapper closed the enormous barn doors behind the car.

Putting on nylon masks, again, the kidnappers roughly yanked the couple out of the trunk and pushed them toward the basement of a pale-yellow stucco house. Once inside, their flex-cuffs were cut off, and each one had a wrist handcuffed to a metal pole extending from the basement's floor to ceiling.

Ambassador Scarmatti thought the room smelled from mold. He saw two dirty mattresses on the floor next to where they were standing. A single light bulb hung down in the middle of the room. Scarmatti turned to the kidnapper who was giving orders to the others.

"I'm the American Ambassador," Tony said in Italian, "I demand to speak to whoever is in charge." The two kidnappers only shrugged their shoulders at him.

"If you harm us, I'll see that you spend the rest of your lives in prison!"

The closest kidnapper slapped him across the face with an open hand. Scarmatti, again, started to say something before a second kidnapper, an enormous man who towered over Scarmatti, stepped forward and punched him full in the face. The blow was hard enough to make Scarmatti slide down the pole to which he was handcuffed, bright red blood spirting from his nose. Scarmatti's head was spinning.

"Tony, are you all right?" Francesca screamed.

"Yeah, don't talk to these animals."

"Animals?" the first kidnapper said. "We'll see who the animals are. And yes, some of us do speak English. In fact, we speak other languages, too, like torture. Ever hear of it?"

* * *

Meanwhile, the Ambassador's Embassy Ford Mondeo was driven to a different location, a deserted barn some ten miles outside Orvieto. The barn was locked after the vehicle was stashed and the driver climbed onto the back of a motorcycle. The two riders sped away toward the town of Marconi.

Chapter 21

THE PHONE CALL

The sharp ring of his cell phone made Alex's arm jump, nicking his chin, as he finished shaving at half past six on Monday morning. He quickly toweled off his face and went into the bedroom to retrieve his phone.

"Sir, this is Corporal Jameson at Post One. The Ambassador's butler just called and said Ambassador Scarmatti and his wife are missing. I called his driver, thinking the Ambassador may have left the house early, but his driver was never called to the Residence to pick him up."

"I assume he's not in the Embassy, then?" Alex asked.

"That's correct, Sir."

"Okay, Corporal Jameson, I'm going to the Residence to check this out. Notify Top Clarke, Joe Roberts, and George Cefalu about this. Tell them meet me at the Embassy at 0800 and await further orders from me."

"Roger that, Sir."

He threw on jeans and grabbed a University of Virginia sweatshirt.

"Rachel, I need to take your car. The Ambassador and his wife can't be found and I'm going to their Villa to check it out. Don't tell anyone about this until I confirm more details. I'll call the DCM as soon as I know something." Her eyes grew wide as she scrambled to dress.

The drive to Villa Taverna normally took some ten minutes; Alex made it in half that time. At the Residence, his first stop was talking with the contract guard.

"Has the Ambassador or his wife left the house this morning?

"No, Sir, I haven't seen them yet."

"Let me see the logbook." He reviewed the pages for Saturday and Sunday. No help there. It only showed the Ambassador had gone out on Saturday with his limo, driver, and bodyguards just one time, then returned in late afternoon. There were no other departures for either of them on Sunday. Alex did note, however, that on Sunday morning Alden Chandler and Charlotte Eaton each visited for maybe an hour at roughly the same time. That was all.

Once inside the house, Alex found the butler.

"Let's go up to the bedroom," Alex said. He scanned the room. The bed looked as if it had been slept in and roughly made up. The Ambassador's wallet, glasses, and cell phone weren't there; neither was Francesca's purse. He turned to the butler, "Did any of the staff see him yesterday?"

"No, Mr. Boyd. We all had the day off. The last time I saw him was Saturday night."

"I assume you've searched the entire house," Alex asked.

"Yes, we have, but neither one is here."

Alex inspected every window and door looking for evidence of forced entry. Nothing. Next, he went outside and saw the bodyguards had all arrived for work. Two were smoking next to their vehicles.

"*Ciao*, Franco," he said to the police sergeant in charge of the team. "The Ambassador is missing. No one has seen him since Saturday night. Did you escort him anywhere on Sunday?"

"No, Mr. Boyd. He told us he was staying home, and we should take the day off."

"Okay, do me a favor and search the villa grounds. I'm going to talk with the police outside."

The bodyguards acted quickly, thoroughly searching the gardens, but found nothing. Alex's discussion with the police outside was also fruitless. He tried the Ambassador's cell phone number, receiving only a message that the phone was currently unavailable. Next, he tried Francesca's number, and got the same message.

His next call was to police Capt. Sergio Bucato on his cell phone.

"I assure you, Alex, the Ambassador was fine when my men dropped him off at the villa on Saturday. He must have gone out on his own."

"You may be right, Sergio. I'd like to have the police check the hospitals in Rome to see if they've admitted the Ambassador, or his wife. Maybe they've been injured in an accident and no one knew to call the Embassy."

"I'll do it and call you back."

Next, he called Rachel. "Hey, Rachel. We still don't know where they are. Did Francesca say anything to you about leaving Rome this weekend?

"No, I wish she had. Is that what you think happened?"

"I honestly don't know, but now I need to call Chandler, then Washington. We'll need to convene an Emergency Action Committee meeting. You better get prepared to handle press inquiries by the million. I have to go. I'll call you if I hear from the Scarmattis. Let me know if Francesca calls you. This isn't looking good."

Calling Alden Chandler was the last thing Alex wanted to do. This was an RSOs worst nightmare; to lose an Ambassador was an unthinkable tragedy. Nevertheless, he placed the call to the DCM.

"What do you mean you can't find him?" Chandler sounded incensed.

"As I said, they've vanished. No one here, not the staff, nor bodyguards, or our residence guards have seen them since Saturday evening. I've asked the police to check the hospitals in Rome, but it's too early to know anything. I saw in the logbook that you were at the Residence on Sunday morning. Did you speak with the Ambassador?"

"Of course, I did."

"Did he appear all right?"

"Yes, everything was normal."

"Sir, did he say anything at all about traveling out of town?"

"Not in the least, certainly not that I recall."

"I'm going to call the DS Command Center," Alex said, "and I suggest you call the State Department Operations Center. Then, we better have an EAC meeting as soon as possible."

"Maybe we should hold off calling Washington until we hear something back from the police," Chandler said quickly. Alex stared at the phone.

What the hell?

"I disagree, Sir. Washington will go ballistic if we fail to notify them immediately. I recommend we tell them everything we know and what we're doing to find him. Washington needs to know we're taking action."

"Fine, I suppose you're right. I'll make the call to the Ops Center and see you at the Embassy in an hour."

Before returning to the Embassy, Alex put in one more call to Carter Ambrose, CIA Station Chief, and briefed him on the situation. He asked Ambrose to check with the Italian intelligence service for assistance.

This is looking more serious by the minute, Alex thought. *I just warned him about using his bodyguards. Unless they vanished into thin air, I think he lied.*

Chapter 22

EMERGENCY ACTION MEETING

Time was of the essence. It was urgent to develop leads on the Scarmattis' disappearance as soon as possible. With each passing hour the likelihood of them having been taken, even harmed, increased dramatically.

The conference room was packed with agency heads for an Emergency Action Committee meeting. Alex asked his deputies, Joe Roberts and George Cefalu to attend. The room was awash with noise, everyone talking at once in small groups.

Alex rapped on the table to get the group's attention, then opened the briefing by telling all known details and what steps had been taken to find the couple so far. Just as he ended, his cell phone rang.

Shit. I forgot to mute it or leave it outside the conference room.

But, looking at the incoming number, he excused himself, and stepped outside the room.

"Sergio! Do you have any news?" Alex spoke to Captain Bucato, police officer in charge of the Ambassador's protective detail.

"Nothing useful, I'm afraid. We've checked every hospital in

Rome; however, the Ambassador and his wife have not been admitted or treated anywhere. I've asked the central *Polizia di Stato* office, as well as the *Carabinieri,* to check hospitals outside Rome. That will take longer."

Alex's optimism plummeted. He'd hoped the Scarmattis were just having a medical emergency. His concern that they had been kidnapped was growing by the minute.

"Okay, Sergio. I believe you have the Ambassador's cell phone number on file, correct?"

"Yes, we do. I've tried it several times, but it seems to be turned off. We'll be able to trace the number, but only if it's turned back on."

"Excellent. Thank you. We'll keep in touch. Ciao, Sergio."

Thank God for my police contacts or I wouldn't be getting anything done.

Alex explained the conversation to the EAC members and tasked the FBI Legatt, Mark Terranova, to follow up with the *Carabinieri.* Then he asked Colonel Watson, defense attaché, to call the Italian military for any assistance they could provide. Before he could even ask, Carter Ambrose volunteered to stay in touch with the Italian civilian intelligence services.

Alden Chandler's secretary entered the room and approached Chandler. In a low voice, she whispered to him.

"I have the Secretary of State on the line for you."

Chandler stared at Alex and whispered, "Jesus Christ." He rubbed his eyes with both hands and looked as if the blood had just drained from his face. Obviously, the State Department Operations Center had pushed the alert up the chain of command to the very top. Alex felt his heart rate increase and knew the problem was escalating. Talking to the assembled group, Chandler brusquely said, "Wait here, I'll be right back." He left the room and went to his office down the hall.

Alex, had muted his mobile, now felt it vibrating in his pocket. He took it out, looked at the display, and saw Jim Riley's name. His old friend was now the Director of Diplomatic Security in Washington, DC. Walking out of the conference room again, he took the call.

"Alex, I got your report from the DS Command Center. Is there anything you want to add or emphasize?"

"Only that they haven't turned up at any hospitals in Rome, so the police are checking further afield. The DCM is on the phone now with the Secretary."

'Off the record, what do you think happened?" Riley asked.

Alex swallowed hard and tried to sound composed. "I can only speculate they must have gone out on their own somehow. Beyond that, I don't know."

"Do you think he's been snatched?"

"I'd rather not say until we know more," Alex replied, worried that if true, he'd be on the firing line.

"Okay, Alex, keep us informed and document everything you do."

"I will. Thanks for calling, Jim." Alex hung up and reentered the conference room. Ten minutes later, the DCM returned, looking very pale, and addressed the room.

"The Secretary said if the Ambassador and Mrs. Scarmatti don't show up by the end of the workday, Washington will launch the IRT to Rome."

Alex clarified the statement. "For those not familiar with that term, it's the Incident Response Team, composed of State, FBI, military, and CIA officers to support our efforts. They are an intelligence, law enforcement, communications, and policy team, not a hostage rescue force."

"Colonel Watson," Chandler continued, "you'll be getting cable traffic for clearance of their US Air Force plane if it comes to that. Charlotte, once we get their manifest, your office will handle logistics."

"Rachel," the DCM called out, "You and I will have to work closely on how we deal with the press." She nodded at him.

"Since we'll be operating 24/7, I'll need some people from the Political Section to handle the shifts," she said.

"Consider it done," Chandler confirmed. "Also, we'd better set up an official record of our actions." Turning to Ames Burnham, the Political Counselor, Chandler said, "I know that I just tasked your section with assisting Rachel, but I also want you to be the official record keeper of all activities on the Ambassador's disappearance. So, keep a good log book."

Burnham nodded.

"That's all for now," Chandler concluded. "We'll meet again based upon developments. Work your contacts; we need to find Ambassador Scarmatti and Francesca. Charlotte, could you stay for a moment to discuss logistics?"

* * *

After everyone left the room, Chandler leaned toward Charlotte Eaton and whispered. "This is horrendous. I think we better keep our roles in providing the car to Tony a secret as long as we can."

"But, Alden, it's going to come out in the end. It would be better to divulge it now."

"I disagree. Tony probably just got into an accident, and it'll all be sorted out before lunch time."

"But if he did have an accident, then it must have happened yesterday. Surely he would have contacted us by now."

Chandler leaned back in his chair. He hadn't thought it through that far. He rubbed both hands over his face.

"This is going to be delicate, Charlotte. Let's just see how it plays out. When he returns, he'll be able to justify our help, or even take full responsibility for his actions."

"I don't like it, but if you insist."

"Good, that's settled. Let's keep our fingers crossed."

* * *

A lex returned to his office with Joe and George. First, he called General Ghiberti, then followed with a call to the Deputy Minister of the Interior Ferrara on his private cell phone number. Both men had been briefed on the situation by their staffs. Ghiberti and Ferrara assured Alex they would use every asset at their disposal to locate the Ambassador and his wife.

Thank God for the Italians, he thought. He felt closer to them by the day.

Chapter 23

WATCHING THE TAPE

Alex was surprised when Sam Carson, engineering security officer, walked into his office with good news. He was feeling desperate for any insight into the Scarmatti mystery.

"I didn't have a chance to tell you before," she said excitedly, "but the extra video equipment for the Ambassador's residence arrived from Frankfurt on Friday evening. I installed it on Saturday. We have some tape of Sunday for you to watch."

"Jeez, Sam, that's great news!"

"Well, it doesn't show much," she said, "but it's something."

"Let's go," Alex said. They left his office and went down the hall to Marine Guard Post One, joined by George Cefalu, Joe Roberts, and Top Clarke.

Everyone squeezed into a small viewing booth. Sam started the tape, which showed a view of the DCM arriving at the Scarmattis' villa. His Mercedes drove into the compound and parked in a gravel area to the right of the villa. There was a lot of irritating background static on the tape, so Sam turned off the sound. Alex clearly saw

Alden Chandler get out of his car and walk to the front door, but lost sight of him when he went under the overhanging portico. Sam fast-forwarded the tape and returned to normal speed when another car, a black Ford Mondeo, drove in, stopping directly under the portico. They could only see the driver's side of the car and watched Charlotte Eaton get out and stand for a moment next to the car door, apparently admiring the garden. Then, she closed the door, and walked around the car to the main entrance of the villa, again, no longer visible under the portico.

"Now, watch this," Sam said. Again, she fast-forwarded the tape then slowed it a few frames later as everyone saw the DCM walk back to his Mercedes and drive out of the compound. A few minutes later, Eaton returned to her car, got in and waited a few moments before eventually driving away. The camera angle only allowed a view of the driver's side of the car; the rest was obscured by the portico. Once Eaton drove off, there was no one on the tape.

"Well, that just confirms what the DCM told us about meeting the Ambassador," Alex said, somewhat downhearted. "Is there anything else on the tape that would be useful, Sam?"

"I'm afraid not. You can see the guard walking around, but nothing else happens. As he stared at the tape something important bothered Alex, but he couldn't put his finger on it. Maybe it would come to him later.

"Damn, what a shame. George, go to the residence and retrieve the guard house tapes of the compound's exterior view. Watch the tapes with Sam and see if anything jumps out."

* * *

Two hours later, George called Alex. "You need to come down to Sam's office. We found something important on the tape."

George and Sam were seated in front of a long worktable when Alex arrived with Joe. In addition to a number of tools lying on top of the table, Sam had placed a CCTV monitor and tape player there.

"I've cued the tape to when Eaton leaves the residence. You'll note it's a high camera angle because it's mounted on the perimeter wall, so you'll only see the top of Eaton's car, but you should watch across the street."

She started the tape. The camera showed the black Ford Mondeo exiting the villa. After it pulled out into traffic, Alex saw a white Fiat pull out of a parking space and follow the Ford. He couldn't make out the license plate on the Fiat, but maybe, he thought, the cops could enhance the tape.

"Do you think that was a coincidence?" Alex speculated. "Why would they follow Charlotte Eaton?"

"Maybe Charlotte wasn't the only person in the car," Joe responded.

"Perhaps. I'll talk to her."

"Anything else I should see?"

"No, Alex, that's it," Sam said.

Alex pulled out his mobile and called Captain Bucato.

"I need your help, Sergio. Can the police enhance a video tape? We have reason to think there's a car tailing one of our Embassy vehicles leaving the Ambassador's residence on Sunday. If you can make out the license plate number, it might be important."

"Yes, we can do it," Sergio replied. "Is the Ambassador in the car that's being followed?"

"We don't know. You can't see inside our vehicle. But the Embassy car left Villa Taverna Sunday morning. I'll ask my deputy, George Cefalu, to bring it to you. Let's treat the tape as evidence."

"Okay, Alex," he said as they hung up.

"George, put the tape in a clear plastic evidence bag," Alex instructed. "Attach the usual signature sheet to it and give it to the cops. Be very sure they sign for it. But I also want you to wait with them while they enhance the tape. Call me immediately if you get any new information."

"Got it, boss." George went back to his office to get the evidence bag and signature sheet. Then he took a cab to Captain Bucato's office with the tape.

Alex and Joe Roberts, meanwhile, went to see Charlotte Eaton. "We have a tape of a car possibly following you out of the Villa Taverna on Sunday morning. Did you notice anyone behind you?"

"No, I didn't." She sat up straighter after hearing this news. Alex watched her reaction and thought he detected a nervous tick in her left eye. "Where'd you get this tape?"

"From our security system monitoring the perimeter of the villa."

"Oh, I see," Charlotte said, looking uneasy. She began fidgeting and taping her fingers on the desktop. Alex kept watching her with interest.

"Where did you go when you left the villa?" Alex asked.

"I just returned to my apartment."

"Why were you at the residence on Sunday?"

"Alex, what's going on? Is this an interrogation?" She seemed to be indignant, but it didn't ring true to him.

"Again, Charlotte, why were you there? This is important."

Eaton paused for a moment. Alex had a fleeting thought she was holding something back.

"We had to discuss a little Embassy downsizing, and I needed a decision ASAP."

"Did the Ambassador mention he would be leaving the villa during the day?"

"No. I would have said so already." Alex wasn't going to let her get off so easily.

"Charlotte, let me be direct: were Tony and Francesca with you in the car when you left the villa?"

"Absolutely not!" she said emphatically. Again, she tried to sound indignant, but this time, Alex was sure she was covering something up.

"All right, Charlotte. If you think of something useful, let me know." He returned to his office.

Now, why would she be lying? What would be the point? Something just doesn't add up. The one thing he felt certain about was his gut feeling.

I smell a little smoke. Maybe the gun isn't far behind.

Chapter 24

IN CAPTIVITY

The afternoon sun hung low in the sky. Setting behind the hills overlooking a white farmhouse, it left the sky a mixture of red and orange hues, promising a good day tomorrow.

Two young men in their twenties lounged at the base of a tall Italian Cyprus tree next to a wooden picnic table near the front door. To most observers they appeared to be friends merely enjoying a late afternoon glass of wine and cheese, then cigarettes. Closer inspection, however, revealed two shotguns lying on the ground behind their chairs as well as pistols tucked into the back of their pants.

Inside the farmhouse, sitting in a comfortable leather chair next to the living room's stone fireplace was Cosimo di Luca, holding court with a half dozen senior New Red Brigade leaders. Also, in the house, but below in the basement, were two younger gunslingers guarding the Ambassador and Mrs. Scarmatti, who were half lying on the floor, chained to pipes in a dark corner.

"So, everyone has seen the newspaper coverage of the kidnapping, I believe," di Luca said flicking ash from his cigarette. It was not a question, rather a statement of fact. "Tomorrow, the Americans will receive our ransom demands. No doubt the American and Italian governments will try to negotiate the amount of ransom money we've set at $10 million, as well as try to hold on to all prisoners we want released. The decision to accept a smaller amount of money has already been decided. We'll call it a sign of good faith. But we must stand firm in our demand for release of all prisoners." No one disagreed with him.

"Paolo, you will handle the calls to the Foreign Ministry. Remember, don't use your phone from here, or from your office in Bologna. Use only the throw-away cell phones for each call. Then remove the chips and destroy everything afterward."

Paolo nodded. He was delighted to be given such an important task. Ever since his days as a student communist at the University of Bologna twenty years ago, he had railed against the establishment.

"I'll make the first call after they respond to our ransom note," Paolo stated. "I'll ask them to prepare cash for delivery within a week, and confirm intentions to release all the prisoners. Naturally, the government will stall for time, giving us reasons for such a delay. Then, when I call back the following day, I will tell them they had better have some positive answers."

"Excellent, Paolo," di Luca replied. "We will keep their feet to the fire, but don't do anything impetuous. Each day that passes represents a public opinion victory for us. If after a week they have not moved in our direction with negotiations, we will send a photo of the Ambassador and Mrs., Scarmatti to several major newspapers in Europe showing their deplorable conditions. The pressure on the government will grow."

"Now, I want to see the Ambassador." di Luca said and pointed to one of the guards. "Make sure they are blindfolded." The guard scurried to the basement.

Di Luca and two others slipped on masks to obscure their identities as a double precaution should their captives' blindfolds come loose.

With masks secured, they walked downstairs into the basement. Immediately, a stench filled their nostrils. It was a combination of damp mold, feces, urine, and body odor. The Ambassador and his wife were blindfolded, each lying on a dirty mattress with one wrist handcuffed to a steel pole between them that reached from floor to ceiling. A makeshift toilet in the corner of the room needed to be emptied. Di Luca saw them both turn their heads in his direction as they heard his footsteps on the stairs.

"Hello! Who's there?" the Ambassador yelled out. Switching into Italian, he repeated the question. Cosimo di Luca had no intention of answering him.

"Please! Let my wife go! You have me, that's all you need."

"Tony, no! I want to stay with you," Francesca Scarmatti sounded panicked.

"It's not okay!' He raised his voice. "Stop treating us like animals."

Di Luca whispered into the ear of one of his guards. The guard turned around, approached the man, and whacked him across the mouth. Francesca stifled a scream.

"Be quiet and comply with what we tell you. You will be released when the two governments agree to our terms."

"What terms?" the Ambassador asked.

Di Luca thought for a moment and decided not to engage in discussion with him. It would be pointless besides, it could even be counterproductive should Scarmatti start talking with the guards about their demands later. Di Luca turned away from the Scarmattis and led his group back upstairs, including the two guards who had been watching the Scarmattis. The smell was too terrible not to give them a break. Once they left the basement, everyone took off their masks and took a deep breath of fresh air.

"Let me see the items they were carrying when you snatched them," di Luca said to one of the guards. He was led into a bedroom where several items were spread out on the bed: wallets, car keys, two wristwatches, some peppermints, the usual female makeup items, a vial of medication marked "Warfarin", and two cell phones. He picked up the vial.

"Has he asked for this?" he questioned a young guard.

"He has, but I wasn't sure what it was, so I waited until you got here."

Cosimo opened it and saw there were only a few pills inside. "If he asks again, give it to him." The guard nodded. DiLuca walked back into the living room.

Since the young guard wasn't invited to accompany him, he stayed behind. Being ambitious, he wondered if the Ambassador's cell phone might contain valuable information with which he could impress his elders. Turning on the Ambassador's phone, he began scrolling through a list of past calls. Then, he looked into the address book on the phone, taking notes as he went. After fifteen minutes, he turned the cell phone off and threw it back on the bed. But it was already too late.

* * *

With his one free hand, the Ambassador rubbed his jaw on the side of his face where the big kidnapper had walloped him. It hurt like hell but wasn't as painful as the damage to his ego.

How could I be so stupid and arrogant? He thought. *Alex warned me about always traveling with bodyguards. I'm ashamed I didn't listen.*

Scarmatti was not a man who made mistakes, at least not often, and never more than once. Yet, depressingly, he had made a big one, and put Francesca in mortal danger. Now, he didn't feel so smart. He looked at his wrist handcuffed to a solid metal pole. They were hidden in a basement, where no one could find them and completely at the mercy of terrorists.

"Tony, did you hear me? Tony!"

"What? I'm sorry, Francesca. I was thinking about out predicament. Are you all right? Are you hurt?" He reached over and touched her shoulder with his free hand. It was comforting to be able to reach out and touch each other in this terrible ordeal.

"My arm is sore from when they threw us into the trunk of the car, but I'm okay."

"I'm so sorry, Francesca. This is completely my fault. My judgment was bad because I was so seduced by the romance of being in Italy."

"Don't say that Tony. I didn't object to us escaping alone without the bodyguards. We both knew we were warned. But now, what will we do?"

Scarmatti looked around the room. It was a dirty basement with gray cement walls, no windows, nothing to identify where they were being held. A single light bulb hung down and glowed from the middle of the ceiling; in another corner of the room was the large chamber pot they had already needed to use. Seeing it sent a chill through his body.

Good god, subjecting Francesca to such indignities!

With no guards in the basement for the moment, he examined the metal pole. "Francesca, help me try moving this."

They stood next to each other, spread their legs slightly for a firm stance, then grasped both hands on the pole, giving it a few hard pulls. Absolutely nothing happened. He realized the pole was rigidly attached to the ceiling and floor with metal plates, each one with four large screws keeping it securely anchored in place.

"Damn!"

"What is it, Francesca?"

"If only I had asked for the ceramics to be delivered to our house, we wouldn't be in this mess."

"Don't beat yourself up, dear. We both wanted to see for ourselves what was in the new shipment. Besides, we also wanted to be on our own for a little while."

He took a step closer to her and wrapped his non-handcuffed arm around her. She sobbed as tears rolled down her face. They embraced a full minute before she spoke.

"Are they going to kill us, Tony?"

"No, they won't. They would have done that in Orvieto if that was their plan. I'm sure they want something in exchange for our freedom. We just have to be strong and trust that we'll be rescued eventually."

"But how long do you think it will take?"

"I honestly don't know. But listen, Alden and Charlotte know where we went and when we were supposed to return. Once they realize we've disappeared, they'll share that information with Alex and the Italian police. It'll be a major search operation, to be sure, but I think we'll be fine."

Scarmatti was trying to keep Francesca's spirits up. He honestly believed the Italian authorities would be immediately alerted by the Embassy. What he didn't know at all was how this situation would really turn out.

Too late now, he realized he should have listened to Alex. He couldn't even count the number of times Alex had told him to keep his bodyguards close. He wished Alex was nearby to help them out of this situation, but it probably wasn't going to happen, not nearly soon enough.

Feeling hunger, Scarmatti realized they hadn't eaten since before they were taken. Even so, he felt an urge to relieve himself and looked over at the chamber pot in the corner. No one was there to help bring it closer.

How can I reach it?

Chapter 25

THE RANSOM NOTE

T uesday morning, the Incident Response Team arrived bright and
early and went directly to the Embassy. They were determined
to find who was responsible for the Ambassador's disappearance
and how to get him back.

First, the leader asked to meet with a small group in the conference
room including Alex, DCM Chandler, Terranova, Ambrose, Eaton,
Colonel Watson from the Defense Attaché Office, Rachel, and
Burnham. Alex prepared to take notes with the fountain pen Rachel
had bought for him. He liked the weight of it in his hand.

"By way of introduction, I'm Ambassador Charles Van Camp, the
State Department's Coordinator for Counter-Terrorism. We're here
to help you manage this crisis. I'll appreciate your support as the
IRT works to get back Ambassador Scarmatti and his wife."

Van Camp's opening statement is ass-backwards, Alex thought. *The
IRT is supposed to support the Embassy, not the other way around.*
He glanced at Chandler, expecting him to correct Van Camp's
misstatement, but Chandler's face was unreadable, and he stayed

silent. Alex's gaze shifted to Charlotte Eaton, resting her chin in her hands. Eaton appeared pale, her hair was slightly disheveled. *She's looked better,* he thought. *She's really taking this hard.*

"We've practiced this type of event many times," Van Camp continued. "I can assure you, our protocols are well established and will help get you through this crisis."

"Practiced?" Alex inquired, with a degree of cynicism in his voice. "How many *actual* incidents have you handled?"

He was aware of Ambassador Charles Van Camp's reputation as an 'empty suit' by people who operated in the clandestine world. The job of Coordinator for Counter Terrorism was not a popular assignment in the State Department and there was rarely competition for the job.

"That's not the point," Van Camp replied haughtily. "And who are you exactly?"

"Alex Boyd, the RSO."

"Maybe we wouldn't be here if you had done your job properly," another man from the IRT said. He was a big guy with thick black hair, who looked like a former football lineman.

"Who the hell are you, and what do you know about Embassy security?" Alex snapped back. He felt outrage, not only at the insinuating comment, but at the entire situation of having the IRT here at all. The hairs on the back of his neck were bristling.

"I'll tell you who I am; I'm John Reynolds of the FBI, and I'm the guy that's going to get the Ambassador back."

Alex saw one of the CIA representatives from the IRT look at Carter Ambrose and shake his head in apparent disgust. Two DS Special Agents, part of the IRT, had their arms crossed but kept silent. They shrugged their shoulders, and changed facial expressions, as if to say: *what can we do?* Alex glared at Reynolds with contempt, then decided not to respond.

"Well, it's possible our security could have been a bit tighter," the DCM spoke.

Alex's eyes bore into Chandler as he thought: *You prick.* But he knew that arguing at this point did nothing to help get Tony and Francesca back.

"One other essential point," Ambassador Van Camp said. "All, and I do mean *all* press briefings or releases, will be handled thru the IRT. We need to control the message to the public and to the terrorists, if that's who we are facing. The IRT's press spokesman is Larry Jones, on loan to us from the FBI in Quantico."

It sounded to Alex that Van Camp had rehearsed this statement, like the rest of his spiel, many times. *Yeah, 'practiced', that's for sure,* he thought.

"How's your Italian?" Rachel asked Jones.

Good girl! Go, Rachel, Alex inwardly smiled.

"I don't speak Italian. That won't be necessary, just as I don't need to know the other twenty languages, or so, in the world."

"*Twenty* languages?" she smirked. "Try a couple of *hundred* world languages." The point was not well received. But, of course, she knew the FBI press spokesman's work would be directed at the American media to enhance the FBI's reputation. Rachel looked over at Van Camp and Reynolds, both of whom looked smug.

Van Camp now turned the briefing over to Reynolds and the CIA representative, who outlined the technical and analytical capabilities of the IRT that would be offered to the Italians. Ambassador Van Camp ended with a statement that the number one priority was to meet with the Italians and establish a working relationship. He also said that he, Reynolds, and the DCM would need to meet with senior Police and *Carabinieri* officials. As an after thought, Van Camp mentioned Alex could accompany them, if he wished.

Since Van Camp said he and Reynolds wanted to clean up before calling on the Italians, he asked if their hotel rooms were ready at the Ambasciatori Palace hotel, across the street from the Embassy. Charlotte Eaton confirmed they were. They adjourned the meeting and left the Embassy while their worker bees set up equipment in the conference room.

* * *

At midmorning a motorcycle rider, wearing a helmet with a darkened visor, approached the Ambassador's residence, the Villa Taverna, at moderate speed. Standing on either side of the front gate were two Italian cops. The motorcycle rider reached into his jacket, got a firm grip on the weighted envelope, and tossed it perfectly between them, and sped away.

Picking up the envelope, the cops opened it, and immediately reported its contents to their supervisor. By eleven o'clock, the police notified the Embassy and delivered copies of the ransom demand. Included were two photos of the Ambassador and Mrs. Scarmatti showing them handcuffed and holding a copy of Monday's *Corrire della Sera* newspaper proving they were still alive.

The ransom demand rambled on about the evils of capitalism and exploitation of the workers of the world. It demanded the release of ten specific members of the New Red Brigade from an Italian prison, plus they wanted $10 million in cash for the safe return of the Ambassador and his wife. Further guidance directed the Embassy to place a specific ad in the newspaper, *Corriere della Sera*, and to provide a telephone number to handle negotiations.

Chandler called Ambassador Van Camp at the hotel and told him a note had been received and requested he to come to the Embassy immediately. The DCM wanted to convene the Embassy's normal Emergency Action Committee but Van Camp refused and was adamant that all discussion be confined to a smaller group invited to assist the IRT.

"*Assist* the IRT!" Chandler blurted out in shock. "I think you have the relationship backwards, Charles."

"On the contrary, Alden. The IRT has the resources and a mandate from Washington to handle this type of crisis. And the Secretary of State sent us out here to deal with the problem." A brief silence ensued.

"All right," the DCM backpedaled. "But we have a shared interest here, and that is to get them back safely." Under the surface, Chandler was steaming. He hated to admit it, but maybe Alex had been right in questioning the real-world experience of Van Camp and his team.

But State Department politics required deference on his part. Once the incident was over and the IRT returned to Washington, they could make or break the DCM's career when they reported to the Secretary of State. That would be a conversation he would never be privy to.

Chapter 26

WHO'S IN CHARGE?

After Chandler called Ambassador Van Camp and John Reynolds about receiving the ransom note, the two rushed back to the Embassy for a briefing. Alex and Joe Roberts walked into the Embassy conference room ten minutes after Van Camp and Reynolds had arrived.

The first thing Alex saw was John Reynolds sitting at the head of the table, pushing aside name placeholders belonging to DCM Chandler and Ambassador Van Camp. Alex grinned, took a seat, and waited for the show to begin.

Chandler arrived a minute later and walked to the head of the table. When he found Reynolds occupying his seat, he looked perplexed, then appeared upset since he was now relegated to a secondary position. Reynolds ignored him. When everyone was seated, Alex handed out copies of the ransom note, and the two photos.

"Everyone, please read this before we start. These were in an envelope, recently thrown at the feet of policemen in front of the Ambassador's residence by a passing motorcyclist."

"Did they get the license plate of the bike?" Reynolds asked.

"The motorcycle didn't have a plate," Alex answered. "The biker was wearing a helmet with dark visor, so the cops couldn't see his face."

Reynolds grunted.

"You will see at the bottom of the letter that the kidnappers have given us a way to negotiate via a newspaper ad," Chandler informed the group. "I've already sent a copy to Washington by an emergency telegram. Naturally, we'll need to coordinate with the Italian authorities and I already have a meeting set up at the Foreign Ministry following this Emergency Action Committee meeting. We'll be speaking with the police and Ministry of the Interior."

Alex noted the DCM was still referring to this as an EAC meeting, trying to assert his prerogative to be in charge over Van Camp. Although he disliked Chandler, Alex believed the Embassy was better off having him run the show than this pair of egomaniacs from Washington.

"We don't negotiate with kidnappers and terrorists," Ambassador Van Camp stated.

Since the DCM remained quiet, Alex spoke up. "Actually, we do negotiate. U.S. Government policy is not to pay ransom, but if you don't talk to the kidnappers, you'll never get your hostages back."

"Nonsense! No negotiation is the US Government's policy," Van Camp reiterated.

"You're wrong," Alex insisted. "We have a history of negotiating: the Iran hostage crisis, the taking of hostages in Beirut, and dozens of times in Africa and Latin America. If we don't speak to the kidnappers, you can't collect information about them or determine on what basis they will return hostages."

Station Chief Carter Ambrose emphatically supported Alex. Surprisingly, so did Reynolds from the FBI. Van Camp frowned but remained silent. Alex thought Van Camp was a moron and lacked any historical knowledge about US government policy and strategy on kidnappings. In Alex's opinion, he was yet another clueless Foreign Service Officer who thought that because he occupied a high-level position for two or three years, he actually was qualified to do the job.

Rachel redirected the conversation. "No doubt the Italian government is having a similar conversation at this moment. We don't know yet if they'll wish to contact the kidnappers exclusively, or if they'll be amenable to a joint operation. I suggest the latter. I have good contacts in *Corriere della Sera* and it will be easy to place the ad in the newspaper." She looked over at Larry Jones, the FBI press officer on the IRT, who appeared relieved that she was taking the lead.

"I agree with Rachel," Chandler chimed in, "we should suggest a joint operation to handle the crisis."

"Another point needs to be addressed," Alex said. "There will be a lot of egos to deal with. The Italian officials won't want to be subservient to us."

"We can work together," Reynolds blustered, "but we'll oversee this so-called joint operation. You can tell them whatever you want, but we'll be making the decisions."

Alex stared at Reynolds and shook his head in disgust. Speaking of egos, he thought. "And tell me again how many FBI agents you have throughout Italy?" Alex asked. "There are tens of thousands of Italian cops, all reporting up to the Minister of Interior or Minister of Defense. They'll be the ones on the ground talking to sources, searching suspect locations, manning roadblocks, and checking databases. It won't be your FBI office in the Embassy that makes any arrests."

"Listen, John," the DCM addressed Reynolds, "it may be our Ambassador who's been kidnapped, but he's being held in Italy and the Italians have every right to be in charge. You may not like it, but the FBI has no authority here, just as we wouldn't allow the Italian police to lead an investigation in the States if their Ambassador was taken. We'll work within the overall framework of Italian sovereignty, so let's try to influence what they do in a way that makes sense to us."

Reynolds was red in the face. Alex guessed he wasn't used to people talking back to him. "Of course, we'll try to control the situation," Alex said, "but the Italians must be involved in a manner that gives them full partnership. I suggest we offer to have an English-speaking representative from the *Poliza di Stato* embedded in our task force in the Embassy. That way any leads can be followed up on immediately. We'll use him as our point of contact to pass information to the Italian bureaucracy, and vice versa. Maybe the Political Section can also ask to have an Embassy rep embedded at the Foreign Office during the crisis."

"I like that," Carter Ambrose said. He was supported by Ames Burnham of Political.

Liz Waters, the DCM's secretary, entered the room, as she had in the last meeting, and told the DCM she had the Secretary of State on the secure line once again. The Secretary, she said, wanted to talk to both Van Camp and the DCM. They excused themselves and the room fell silent.

After a minute Joe Roberts leaned over to speak with Alex. "Brilliant move on your part to get the cops imbedded. Did you have a unit in mind?"

"I'll call General Ghiberti and ask him, but that will be after we speak with the Italians at the Foreign Ministry."

Van Camp and Chandler returned fifteen minutes later, and Chandler addressed the group.

"The Secretary confirms, pending agreement with the Italians, we should place the ad in the newspaper and open negotiations." Chandler looked around the room, but no one commented. "The

Italians are expecting us at the Foreign Office, so we should go now. The group will be Ambassador Van Camp and me, the military advisor on the Incident Response Team, John Reynolds, Mark Terranova, and Alex Boyd. Carter, do you want to attend?"

"No, we'll work the intelligence angle separately; I don't need to see the politicians or the cops." Chandler nodded.

"Because we also need to address the newspaper ad, I suggest we take a press person," the DCM added. "Larry, I know you will be in charge of press releases, but since you don't speak Italian and Rachel Smith does, I believe she should accompany us since few of the Italian authorities speak English."

Alex covered his smile with his hand. He knew the DCM was lying since many senior Italian officials were reasonably fluent in English and realized the DCM was subtly trying to reassert Embassy control over the IRT. Jones reflected on this for a moment, looked over at Reynolds, and said, "That will be fine; I have plenty of work to do here."

"In that case," the DCM said, "Rachel, I'd like you to be the official notetaker for our side, and then prepare the telegram to Washington afterward. Ames, you're in charge in the Embassy while we're gone."

The meeting ended. The team going to the Foreign Office headed down to a van waiting at the main entrance. Charlotte Eaton quickly followed Chandler into his office as he was retrieving his suit-jacket.

"Alden, we must tell the Italians about the Ambassador using the Embassy car."

"No, we don't, Charlotte. Besides, it's too late now. I don't know how we'll explain the missing car from the motor pool, but you need to think of something. When the Ambassador is released, I'm sure he'll take responsibility. If, God forbid, he doesn't return alive, then maybe the car will never be found. In any case, it must remain a secret at best or an unexplained anomaly at worst."

Chandler left her standing in his office. Charlotte looked down at her trembling hands. Back in her office, she took a Valium and a few acid reduction pills as tears formed in her eyes. Now, she could fully admit it: she was scared more than at any other time in her life.

Chapter 27

ITALIANS TAKE CHARGE

The Italian Foreign Office was located north of the city center, near the old Olympic stadium. Known as the *Ministerio degli Affari Esteri*, it reminded Alex of the State Department building in Washington, DC.

The group was escorted up to a conference room next to the Foreign Minister's personal office. Unlike some grand Italian palaces Alex had been in, this large room was plain and appeared more functional than anything else.

In the middle was a long elegant wooden conference table, where the Foreign Minister and DCM would take seats across from one another while each team flanked their head man. Alex took a seat on the right side of Chandler, Ambassador Van Camp took one on his left, forcing Reynolds to sit further away. Alex saw Reynolds standing behind his chair for a few seconds before sitting down. He guessed Reynolds always expected to be the center of attention and having a chair off to the side didn't sit well with him.

The Foreign Minister was supported by both his Interior Minister and Deputy Interior Minister, Umberto Ferrara, whose life Alex had saved at the bank on his first day in Rome. He and Alex nodded and smiled at one another.

Also, at the table were General Raffaele Ghiberti, director of the *Polizia di Stato,* and Colonel Vittore Adriani, head of the NOCS, who had hosted Alex at the terrorist exercise in Abruzzi. Alex also exchanged nods with both men. He looked down the table and saw two senior *Carabineri* officers and one senior Italian Army officer whom he did not know. Finally, Alex saw two interpreters wearing headphones in the corner of the room, seated side by side.

DCM Alden Chandler moved closer to one of the small microphones near him leaving his headphones resting on the table. He opened the meeting in Italian by thanking the Foreign Minister for the Italian government's efforts in the search for the American Ambassador and Mrs. Scarmatti.

"This is indeed a tragedy," the Foreign Minister replied. "Rest assured we are doing everything possible to find Ambassador Scarmatti and his wife. But before we go further in our discussions, I think we should introduce everyone present."

Both groups did so, then the Foreign Minister continued.

"We in the Foreign Office are leading a task force to direct the Italian government's response. It will operate twenty-four hours a day. We assume you have a similar setup in the Embassy."

"Yes, we do, Minister." Chandler replied. "I would like to ask Ambassador Van Camp to explain what assistance we can offer your government in this crisis."

Van Camp described, in English, the team's technical abilities that could be offered in communications intercept and analysis, FBI investigative help, and liaison with the US Military's Joint Special Operations Command. The Italians listened politely for ten minutes.

"Thank you for your explanation and for your offer of assistance," the Foreign Minister said. "I believe we already have what we need, but we may well call upon you for technical equipment. As you know, Italy and the United States have shared training, operational doctrine, and technology over many years. For now, I think we must focus at this preliminary stage of contacting the terrorists and deciding what will be an appropriate response."

Alex had been listening to the interpreters through his headphones but removed them when he realized his Italian was good enough to listen directly to the Foreign Minister. This was basically the same approach taken by the DCM, Mark Terranova, and Rachel, whereas the Washington-based IRT members were glued to their headsets.

The Minister's comments were apparently too much diplomatic bullshit for John Reynolds. He tossed his headphones on the table, rather unceremoniously, and spoke for the first time in an aggressive manner.

"That's all well and good, but we have leads that can be followed. What about the white Fiat that tailed our Embassy car from the Ambassador's house? Have you questioned these people yet? What about the police bodyguards? Why weren't they present on Sunday? They need to be questioned. And what about these other New Red Brigade people already in jail. I'll bet they've had contact with the kidnappers."

Although, these were all legitimate lines of inquiry, each matter had either been addressed or was currently being pursued by the Italians. Reynolds knew this because it had just been discussed at the Embassy. The real problem, however, was his tone of voice, which Alex realized, was very insulting. It was as if Reynolds was talking to cops in New Orleans or Des Moines, rather than to a distinguished gathering of the most senior officials in Italy.

The Foreign Minister motioned to General Ghiberti to reply. Ghiberti did so in Italian, forcing Reynolds to scramble to put his headphones back on.

"We are tracing the white Fiat. The original owner sold the car some time ago. It was never registered again, as it should have been under Italian law. The original owner could not find the name of the buyer because his records are incomplete. I suspect this will be an unsuccessful endeavor on our part.

"Secondly, as you have no doubt been told by Mr. Boyd, the bodyguards were given the day off by the Ambassador, as he occasionally did on weekends if he had no plans to leave the house. We still had police outside the house to protect him, but more importantly, he was not taken from his home. Your insinuation that the bodyguards may have been cooperating with the kidnappers is offensive.

"As to your last point, the New Red Brigade members in jail are being interrogated as we speak. But they won't talk. Naturally, we are checking records of who has visited them in jail, and whatever contact the prisoners may have had with outsiders. So far, the only visitors have been their lawyers or immediate family members."

"Thank you, General," the Foreign Minister stated. "As I said a few moments ago, we propose to place the ad in the paper, as requested by the kidnappers. Do you agree?"

"Yes, we do," Chandler responded. "I would like to have Rachel Smith, our Press Spokeswoman, handle the placement."

"We know Miss Smith well, we have worked with her many times, and respect her abilities," the Foreign Minister said as he nodded toward Rachel and smiled. "She is most welcome to work with our people in the Foreign Ministry on this task. But I must insist that we place the ad. The number we use for the kidnappers to call back will be here as well."

Alex immediately understood the Minister's point and was embarrassed he hadn't focused on this back at the Embassy.

"But our FBI agents have handled hundreds of kidnappings," Ambassador Van Camp countered. "We believe it should be handled out of the Embassy." Alex saw the DCM's jaw clench and watched as Chandler rubbed his forehead with three fingers.

Finally, Deputy Interior Minister Ferrara spoke up. "I am sure you do believe it should be handled out of the Embassy, Ambassador Van Camp. But perhaps you have heard of our Mafia problems in Italy? Kidnapping is their specialty and has been for decades. This was also true of the old Red Brigade. It is now true of this new breed of terrorist. Our police and *Carabinieri* have most probably handled many more kidnappings than your FBI.

"As I understand it, in America it is normally the local police who often do the actual negotiating in most cases. But even more importantly, should the kidnappers call the Embassy, who will speak to them in Italian? Mr. Boyd and Mr. Terranova speak excellent Italian, but if they are not available, will you turn it over to an untrained semi fluent Italian-speaking American, or maybe ask one of the Embassy Italian nationals, who perhaps handles customs clearances for the Embassy, to talk to the kidnappers? Personally, I would rather put this delicate task in the hands of an experienced and professional Italian law enforcement officer who has done it before."

Right on the mark! Alex thought. *Good for Deputy Minister Ferrara.* Italy wasn't some third world country that could be treated with disrespect. They had real world skills and experience that, in Italy, exceeded the FBI's much publicized hands-on abilities. Of course, it always came down to who was on the ground at the time of the operation, but Alex guessed the Italians would put their best people on the job.

He glanced at the American team members. Van Camp appeared perplexed again, and Reynolds' fingers were tapping the table while he stared down at them. Alex figured they realized Ferrara was right.

"Let me make an offer," the Foreign Minister said. "Just as we want Miss Smith to assist with the ad in the *Corriere della Sera,* I would like the Embassy to place one or two officers in our Task Force in the Ministry to liaise. Naturally, they will need to speak Italian if they want to be effective."

Chandler and Van Camp leaned toward each other and whispered together. Then Chandler said, "Mr. Minister, we accept your offer." He turned toward Alex, "Do the two DS officers with the IRT speak Italian?"

"No, they don't," Alex replied. "But you could pair them with an Embassy Political or Economic Officer who does. That way you'll always have a linguist and a law enforcement professional embedded in the Foreign Ministry Task Force."

Chandler nodded and told the Foreign Minister his plan. Next, he said, "Mr. Minister, let me also request that you place an Italian Police Officer in our Embassy task force room to assist with liaison."

Both General Ghiberti and the senior Carabineri officer smiled when they heard the offer.

"Very good. We will place two officers, one from the *Polizia di Stato*, and one from the *Carabineiri* in the Embassy," the Minister responded.

The Foreign Minister then had draft copies of the kidnappers' requested newspaper ad passed out to everyone.

"Please review it for approval, then we can have it in the next edition of *Corriere della Sera*."

Rachel read it and gave her approval as did Van Camp and Chandler. When the meeting ended, Alex walked over to General Ghiberti, Deputy Interior Minister Ferrara, and Colonel Adriani, quietly greeting them and shaking everyone's hands.

"If there is anything you need, call me directly," Ghiberti said. "We won't rest until we get them back."

"I know, Raffaele. Thank you for your help. All of you, thank you. I apologize for some of the things that were said to you today by members of our side."

"Yes," Ferrara said, "Your FBI believes they can operate anywhere with impunity. Well, we will do our work regardless of their attitude. As General Ghiberti has said, call us if you need anything." They shook hands again and Alex rejoined the American group as they departed.

Alex was confident about the professionalism on the Italian side. He also knew that if the attitude of Ambassador Van Camp and John Reynolds did not change, it would not bode well for the future.

Chapter 28

THE ITALIAN STRATEGY

Returning to the Embassy, Alex immediately called Jim Riley, director of Diplomatic Security in Washington D.C. on the secure phone.

"Hello, Jim?"

"Hey, Alex. Any news? Washington is desperate for updates." Alex briefed him on their meeting at the Foreign Office including all the attitudes and posturing from the FBI.

"Not surprised about those guys, but it sounds like the Italians have the reins in hand and are starting to go down the right road. I take it nothing else has developed since you received the ransom demand."

"Right. The Foreign Office will place the ad in the *Corriere della Sera* and the point of contact will be within their task force. All this info will be in a telegram the DCM is sending. I'd like your advice on handling Van Camp and Reynolds from FBI. As I just mentioned, Reynolds embarrassed himself at the Foreign Ministry big time and Van Camp didn't make a good impression either."

"Van Camp is a jerk," Riley said. "I've heard he wasn't even a good Political Officer, much less terrorism expert. Just try to be civil. As for the FBI, watch out for them. We know they're out of their depth operating overseas, but remember, they are powerful and their PR machine is relentless. If you can get along with them, that's best. But speak your mind when it comes to the investigation. I have to brief the Secretary now. Call me if anything else develops. Talk to you later, Alex, and good luck."

Alex didn't feel much better after speaking to Riley. He was about to get a cup of coffee when the secure phone rang next to his desk.

"Boyd here."

"Alex, its Danny Aaron."

"Danny! How are you? How's the "fudge factory?"" using slang for the State Department.

"I'm fine, but the question is how are you are doing?"

"You can imagine, Danny. Did you see our reporting telegrams on the kidnapping?"

"Yeah, I did. I've never seen anything so mysterious. Few, if any leads, and how he was taken is unknown."

"Exactly. Between you and me, I think Chandler and Charlotte Eaton are covering something up; they know more than they're admitting, but I can't prove it now."

"I wanted to let you know that some friends at Justice told me the FBI is already spinning a story that the kidnapping is all your fault," Danny Aaron continued. "Watch your back."

"Thanks, Danny, they've said as much to my face already."

"I mean it, Alex. They want to set you up as the bad guy for not protecting Scarmatti. They want the win."

"Thanks Danny, I appreciate the heads-up. Right now, I'm going to brief my staff, but stay in touch."

"So long, buddy."

* * *

Twenty minutes after the Americans departed the Foreign Office, the Minister convened a meeting with only Italian participants. The original Italian team was joined by a senior representative from the Prime Minister's Office.

Laura Ricci, the Prime Minister's representative, opened the discussion. She was a middle-aged, long-time political advisor to the Prime Minister's party, and a behind-the-scenes operative from Milan with considerable talent. Although she had a law degree, her specialty was public relations.

"How did the meeting go with the Americans?" she asked.

"Difficult, but we made some progress," the Foreign Minister responded.

"What was 'difficult'?"

"The FBI and State Department representative from Washington think they are equal partners with us, perhaps even in charge."

General Antonio Romano of the Carabinieri, sitting at the table, spoke up.

"I believe we can control the FBI. In general, they are competent as we know from working with them for years against organized crime. But this Mr. Reynolds appears to think highly of himself. We will keep him close to us."

"What about Ambassador Van Camp?" Mrs. Ricci asked. "Should the Prime Minister meet with him one-on-one to discuss the kidnapping?"

"I think not," the Foreign Minister replied. "He is an Ambassador in name only. His credentials and experience are, at best, slim. I believe the Americans call his position merely a figurehead. My advice is to have the Prime Minister publicly express his concern over the kidnapping, promise to use every tool we have to rescue Ambassador and Mrs. Scarmatti, but to distance himself operationally from the effort."

Laura Ricci quickly calculated that if things went badly, the Prime Minister, her main concern, could blame the Foreign Minister and security services.

"So, tell me, how did this happen?"

"I believe the Ambassador drove off on his own, somehow bypassing our police outside his residence," General Ghiberti explained. "Or, perhaps he agreed to meet with someone privately and was grabbed at that meeting."

"Aren't police with him all the time?" she asked.

"They should be," Ghiberti continued, "but he has lied to us before and released his bodyguards upon occasion. In any event, we should focus on getting him back."

Ricci knew Ghiberti was right, but she had to have a political contingency plan should the Ambassador be killed.

"So, you are telling me it's the fault of the Americans that their own Ambassador was kidnapped."

"No, I don't think so. I personally know the head of security at the Embassy and he seems to be a good officer," General Ghiberti replied. "But, yes, if the Ambassador disregarded the advice of his own security team, then he, himself, is partially at fault."

Ricci was tapping the table with her fingers, debating whether to pursue this line further, but decided she could address it later.

"Tell me what you are doing to find the Ambassador."

"We, and the *Carabinieri,* have checkpoints set up throughout Italy, searching for the white Fiat, but also conducting random stops and searches," Ghiberti said. "We have pulled in every major leftist in the country for questioning and told them any information they provide related to the kidnapping will be rewarded, should they get into future trouble."

"What techniques are you using during the questioning?" she asked.

Ricci imagined that Ghiberti didn't like her micromanaging his operation, but he also knew her position and how powerful she was.

"With some, we use extreme pressure, physical pressure. With others, we use a more subtle approach. It depends on our history with the suspect."

She looked at General Romano.

"The same goes for the *Carabinieri*."

Laura Ricci found dealing with the police distasteful. But if their techniques worked, she was prepared to look the other way.

"What else are you doing?"

"We have tapped phone lines of lawyers and family members of the prisoners, and we're checking all past phone records, as well as questioning all visitors who have recently seen them in prison," Ghiberti said.

"What do you recommend for negotiating with the kidnappers?" She looked around the table for an answer.

"First and foremost, we will not release the terrorists from jail," the Foreign Minister said. "That would only encourage the New Red Brigade to repeat such actions in the future."

"I agree," Deputy Interior Minister Ferrara said. "We should consider making a ransom payment. But first we need to negotiate on the amount, if only so they take us seriously. Otherwise they will simply hold onto the Ambassador and up the stakes."

"Do you agree?" Ricci asked, turning to Generals Ghiberti and Romano.

"We do," Ghiberti responded. Romano nodded. "However, the Americans will disagree on this point. They will be against paying any money at all."

"What if the kidnappers absolutely insist on the release of their comrades from prison?" Ricci pushed the issue. "What if they send us a message by cutting off an ear of Mrs. Scarmatti or a finger from the Ambassador? Then what? Can we stand firm? Should we stand firm?"

Deputy Minister Ferrara offered a proposal.

"I believe we must preempt them from doing such by establishing a backdoor channel to negotiate, a channel of which the Americans are unaware. I don't trust either the FBI or the State Department. We have precedents for releasing serious criminals early from prison in exchange for concessions, agreements to which the Americans would not agree. In this case, we could bargain for the terrorists to accept a smaller ransom to let the Ambassador and Mrs. Scarmatti go free and unharmed now, while we secretly agree to reduce their comrades' sentences significantly and release them, say, after five years instead of immediately."

Ricci reflected on this idea for a moment. Dealmaking was a classic part of Italian culture and politics. In her experience, standing on principle rarely resulted in a good outcome.

"All right, I can speak for the Prime Minister. We accept this idea. How do we do it?"

"The *Carabinieri* and the *Polizia di Stato* can put out the word through known leftist sympathizers that we want to talk with the kidnappers in secret," General Romano of the *Carabinieri* told the group. "We can give them a telephone number to use. This number will be separate from the task force telephone lines. First, we will establish the authenticity of the caller, and then begin to talk."

Ricci leaned back in her chair while looking up at the ceiling and contemplated this option. It sounded feasible on the surface, but down deep, she still had reservations.

"When the Ambassador and Mrs. Scarmatti are released, what do we tell the press? They will think we gave in to the terrorists and paid a ransom, which we will have."

"We will say," the Foreign Minister explained, "the kidnappers were feeling the pressure of our search efforts and decided to cut and run. The money need not be revealed. When their comrades are released early from prison, we will say we independently took into consideration that the Ambassador and his wife were released unharmed, assuming that they will be."

"What if the kidnappers then go to the press and tell the truth?" Ricci countered. "Or they threaten to do so if we don't pay another ransom?"

"I'm afraid we will have to cross that bridge when we come to it," the Foreign Minister replied.

"Besides, the odds are that all the New Red Brigade members will be either captured or killed by the five-year mark," Deputy Minister Ferrara added.

Ricci didn't know if Ferrara was making a prediction or implying a threat and didn't want to know.

"All right, I will approve your plan. Keep me informed." With that, she rose and left the room, leaving the others to work out the details.

Chapter 29

THE MISTAKE

Two hundred kilometers away from the kidnappers' hideout, a computer screen flashed when Ambassador Scarmatti's cell phone was activated at the safe house. A representative at the phone company's monitoring station was working with the *Polizia di Stato*. Sliding his chair closer to the screen, he put down a half cup of coffee.

"Luigi, look at my screen," the tech said to a cop nearby. "We have the Ambassador's signal."

"Okay, move over," Luigi said, as he rapidly typed instructions on the keyboard. After they had waited so long for the Ambassador's signal to pop up, it was only minutes before the screen indicated which regional cell phone towers were now connecting to the Ambassador's phone.

"We've got him! Finally!" Luigi said with excitement and satisfaction. They sent the information to *Polizia di Stato* headquarters in Rome, and to the Foreign Ministry's task force.

Moments later, Alex received a call from DS agent, Mike James, embedded at the Foreign Ministry's task force.

"We've got vital info. Go to the Embassy conference room and wait for a call." As Alex entered the room, the Italian policeman working as liaison had just started to brief the Americans at the table.

"An activation signal has originated from an area south of Bologna. No one made a call, but cell towers were pinged, and we were notified that the phone was turned on." The decibel level sky-rocketed in the conference room as several small conversations overlapped.

"If I can have your attention," the policeman pleaded for silence. "The *Polizia di Stato* and the *Carabinieri* will be searching that area more intensely." As the chatter in the room increased once again, Alex moved next to the policeman.

"What type of area are we talking about? he asked.

"Farms, small villages, some light industry. But this will take a lot of manpower and time, I'm afraid, because the area is so rural. The search will be over several square kilometers."

Alex spoke with him for another moment about the intelligence, then thanked him and turned to face the others. He noticed Ambassador Van Camp talking into a handset connected to a nonsecure phone. Since Alex knew that Sam Carson, his engineering officer, had unplugged all nonsecure phones in the conference room yesterday, he realized she must have left the disconnected phones just lying in the bookcase next to Van Camp. He quickly realized Van Camp must have grabbed one and plugged it into a convenient phone jack to make his call. Alex moved closer to listen and couldn't believe what he was hearing from Van Camp.

"Yes, that's right. Inform the Secretary we believe the Ambassador and his wife are possibly being held near Bologna."

Moving with lightning speed, Alex grabbed the phone out of Van Camp's hand and slammed it down onto the phone cradle, ending the call while he grabbed the cord from the jack.

"Who were you talking to?" Alex demanded, getting right in Van

Camp's face.

"None of your business," Van Camp furiously retorted.

"The hell it isn't! You were talking to Washington!"

"Yes, I was, and you just hung up on my deputy. Who do you think you are!?" Van Camp said in a loud, livid voice. But he couldn't match the anger Alex was feeling. By now, everyone in the room was listening to the exchange, including the DCM, and Station Chief Carter Ambrose.

"You were using a nonsecure phone to pass on the most sensitive information we've developed so far!" Alex yelled, then lowered his voice to normal levels. "You should have used the secure phone on the other side of the room. How could you be so naïve to think no one would be monitoring your call? I'll remind you that the task force doesn't know yet who's backing the New Red Brigade, including possibly foreign powers with intercept capability. You may have just signed the Ambassador's death warrant!" Alex knew his comment was melodramatic, but it didn't matter, two people's lives were at stake.

Station Chief Ambrose Carter glared at Van Camp. "I take it you were telling Washington where the Ambassador might be located."

"Yes, and Boyd hung up my call. He had no right!"

"Alex was right. You've just committed a serious breach of our security. There are a host of countries and private entities that can intercept any open-line phone call, including the paparazzi. That was worse than a rookie mistake. It could have jeopardized our position."

Not commenting on the call, Chandler announced they would meet in another room to discuss the new information regarding the Ambassador's phone activation. He asked everyone to gather in the next room, leaving all regular staff to work on the new lead. Van Camp remained silent and walked by Alex without a look.

Alex sat down at the conference table next to Rachel.

"You did the right thing with Van Camp," Rachel whispered, "That was pretty gutsy on your part. But, be prepared for blowback later."

"I know."

Alex looked at his watch for the third time after they had moved from one conference room to the next. He knew something was going on when DCM Chandler, Mark Terranova, John Reynolds and Ambassador Van Camp inexplicably had not arrived in the conference room after fifteen minutes had passed. He hoped the reason would be revealed at the meeting. What's keeping them?

"Are you all right, Alex? You look worried," Rachel asked.

"I'm wondering if I did everything possible to protect Tony and Francesca. Suppose I had demanded the cops never take a day off, regardless of what the Ambassador told them? Or what if I had offered Joe, George, or me to be available on weekends to protect Tony?"

"Look, Alex, you can play the 'what if' game forever. How could you know the Ambassador would lie to his bodyguards about going out?"

"Thanks Rachel, I appreciate what you're saying. You know, we haven't worked all that long for the State Department, but I'm really tired of this bullshit.

She reached over and squeezed his hand, understanding what Alex was going through mentally. "Let's just deal with one issue at a time. That's all we can do."

He stared into her green eyes and smiled. "I know. I love you, thanks, Rachel."

The DCM, Van Camp, Reynolds, and Terranova finally walked into the conference room together. Wasting no time, the DCM made an announcement.

"Now that the Italians have narrowed down the area where the Ambassador might be located, it's time we think about hostage rescue. I believe we should tell the Italians that we insist the FBI's Hostage Rescue Team fly in from Washington and handle any rescue operation."

Simultaneously, Alex and Colonel Jim Watson, defense attaché, exclaimed aloud: "What?!" Not believing the audacity of such a remark, Alex spoke out first.

"The Italians have excellent units, Alden," he said still in semi-shock. "Both the NOCS and the *Carabinieri* teams are first class and very experienced. It's insulting to them to take the action you're suggesting."

"I agree with Alex," Colonel Watson declared.

"It not a suggestion, Boyd, besides, it's the American Ambassador who's being held hostage," Van Camp interrupted.

"Well, I hadn't thought of that," Alex said mockingly.

"I don't think you're in a position to offer an opinion," Reynolds rebuffed him.

"I damn well am! I know the NOCS unit very well. They're part of the *Polizia di Stato* and have world-renowned experience. Equally important, they're a seamless part of the police chain of command. If we have any real hope of getting the Ambassador back safely, it's with them leading the charge." Alex, however, knew exactly to what Reynolds was referring. That he, Alex, was being held responsible for the Ambassador's kidnapping, and the FBI wasn't going to let go of that bone.

"More to the point," Colonel Watson stated," overseas hostage rescue is part and parcel of what Delta and the SEALS are trained to do, when locals don't have that capability. Both units have worked with the Italians in the past and respect their ability. The FBI has no business trying to pull off a hostage rescue overseas. I believe our first option should be to rely on the Italian units."

"I've made my decision," Alden Chandler stated. To him, the issue was settled.

"The FBI team has been standing by since the beginning of this crisis and they're ready to deploy," Reynolds added.

"What do you think Delta and SEALS have been doing, Reynolds?" Colonel Watson responded. "Both units already have advance teams in Europe. In fact, the SEALS are currently standing by in Sigonella, Sicily, awaiting orders."

"You moved them without State Department permission?" Chandler raised his voice in anger.

"Alden, they don't need permission until they're chopped to the civilian side of the house. They flew to Sicily under the authority of the Commander, U.S. Forces, Europe. Where's the FBI team now, in Quantico?"

"Yes, but they can be here in a day," Reynolds stated.

"Look, the Italian teams have several advantages," Alex explained. "They speak the language, they know the area, they're here already, and they know how to interact with the Italian chain of command. That's why Colonel Watson and I believe it's a bad idea to press the Foreign Ministry on using an American team."

"Excuse me, I'd like to make a comment," Ames Burnham, Embassy political counselor, interjected. "From a political perspective, I think the Italians are unlikely to allow the US to make any rescue attempt at all. It's a matter of their sovereignty, their pride, and their responsibility."

Alex thought it was a brave statement since Chandler had already argued a position to the contrary.

"Don't forget the Italians also have international law on their side," Burnham continued, "meaning it's the responsibility of the host country to protect foreign diplomats. They will, no doubt, argue this extends to hostage rescue. Remember, we are in their country and since being kidnapped, the Ambassador is not in the Embassy, meaning American territory, at this time."

"Carter, do you have any thoughts," Chandler asked Carter Ambrose, the Station Chief.

"Not on this subject, Alden. It's not really our area of expertise. We'll focus on developing intelligence for whichever team makes a rescue attempt, if it comes to that."

How interesting that Ambrose chose not to get involved. Alex thought. *But I can't fault him since the Italian intelligence services doesn't have a rescue team the CIA has ever worked with. Nevertheless, I would have liked his support; but without a dog in the fight, I guess Carter chooses his battles very carefully with the DCM. But the real question is: How did the FBI gain Chandler's full support?*

Alex knew it wouldn't be the first time the FBI could raise the possibility of opposing a Foreign Service Officer's future nomination to be named Ambassador somewhere. He knew the FBI had powerful friends on Capitol Hill. It would only take a quiet behind-the-scenes conversation with select Senators to deep-six any nominee, or even get the State Department to withdraw a nomination altogether.

"I repeat, I've made my decision," DCM Chandler stated. "We'll lean on the Italians to bring in the FBI's Hostage Rescue Team. Ambassador Van Camp, will you and John Reynolds present this offer to the Foreign Minister? I'll call ahead and tell the Minister that you're coming to see him."

"I'll be glad to," Van Camp replied, looking very self-important with the prospect of leading the discussion. Reynolds agreed as well, and added that the Embassy Legatt, Terranova, would be joining them.

Unbelievable, Alex thought. *Clearly Chandler should have been delivering this message to the Foreign Office. Equally clear, Chandler had extricated himself from the likely confrontation, placing the burden on Van Camp and the FBI. Brilliant tactic, but sneaky and gutless.* Alex was certain Chandler was positioning himself to blame Van Camp and Reynolds when the approach to the Italians failed. He could later spin it that way in his reporting to Washington.

What's the adage? Alex thought: *He who writes the narrative, controls the history.*

Chapter 30

REJECTION

During the ride to the Foreign Ministry, Mark Terranova tried to convince Reynolds that, perhaps, the best approach would be to say the FBI team would 'support' the Italians in a raid. But Reynolds would have none of it.

"Support the Italians?" Reynolds defiantly blustered. "Hell, we train the rest of the world how to do it. Why should we defer to the Italians?"

After that, Terranova knew it was pointless to argue. He also knew it was the Defense Department, CIA, and State Department's Anti-Terrorism Assistance program that actually did such foreign training. Perhaps, he needed a more subtle approach with Reynolds. For now, Mark decided he would remain silent in the meeting, or minimize his own words. He could see disaster looming yet tried one more point.

"I think we need to consider that the Italian government won't want to lose face. Once the teams are on the ground, we can sort out specific tasks."

"Listen Mark," Reynolds replied curtly, "you need to remember who you're working for."

So that was it, Terranova figured. *Reynolds was stubbornly charging ahead, disregarding all advice.* He looked over at Ambassador Van Camp, whose expression remained neutral. Upon arrival, they all exited the car and walked into the Foreign Ministry for the showdown.

While the number of participants was smaller for this meeting than last time, the Italians still had their big guns in attendance. Flanking the Foreign Minister were Deputy Interior Minister Ferrara and General Ghiberti from the *Polizia di Stato.* Next to Ghiberti was General Romano from the *Carabinieri.*

"I understand from Mr. Chandler," the Foreign Minister said, "that you want to use the FBI's Hostage Rescue Team should we locate the Ambassador and his wife." At that moment, Terranova realized the Minister spoke English.

"Yes, we have our team standing by in Quantico. They can be here immediately," Reynolds said.

"I believe it would be advantageous to accept this offer," Van Camp added.

"Advantageous? To whom?" the Foreign Minister asked.

"Why, to everyone concerned," Van Camp replied. "The FBI is very experienced."

"I believe we've covered a similar subject at our last meeting," Ferrara said, "It was decided the Italian government would handle such matters."

"I have to insist," Reynolds jumped in harshly. "The successful recovery of the Ambassador is a top priority of the US Government."

"Indeed, it should be," the Foreign Minister agreed. "That is why our best teams from the *Carabinieri* and the *Polizia di Stato* are prepared to make the raid, if it comes to that."

"But we have techniques and equipment developed over many

years," Reynolds relentlessly pressed his case.

"These secret techniques, perhaps, ones no one else knows, not even your closest allies?" the Foreign Minister asked.

Terranova listened with deep embarrassment. It was apparent the Italians were not going to relinquish responsibility in this matter. Was Reynolds under pressure from higher-ups in Washington, or was this dogged approach his own issue?

Ignoring the Minister's question, Reynolds plowed on, "This is exactly why the FBI's Hostage Rescue Team was created; to secure victims from high threat environments."

"No, Mr. Reynolds, I am afraid there will be no negotiation on this point. The FBI team will not be granted entry into Italy."

Reynolds was furious.

"How can you make such a judgment? You have no experience in this area! You sit at your desk all day in your pinstripe suit and push papers."

Terranova was aghast at Reynolds impertinence. The Foreign Minister's body was stiff and his face was reddening as he clenched his fists on the table.

"I have just a few words to say," Deputy Interior Minister Ferrara interjected, putting a calming hand on the Foreign Minister's arm. "Ruby Ridge and Waco." The words hung in the air in an uncomfortable silence.

"If these are examples of the FBI's techniques and competence, then *Oddio,* oh my God, I fear for the Ambassador's safety."

Terranova watched Reynolds and wondered if he would accept the inevitable decision of the Italians. Crossing his arms, Reynolds leaned back in his chair. Terranova could see Reynolds try to burn a laser-like beam through Ferrara with his eyes.

"Gentlemen, I think our business is concluded," the Foreign Minister tersely said. The Italian group stood, bowed slightly, and left. There were no handshakes or cordial comments. On his way out,

General Romano caught Terranova's eye and used his hand to make the sign of using a telephone. Terranova nodded, hoping his bridge to the *Carabinieri* had not just been burned to the ground, much like the FBI had done to the Branch Davidian compound at Waco.

Silence enshrouded the group riding back to the Embassy; everyone lost in their own thoughts. Upon arrival, Reynolds said they should reconvene in the Legatt offices rather than the task force conference room.

"To hell with the Foreign Minister, I'm going to bring the FBI Hostage Rescue Team as far as Frankfurt. They can stay at a US military base until we call them in.

"Is that wise?" Van Camp asked. "You heard the Italians."

"They can't stop us from flying to Germany. We'll think of a way to make this happen. I'm not sure how, but we're not going to be obstructed by that pasta-eating creep."

Terranova was appalled. He'd had enough and didn't want any further part in this. His assignment in Italy had been wonderful, until now. Yet, he knew his future rested with men like Reynolds, so he could only say: "The secure telephone is in the next room. If you must launch the team to Frankfurt, you can use it to call Washington."

Reynolds followed his direction into the next room and prepared to explain to headquarters why subterfuge was needed to get the rescue team into Italy.

* * *

When no response came from the ad in *Corriere della Sera*, Alex and Rachel were both disappointed. They hated this waiting period. There was no information from any sources nor from the CIA's Italian counterparts. Nothing at all.

"You know about kidnappings, Alex," Rachel said. They were eating sandwiches in Alex's office at noontime. "You understand the history, tactics used by police, and motivations of kidnappers to release their victims. What are the real chances we'll get them back safely?"

"I honestly don't know. All I can say is these terrorists have a specific agenda of money and prisoners they want released. That's a good thing. There's a history of this type of event in Italy, so both sides have a basis on which to negotiate. Their demands are not like the Islamic terrorists who only want to kill or make outrageous demands to which no one is going to accede. At least no one with any principles would agree to. The one key thing we need is good intelligence."

"Are you saying we should favor negotiation versus having the police make a rescue attempt?"

"No, I'm saying we can't do anything until we have intelligence. Then we can talk with the kidnappers and hope they'll be reasonable and humane."

"What if we get specific intelligence regarding the whereabouts of Tony and Francesca?" she asked.

"Then the powers that be need to make a critical decision on whether to force a rescue or lay siege to the kidnappers."

"Will the Italians make good decisions?"

"Let's hope so. They have experience on their side." Continuing to eat in silence for several minutes, Rachel looked at him and realized his eyes looked a little tired.

"Are you feeling any better now? You were pretty down a while ago."

"Actually, no. I'm not feeling any better. It's not just the kidnapping. It's the whole business of constantly needing to fight guys like Chandler, Van Camp, and Reynolds in order to do the right thing. Is this what a career in the State Department is all about: Constant internal battles, constant arguments over turf instead of substance?"

Rachel listened carefully knowing Alex wasn't prone to whining and complaining. Quite the opposite, he usually greeted challenges with humor and resoluteness. Then, she decided to take a risk.

"Look, stop feeling sorry for yourself. You're better than that. Everyone here is depending on you, even the jerks you must argue with. This is no different than if you were working any place else. There are always egos and people who push bad ideas. I'm still counting on you to get us through this."

Alex was taken aback at first. She'd never spoken to him like that and he knew she meant it. But her risk paid off as he rolled her words around in his head for a moment.

"I guess you're right," he said, reaching over and taking her hand. "You're quite a woman, Rachel. Thanks for the advice."

Chapter 31

SURVEILLANCE AND MOVEMENT

Ambassador Scarmatti's cell phone signal came from an area just south of Bologna. The *Polizia di Stato* immediately set up a forward operating base at police headquarters in central Bologna.

General Ghiberti then asked Alex if he wanted to have someone from his office embedded in their operation. After checking with the DCM and Ambassador Van Camp, all agreed that Mike James, one of the DS Special Agents from the Incident Response Team, would join the Bologna operation. Carter Ambrose asked if he could insert one of his CIA case officers, Harold Jordan, who was fluent in Italian, and the police agreed. The FBI declined to assign anyone to Bologna because they were partnering with the *Carabinieri*, who operated separately from the police.

After moving to Bologna, James and Jordan sat in the large open work area of the police station observing officers scouring through online property records of known extreme leftists in the province of Emilia-Romagna, in which Bologna was the capital. The police believed the kidnappers had realized in advance they would need a secure location to hold the Scarmattis, so they probably had made arrangements utilizing sympathetic supporters.

After hours of painstaking cross-referencing data, the police began focusing on one man, Emilio Testa, a communist Professor of Political Science at the University of Bologna. He had a long record of arrests for violent demonstrations against the government, as well as for fund raising for imprisoned terrorists. Testa had a farmhouse south of the city, in the area where the Ambassador's phone was activated. The police decided to have the NOCS set up surveillance on Testa's farmhouse.

"Hello, Alex?" James said, calling on the secure cell phone network. "I want to give you a heads-up that the police have surveillance on a potential suspect's farmhouse."

"Where?"

"Not far from Bologna—outside of the town of Marconi. Harold Jordan is passing on the same info to your Station Chief, and the cops are relaying it to the Embassy task force through their liaison officer."

"What's it based on?" Alex asked.

"Nothing concrete, just record checks of known communist sympathizers or criminals in the region who own rural properties. But it's close to the towers that got a ping from Scarmatti's cell phone."

"Okay, thanks Mike. I appreciate the call."

* * *

Two days after the ad appeared in the newspaper, Cosimo di Luca's comrade, Paolo, called the Foreign Ministry number listed. He kept the conversation short and insisted upon release of all hostages. In response to the government's statement that raising $10,000,000 would be difficult, Paolo left the door open to accept a smaller ransom, only if all the prisoners were freed. The Italian government shared details of the call with the U.S. Embassy, who reported it to Washington. The ball was starting to roll.

* * *

By mid-afternoon the NOCS set up surveillance of Emilio Testa's farmhouse south of Bologna. Three two-man teams, dressed in camouflage fatigues and using extremely powerful night vision scopes and video cameras with infrared capability, established three observation posts at an approximate distance of two hundred to three hundred meters within wooded areas surrounding the farmhouse and attached barn. The teams operated under camouflage nets that blended in with the vegetation, hiding their small satellite-uplink antennas. While a lightly falling rain made their positions uncomfortable, it was beneficial as the rain decreased a possibility the suspects might decide to take a long walk where they could possibly spot the surveillance teams.

"Team One to Control. We see two suspects making periodic patrols outside the house; both are carrying shotguns."

"Control to Team One, acknowledged. We see them from your video feed," the Tactical Commander replied. He was in a large van outside the nearby town of Marconi. Also, in the van were three officers who monitored video screens, radio networks, and computer links.

"Team Two to Control, nothing to report"

"Team Three to Control, we see the two men with shotguns stopping to smoke behind the house."

"Control to all Teams, acknowledged."

This routine activity went on for several hours. The NOCS Commander, Lt. Guido Campanella, knew surveillance work was tedious. His teams would have to stay alert and hope to spot something of significance. That happened in late afternoon.

"Team One to Control, one of the men just opened the barn door. Look at our video feed. You can see a white Fiat inside the barn."

"Control to Team One, can you read the license plate?"

"Team One to Control, we can make out the last three numbers… 694. The full plate is obscured, maybe with mud."

Lt. Campanella rapidly scanned his briefing notes and saw that 694 were the same last digits of the white Fiat seen following the Scarmattis from their residence in Rome.

"Control to all teams, we've just hit the jackpot. The license plate is a partial match. Maintain surveillance and report as needed."

As Lt. Campanella was about to call Bologna headquarters, the surveillance radio crackled to life once again.

"Team One to Control. The barn door was just opened wider and a dark blue, four-door Lancia is leaving now. Two suspects in the front seats. License plates are not, repeat, not readable."

Lt. Campanella looked at his video screen and saw the Lancia driving down the road away from the farmhouse.

"This is Control to Bravo One and Bravo Two," using call signs for two mobile units set up in the town of Marconi. Each unit had two men operating from plain-looking, midsized cars with turbo-powered engines for high speed pursuit.

"This is urgent. I need you to follow a dark blue Lancia just leaving the target. There are two suspects inside the vehicle."

Both units rocketed toward the farmhouse, hoping to spot the Lancia en route, but failed. One unit stayed in the area, searching nearby villages, while the second unit got on the A-1 autostrada heading north toward Bologna, anticipating the suspects might be linking up with the owner of the farmhouse, Emilio Testa. Unfortunately, that proved a wrong assumption, as the Lancia headed south on the autostrada toward Florence.

Lt. Campanella reported events to the forward operating base in Bologna which, in turn, notified Colonel Adriani at NOCS headquarters in Rome. Adriani assessed the situation and requested authorization to raid the farmhouse. General Ghiberti told him to prepare his team but wait until he had spoken to the Foreign and Interior Ministers.

At the same time, DS Agent Mike James and CIA case officer Harold Jordan, both operating from the Bologna base, alerted Alex Boyd and Station Chief Carter Ambrose respectively via secure phone lines: The dice had been thrown.

Chapter 32

ALEX JOINS THE ATTACK

Alden Chandler listened carefully on the secure phone in the task force conference room. The Foreign Minister was explaining the impending raid on the farmhouse that evening planned by the *Polizia di Stato.*

"Mr. Minister," he said with slight annoyance, "I know we've already discussed this, but I must insist you hold off until the FBI's Hostage Rescue Team arrives!"

"Mr. Chandler, at our last meeting, we told you very strongly that the FBI team is not needed, nor wanted," the Minister returned his agitation.

"I realize you said that, but the US Government would like you to reconsider." In his heart, Chandler knew the Italians were not going to change their minds, but Reynolds, Terranova, and Van Camp were standing next to him. He was trying his best to show solidarity with the FBI.

"For the last time, Mr. Chandler, our answer is no. *Finito!* However, if someone in the Embassy from the FBI wants to observe the raid, I can allow that."

"May I call you back in five minutes?" Chandler asked.

"That's fine."

Chandler relayed the offer to Reynolds while the others were nearby listening to the conversation. Trying to look relaxed, Alex was leaning against the wall with arms crossed, watching Reynold's body language as he considered the Foreign Minister's offer.

"What do you think, Ambassador?" Reynolds asked Van Camp.

"It's an opportunity to get closer to the Italians," Van Camp said. "Admittedly, you won't be in charge, but at least you'll be there."

"But if anything goes wrong," Reynolds declared, "they'll say the FBI was present and supported the raid. I think we shouldn't accept the offer."

"Well, we do have one DS Agent and a CIA officer at their Bologna base," Ames Burnham, the political counselor, said. "So, we already have a presence. They could accompany the raid."

After further discussion, Chandler called the Foreign Minister again.

"Thank you for your offer to observe, but if the FBI cannot lead the raid, then our liaison will consist of the two officers already in Bologna."

"Very well. The raid will be made in the middle of the night when the kidnappers will be less alert. Someone will call you back after it's over."

Ten minutes later, Alex and the other task force members were still lingering around the conference table. Rachel and Larry Jones, the FBI press spokesman, were discussing the timing of when to talk with the media. Jones was pushing for an immediate FBI press announcement in Washington, in case the Ambassador would be rescued. Rachel felt the FBI should hold off announcing anything until it could be coordinated with the Italians, the State Department, and the White House. Alex was sitting alone, silently tapping his fingers on the table, full of nervous energy, trying to figure how he could do something more meaningful.

"Alex," Nancy Williams called to him, as she entered the room. Standing at the door, she beckoned him over. Glad for the interruption, he rose and joined her. She led him outside into the hallway.

"You just got a call from Colonel Adriani of the NOCS." Alex's body tensed.

"What did he want?"

"For you to call him. I think he's offering you a chance to work with them. But the line wasn't secure, so he only hinted about joining them for a meeting tonight."

"Thanks, Nancy." Alex rushed downstairs to his office and called Adriani.

"Vittore, it's good to hear your voice. Is this what I think it is?" Alex asked.

"Good to hear your voice as well, Alex. Yes, Deputy Minister Ferrara and General Ghiberti have approved you to meet with my friends and me tonight."

Alex thought for a second and remembered the old adage: 'It's better to ask forgiveness than to ask permission,' so he accepted without first talking to Chandler. He knew it would bring big trouble later. But this was now.

"Okay, Vittore, I'll be there. Tell me the arrangements."

"Be outside your Embassy in thirty minutes; I'll have someone pick you up and bring whatever equipment you'll need for the meeting."

"Thanks, Vittore. I mean it."

"We look forward to seeing you, *Ciao.*"

Alex turned to see Nancy, Joe and George all standing there.

"Boss, can I come with you?" Joe Roberts asked. Alex realized he hadn't thought to ask Colonel Adriani if he could bring someone.

"Joe, I really need you here dealing with the task force, and watching my back. George, same goes for you. Besides, I'll have Mike James up in Bologna; I'm afraid that's the best I can do." They both looked crushed. *Good men, Alex thought, brave and bold, the kind of guys you want watching your back; not afraid to do things for all the right reasons. Chandler could take a lesson from them.*

"If you need me, I've got my cell phone and James has a secure phone linked to the task force." He quickly went to his safe and took out his SIG Sauer 9mm pistol, holster and spare magazines, put them on under his jacket, then walked back to the conference room. He signaled Rachel to join him. She left Larry Jones sitting at the conference table, and walked with Alex into a nearby office for privacy.

"Rachel, the Italian cops have given me less than half an hour to meet my ride to Bologna. They want me at their rescue attempt tonight." Not surprisingly, her face showed a mixture of concern, fear, and negativity.

"Are you crazy? The DCM just declined to have the FBI as an observer. Now, you're going, instead? You didn't even ask Chandler if you could."

"Right, and what do you think he would say?"

"Of course, he would say 'no'. Damnit! This is a bad idea. Alex."

"Rachel, this isn't a discussion. I didn't join DS to push papers all day, dabble in politics, or craft press releases." Immediately, he knew he'd gone too far.

"Oh, you think handling press releases is beneath you?" Her green eyes blazed with a ferocity he seldom witnessed.

"No! That's not what I meant. Those things are just not what I do, that's all."

"I repeat, Alex, this is very bad idea. Chandler will have your head for it when he finds out. There will be serious political fallout for you."

"You're probably right, but, I have to go," He wanted her approval, and was upset that she hadn't given it. He tried to hug her, but she pushed him back with force.

"God damn it, Alex! We almost died in Islamabad and I never want to go through that again. Now you're choosing to go right back into a dangerous situation. I need you, not just your memory."

"I have a job to do, Rachel. Morally, it's the right thing, and I want you to see that. What kind of a person would I be if I didn't help rescue Tony and Francesca? I'll call you later."

As he turned to go, she grabbed his arm, then stepped toward him, embracing him tightly. "You come back to me, Alex Boyd. I need you!" Both of them teared up. He knew it was time to go, now, for sure.

* * *

Alex stopped briefly at his office to pick up his Barbour coat, then walked out the front door of the Embassy. Rain had intensified, but the temperature wasn't bad. Within minutes, a car with two NOCS officers pulled up just as Adriani had promised, and Alex jumped in. Immediately, he recognized Captain Nino Agostino, his friend from the NOCS exercise in Abruzzi.

"So, Nino, how far a drive is it to Bologna?"

"No drive, my friend. You're getting special VIP treatment."

"The last time someone said that to me, I was in basic Navy training. It wasn't a nice surprise." Nino chuckled at Alex's nerves.

"We're going to Ciampino Airport where we'll take a police helicopter to a base near the farmhouse."

They sped through the wet streets of Rome, windshield wipers working overtime. Alex watched pedestrians fighting to keep umbrellas from turning inside out.

Shit, he thought. *I hate flying in bad weather.*

The flight from Ciampino to the base near the farmhouse lived up to Alex's fears. Turbulence buffeted them the entire trip; wind gusts violently threw the helicopter from side to side, often pitching up and down with unexpected blasts of air. Fortunately, none of the other NOCS members were in a talking mood. After landing, a nauseated Alex followed the rest of his travel team to a hanger where they would meet the rest of the assault force.

The hangar was devoid of aircraft, but full of cops relaxing on the floor with equipment spread out around them. On one wall were several large displays containing photographs of the farmhouse and a large map of the area. Colonel Adriani walked over, sporting a large grin, and shook his hand.

"Alex! Thank you for coming"

"To the contrary, thank *you*, Vittore." Colonel Adriani nodded.

"We would normally wait until, perhaps, four in the morning to make our raid, but because the weather is terrible now, I want to take advantage of the storm to make our assault. It will help conceal our approach and, hopefully, the kidnappers will remain inside the farmhouse to stay dry. We will attack at eleven this evening."

Alex nodded and looked around the hanger for Mike James and Harold Jordan but didn't see them. Capt. Paolo Capelli, one of the other NOCS squadron leaders, slapped him on the shoulder and they shook hands. A few other NOCS troopers, whom he remembered from Abruzzi, came over to greet him.

"Come with me, Alex. We have some equipment for you to wear," Capelli said.

They walked to a large truck parked in the corner of the hangar. Paolo pulled out a helmet, ballistic vest, gas mask, and camouflage jacket with hood.

"These should fit. But you'll have to wear your own shoes and pants."

Not having had time to grab his own outdoor clothes, Alex was stuck wearing his lace-up black office shoes and suit pants. Alex smiled as Paolo started laughing, knowing his getup looked odd.

"Paolo, at a time like this, who gives a shit. It's a come-as-you-are party."

A booming voice roared across the hanger. Colonel Adriani declared to the entire group: "Okay, everyone, listen up! The briefing by Lt. Campanella will begin now."

Alex looked at the briefing boards and saw Mike James and Harold Jordan standing next to a guy whom Alex assumed was the key briefer. He noted both were fully clothed in NOCS assault gear, head to foot—*lucky guys.*

For the next hour, several briefers repeatedly went over the assault plan in minute detail. The only thing they lacked were internal photos of the farmhouse and barn. *Hopefully,* Alex thought, *the element of surprise would compensate for this lack of information.*

He was pleased to learn he would be part of a team entering the farmhouse through the front door, not merely observing. Simultaneously, another team would assault through a rear door, and a third team would attack the barn.

The three, two-man surveillance teams, operating within sight of the farmhouse and barn, were still streaming live video back to the computers in the hanger. Heavy rain was distorting the images, but it appeared the suspects had withdrawn their two-man patrol from around the buildings. There were lights on inside the farmhouse and silhouettes could be seen moving behind shaded windows. According to the briefer, the white Fiat had not left the barn all day.

Hours later, Colonel Adriani ordered everyone to be on alert. The NOCS assault force and Alex were told to put on their gear. Dropping his personal Barbour coat and suit jacket on the ground, he hoped he would remember to pick them up on the way back, assuming he made it back alive.

"Okay, everyone to the trucks!" Adriani ordered. Alex followed his team leader, Captain Paolo Capelli. Mike and Harold were on

Team 3 and would assault the barn, so they boarded a different truck. A ten-minute drive later, the trucks stopped, and everyone disembarked. Alex's team formed up next to the truck. He pulled the camouflage jacket hood up over his head since the rain had now increased and was pounding him.

"The farmhouse is just over this hill, three hundred meters away," Capt. Capelli reminded the team, "You'll be able to see it soon. We'll maneuver on foot until we are one hundred meters from the farmhouse, then we'll crawl until we reach the attack point, twenty meters from the house. On my signal, we will rush the front door. You know your assignments after that."

Walking in staggered formation with his team, Alex tried, like everyone else, to take advantage of whatever natural cover there was. For the most part it was flat, but there were occasional trees and dips in the ground. While the crops were not high, they would provide some concealment should the men have to drop completely prone.

At the one-hundred-meter mark from the farmhouse, everyone lay on the ground. The rain never let up as they slithered through wet crops, mud, and puddles of water. By now, Alex was totally drenched. Water drizzled inside his jacket and ran down his neck and back; mud splashed up onto his face and occasionally into his eyes. He knew he would throw away these pants and shoes if he survived the night.

At the twenty-meter mark, everyone stopped and waited for the signal. First, Capelli asked for the thermal imaging device being carried by another NOCS trooper. Alex wasn't far from Capelli and saw him scanning the farmhouse. Capelli whispered a number into his microphone. Alex presumed it was the number of kidnappers inside. Then, Capelli gave the order for all to don their gas masks.

"On my signal," Capelli commanded. Waiting ten seconds, he rasped out, "Ready: go, go, go."

The entire team rose as one and sprinted to the front door. Hell was about to be unleashed.

Chapter 33

HELL UNLEASHED

Alex stacked behind three team members in front of him and to the left of the front door, all prepared to enter the farmhouse. A fifth man got behind him. Immediately in front was Captain Paolo Capelli, squadron leader. Unzipping his jacket, Alex drew his 9mm Sig Sauer pistol. Spare magazines were in holders on his left hip belt. A heavy metal battering ram was ready at the front door held by a sixth NOCS trooper.

With a heave, the trooper smashed open the door and quickly stepped aside. A seventh trooper threw in a flash-bang making an incredibly loud explosion. It sent brilliant, disorienting light flashes along with smoke and tear gas beyond the entryway. Alex's five-man stack moved in, followed by the men who used the battering ram and flash-bang.

Heart racing, Alex felt the danger, yet anticipation, of finding the Ambassador and his wife. Smoke and tear gas still hung in the air as they entered the hallway. Walking quickly, the team worked methodically down the hall. Flashlight beams, mounted on submachine

213

guns, reached forward like long fingers through debris hanging midair searching for enemy targets. The first two turned into the living room through a doorway on the right. Alex heard submachine guns firing at one or more targets. Simultaneously, he heard fire returned from a different weapon. With no time to worry, his team's job was to continue down the hallway and clear the other rooms.

Fifteen meters away, a man jumped into the hallway at the far end, unleashing a burst of machine gun fire aimed at Alex and his teammates. It happened so fast, Alex could only react on instinct. Pointing his pistol without using its sights, he rapidly fired two sets of double-tap shots at the target in under two seconds. The man crumpled to the ground, just as Alex realized he, himself, was having trouble breathing. Dropping to one knee, he felt dizzy; his chest was hurting like he'd been hit by a huge fist.

Leaning against the wall, he slid down to the floor to assess his condition. Helmet off, he slid his gas mask on top of his head. Too dark to see blood, Alex felt the front of his ballistic vest with one hand. Sure enough, a bullet had stuck in his Kevlar body armor. Ripping open the Velcro fasteners of the vest, he physically inspected his chest. Nothing. No wound and nothing wet or slimy like blood. Then he noticed Capelli, also on the ground, holding his left arm. Two NOCS, moved past both men and cleared the remaining rooms. A teammate stopped to attend Capelli's arm injury. Slowly regaining a normal breathing pattern, Alex felt the dizziness disperse. Painfully, he leaned over to talk to Capelli.

"Are you all right, Paolo?"

"I think so. Just a little hole in my arm. With an aspirin and cappuccino, I'll be fine."

Alex laughed, which made his chest hurt like hell. Capelli's deathbed humor, was typical of men living close to the edge.

"Adriani owes you a cannoli as well," Alex joked and got to his feet, a little unsteady.

"Thank you, Alex, that was good shooting."

He smiled while helping Paolo stand. "I only wish we could have questioned that guy first." Reaching down for Capelli's submachine, he continued, "You won't be needing this for now."

Walking down the hall to inspect the dead man, Alex saw two of his shots had hit the man squarely in the center of the chest ; the third one hit in the upper left shoulder. Apparently, his fourth shot had missed. Searching the dead man's pockets, he found nothing useful. Walking back to the living room, one kidnapper was dead and another, still alive, tied with flex-cuffs, lying on the floor. The NOCS troopers who had entered the room were both okay.

"Anyone search upstairs for the Ambassador, or more bad guys?" Alex asked.

"They're doing it now," a NOCS trooper replied. He walked to the base of the stairs as two NOCS came down.

"Nothing upstairs, it's clear," the first NOCS said.

"Let's see if there's a basement."

Finding a door with stairs leading down. Alex looked at two troopers nearby.

"Flash-bang?"

They nodded and Alex pulled his gas mask down onto his face. A NOCS tossed one flash-bang into the basement which immediately exploded and lit the stairs with flashes. Moving quickly downstairs, all three men used submachine guns to scan the area for potential targets. The basement smelled like a sewer but was empty.

Using the light attached to his submachine gun, Alex saw two dirty mattresses, food trays thrown around the room, a couple of chamber pots filled with human sewage, and discarded clothing items. There were also two smashed cell phones on the floor.

He picked up a man's jacket, and a woman's coat. The jacket

contained a receipt for ceramics, listing the buyer as Anthony Scarmatti. The coat pocket had used tissues, a small makeup compact, and a piece of paper with notes about restaurants in Orvieto. On the letterhead was the name Francesca Scarmatti. They had been so close.

Alex turned to the two NOCS members and said, "Let's check the barn."

He and his team moved cautiously through the inter-connecting door from the farmhouse into the barn already under control of the other NOCS squad. One kidnapper from the living room, still alive, had been moved there. Alex saw two additional kidnappers in handcuffs, both unharmed.

"I take it this part of the raid went well with no casualties," Alex spoke to Harold Jordan, the CIA case officer. "Any sign of the Scarmattis?"

"No, but at least no one was hurt. We didn't find anything of use other than the white Fiat."

"Did we get anything yet from these guys?" pointing to the two kidnappers captured in the barn.

"Nothing so far. As you can see, the NOCS are grilling them now."

Mike James joined Alex. "Are you all right? You have blood on your neck and jacket."

For the first time Alex had enough light to see and looked down. He didn't remember taking off any body armor, yet his camouflage jacket was still on.

"Yeah, I'm fine. The blood is Capelli's, but he'll be okay."

Moving closer to hear the interrogation of the two kidnappers, Alex realized Adriani and Agostino were standing next to him.

"The Ambassador and Mrs. Scaramatti were clearly in the basement, Vittore," Alex told Adriani. "We found some personal items to confirm it."

"My men told me," Adriani responded. "I've reported it to

Bologna; they'll pass it on to Rome. The Scarmattis must have been moved very recently. We just missed them."

Alex listened to the interrogation for another forty minutes, but the kidnappers were denying everything. He felt tension and anger beginning to course throughout his body. His head felt ready to explode; his breathing was becoming deeper with each nonresponsive answer by the kidnappers, and he couldn't stop rubbing his hands together as he continued to listen.

To come so close to getting the Scarmattis back was almost too much to bear, especially with all the bullshit and pressure at the Embassy. Then, thinking about his next question long and hard, Alex looked at the Colonel.

"Vittore, may I interrogate them for a few minutes? If you agree, I recommend we limit the number of people in the barn."

Colonel Adriani shifted into English, suspicious of Alex's intent. "What do you have in mind, Alex?"

"Honestly, this will go against everything I've been taught, indeed, everything that's legal and moral in the United States, but I'm certain the Ambassador was here and these men know where he was taken. It's worth the risk, and time is vitally important."

Adriani took a deep breath and frowned. Alex knew Adriani suspected what he had in mind would be outside the law. Just then, Capelli walked over to them, helped by a colleague, his arm now in a sling.

"I overheard your conversation, Colonel, please allow me to say that Alex saved my life in the house. I think he's earned a few moments with the suspects."

Adriani seemed moved by Capelli's plea, but Alex figured he was really grabbing a second to decide his next move. Then, he turned to the assembled NOCS, ordered most of them to leave, and told the few remaining never to say a word about the next few minutes in the barn. He nodded to Alex.

Approaching one of the kidnappers tied to a chair with flex-cuffs, Alex punched the man hard on the side of his face. Clearly shaken, the man, however, simply smiled back at Alex.

"Where did you take the Ambassador and his wife?"

The man stared at Alex whose attire looked different from the others. The man glanced at Alex's pants and shoes.

"Who are you?" he asked.

Alex hit him again, in the jaw with his fist. This time the man didn't smile. Instead, he spit out blood.

"The Scarmattis were in the basement; I found their things! Where are they now!" His nose was just an inch from the man's face.

"I don't know what you are talking about."

"If I have to repeat myself, I will really hurt you!" Alex looked over at the other kidnapper and saw fear in his eyes. Grabbing the second man by the throat, he squeezed tightly. When his face started turning blue, Alex let him go. As the man coughed, trying to get some air, Alex slapped him on the side of the head. The man looked terrified.

"Alex, are you sure you want to do this?" Mike James asked, standing behind him.

"Absolutely. You can leave if you want to." But, James didn't budge.

Then, Alex grabbed the second kidnapper's face and yelled, "Where is the Ambassador?" The man tried to look over at his colleague who was telling him to shut up, but Alex pulled his head back to face him and said, "You have one last chance."

The man said nothing. First, Alex noted a stain growing around the crotch of the man's pants, then he smelt the urine as it dripped to form a wet puddle at his feet. Alex punched him in the stomach as hard as he could and the man gasped for air, then coughed repeatedly. The man's eyes were now wide with fear. Slowly, Alex reached into his shirt pocket and took out his Italian fountain pen, the pen Rachel had given him as a gift. He methodically unscrewed the cap and placed it over the rear end of the pen. The first kidnapper tried to make light of the situation.

"So, you are going to take notes?"

"Not exactly," Alex replied. Placing his thumb over the rear, flat end of the pen, he jammed it full force down through the light weight cotton pants into the kidnapper's thigh. The man howled like an animal, jerking around in his chair.

Colonel Adriani flinched as he watched, about to move forward when Captain Capelli grabbed his arm, shaking his head.

"Where are they?!" Alex screamed into the kidnapper's face, his nose mere inches away. The man shook his head, his mouth open in a silent scream of pain.

"I don't know where they were taken!" he managed to gasp out. It was the first acknowledgement the Scarmattis had been in the farmhouse; the man knew something.

Violently, Alex yanked the pen out of his thigh as the man screamed again. Quickly turning to Adriani, Alex winked, hoping it was seen as a sign of reassurance. Then, Alex pressed the tip of the pen against the kidnapper's throat, breaking the skin slightly as blood intermingled with ink. The man broke down, partial crying.

"Okay, okay, stop! They left early today!"

"How," Alex demanded.

"In the Lancia."

"Going where?"

"I don't know!"

"Liar!" Alex screamed into his face and pressed the pen harder against the soft tissue of his throat. The man coughed and shook violently.

"I only know they went south on the autostrada."

"Shut up!" the other kidnapper yelled, but it was too late.

"Why did you move him?"

"We got a tip-off. A phone call from a comrade said the police had traced a signal from the Ambassador's cell phone, so we had to move him."

Alex heard Adriani whisper the Italian equivalent of 'Holy shit!'

"Again, where is he now?" Alex grabbed the man's hair and yanked his head back.

"I don't know! He is with another cell, another group," the man said through a cascade of tears. Alex starred into the man's eyes, then slowly removed the pen from his throat, straightened up, screwed the cap back on, and put the pen back into his pocket. He was perspiring when he turned to face Colonel Adriani.

"That's all the questions I have, Vittore. I'm sorry for this, and hope it doesn't get you in trouble. I appreciate you trusting me. Thanks for letting me join the raid."

"We will deal with whatever happens," Adriani responded in English, "but for now, you have given us some useful leads. Thank you."

Chapter 34

IN HOT WATER AGAIN

Looking for evidence, the NOCS experts combed through the white Fiat, farmhouse, and barn. They missed nothing, but found no evidence pointing to where the Scarmattis had been moved. Alex motioned for Mike and Harold to join him in a corner of the barn.

"We have to inform the Embassy Task Force," Alex said. "Do you have your secure cell phone on you, Mike?"

"I do," he said, handing the phone to Alex.

"It's close to one in the morning; I don't know who'll be there at this hour." Alex looked at his dive watch, "but we're about to find out. Harold, I assume you're going to call Carter Ambrose with an update."

"I've already called him once, but I'll do it again, now that you got more information out of the kidnapper."

"Okay, here goes," Alex said, punching in the secure number of the Embassy conference room.

"Task Force Operations Center, Ames Burnham speaking," answered the Embassy's Political Counselor.

"Ames, its Boyd. Is the DCM there?"

"Everyone's here, Alex. We're waiting for a police report about the raid. Where have you been?"

"I'm near Bologna. Is Rachel there?"

"Yeah. She's walking toward me now."

She grabbed the phone out of Burnham's hand. "Alex! Are you okay?"

"I couldn't be better, Rachel. Listen, the Scarmattis were held here at the farmhouse, but were taken away before the raid. Still, we have some leads."

"The DCM wants to talk with you," she said. "Will I see you tonight?"

"Yeah, I should be back in a few hours. See you at the apartment."

She handed the phone to Chandler.

"Boyd! Where the hell are you?!" He screamed.

"I'm in a farmhouse, south of Bologna, where the Ambassador and his wife were being held. But we missed 'em."

Alex described the raid and what they found in the farmhouse, then told in detail about the information gained from the captured kidnappers.

"You'll be interested to know the terrorists were tipped off. We have a mole," he said, listening for Chandler's reaction, carefully omitting anything about his own specific role in the raid.

"I specifically forbade *anyone* from participating in the raid!" Chandler forcefully yelled. "That included you, Boyd, I'm furious!"

"That's not totally accurate, Sir. You told the Italians the *FBI* would not be 'observing' the raid. I was invited separately, at the last minute, by General Ghiberti to observe. The police were going to make the raid with or without us. I just watched."

"Don't mince words with me, Boyd. Your presence, and indeed the raid itself, jeopardized our efforts to find the Ambassador. I've had it with you. You are off the task force and banned from participation!"

Alex had been half expecting this, but still it shocked him, especially Chandler's bullshit about the raid jeopardizing efforts to find the Ambassador. It was pure FBI propaganda.

"My relations with the police are our best hope of influencing what happens," Alex said "and the raid did not jeopardize finding Tony and Francesca." He hoped by using their first names, it would remind Chandler about his close relationship with them. He knew it was closer than Chandler liked.

"Don't be so conceited, Boyd. You're done! And by the way, did the other DS Agent participate in the raid?"

Alex looked over at Mike James, listening to the conversation.

"No, I haven't seen him all evening. He's been at the Bologna base doing liaison."

"Then he's smarter than you, Boyd."

"I guess so."

Chandler abruptly hung up.

"You didn't have to do that, Alex," Mike James said.

"Yes, I did. Chandler will fry your ass if he has a chance. Avoid him at all costs. Give me another minute; I have one more call to make."

Alex dialed the DS Command Center's secure number in Washington, DC.

"Hi, it's Alex Boyd in Italy, can you patch me through to Director Jim Riley?" He also asked they not record the call, but said they could listen in. If the issue of "extreme measures" arose later, he didn't want to be on tape admitting it.

Fifteen minutes later, Alex was finished; returned the phone to Mike, and asked Colonel Adriani how he could get back to Rome.

"The chopper is going to take us back to Ciampino. It's ready when you are," Adriani said. Before boarding for the ride back to Rome, he exchanged the NOCS' blood-spattered camouflage jacket for his own suit jacket and Barbour that he'd left in the hangar. The trip was quiet and this time the weather cooperated; it had stopped raining and turbulence was minimal. When he landed, a police car took him directly to his apartment.

Alex entered his building on Via Tagliamento and climbed the stairs to their apartment. Glancing at his watch, it showed three in the morning. Unlocking the door, he entered quietly trying not to wake Rachel, if she was asleep. He placed the suit jacket and Barbour on the living room sofa.

"Alex? Is that you?" she called sleepily from the bedroom.

"Yeah, sorry I woke you."

She turned on the bedside light and looked at his pants.

"Have you been playing in the mud? Why are you so filthy?"

"Uh, the weather was bad, raining, and the ground was a mess."

"To say the least. Let me help you take off your wet clothes. I want to hear about everything that happened."

"No, that's okay, Rachel, you'll get dirty. Stay in bed; I'll undress in the bathroom."

He placed his wallet, keys, pistol and extra magazines on the dresser. Then grabbed the fountain pen, realizing it was covered in dry blood, and put it into his shirt pocket while walking into the bathroom. Closing the door behind him, he quickly washed the outside of the pen. Red-brown blood flowed into the drain. He unscrewed the top and saw the inside was coated with more blood and tiny bits of flesh. Cleaning it the best he could, he tested it by trying to write on a piece of paper. Clearly the nib was damaged.

If Mussolini was alive today, he wouldn't be amused that I destroyed his pen. Setting it aside, he knew a repair was needed.

His shoes and pants were ruined, but he intended to throw them away. Seeing blood smears on the side of his neck, he was grateful Rachel hadn't seen them. Pulling off his shirt, he saw a large, ugly bruise on his chest where the bullet had hit his ballistic vest.

Shit, he hadn't thought about that. He felt fine, but the bruise looked terrible. He also smelled of body odor mixed with a hint of tear gas.

"I'm going to take a quick shower, be out in a few minutes," he yelled out to Rachel.

After five minutes, he was just finishing his shower when the bathroom door opened and Rachel walked in.

"So, tell me what happened." She pulled back the shower curtain.

"My god, Alex.! How did you get that hideous bruise?"

"What, this thing?"

"Don't bullshit me! You went on that raid, didn't you? I thought you'd be in their headquarters, or something like that."

"Okay, I got a little closer than expected. The ground was uneven, wet, and muddy. I slipped and fell onto a fence. That's how I got it."

Rachel stared at him for a minute. "Alex, you're one of the most athletic guys I know. You expect me to believe you lost your footing and fell on a fence?"

"We were running at the time?"

Crap, he knew he was digging himself in deeper. But he couldn't tell her he'd been shot, not after she had implored him not to go in the first place.

"I'll be in bed. Tell me what happened in Bologna when you get out of the bathroom." She turned on her heels and left the room.

The conversation in bed was heated and angry. Rachel had warned him there would be political fallout for his decision to go to Bologna without getting Chandler's permission. She told him how angry Chandler had been after speaking with him on the phone. Now, he was banned from the task force. Unfortunately, Alex knew he couldn't tell her how he'd successfully gotten information from the kidnappers about the blue Lancia moving the Scarmattis south on the autostrada, or about a mole inside the task force. If he did, he'd have to explain how. Better to let her assume the Italians had developed the information.

By 4:00 a.m., they finally turned out the light and tried to sleep. Alex didn't nod off until around five.

Chapter 35

CHECK! YOUR MOVE.

Early the next morning, General Ghiberti ordered the police to contact Lancia, the car manufacturer whose name was gained through Alex's violent interrogation. They were searching for a list of all recent purchasers of dark blue models. Because 300 such cars were sold nationwide in the last year alone, Ghiberti decided to narrow the search by focusing on provinces nearest to the farmhouse: Umbria, Tuscany, Lazio, Marche, and Emilia-Romagna. That cut the list down to only forty-two purchasers in the last year.

Investigative teams spread throughout the five provinces to interview dealers and obtain information they might recall about buyers. Police databases were also cross-referenced to examine possible extremist links to these purchasers.

In a one-on-one meeting in the General's office, Ghiberti asked Colonel Adriani, "Vittore, who else saw Alex's interrogation of the kidnappers besides you?"

Adriani leaned back in his chair, opposite Ghiberti's desk, and replied, "The other two Americans, Captains Agostino and Capelli,

Lt. Campanelli, and three more of my men. Of course, three kidnappers were there. Alex only interrogated two of them. But they all saw it happen."

"This could be trouble. The kidnappers will certainly say one was tortured and the other was beaten. Their lawyers will have a field day."

"I know, General."

"And you officially booked them into the Bologna police station? I mean, there is a record of them being brought in?"

"Yes, General, correct."

Ghiberti could see from Adriani's expression that he was worried about the implication of his last question but decided to ignore it.

"Then we must close ranks and deny the torture ever happened. It will be their word against ours. Remember, we have evidence they are the kidnappers. This will play well in the media if the allegation of torture ever goes to a jury. Clearly Italian and European Union laws were broken by Alex. So what? This happens all the time with criminals in ordinary cases."

"What do you plan on doing, General?"

"Leave that to me. We will use standard police techniques to make the kidnappers see things our way. Vittore, I cannot thank you enough for your actions last night at the farmhouse. If we are lucky, the NOCS will be called into action again very soon. How is Captain Capelli feeling?"

"He's fine, Sir. His arm will be as good as new in no time."

"Give him my regards, Vittore. Ask him to see me when he recovers. I want to thank him in person for his bravery."

Colonel Adriani left the office and Ghiberti called the Chief Investigating Officer on the Ambassador's case, who would be preparing all evidentiary material for the prosecutor.

"Hello, Major Vicencia? This is General Ghiberti. Are you getting all the help you need on this case?"

"Yes, sir. I have everything I need."

"Excellent. One more thing: I have a favor to ask."

"Anything you want, General."

"You know where the three kidnappers are being held, yes?"

"Naturally, at the central jail in Bologna, Sir.

"Correct, Major. I want you to bring all their immediate families to the jail and question them individually."

"Yes, as you wish, but we would normally do this anyway, General. Why are you mentioning it specifically?"

"Major, I want the kidnappers to believe if they don't cooperate, then their loved ones might be charged as accessories to this crime. Don't use any physical force. Don't subject them to any questionable techniques. Except verbally, be harsh, be tough, and ensure the kidnappers hear you interrogating their families. Do you understand?"

"Completely, Sir."

"You are excellent at your job, Major Vicencia. I just want to be sure the kidnappers are intimidated. I won't forget your cooperation."

"Yes, sir."

Ghiberti hung up the phone, smiled. His judgment told him these kidnappers would not have enough courage to bring up Alex's actions, if potential charges were hanging over the heads of their families.

Had Alex not acknowledged his lawless intent prior to his violent actions in the barn, Ghiberti thought, *or not apologized to Colonel Adriani for possibly causing him trouble, then, I might not be so inclined to protect him. But Alex saved Captain Capelli's life and possibly others.*

Yes, Ghiberti was comfortable with his orders to the Major.

* * *

The phone rang in the FBI's main office in Washington, DC. "Special Agent John Reynolds returning a call to the Assistant Director."

"One moment Agent Reynolds," the FBI secretary said. Reynolds was calling on a secure Embassy line from the Legatt offices. Only Mark Terranova, resident Embassy FBI agent, was present.

"Hello, John? Thank you for getting back to me. I'm concerned over the Embassy report regarding a failed raid at the farmhouse. I thought the Italians were better than that."

"Sir, in all honesty, the police probably did the best they could, given the rapidly evolving situation. At least I managed to ensure the FBI was not part of that failure."

"Yes, and for that, John, we're grateful at headquarters. I also saw Agent Terranova's report that the *Carabinieri* is more than willing to work with us in finding the Ambassador. Do you think they can help us get our Hostage Rescue Team into the country?"

"I think they may be able to assist, covertly, but they also have to take orders from higher up, so we'll need to be cautious."

The line was silent for nearly ten seconds. Reynolds began to wonder if the Assistant Director was still there. He looked over at Terranova, who merely stared back at him.

"All right, then," the Assistant Director finally said, "Let's see if we can get in some members of the HRT to assist the *Carabinieri*. We can call them "advisors", regardless of whether the *Carabinieri* want to use them or not in an actual raid."

Terranova grabbed Reynolds arm and whispered, "Will they be able to get their equipment into Italy?" Reynolds acknowledged the point but shrugged.

"Sir, will the team be able to bring their gear, including weapons, into Italy? This may be difficult."

"We'll sort that out later, John. I'll leave it up to the team in

Frankfurt." Reynolds figured the Assistant Director didn't have a clue on how to handle it.

"Oh, one last thing, John. I noticed in Terranova's report that the Embassy's Regional Security Officer, a guy named Alex Boyd, was present at the raid. How did that happen?"

"Boyd's a pain in the ass, Sir. But he does have excellent connections with the police. However, I think we've taken care of him. The DCM hates him as much as we do. He may be history."

"I hope so. Let me know if you need any further help with him."

"Will do, Sir."

The Assistant Director was the first to hang up, ending the call.

* * *

While Reynolds and Terranova were calling Washington, DCM Chandler and Management Counselor Eaton held a private conversation in Chandler's office.

"Yes, Charlotte, I agree with you that the kidnappers must have ditched the Embassy car somewhere. It obviously wasn't at the farmhouse."

God, he thought, *she's driving me crazy with her constant pestering about the car.*

"I don't know how we'll resolve this," he said.

"Alden, my staff knows the car isn't in the motor pool. Of course, they don't know where it is. I've managed to put them off by saying I'm too swamped with supporting the task force to deal with a motor pool issue now."

"Excellent."

"That's not the point, Alden. It will come out eventually, and will look extremely suspicious."

"Charlotte, if we get Tony back, he'll acknowledge his role in using the car, I'm sure. As I implied previously, should he not make it back, well, I doubt the car will be found."

She clarified, "You mean if he's killed, along with Francesca."

"You can put it that way if you want, but I find it too harsh a thought. But yes, if he doesn't return, then we can let people presume he took the car for himself without our knowledge."

"But I'm on tape as having driven the car to his house that morning," she was almost in tears, her left eye was twitching.

"Relax, Charlotte, please. You are also on tape as having left the house. No one has linked you to driving him off the residence grounds. We just need to stand by our story."

"I have to go," she said, walking out of the office and down the hall to the women's bathroom. She sat in a stall and silently cried. When she finally collected herself, she washed her face in the sink and took a small container from her pocket. Removing a Valium, she popped it in her mouth. It was still early morning, yet she needed help to calm down.

* * *

Alex slept late the morning after the raid since Chandler had banned him from the task force. Joe Roberts would cover his assignment. He vaguely recalled Rachel saying "Bye" to him somewhere around seven that morning. He must have needed the sleep since he didn't wake until nine.

His chest still hurt where he'd been shot. When he looked into the bathroom mirror, he saw the color had deepened into purple. Maybe this would be the worst of it. After having a few cups of strong coffee and two slices of buttered toast, he showered and shaved, threw on a black turtleneck with dark grey slacks, and added a grey herringbone sports coat. Before heading off to the Embassy, Alex retrieved his pistol and extra magazines from the top of the dresser.

Nancy, George, and Sam greeted him warmly when he entered the office. Joe had briefed them earlier that morning on results of the raid the previous night.

"Alex," Nancy said, "we're all worried about whether you'll be able to stay at post after last night."

"Unfortunately, I may have dug my own grave, Nancy. But it was a risk I had to take. I guess it didn't work out."

"It's not over yet. Besides, there are a lot people in the Embassy who support what you did; that was brave of you."

About to say something self-deprecating, Alex paused as Nancy's phraseology sunk in.

"What do you mean, 'that it was brave'?"

She looked at him curiously, opening her hands, indicating she was unsure of why he asked.

"The police liaison officer told Joe all about the raid this morning; that you killed one of the kidnappers."

"What else did he say?"

"I think that's all. Why, Alex?"

"The DCM doesn't know I was even on the raid, and Rachel isn't exactly certain what I did. I'd like to leave it like that."

"Oh, I see. You'd better talk to Joe. I'm not sure who else knows."

She returned to her desk and began working on paper piles. An hour later the phone rang. Answering it, she put it on hold.

"Alex, you have Jim Riley from Washington on the line for you." He took the phone after a long look at her.

"Good morning, Jim."

"The question is, how are you feeling after stopping a bullet last night?"

"You know. Sore, black and blue, but okay. I guess you've heard I've been banned from the task force operation."

"Yes, and not only that, your DCM called the European Bureau's Assistant Secretary, Archibald Watson, last night and wanted you removed from post. I got a call from Watson shortly afterward at home."

"I'm all ears, Jim. So, is that it for me?"

"No. I told Watson we don't have an Italian speaking RSO available to replace you, and it would be a terrible decision to replace you in the middle of a crisis. Especially since you obviously have excellent contacts with the Italian police. I got him to agree that the Ambassador should look at this matter, if, and when, he's freed."

Alex was silent. *So, he would live to fight another day.*

"Thanks for having my back, Jim."

"You're welcome. Oh, and by the way, Alex, the Secretary will be deciding about using the Rewards for Justice Program today. You should hear sometime tonight or tomorrow."

They hung up and Alex dwelt upon the implication of using the Rewards for Justice Program. It meant that non-law-enforcement individuals with information regarding the kidnapping would receive a large reward if their information proved correct and led authorities to the kidnappers. It had worked in the past at other embassies. He hoped it would work again here, too. Anything to bring Tony and Francesca home safe.

Chapter 36

A NEW DISCOVERY

Alex leaned back in his chair and put his feet up on the corner of his desk, finally having time to think. He grabbed a yellow pad and instinctively reached for his fountain pen, forgetting he was wearing a turtleneck without a pocket. Then remembered he'd left the pen at the apartment since it was unusable. Instead, he reached for a pencil. Methodically, he noted every important aspect of the kidnapping, trying to find a new lead.

Something kept bothering him whenever he thought about the morning of the kidnapping, but he couldn't put a finger on it. He began writing down each event on a timeline, noting in a side column what actions the Embassy or the Italians were taking as a result of those events. Nothing seemed to generate new ideas.

I don't think the Ambassador ever filled out the personal security information questionnaire I sent him a month ago. It included information about his relatives, personal history only he or closest loved ones would know, even the creation of a secret password in the event of a kidnapping, and his medical condition.

Well, too late now, Alex thought. With time on his hands, he decided to check in with the Embassy's Regional Medical Officer to see if he had anything useful on the Ambassador's health.

"Hello...I'd like to speak to Doctor Wilson," he said to Renata, the Italian female receptionist, as he walked into the Embassy medical offices.

"Oh, I'm afraid Doctor Wilson isn't in town, Alex. He had a death in the family and flew home to Rhode Island almost a week ago."

"I'm sorry to hear that. Nothing matters more than family. Would Betty Fisher be available?"

"Yes, I'll call Nurse Fisher. Please have a seat," she said, indicating the sitting area.

Waiting for the nurse practitioner, Alex thumbed through some reception room magazines. Most were medical journals, providing riveting stories such as 'How to Survive a Heart Attack,' or 'The Benefits of a Regular Colonoscopy.'

I wonder if Chandler should read that one?

"Hi Alex, come back to my office," Betty said. He followed her.

"What can I do for you?"

"I realized the Ambassador never sent back the personal security questionnaire I gave him. It would have contained pertinent medical records. Maybe you can help me out." He smiled, expecting her cooperation.

"I don't know, Alex. You realize medical records are restricted only to those who've been authorized to see them. Do you have anything signed by the Ambassador?"

"No, as I said, he never sent back the questionnaire I gave him." Alex was surprised at resistance of any kind. Since he knew this was her first overseas post, he tried to make an allowance.

"Betty, I'm not asking out of morbid curiosity, it's my job to know about the Ambassador's health since we have to protect him. I regret not doing this earlier."

"Alex, I could get in trouble if I divulge his file without permission," Betty pleaded.

"Look, I can see you're nervous with this conversation, but since Tony and Francesca have been kidnapped, it's important to know *anything* that might help them."

She considered the request. He decided to press further.

"Listen, I'll take full responsibility and be prepared to tell Doctor Wilson you protected Tony's privacy. Trust me, Doctor Wilson would give me this information in a minute."

"Well… okay, I suppose so. Wait here."

She left the room and came back five minutes later with two files in hand. Sitting down, she opened the first one and held it close to her face, clearly not letting Alex see it.

"All right, Francesca's in excellent health. She doesn't take any medications." Betty put the file down on the desk and opened the second file.

She raised her eyebrows. Her expression showed concern. He waited, tapping his foot somewhat impatiently.

"For God's sake, Betty, what are you looking at?" he finally said.

"Well, it appears Ambassador Scarmatti takes Warfarin, sometimes called 'coumadin' for his heart. Specifically, he takes it for an operation he had years ago placing a mechanical aortic heart valve. He needs to take Warfarin daily to keep his blood on the thin side."

"Did you know this before?" Alex watched as she became somewhat nervous. He noticed a little perspiration on her forehead.

"No, because Doctor Wilson always handled the Scarmattis personally and never discussed their health with me."

"Okay, I understand. Sorry if I upset you, Betty. What happens if he doesn't take this Warfarin regularly?"

"That would be very dangerous. If he doesn't keep his blood at the proper level of thinness, his blood will get thicker in just a few days without the medicine and he could develop a blood clot. Should it travel to his heart, it could possibly clog his artificial valve."

"Meaning what, exactly?"

"The valve might stick open or closed." She said. "With the valve not working properly, bits of sticky blood particles could break off and move into his brain, causing a blockage of his blood flow. He would likely have a stroke; how bad, can't be known in advance. But if the valve sticks in the closed position, he would die for sure." She was beginning to breath quicker.

"Relax, Betty, take some deep breaths. Where does he get his Warfarin?"

"Doctor Wilson scribbled a note in the file that the Ambassador goes to the Farmacia Borghese, down the street from his residence."

"Would the pharmacy tell us when his next prescription needs to be filled?"

"Yes, we have a code to verify who we are."

"All right," Alex said, "I'd like you, or the receptionist, Renata, to call the pharmacy and ask them that question. When Tony and Francesca went missing, I searched their house and don't recall seeing any medication on their nightstands. I'd have to look again in their bathroom cabinets to be sure. Nevertheless, I suppose it's possible he carried it with him, although I don't know why unless he was going somewhere."

Betty and Alex walked out to the reception desk. Renata dialed the Farmacia Borghese's number and made the request.

"When we saw the news about his kidnapping, we prepared the information about his Warfarin use in case the police asked," the pharmacist said, "but no one has called. He should have picked up his thirty-day refill three days ago."

Alex knew Tony Scarmatti was in big trouble; now his life was in danger, in more ways than one.

* * *

The piece of paper slipped through Tony Scarmatti's fingers and fell to the floor. Francesca looked horrified since this was Tony's second attempt to hold onto it. He reached down and used his thumb and index finger to try picking it up, but he couldn't do it.

"What's happening, Tony? I'm scared."

"My guess is I've had a stroke, maybe a small one."

"How do you know that?" Because you've lost your sense of touch?"

"Yeah. I'm not getting enough Warfarin and my blood must be too thick. The doctor in Los Angeles warned me about this. The medicine is a blood thinner. I'm not getting enough so my blood is getting thicker and probably blocking the blood flow to my head."

"Oh, Tony, No! Maybe you should lie back on the mattress and rest."

This new location was as dirty as the old place. Same setup, though: dirty mattresses on a basement floor with each of them having one hand tied to a center pole running from floor to ceiling.

He hadn't felt well for the last day or two even before the move. Even before they shoved them into the trunk of a car, for a second time and transported them to this new place without telling them what was going on. Since then, whenever he had to use the chamber pot, he couldn't seem to grasp the paper they had left in a roll on the floor.

Now, they had been sitting on the mattresses for an hour. The mattresses stunk, they stunk, and the entire room smelled like a sewer. The pots they had been given to toilet in were full and the kidnappers hadn't come down to the basement to empty them for hours. Plus, Tony and Francesca were still wearing the same clothes since they had been snatched. With their wristwatches and phones taken away, Francesca had lost count of the number of days they had been in captivity.

"There's another thing I need to tell you."

She looked into his face, knowing this news had to be bad.

"At times today, my vision has grayed out." She raised her hand up to her mouth, but then remembered that it wasn't clean, and smelled of feces.

"You mean you can't see?"

"No, not that bad. It's just that my vision is partially obscured for a while, usually the top half of my vision. But then it clears up."

"Damn it!" She yelled, at the top of her voice. "Get us out of here. I want a doctor!"

No one came into the basement. Francesca stared at the door at the top of the stairs and felt hopeless.

"Relax, they'll check on us soon, they always do."

She leaned over and placed her hand on his shoulder as he lay on his back with eyes closed. Then she rubbed his forehead. Feces or no feces on her hand, Tony needed comforting. After a few minutes, he started snoring.

At least he's still alive, she thought. She stopped touching him and sat up with her legs bent and hands wrapped around her knees. *This is so hard,* she whispered to herself. *We're treated like animals, the food is terrible, and we have no idea if anyone is trying to rescue us.* She let her head hang down. *And why did they move us from one location to another? What was that about?*

It was not knowing that caused despair and anxiety. She looked over at Tony, still snoring. *I'm going to have to be strong if we're to get through this,* she sighed. She desperately wanted to feel safe again and surrounded by people who cared for them. She thought of Rachel, her closest friend and confidant, and wondered what she was doing. *Certainly, they're looking for us by now, and the police, too. I must believe we have a chance to survive. Tony and I need to hang on a little longer. But for how long?*

Then she heard the door open at the top of the stairs and saw one of the kidnappers walking down the steps. Tony awoke and looked up. The man coming down the stairs was carrying two clean chamber pots. As he reached down to exchange them for the old ones, Tony said in Italian,

"I need a doctor. I'm not feeling well." The man stared at him.

"He's a heart patient and needs more medicine and a doctor," Francesca pleaded.

"Are you really sick?" The young man asked.

"Yes, I am. You don't want me to die while you're on duty, do you?"

The man thought a moment. "Okay, I'll see what I can do." He walked back upstairs and locked the door.

"Hang in there Tony, it's going to be all right." Francesca said as Tony looked at her. They held hands. Neither was sure it was true, but both wanted to pretend it would be.

Chapter 37

A STRAINED RELATIONSHIP

Alden Chandler walked into the conference room, and spotted Alex.

"You're no longer wanted here, Boyd!" his voice was loud enough for everyone to hear.

"That's right, Boyd, you're not part of my task force," Ambassador Van Camp added.

"Oh, shut up, and just listen," Alex said. Van Camp's body went rigid. Chandler began to protest:" You can't…" but stopped when Alex abruptly raised his hand.

"I have vital information about the Ambassador's health." Silence filled the room as Alex explained about Scarmatti needing Warfarin for his heart condition and the life-threatening effects of not taking it. He concluded with a solemn fact.

"We don't know if the Ambassador had any Warfarin with him when he was snatched, but even if he did, it should have run out by now. He's in real danger from this alone."

Turning to the police reps, Alex said, "I want the police and

Carabineiri to check every pharmacy in the five-province area for any new Warfarin prescriptions being filled. Maybe the Ambassador mentioned his condition to the kidnappers. If they want to keep him alive, they'll need to fill a prescription."

The *Polizia di Stato* and *Carabinieri* officers immediately reached for phones to call their headquarters and pass on the information. One officer placed a call directly to Colonel Adriani of the NOCS.

Joe Roberts, Alex's deputy, rose from his chair, walked over to Alex, and shook his hand with a firm grip.

"It's great to have you back from last night's raid, Alex. How are you feeling?"

"Couldn't be better, Joe. A little sore," he paused to rub his chest, "but I'm all right. Sorry I couldn't take you with me, but at least you're here to carry on."

Friends from DEA, CIA, and the Defense Attaché quickly joined Joe and Alex, praising his actions the night before. Rachel quickly strode to Alex from across the room, saying without hesitation, "Let's talk outside."

Once in the hallway, she cornered him, her face inches from his. He could feel her warm breath and smell her perfume.

"Were you ever going to tell me you got shot last night?" Her blazing green eyes focused directly into his eyes.

"Probably not, Rachel."

"I didn't think so."

"Who told you I was shot?"

"I heard it from the NOCS cop. He was describing how 'wonderful and amazing' you were last night."

"What did he say, exactly?"

"After hearing him tell Joe you were shot, I tuned it all out. So much for your bullshit about falling onto a fence." Her jaw was clenched tight.

"I didn't want to worry you."

"Goddamn it, Alex, I told you we were in this *together*. I thought we were a team. Now, I wonder if I can trust you." A pang of guilt gave him a gut punch.

"Of course, you can trust me. But is it wrong for me to want to shelter you from the ugly parts of life? Listen, Rachel, I love you deeply." He reached out to touch her arm, but she slapped his hand away.

"Really?" Her face was red, breathing was heavy, and her body was tense. She spun on her heels and stormed down the hall toward the Ladies Room leaving Alex standing alone in the hallway.

Thanks for asking how I'm feeling today, Honey Bunch.

* * *

Later that evening, Alex and Rachel both picked at a light evening meal in their apartment saying very little.

"Okay, Rachel, I'm sorry," Alex broke the silence. "I should have told you about being in the raid, but, honestly, when I came home, you were sleepy, and I really needed to rest."

"You could have told me first thing in the morning, even by phone. You know how I feel about this, dammit," her penetrating gaze bore into him.

"I do know. I just didn't want to upset you. It was intense. I felt really ragged when I got home. But it was a large team that attacked the farmhouse."

"Apparently not large enough, Alex. You were shot." She was right. Had the bullet hit his head instead of his body armor, he'd be dead now.

"Look, Rach, I promise to let you know in advance if I ever go on another raid." He wanted to touch her arm but remembered how she had slapped him away before. Now, covering her face with both hands, she leaned both elbows on the table. He waited silently, watching her; wondering what she was thinking. When she finally looked up, her eyes were moist.

"Okay, I guess you feel making these raids is part of your job. I'll have to live with that. But, Alex, don't you know you are a part of me? If I would ever lose you, I wouldn't be able to go on. Can't you understand that? Can't you be more... I don't know," she paused, "... less *dynamic?*"

"I don't want to lie to you," he responded. "But, when you're placed in that type of situation, hesitation gets you killed. Unfortunately, violence is a necessary part of my job. I can either initiate it, or let it be inflicted on me. We both know working in an American embassy today means accepting lots of risk. It's flat out dangerous in many places, even in Europe. Since Uncle Sam is never going to assign a battalion of Marines to every embassy, we have to aggressively do what we can with the limited resources we've been given. That means manpower. Sometimes, that means me."

Rachel reached across the table, placing her hand on his. He accepted it and held it tightly. She smiled.

"Gee, I never thought of you as a limited resource before, now that you mention it."

He squeezed her hand harder, acknowledging her little joke. But at least she was lightening up. He thought of the pen, then buried it deep in his mind.

One step at a time.

"Alex, I'm sorry for being so harsh. Let's change the subject. How do you think this will all turn out?"

"If the Scarmattis are released, or the Italians rescue them, then I'll have Tony's support for the security I provided. If they're killed by the kidnappers, then Chandler and the FBI will see that I'm buried." She knew Chandler had already requested Alex's recall to Washington.

246

"In any event, when this is over, I'll have to honestly reassess whether I want to stay in the State Department."

"I know you're disillusioned," Rachel said, "but please let the dust settle before making any decisions."

"Okay."

He noticed Rachel didn't offer to leave the State Department with him. Feeling momentarily alone, he wondered whether they had a future together after all.

Chapter 38

THE DOCTOR CHECKS IN

One of Doctor Gregorio Moretti's passions was simply getting out of Florence upon occasion. He relished any chance to drive into the countryside in his new Audi S-4 and try out its powerful engine. He loved this beautiful machine, a luxury afforded by his private medical practice.

Earlier that morning, he told his staff he'd gotten word an old friend was ill and had an obligation to check on him. By 9:00 a.m., he left the hospital, Ospedale di Santa Maria Nuova Florence, and headed south on the autostrada; his destination being the exit for Montepulciano, 115 kilometers away. But, at the interchange, he bypassed Montepulciano continuing in the direction of Pienza.

Since the main street in Pienza was for pedestrians only, Dr. Moretti skirted it and headed west along some winding country roads. A few kilometers further on was the villa belonging to Adrianna and Massimo Esposito. Adrianna had inherited the villa from her parents, who died ten years earlier. She and Massimo used it mostly on weekends since their main residence was in Sienna.

The Esposito family once owned considerable farmland, but Adrianna and Massimo, not being farmers, sold off most of it. They pocketed a pretty penny which allowed them to modernize the villa, put in a swimming pool, and expand the rear stone patio next to a vine-covered arbor. All this happened while they still held onto several acres of surrounding property for privacy, and a small vineyard.

Dr. Moretti now drove along a two-lane road surrounded by small vineyards, cultivated farmland, and gently rolling hills. Many lovely limestone and stucco houses with red tile roofs were widely separated along the way and varied from large villas down to small cottages. He downshifted on a turn as he approached Villa Esposito, knowing he was looking for the entrance to a long driveway. Finding it, he turned onto the gravel road. Moretti drove to the front of the two-story villa while listening to the crunch of pebbles under his tires, and parked.

The villa had six large, French windows across the front of a pale shrimp-colored stucco farmhouse. Low-level purple bougainvillea bushes, in full bloom, surrounded the main building setting a beautiful scene. For privacy, the family had planted cypress trees on either side of the long driveway with more trees approximately fifty meters from the building across the entire front of the property. Now well over a generation old, the cypress trees had grown quite high and full.

Cosimo di Luca greeted Dr. Moretti as he walked toward the front door. Friends since university days when both were radical leftists on campus, neither had changed their leftist leanings to this day.

"Gregorio, it's good to see you again. Thank you so much for coming on short notice."

"The pleasure is mine, Cosimo. So, you have a sick patient you want me to look at?"

"Yes, Gregorio. This may be the most important patient you will ever have."

"I think I already know who you must be talking about, and frankly, I'm worried about what you've gotten into this time. You are the one who grabbed the American Ambassador, aren't you Cosimo?"

"Yes, I am."

Moretti had correctly surmised this was the case since he occasionally helped Cosimo in minor ways with his extremist activities. He knew Cosimo was a big man in the New Red Brigade. He just didn't know that Cosimo was now its leader.

"We've been friends a long time, Cosimo, so I can say this. I only hope you've thought this through; otherwise we will all be in jeopardy."

"We'll be fine, Gregorio," he said while reassuringly putting his hand on the doctor's shoulder. Moretti stared at him for a moment, trying to see what was in his eyes.

"Okay, lead me to the patient."

Dr. Moretti followed Cosimo di Luca inside the villa belonging to the Espositos, feeling pleased he could use his medical knowledge to help an old comrade.

"First, we must put on these masks," di Luca informed him, handing one to Moretti.

"Really, how can I examine a man if I am burdened by wearing a face mask?"

"You must. It is to protect your identity. I must also warn you of a bad odor. It is difficult to keep things clean in these situations."

"I understand," Moretti said as he grudgingly put on the mask.

They walked down a few wooden steps into the basement where another kidnapper was present, sitting in a chair to the side. The odor assaulted his nostrils as Moretti saw Ambassador Scarmatti, and his wife, lying on separate mattresses in a corner of the filthy room. Each had one wrist handcuffed to a metal pole. They looked terrible.

"This is a medical doctor," di Luca said to the Scarmattis. Moretti knelt next to Anthony Scarmatti and addressed him in English.

"What is wrong with you?"

"I have some weakness in my left arm. Also, last night I tried to pick up a piece of toilet paper and it kept slipping through my fingers. I could not feel or grasp it. Yesterday and earlier today, my vision was graying out, but that seems to have cleared up. I also think I'm having heart palpitations."

"When did this start?" Dr. Moretti asked as he put a stethoscope on Scarmatti's chest to listen.

"Two days ago, I think, at least the weakness in my arm; the rest of the symptoms have occurred since then. I have an artificial aortic heart valve, Doctor."

"Do you take a blood thinner medicine, such as Warfarin?" Moretti asked.

"I do."

Taking his blood pressure, Moretti made no comment, but simply put the stethoscope on Scarmatti's carotid artery. Then, shaking his head slightly, stood up, turned, and motioned to DiLuca.

"Let's talk upstairs." Di Luca motioned to Renzo, the other kidnapper, to follow them.

"I believe he has had a transient ischemic attack, a ministroke," Moretti said when they reached the kitchen. "His symptoms are consistent with this. Some know it as a TIA. I could be certain after blood tests and some scans, but I know those are not possible in his case. Did he have medication on him?"

Di Luca extended his hand and the other kidnapper gave him two medicine containers. One was empty; the other had three pills in it. Moretti examined both bottles. The Ambassador's name was on one along with the name of the medication: "Warfarin 2 mg tablets. Take three tablets once daily."

"I presume the Ambassador had this empty one on him when he was captured. I see it is from a pharmacy in Rome."

"Yes," di Luca replied. "He told us he must take the pills every day. He had intended to stop at his pharmacy on the way back from Orvieto for a refill. When we grabbed him, the bottle did contain a few pills, but he finished them off on the first two days."

"'This other one from a Bologna pharmacy, how did you come by this bottle?" Moretti asked.

"I was sent to get it for him when the Ambassador's medication ran out," young Renzo replied. "I was only able to get a week's supply." Looking at the quantity prescribed, Moretti did the math in his head.

"Then the second bottle should be empty by now. Why are there still pills left? How many have you been giving him?"

"We weren't sure when we could get more, so we gave him only one pill a day," Renzo said.

"One tablet is only two milligrams; he needs six milligrams a day; that's three pills," Moretti complained harshly. Di Luca looked worried; Renzo apologized.

"Here is the situation: The Ambassador needs an immediate increase in Warfarin, or he could have a massive stroke or heart attack at any time. Without the proper dose, his blood will thicken soon and can easily clot in his artificial valve. Then, it will not function properly, and the consequences will be devastating."

Knowing there was no way to test Scarmatti's PT/INR blood level, Moretti took a medical pad from his bag and wrote a prescription for one month's supply of Warfarin 6 mg daily. He knew using a lab to check the blood level now would risk exposure to law enforcement authorities and take time they didn't have.

"Give him the three remaining pills now, and get this filled immediately," Dr. Moretti told Renzo. Moretti handed him the prescription paper. "After that, give him three pills every day without fail, or you may have a dead man on your hands." Renzo nodded. Moretti reached into his bag again and took out a bottle of aspirin with a 325mg strength.

"After you give him the last three pills now, give him two aspirin in the morning and two more at night if the other medicine hasn't arrived yet. That's all, no more. By then, we must have the prescription filled. His blood must be thinned, and this will help. There is a pharmacy in Montepulciano which will have the Warfarin, although there is a smaller pharmacy in Pienza that may also have it. You should check in Pienza first since it's closer. This is very important. He needs this medication immediately."

"Yes, Doctor," Renzo said. After taking the remaining three Warfarin pills from the bottle to the Ambassador in the basement, he left the villa to check the first pharmacy. Di Luca asked Moretti to join him in the living room.

"Tell me truthfully: Will he be okay?" di Luca asked.

"It's hard to tell. If you can get enough Warfarin in him quickly, then he should survive. I want to emphasize, Cozimo, this is a very grave situation."

Di Luca wondered whether it was time to negotiate secretly with the Foreign Ministry, as they had offered. A dead Ambassador was of no value to him. Before Dr. Moretti left, he put his mask back on and returned to the basement, again, to speak to Scarmatti.

"Mr. Ambassador, I fear you may have suffered a ministoke."

"No!" Francesca involuntarily cried out, covering her mouth.

"Your symptoms were caused by a Transient Ischemic Attack. You may have heard of it called a TIA, or small stroke. It refers to a loss of blood flow in an area of your brain, or perhaps elsewhere that did not cause tissue to die. But I fear that, in this case, your valve may be sticking a little and preventing strong blood flow. This is not good. However, I have sent for a full supply of Warfarin for you. You have just taken the last three pills and will be given aspirin in the morning until your medicine gets here. Then take your normal six milligrams thereafter."

"Thank you, Doctor."

"Has this ever happened to you before?"

"No, never."

"You took the last of the Warfarin just before I came down, yes?"

"I did."

"Good. Now, I will examine Mrs. Scarmatti," Doctor Moretti said.

Francesca Scarmatti appeared to be in good health despite desperately needing a bath. Her blood pressure was a little high, but that could be expected since she was a victim being held against her will. Also, she had just heard the news he had given to her husband. Finishing, he bid them rest and left for Florence.

I honestly think Cosimo may have waited too long to call me about the Ambassador's condition, he thought as he drove back to the hospital.

Chapter 39

CONFRONTATION

Alex lay in bed waiting for his alarm to go off. He hadn't slept well and knew Rachel had tossed and turned all night. He tried massaging his shoulders and neck to relieve the stress, but it didn't help. This kidnapping situation was beginning to have a negative impact on their relationship. The luminous dial of his watch showed another thirty minutes before his alarm would go off.

Maybe I can reset the mood.

"Rachel," he whispered, sliding closer and touching a firm breast.

"Huh, what..." she moaned, half asleep. Alex brushed aside her wavy brown hair, kissing the side of her neck. The lingering fragrance of her perfume mixed with night cream was usually a pleasant odor for him, one that signaled time for night games.

"Not now..." she mumbled, clearly not awake yet.

"Yes, now."

She gently pushed his hand away and reached over to grab her alarm clock.

"I might as well get up," she said, now more awake. "It's almost time anyway; I have the mornings press reports to look at." Pulling the sheets back, she slid her long, shapely legs to the side of the bed until her feet touched the floor. Then slowly stretched her arms upward before looking over at Alex.

"I guess neither of us slept much last night."

"You can say that again."

He reached over and touched her back, still hoping for something more. Rachel didn't acknowledge his soft caress but simply got up and walked into the bathroom. Alex lay back in bed, frustrated. While he lay there, her cell phone rang. The display indicated a State Department number from Washington. Jesus, it was midnight in Washington, so he thought it must be important.

"Hello, Alex Boyd speaking; Rachel Smith's number."

"Oh," there was a slight pause. "Hello, I'm with the European Bureau's press office," a female voice said. "Is Rachel there?"

"Yes, hold on a minute."

Alex smiled. He figured at least the no name woman from Washington might think he had wild sex last night with Rachel. Walking to the bathroom, he handed her the phone, then returned to bed.

He overheard conversation from the bathroom about the Diplomatic Security Rewards for Justice Program. When she walked back into the bedroom, she went to Alex's chest of drawers, looking for pen and paper. Alex's eyes opened wide as she picked up his fountain pen, unscrewed the top and tried to write with it on a pad they kept there. Sure enough, the pen failed. Rachel found another pen, took some notes, then hung up. He waited apprehensively for her reaction. She unscrewed the fountain pen, noted the full ink cartridge, and screwed it back together again.

"Alex, why doesn't your pen work?"

"It got damaged in the raid. I had to stab a guy with it to make him talk."

"Oh, you're such a bullshit artist, Alex. Why do you tell me such unbelievable stories?"

"Okay, it fell out of my pocket. The nib must need replacement."

"Now, *that* I believe." Rachel walked over to the bed, bent over, and kissed him on the cheek.

"What was the call about?"

"Washington's approved the million-dollar reward for information leading to the arrest of the Scarmattis kidnappers. They're sending us a telegram with verbiage to use with the Italian media."

Now, Alex's cell phone rang; he picked it up, and heard the exact same story from the DS Command center. Rachel showered, and dressed quickly; he took his time.

"I'm going to take our car and grab some coffee at the office. You don't mind, do you, Alex?"

"Nope. I'll take the bus later."

They embraced, and she kissed him briefly on the mouth.

* * *

Rachel barely had time to review the overnight news from the States, and only glanced at the Italian press before the DCM wanted to see her in his office. When she arrived, Mark Terranova and John Reynolds, the FBI duo, were also there.

"Rachel, I assume you saw the Department's suggested press release on the Rewards for Justice Program regarding the Ambassador?" the DCM asked.

"Yes. One million dollars for information leading to the arrest of the kidnappers."

"Good. I've put the State Department's suggested language into this memo," he said, handing it to Rachel. "You can give this to the media."

Instinctively, her antennae were up. *Why is he doing my job for me,* she wondered. *And why is the FBI already waiting in his office when I arrived?* She examined Chandler's memo carefully.

"Did Washington approve this modification?"

"What do you mean?" Chandler asked.

Jesus, she thought, *did he think I wouldn't notice?*

"You've left out the part about contacting the RSO. Washington's language always says persons with information should contact either the RSO or the FBI. Your language only mentions contacting the FBI."

"I thought it would be more appropriate considering the heavy FBI presence here now."

"Alden, Washington's language is based upon the law, as written by Congress. It's the same language that's used worldwide every time the Rewards for Justice Program is activated. I strongly recommend you get Washington's approval if you want to change it. Naturally, the Bureau of Diplomatic Security will have to clear off on this, which I doubt they'll agree to do."

Rachel understood what was going on and it pissed her off that the DCM was so blatantly disregarding the State Department's own interests to further the ambitions of the FBI. The State Department liked to think of itself as the US Government leader in the foreign policy arena, as it had been since the country's founding. *Like Alex always says, State has voluntarily given up so much ground to other agencies over the past two decades that its leadership role is now in question. Just a few lines like this in a press release, failing to mention contacting the RSO, might not seem earth-shaking, but will continue to erode State's authority. If allowed to continue, it will mean the State Department's retreat from its responsibilities. The way this is written makes State beholding to the discretion of the FBI to share information,* she thought before saying anything.

Standing rigidly in front of Chandler to her full height in heels of six-foot one-inch tall, she stared down at him, waiting for him to reply. Chandler looked over at Reynolds, who glared at Rachel. Finally, Reynolds gave a nod to Chandler.

"All right Rachel, we'll use the original language. But I'm instructing Charlotte to tell the telephone operators, if anyone calls in with information, the call is to be routed to the FBI."

"Understood, Alden. Is that all?"

"Yes."

"I'll contact the media within the hour about the Reward offer." She left the office fuming and headed straight for Alex's office. She found him sitting at his desk with a morning cup of coffee.

"Got a minute?" Then, without waiting for a reply, she immediately began describing her contentious meeting with the DCM and FBI. Alex realized this was clearly a different Rachel from last night and early this morning.

She is really livid about this, he thought.

"I am really livid with Chandler," she echoed his thoughts. Sophisticated when she wanted to be, now she was using her best locker room language to tear apart the DCM. She wasn't so kind to the FBI either. Having been a competitive jock at UCLA, she knew all the right words. Alex smiled, finding it amusing.

Given the right situation, women can be as vulgar as men.

"Oh, do I amuse you Alex?" she asked, noting his smile.

"Relax, Rachel. Calm down. I love you for all your support. I really do. You did the right thing standing up to Chandler. I'm grateful, and the State Department should thank their lucky stars you're on top of this, even if our own esteemed DCM, 'His Highness, The Royal Prick,' doesn't want to hear it. Maybe I'll have a quiet conversation with the supervisor of the telephone operators about where the calls should be routed. On the other hand, ninety percent of calls in response to reward offers are traditionally bullshit."

"Really?"

"Yeah, they are. Every call has to be checked out, but usually it's only a caller who wants a quick payout. So, they make up bogus information. It happens all the time. Mind you, DS has had great successes from the Rewards for Justice Program. But for every success, we've had many, many false leads. Thanks for defending my interests, but right now, I believe working with the Italian cops is our best bet. Letting the FBI handle those calls actually saves me time."

"Okay, Alex, I feel a little better. But it's the principle of Chandler not even defending State's interest that pisses me off. He's such a dickhead."

"I know, Rachel. Chandler is behaving like a typical old-line Foreign Service officer."

"I know, you're right."

* * *

She returned to her office and Alex decided to clean his SIG Sauer 9mm pistol since he'd dragged it through the mud at the farmhouse. Afterward, he handled a few paperwork tasks and was about to take an early lunch when the Italian police called.

"Hello, Mr. Boyd, this is Major Carlo Vicencia, I am the Chief Investigating Officer for the *Polizia di Stato* on the Ambassador's kidnapping case. That means, among other things, I am coordinating our evidence and working with the prosecutor should the case come to trial."

"I'm glad to talk to you Major. How can I help?"

"General Ghiberti has asked me to invite you to lunch today at police headquarters so we can discuss progress so far."

"What time should I come?"

"If you can come now, we can discuss the information, then eat afterwards."

"Excellent Major, I'll be there in fifteen minutes."

Vicencia gave Alex his phone number to call when he arrived, saying he would pick him up by the reception desk at police headquarters. But Vicencia was already waiting when Alex arrived. They proceeded directly to the investigating offices. It was a very large room containing metal desks with computers separated by four-foot high cubicle dividers. About twenty men and women occupied the cubicles, some in police uniform, some in plainclothes. At the end of the room were several large white boards for hanging photos, papers, and writing notes.

He saw Ambassador and Mrs. Scarmatti's photos positioned at the top of the center board, with a dotted line running to Orvieto, no doubt because of the ceramic store receipt Alex found at the farmhouse. Another solid line went to the farmhouse outside of Bologna. The names of the known kidnappers, dead or alive, were written next to it. Another section of a white board dealt with the dark blue Lancia and a third section listed information about pharmacies. There was more data, but Major Vicencia interrupted Alex's perusal of the boards.

"As you can see, Mr. Boyd, we have organized our investigation according to leads and evidence so far collected."

"Major, this is indeed impressive."

"Here is what we know so far: First: two new Warfarin prescriptions have recently been filled outside of Bologna in the last few days. We have put two people under surveillance who have turned in those prescriptions. They may be linked to the case or may prove not to be involved in the kidnapping at all. Information about any new prescriptions could come into this office during the day.

"Secondly: Regarding the dark blue Lancia, we have already eliminated twenty of forty-two owners from our inquiries; they have no known left wing ties and we believe they are ordinary citizens. Our inquiries are still continuing."

They spoke for another ten minutes as Major Vicencia answered Alex's questions until an aide stuck his head in the door and announced:

"General Ghiberti is waiting for you both in his office for a light lunch. He asks that you join him now."

Alex was ready for lunch.

Chapter 40

TRACKING A LEAD

Shortly after lunch, Alex checked in with Carter Ambrose, CIA Station Chief, to ask about possible leads he might have received from his Italian counterparts.

"Nothing of use so far, Alex."

"You haven't been targeting the New Red Brigade?"

"No, however, on the good news side, the Italian service is helping cops reinterview New Red Brigade members in prison. I figure at least one of them must have information. I'll let you know if anything develops. As you might expect, Langley's putting a lot of pressure on us to find the Ambassador.

"By the way, the rest of the Embassy Country Team thinks the DCM was wrong to exclude you from the task force. Hell, your police contacts are the only ones who've done anything so far. Not to mention you going on that raid... pretty gutsy."

"Thanks, I appreciate that Carter. You know Chandler's trying to send me home?"

"He's made that abundantly clear. Try not to think about it."

"Easier said than done."

Carter paused for a long moment. "Harold Jordan told me you were responsible for getting intelligence from the kidnappers at the farmhouse after you stabbed one SOB in the leg with your pen."

"That's true."

"Not to worry, Alex. Officially, Harold will say he never saw it happen."

"That's a relief."

"Okay, I was just wondering. By the way, if things don't work out for you at State after this is over, give me a call. Anyone who can do what you did, and keep focused on what's important, is certainly of interest to the CIA.

Alex nodded and they shook hands.

* * *

By mid-afternoon, the officer from the *Polizia di Stato* assigned to the Embassy task force came to Alex's office.

"Major Vicencia would like to talk with you, *Senore* Boyd." He spoke into his secure cell phone, then handed it to Alex.

"Hello, Major Vicencia?"

"Yes, Mr. Boyd, we have just received information that a pharmacy south of Bologna partially filled a new Warfarin request shortly after the Ambassador went missing. It is suspicious because the man wanting the Warfarin did not have a prescription. At first the pharmacist wouldn't do it, especially after the man offered a bribe in lieu of a proper prescription. But then, the pharmacist said the man pleaded his case, said it was urgent, that his friend was sick, and his normal doctor was on holiday. So, the pharmacist reluctantly agreed to fill a one-week supply."

"Major, you said this was about a week ago?"

"Yes, approximately, Mr. Boyd."

"Please, call me Alex. Why is he telling the police about this now?"

"Because now we are contacting every pharmacy which has recently filled prescriptions for Warfarin."

"Did he give you a description of the man?"

"Better than that, Alex. He has a CCTV camera in the pharmacy which he says clearly shows the man. The local police now have the tape and a copy is being sent here to Rome. It should be here early this evening. I will let you know when we receive it."

"I can't thank you enough for letting me know, Major Vicencia. May I call you Carlo?"

Major Vicencia was surprised and impressed that Alex remembered his first name.

"Of course, Alex. I would be pleased."

"I assume this information is being passed on to the task force in the Embassy. Am I right?" Alex asked.

"Yes, we have already done so. I wanted to ensure you received this directly. Naturally, we are aware of your internal problems within the task force."

"As I said, Carlo, thank you. Assuming you receive the video tape by tonight, may I come to your office in the morning to see it?"

"I look forward to it, Alex. Tomorrow then."

At nine the next morning, Alex called Major Vicencia and confirmed the police had the CCTV tape. He took a taxi and was escorted up to the same large room as yesterday. The Major took Alex to a TV monitor where they played the video from the pharmacy south of Bologna.

The man was clearly visible, around twenty-five years old, entering the pharmacy and approaching the counter. Alex took note of physical characteristics. Without sound, they watched both the man and pharmacist speaking, cordially at first, then apparently in a heated discussion. The young man reached into his pocket and took out money which was rejected by the pharmacist. More argument followed, then the pharmacist left the counter while the man waited. He returned and an obvious exchange took place, money passed to the pharmacist for a medicine bottle, a receipt was given to the man. A final exchange of heated words ensued before the man left the store.

"You just saw the transaction which I described to you yesterday," Major Vicencia said.

"Carlo, why didn't the pharmacist just tell the man to bring his friend to a hospital if he was sick?"

"I don't know. Maybe the police in Bologna didn't think to ask."

"I saw on the video the man paid cash, so there's no credit card record. I didn't see him sign anything." It was a question more than a statement.

"You're right, Alex. He should have signed the prescription book, even though he didn't have a prescription. The pharmacist forgot to ask him. These things happen. But, in truth, it probably doesn't matter because he would use a false name if he's connected to the kidnapping."

Alex acknowledged Vicencia's point.

"Last night we sent a photo of the man in the video to all police stations in central Italy to show to pharmacies this morning. It's too early to get results, but maybe as the day goes on, we will hear something back."

"Carlo, everyone at the Embassy is grateful for your efforts. Indeed, for all efforts of the Italian Police. I'm curious, about one thing, though: has anyone from our task force called to say they will be visiting this morning to hear what you've just told me?"

A faint smile played on Carlo's lips.

"No, Alex. Our man in the task force has briefed them and given them a copy of the tape; and, of course, the FBI is working closely with the *Carabinieri*, who we have briefed as well. But, no one has asked to visit us specifically."

Alex didn't say anything further. He knew Mark Terranova, the FBI Legal Attache, had excellent relations with General Ghiberti and could access the same people as he could, therefore, he assumed Reynolds and Van Camp decided to put the kibosh on working more closely with the cops, as opposed to working with the Carabinieri. It all seemed very shortsighted.

"Alex, you are most welcome to stay with us to await results from the pharmacy checks. If you will stay, let's first get some cappuccino down the street. The coffee in the headquarters canteen stinks. It is as bad as American coffee. I hope you are not offended."

After a second cappuccino, they walked back to the imposing grey-colored stone *Questura*. Major Vicencia's pager buzzed just as they were entering the lobby.

"New information has just come in," he said to Alex. A minute later they were back in the open-plan office, standing next to one of the large whiteboards, listening to a briefing by an extremely attractive, mid-thirties, blond-haired woman. She wore a well-cut, figure-hugging, dress and held a clipboard.

"Major," she said in Italian, "we've just received a report of a sighting last night in Pienza of the same man who bought the Warfarin in Bologna a week ago. He entered Farmacia Pienza, but they had no Warfarin in stock, so he left. The pharmacist identified him from our photo just distributed. He also said the man did not ask if any other pharmacies might have it."

"Thank you, Gina," Major Vicencia said.

She smiled at Alex, her big brown eyes drawing him in. He smiled back, always able to admire a shapely figure, especially as she walked away. Then, a thought hit him.

"Gina, do you know if the man in Pienza had a prescription?"

"So sorry, we didn't ask. But I'll do it now." Within a few minutes she was back.

"I talked with the pharmacist directly who said the man was holding a script, but he didn't actually see what was written on it. The young man asked for Warfarin first and the pharmacist simply told him they didn't have any in stock."

"Thank you, Gina. That was very helpful," Alex said.

Walking to her cubicle, her hips gently swayed with a sensual motion. With some difficulty, Alex refocused his attention on the major.

"Captain Santino," Vicencia called out, a man in uniform quickly approached him.

"Yes, sir."

"I want you to transfer half the search units from the Lazio and Marche areas and concentrate them in a radius of twenty kilometers around Pienza to make inquiries at pharmacies there. I want this done immediately."

"Yes, Major."

"Alex, I believe it is safe to say if the same man is looking for Warfarin again, this time two hundred kilometers from Bologna, then it's likely the Ambassador may be in the Pienza area. We may be getting closer."

Chapter 41

AN UNEXPECTED VISIT

A feeling of guilt hit Alex. He couldn't focus on trivial stuff nor do routine office work, while Tony and Francesca were being held. The down time waiting for things to happen was maddening.

He decided to call a full staff meeting to give everyone the latest information on the kidnapping, including Mike James and the other DS Special Agent, part of the task force from Washington.

"Alex, I have a question that occurred to me this morning," Sam Carson said as the meeting was beginning. "Remember our video which showed Chandler and Charlotte Eaton each driving into the Ambassador's parking lot the morning of the kidnapping?"

"Yeah, Sam, what are you thinking?"

"Why did Charlotte use a motor pool car when she has her own personal vehicle?" Her question was incredibly insightful. "I started wondering if maybe she was delivering the car to the Ambassador." Sam stated. Now, everyone began to murmur around the table.

"Sam, that's it! I couldn't put my finger on something all week. Why, would she have used an official car on a weekend, just to see the Ambassador? Maybe she had other business errands to run afterward, but it was a Sunday. We need to find out."

The secure phone rang and Nancy picked it up. After a few words, her expression took on a worried look.

"Alex, its Jim Riley calling you from his home."

Alex looked at his watch. *Geez, it's five in the morning in Washington. This can't be good if the Director of Diplomatic Security is calling this early.*

"Hey, Jim…What's up?"

"Alex, I wanted to tell you personally, before you got the official telegram: Chandler has continued agitating the European Bureau about removing you from post. Ambassador Van Camp has also weighed in with the Secretary, and not in your favor. I've stood my ground, but last night the Secretary of State personally asked me and Archibald Watson, the European Bureau's Assistant Secretary to fly out to Rome and evaluate your situation. We're leaving tonight and will arrive tomorrow morning at 6:00 a.m."

Alex's eyebrows rose as he took a deep breath, slowly blowing out air. He saw everyone in the room looking at him, trying to judge what was happening. His mind spun.

I'm not surprised by Chandler's actions. Nevertheless, when your boss in Washington tells you the Secretary of State has become personally involved in your future, it's stunning.

"Okay, Jim. It goes without saying I appreciate all your efforts to contain this attack on me. What can we do for you at this end?"

"Everything we need will be in the telegram. We'll meet with several Country Team members, the task force leaders, and of course, with DCM Chandler."

"Will I be able to sit in on these meetings to defend myself?"

"You know how it works, Alex. Some meetings, yes, you will. Others, no you won't."

"I understand. Should I pick you up at the airport?"

"No, but only because Watson will be with me. I want to see you privately in your office before I do anything else. We'll come directly in from the airport."

"All right, Jim. It'll be good to see you again despite these unfortunate circumstances."

"Agreed. Tomorrow then, Alex." They hung up.

Alex explained the full conversation to his staff. Everyone volunteered talking to Riley in his support. He was touched by their loyalty but could only thank them and say they'd have to see how it played out.

"Okay, everyone, back to business. Sam, your insight into Charlotte using the motor pool car is brilliant. I want you and Joe to talk to the motor pool supervisor. Find out anything you can about the car, including whether all other motor pool cars were accounted for that day. Then we'll decide how to question Charlotte. Right now, I've got to think about Riley's visit."

The meeting broke up and Alex tried figuring his best strategy. But first, he called Rachel to give her the bad news about his situation reaching the Secretary of State. When he mentioned Riley and Watson's visit, they agreed, it wasn't good. An hour later, Sam and Joe returned to report a black Ford Mondeo was, indeed, missing from the motor pool. They gave the license plate number to Alex.

"No one even signed it out!" Joe exclaimed. "It's incredible!"

"When did they notice it missing?"

"They didn't, until we showed up," Sam answered, "They claimed they were looking for it, but I don't buy it."

"This is bad," Alex said. "I've never heard of an Embassy motor pool not keeping track of its vehicles. Cairo or Islamabad have dozens of cars in their fleet. This post isn't even that big. What shoddy management. Unbelievable."

"Not trying to excuse them, but you should know this particular car is informally set aside for use by the Management section," Joe continued, "You know, for runs to the airport, inspecting Embassy housing, or calling on vendors to the Embassy. I think they thought someone in Management just failed to return it or left it parked at their residence."

"That could explain why they didn't miss it, Joe, but it's too loose a management practice. I suppose nobody wanted to ask their American boss what happened to the car, especially if it's been a regular practice. They probably thought it was just another perk of the job."

"This is Italy," Sam said.

"So, the question is… does our vehicle gate camera for the Embassy parking lot have an archive going back far enough to that Sunday when the Ambassador was kidnapped?"

"You're wondering whether Charlotte returned the car after her visit to the Ambassador?" Joe asked. Alex nodded.

"The problem is… first, we don't have a video image of the license plate on the car leaving the residence, we're assuming it's the car set aside for Management. Secondly, all the motor pool cars are black Ford Mondeos, except for a few vans and the limos used by the Ambassador and DCM."

Alex exhaled and clasped his hands behind his head. "Incredible."

"Do you want me to interview Charlotte?" Joe asked.

"Yeah, I do. But first ask her why she took the car in the first place on that Sunday before asking if she knows it's missing from the motor pool. Give her the plate number and ask if it's the one she drove to the Ambassador's residence. Watch her reactions. Sam, go with Joe to be a witness."

"I assume you don't want me to read her Miranda rights, just yet," Joe said.

"Correct, Joe. Let's hear what she has to say, then we'll review it together. In any event, if she lies to you, then she's lying to a federal agent about a criminal investigation, and that's a felony. After talking with her, ask the American in General Services if he knows anything about this, although I'd be very surprised if he did." Alex paused. "On second thought, ask Charlotte to call him up to her office, and ask him about the missing car in front of you. It'll be interesting to see how she handles it."

* * *

Joe and Sam returned from interviewing Charlotte Eaton not long after lunchtime.

"I'm all ears.," Alex said.

"Charlotte admitted she used a Ford from the motor pool to drive to the Ambassador's residence to deliver some papers," Joe said, "but couldn't recall the license plate number. She told us she didn't know where the logbook was kept, and because it was a Sunday, no one was in the motor pool office, so she just took the keys and didn't sign out the car."

"That still doesn't answer why she didn't use her own car," Alex said.

"According to Charlotte, the reason she was even using a motor pool car," Sam stated, "was because later that day she expected to go to the airport to speak with Italian Customs officials about why Embassy shipments from the States were taking too long to get cleared."

"Really? She wants to speak to Italian government officials on a Sunday about a routine matter?" Alex said, "Sure, that makes sense."

"Yeah, Alex, we didn't believe her either," Sam said.

"How about later that day or at night? Did our cameras capture her returning the car to the motor pool?"

"We thought about that," Sam replied. "Before coming back here, we looked at the video again from the Embassy compound's back gate, but unfortunately, the resolution wasn't good enough to identity her or the license plate. She claimed to know nothing about the missing car; said she was shocked it hadn't been reported as missing earlier. But we watched her reaction and her surprise just didn't ring true. It reminded me of the line in the movie *Casablanca* when Captain Renault claims he's 'shocked' to find gambling in Rick's Café, just as a waiter hands him a pile of money from his winnings."

Alex smiled. "So, what happened when she talked with the American General Services Officer in front of you?"

"She called him up to her office," Joe replied, "and with a straight face, asked if he'd heard about the missing car. He said 'no'. But my guess is that he routinely lets his Italian employees run the show and probably doesn't know what's going on. So, we didn't get much from him."

Alex took a deep breath and blew it out, crossing his arms across his chest.

"Okay, guys. Write up your notes and hold onto them until we have something more to go on. Thanks for everything you did; it was helpful. For the record: I think Charlotte is lying."

Chapter 42

MYSTERIES REVEALED

Later that afternoon, Gina from Major Vicencia's staff called Alex with a message that the Major had new information on the kidnapping. Then, invited him to their office. She was circumspect about the nature of the information because they were speaking over an open line.

"Gina, I'm delighted to come to your office," he spoke in Italian. "Also, I never thanked you properly for immediately following up on my request."

"Ah, you remember me, then?"

Alex smiled to himself, recalling her big eyes, beautiful face, and terrific figure. "Of course, I remember you, Gina, you were extremely helpful. Please tell the Major I'll be there in fifteen minutes."

Anticipating a greeting from the vibrant Gina, he was more than a little disappointed to be met by an overweight, extremely hairy, and somewhat smelly male sergeant with a two-day-old stubble.

He must be saving money to have his uniform cleaned and pressed for a special occasion, Alex thought. *Today, isn't that day.* He followed the sergeant upstairs, eyes avoiding the back view.

"Alex, welcome to our headquarters again! Thank you for coming," Major Vicencia said warmly as they shook hands. "We have significant developments in the case."

Alex noticed Gina walking toward them. He knew she would smell better than the guy who escorted him upstairs, and without any stubble. They shook hands, her fingers lingering a tad longer than needed.

"Let's go to the white board on the right," she said confidently. They all walked across the room.

"Alex, I will ask Gina to present our information because she is the officer who has been working with the police in the Pienza area," Major Vicencia explained.

"We have two significant breaks in the case," she began. "First, the man who originally filled the one-week Warfarin prescription in Bologna, tried to get more in Pienza, but was not successful, then brought a prescription to a pharmacy in Montepulciano at midday today. Montepulciano is located not far from Pienza, therefore, we are still dealing with the same area. The pharmacy filled the prescription, and later recognized the man from our photos and called the police. We now have the prescription which gave us the name and address of the doctor who wrote it. He is Doctor Gregorio Moretti, who practices in Florence. It's worth noting Florence is halfway between Bologna and Pienza."

"Is he known to the police?" Alex asked.

"When he was young," Gina continued, "he was involved in many left wing protests and some minor acts of vandalism. Now, in his mid-thirties, and according to our information, he still supports left wing causes, but does so lawfully. He has a good reputation as a doctor."

"I assume you are watching Doctor Moretti."

"Of course. We have teams running twenty-hour surveillance on him. We may, however, pick him up for questioning. I emphasize this is merely one possibility."

Alex grimaced at the thought and was uncomfortable with the latter approach, but knew he had to handle this matter delicately.

"That certainly is one option, in fact, an option that can be exercised at any time. Why not just continue to surveil him? If he's supporting the kidnappers, perhaps he'll lead you to the Ambassador's location. Also, if he were picked up for questioning, and is involved, then the New Red Brigade would know you're on to them. They would simply move the Ambassador again." Major Vicencia and Gina looked at each other, making a few quiet comments that Alex had trouble hearing.

"We agree that your approach is the best one for now," Vincencia said. "As you suggest, we'll continue to watch Doctor Moretti until he makes his next move."

"Will you give the Embassy Task Force this information?"

"No," Major Vicencia stated flatly.

"I see." Alex said. "You realize that puts me in a difficult position."

"We realize that, Alex," Vicencia replied. "But, to be honest, the FBI has already demonstrated a proclivity for rushing in before they think. They will want to be part of our surveillance team, an absurdity since none of them except Mark Terranova speaks Italian or even looks Italian. No, it is best if we deal with this skillfully, and let the Embassy Task Force know about it later."

Alex weighed this situation carefully. It was obvious the Italians felt the FBI couldn't be trusted. Well, he didn't trust them either, so screw them.

"Okay, what you've just told me will go no further unless you say I can share it at the Embassy. What about the Italian intelligence services? Do they have this information?"

Gina answered this time. "Yes, they do. If you want to know if they will share it with Carter Ambrose, they will."

Alex chuckled. So much for Carter being the top American spy in Italy. It seemed everybody knew Carter, more importantly, liked working with him.

"Our second break in the case," Gina continued, "is that we believe that we have found the owner of the late-model, dark-blue Lancia seen leaving the farmhouse near Bologna just before the raid. We presume the Scarmattis were in the trunk. You may recall we never had the license plate number. The owner's name is Massimo Esposito. He lives in Sienna, not far from Pienza and Florence. He is a businessman now, but in the past he, too, was associated with extreme left wing causes; very extreme causes. We are finding out more about him now. He is also under twenty-four surveillance, but it is too soon to know anything more."

"That's it, Alex. Now you know what we know," Major Vicencia said. "General Ghiberti and Deputy Interior Minister Ferrara say we can trust you with this information." Vicencia looked at him directly. "Is that true?"

"You can, Carlo. You have my word. It'll be our 'American Omerta,'" referring to the Mafia's code of silence. "Please thank General Ghiberti and Deputy Minister Ferrara for me."

"May I ask you a personal question, Alex?" Carlo said.

"Sure."

"How exactly does the Deputy Minister of the Interior know you?"

"Oh, I helped him out during a bank transaction."

Major Vicencia shook his head, not understanding. "It must have been a very valuable transaction."

"You might say it changed his life," Alex replied. "But you'll have to ask him, if you want to learn more. I want to thank you for sharing this info with me."

Vicencia nodded, and asked Gina to escort him out.

On the way down the stairs to the lobby, Alex said, "Gina, since you've been wearing civilian clothes, I don't know if you're a police officer, or a civilian employee." Gina smiled, and gave him her business card.

"I am a Captain with the *Polizia di Stato,* Criminal Intelligence Division. My full name is Gina Bianchi."

"Well, I'm pleased to know you, Captain Gina Bianchi," he said as they shook hands.

"And I am pleased to know you also." She was smiling as if she had a secret.

He looked into her brown eyes a few seconds.

"I detect there's something else you want to say to me, or am I wrong?"

"Only that I hope you and your tall girlfriend enjoy living in Rome," she said in perfect English. "She is quite beautiful." Alex was stunned. Not only did Gina know about Rachel, but her perfect English was totally without accent.

"Incredible, Gina. You knew from the start that Rachel and I are together."

"Of course. I'm in police intelligence, aren't I? I find out what I want to find out."

"Have you also been talking to police on the task force?"

"Maybe yes, maybe no."

"Goodbye, Gina," he said taking her hand. He brought it to his lips, gently kissing the back of her hand gallantly. She laughed; he smiled, then walked toward the exit.

"Alex," she called out. He stopped as she walked a little closer so no one could hear.

"Thank you for saving the Deputy Minister's life at the bank." She smiled again and walked away.

He stood in the lobby watching her walk up the staircase, and chuckled. He just realized what an extremely capable, smart, and very intriguing policewoman Captain Gina Bianchi turned out to be. He had underestimated a beautiful woman.

Chapter 43

WATCHING FROM THE SHADOWS

Doctor Gregorio Moretti drank his second cup of morning coffee, strong and rich as usual, while sitting on his flagstone patio in Fiesole, a hilly suburb just a few kilometers north of central Florence. Ever since his wife, Maria, had died in an automobile accident three years ago, he had found solace and tranquility just sitting on his patio amid a beautiful garden of purple bougainvillea and wisteria.

Dr. Moretti's large, three-story house was a 1930s traditional pale-colored terracotta and masonry design, surrounded by houses of similar size in Fiesole, an upscale neighborhood. With his young wife now deceased, and no children from the union, Moretti often felt the house was much too big for his taste or needs.

Consequently, he had converted part of the downstairs into a three-room clinic where he saw wealthier patients two days a week. There was ample parking in his circular driveway and privacy assured by the villa's surrounding stone walls. During three other days of the week, he offered his services as an Internist at the Ospedale Santa

Maria Nuova, the large public hospital only two blocks from the Piazza Duomo and Florence's massive Cathedral. Today was one of his hospital days, and he would be driving there in a few minutes.

Moretti finished his coffee and headed for the front door, putting on his suit jacket as he always did. Once outside, he climbed into his Audi S-4, started it, pressing down on the accelerator several times to hear the deep, throaty roar of the engine. This car was one of his few 'expensive toys' and one of his greatest pleasures. As a successful doctor, he felt entitled to such a magnificent car. As a socialist, and sometimes communist, however, he felt guilty he didn't drive a Fiat 500, the diminutive vehicle that used very little gasoline. Pressing the remote gate opener, he roared out of his driveway.

What the hell, life is full of contradictions, he thought looking at the road ahead.

Moretti's natural inclination was to drive as fast as possible; but memories of his wife's fatal traffic accident and his social consciousness demanded he drive responsibly and slowly, which he did, but only in town.

"Viola One to all units, he is on the move." Viola, meaning purple, was the nickname for the Florence football club, Fiorentina, but today it was the call sign for the police team running surveillance on Doctor Moretti. Ever since his prescription for Warfarin had been presented to the pharmacy in Montepulciano, the *Polizia di Stato* had set up rotating teams of watchers on him around the clock.

Viola One was sitting on his motorcycle down the street from Moretti's residence when the doctor drove past. Once out of sight, Viola One started his engine, and began to follow, maintaining a discrete distance.

"Viola Two to all units, I have him," came the report as Moretti passed two plainclothes cops sitting in a parked VW Golf. Pulling the car out of its parking space, the cops tailed him for the next mile.

"Viola Two to Viola Three, we are approaching your location."

"Viola Three to all units, we have him in sight and will take over." Before Moretti reached the intersection where two undercover officers were waiting, they pulled into traffic on their motorcycle in front of Dr. Moretti's approaching car and headed in the direction of central Florence. The male officer was driving, while the female was sitting behind him in the tandem position on the cycle. For all the world, it appeared to be just another young couple sharing their ride. They were assuming, correctly, the doctor was headed to the hospital.

The cop driving the bike used his rearview mirrors to monitor Moretti's progress behind them. He could see Viola One now pulling into position, joining the others a few cars behind Moretti's car.

The trip into town didn't take long. Moretti parked in the usual lot reserved for doctors, and the teams took up their assigned surveillance positions. The female officer from the cycle, with one of the males from the VW Golf, walked into the hospital and found the patient waiting area near Doctor Moretti's office. From there, they would watch him and report anything out of the ordinary.

Luckily for the other three cops, the hospital was surrounded by busy streets, giving them a chance to have coffee and snacks while observing the doctor's car in case he came out unexpectedly. It also provided anonymity as they hung out in one café or another. Various group combinations would take turns sitting in the patient waiting area.

At one o'clock, Moretti left the hospital on foot, walking three blocks to Via Cavour, and entered a well-known restaurant. The team observed Moretti joined by a female companion. Twenty minutes later the original police team was replaced by a new team, two of whom entered the restaurant, managing to get a table not far from the doctor, hopefully to overhear any conversation. Later they would report the lunch companion seemed only to be a friend.

Following lunch, the doctor walked back to the hospital, spent a few hours seeing patients, then returned to his house for the remainder of the day and evening.

This pattern was repeated for the next few days. While seeming a hardship in its monotony, everyone knew the Ambassador's life might be hanging in the balance. They couldn't afford blowing this surveillance operation by being impatient.

Chapter 44

BRINGING RILEY UP TO SPEED

While the *Polizia di Stato* was surveilling Doctor Moretti in Florence, Alex waited for his old friend and former Islamabad boss, Jim Riley, to arrive from the airport. Jim's newest position as director of the entire Diplomatic Security Service, headquartered in Washington, DC., had been well-earned. The fact that he was coming to see Alex on official business, and not a friendly visit, was the hardest part of this reunion.

Alex hadn't slept well the night before. He wanted to believe he wasn't worried about his so-called career. *In fact, the joke within Diplomatic Security is that no one truly has a career in the Foreign Service, only a series of assignments linked by one's physical body,* he thought. This decades-old cynical comment means a lack of career planning. *Probably right.*

No, he hadn't slept well because of what was involved in Ambassador Scarmatti's kidnapping:

First, he had warned the Ambassador repeatedly not to go anywhere without his bodyguards; had even put it in writing and sent warnings to the DCM and the Ambassador.

Secondly, he had carefully cultivated a professional relationship with the Italian cops because one never knew when a crisis might occur. But now, his immediate supervisor, DCM Alden Chandler, as well as the Embassy Task Force, were refusing to let Alex take an active role with his Italian contacts. Not that it was stopping him from doing so.

Thirdly, rather than utilize his expertise, Chandler was bending over backwards to accommodate the FBI who, effortlessly, had managed to alienate the Italians at every turn. It had taken Alex hours to fall asleep, hours to stop being pissed off, and hours to stay focused on what the prime objective was—rescuing American Ambassador Anthony Scarmatti and his wife, Francesca.

About to pour another cup of harsh coffee, there was a knock on his office door. He glanced at the wall clock.: 7:00 a.m. He opened the door to see Jim Riley smiling back at him, dressed in a grey business suit, looking ready for work.

"Jim! I didn't expect you until eight, at the earliest."

"We got a tailwind on our flight from DC, plus I traveled with only a carry-on."

He dropped his bag on the floor and gave Alex a warm embrace.

"Come on in, have coffee, and tell me what you know," Alex said. "By the way, where's Watson?"

"He went to see the DCM, if Chandler's in the office this early."

"Oh yeah, he'll be there. I'm sure he can't wait to spin his tail of why I need to be thrown out." Riley grabbed a coffee and found a seat.

"The reason the Secretary told us to come here is that he's concerned the Embassy is less than unified in its efforts to find the Ambassador and his wife."

"He's right to be concerned," Alex answered. "The question is, what exactly is he hearing?"

"I'm not completely sure, but I suspect it might be better than you think."

"Really? How so?" Alex perked up in surprise.

"I know the CIA praised you for what you've done so far. They told me that in DC, and I believe their view made it to the Secretary."

"Well, Jim. That is good news."

"Also, the State Department Office Director for Italian Affairs commented favorably about you to me, albeit discreetly, and your Political Counselor, a guy named Burnham, privately supported you and said as much to DC. But that's strictly off the record since the Italy desk doesn't want to run afoul of Alden Chandler."

"Got it." Alex made a mental note to thank Ames Burnham.

"As you can imagine," Riley continued, "Chandler, Van Camp, and the FBI have nothing good to say about you. They complained you're uncooperative and trying to showboat. That's what they told the Secretary."

"Uncooperative and showboating, that's rich. But I'm not surprised. What can you tell me about your traveling partner, Watson? Is he a fair guy?"

"I don't know him well. He's more of an acquaintance. But we attend a lot of the same meetings in DC. We'll just have to watch him operate and trust he'll support me in making the right decisions. After all, he'll have to live with the consequences if he backs the wrong horse. I'll say this, however, as Assistant Secretary of State for European Affairs, he's a real power in Washington whenever European policy is debated."

"Okay, does he personally know Chandler?"

"He does. But I don't know if they're personal friends. Professionally, Watson probably respects Chandler, although Chandler got this DCM job in Rome before Watson took over the European Bureau."

"What's Watson's background?"

"He's been our Ambassador to Greece, and Portugal, and he's spent a bunch of time in Washington in high level positions."

Alex reflected on this information: *Other than possibly serving together in Washington during their careers, it doesn't appear Watson has worked with Chandler overseas. But still, it remains to be seen if they are close.*

"You and I have talked several times since this crisis started," Riley said, "but why don't you tell me the whole story again, from the beginning."

Alex took the time to give every detail, especially the part about the Ambassador taking frequent weekend jaunts without bodyguards, even after being warned to be careful.

"Of major importance, now" Alex explained, "is the outwardly hostile, insulting, and condescending attitude of Van Camp and Reynolds toward Italian officials."

"What does Chandler think about that?"

"Chandler hasn't rebuked them," Alex replied. "I think he's afraid of the FBI, at least as far as Reynolds is concerned. Besides, Reynolds just spins out of control without warning, so it's not as if Chandler can predict his outbursts in front of the Italians."

"There's another thing you're not aware of, Jim. After the Italians told us about picking up the Ambassador's cell phone signal south of Bologna, Van Camp actually used an open line in the conference room to call Washington and pass on the information to his deputy. That info was extremely sensitive and being held closely. Not only could Van Camp's call have been intercepted, but we subsequently learned that the kidnappers at the farmhouse were tipped off that the police were able to track the Ambassador's cell phone signal. Is Van Camp's indiscretion responsible for that? I can't be certain. Either that, or we could have a mole."

After swearing Riley to secrecy, he included the most recent information about Doctor Moretti in Florence.

"There's one more vital thing I need to mention, Jim. I believe Chandler and Charlotte Eaton are holding back information about the Ambassador's whereabouts on that Sunday, and his probable use of an Embassy motor pool car. I also believe the Ambassador and Chandler connived to ditch the Ambassador's bodyguards on several weekends, including the day he was snatched."

"What? Tell me more about that, Alex." At the end of Alex's update, Riley mentioned he would speak to Watson about it.

"All right, Alex. I was up to speed on everything except the information on Doctor Moretti and the motor pool car. I'll keep the Moretti info confidential until the cops release it to the Embassy. By the way, I should have asked earlier, how are you feeling after being shot in your body armor?"

"I'm okay, just black and blue, plus a few other colors," Alex said, trying to make light of it. Jim had seen Alex in action in Pakistan, knew he was tough, and wasn't prone to look for sympathy.

"Here's the deal: Assistant Secretary Watson and I will meet with the DCM and Ambassador Van Camp together. Then we'll meet with the FBI Legatt Mark Terranova and Reynolds. More meetings will be held with the CIA Station Chief, and finally, with the Political Counselor Ames Burnham. There should be a wrap up session with the DCM and Van Camp. I want you to attend that final meeting. Should I see anyone else? Do you want me to talk to Charlotte Eaton, and pressure her about what she knows?"

Alex thought for a moment.

"You can handle that any way that you want. If she provided the car to the Ambassador and is holding back information, that could be a criminal charge against her for obstruction, at least, and possibly against Chandler, too, if he knows about it," Alex paused, "but, now that I think about it further, it's probably better if I can develop more evidence before confronting her later in a formal interview. I suggest you separate these political proceedings about me from a potential criminal or administrative case against Eaton."

"Okay, I'll leave that as your call," Riley said. "Anyone else I should see?"

"Do you want to talk with General Ghiberti, the Chief of the *Polizia di Stato*?"

"I wouldn't specifically ask his opinion on internal Embassy politics," Riley stated, "but I could thank him for his cooperation and ask about the investigation. In fact, I believe it's essential I do so, otherwise I'd look pretty stupid returning to Washington and not have talked with the cops. So, okay, please set that up. I'll strongly suggest to Assistant Secretary Watson that he should accompany me."

"Good, I'll do it immediately."

* * *

Riley walked to Carter Ambrose's office, the CIA Station Chief, whom he hadn't seen since his last days in Moscow some six or seven years ago. As he entered, Ambrose rose and greeted him.

"Jim. It's damn good to see you again! How's your wife and family?"

"They're fine, Carter, and yours?"

"Excellent. I don't know how Becky keeps the weight off here in Rome, but she's as fit as ever. Our kids are doing great back in the States. But listen, I'm so sorry you had to fly out here to deal with this vendetta Chandler has against Alex."

"You mean because of the link to Winston Hargrove in Pakistan?"

"Yeah, Jim. Chandler let the cat out of the bag once when I was briefing him a month ago on something else. I mentioned it was good to have Alex here because he seemed to have an excellent head on his shoulders and could deal with any security problem. Chandler told me Alex was a 'cowboy' and lucky to be here at all. Naturally, I was curious, and followed up with Bill Stanton, my counterpart in Pakistan, who told me what a great job Alex and you did before, during, and after the terrorist attack. I found out Hargrove and Chandler are good buddies, and that Chandler is steamed that Alex's actions crushed Hargrove's career."

"Yeah, that about sums it up. I take it you don't support Chandler's banishment of Alex from the task force meetings."

"Of course not. It was unprofessional of Chandler, and certainly counterproductive. As for Van Camp, he's a moron. Reynolds, I know, is playing the typical FBI game of pointing fingers at everyone else outside the FBI. He's killing our relationship with the Italians, as is Van Camp."

"Carter, if asked, would you privately tell the DCM that Alex should be reinstated in the task force meetings?"

"Privately, I would. But I don't want to make a public show of it. Despite all his failings, Chandler knows Italy well, and his knowledge of Italian politics is worthwhile listening to. He has some qualities to offset his personal animosity toward Alex."

"That's fair enough."

"Can I invite you over to our apartment tonight for dinner? I already cleared it with Becky."

"Sure, Carter. Jet lag may get the better of me, but I'd be delighted."

As Riley got up to leave, Ambrose asked him to sit down again.

"I have one other thing you should know about, Jim. The Italian intelligence service asked me if the FBI brought in some of its Hostage Rescue Team yesterday. I assume you're up to speed on the controversy about the FBI wanting their team to make whatever raid happens, and the Italians told them absolutely not.

Yeah, I am. Why did they ask you that?"

"Yesterday, they spotted John Cook, who is Terranova's deputy here in Rome, meeting five guys from a commercial flight from Frankfurt. The Italians said all five looked military, very fit, and dressed in the typical black cargo pants that SWAT guys wear, although the rest of their attire looked basically civilian. They all carried military-style large duffle-bag carry-ons. I spoke with our Defense Attaché, who knew nothing about it, so it's not his guys. Of course, I didn't think they would be since Cook met them and he's FBI."

"If I understand it, Carter, the Italian government officially and clearly banned the FBI from bringing in its Hostage Rescue Team, but they did it anyway?"

"Yes, at least, it appears they brought in a few guys. After he picked them up, Cook took them to *Carabinieri* headquarters."

"Interesting. Who else in the Embassy knows?"

"No one, Jim. Well, the Defense Attaché knows part of it."

"If I have to, can I use this info with Chandler for leverage?"

Ambrose remained silent a few seconds. He knew Riley was exceptionally discreet with sensitive information, but his own instincts were to protect anything that came from the Italian intelligence service.

"Come on, Carter," Jim said, "Who would be surprised the Italians monitor arrivals at their own airport? Besides, you already told the Defense Attaché. And, obviously, the FBI knows. So, why not Chandler? He's in charge of the Embassy, like it or not."

"All right, you have a point, Jim."

Chapter 45

THE HEAT TURNS UP

Riley asked Nancy to arrange a meeting with Chandler and Ambassador Van Camp along with Assistant Secretary Watson who just arrived with him from Washington. Shortly, thereafter, she reported the men would be assembled in Chandler's office within ten minutes.

"Nancy, I would love to take you back to Washington with me to work your magic. Too bad you're needed here." He quickly removed two papers from his briefcase and put them in his breast pocket before climbing the stairs to the meeting.

As he walked down the hallway, he saw the Renaissance ceiling frescos and paintings hanging along the corridor outside the upper floor offices. He realized Rome displayed the most opulent classical art of any embassy in the world, even more than in Moscow, Bonn, Warsaw, and Pretoria where he had served during his career.

No wonder the European Bureau refers to itself as 'The Queen of Bureaus' within the State Department, he thought. *Pompous, yes, but not far off the mark.*

Entering the DCM's office, he saw Chandler already speaking with Van Camp and Assistant Secretary Watson now gathered in his inner office. The door was open for him.

"I'm glad you're here, Riley" Chandler said, trying to grab the initiative before Riley could say anything.

"'Glad' is not exactly how I'd put it, Alden." Riley said, deliberately using Chandler's first name knowing he hated being called "Alden" by people he regarded as "inferior." Riley apparently fell in that category since Chandler frowned while asking everyone to take a seat on the sofas and chairs in the sitting area of his expansive office.

"As you know," Archibald Watson began, "the Secretary of State asked us to review the Embassy's efforts at getting the Ambassador back."

Riley was pleased Watson had phrased his opening remarks by addressing the real issue of concern, rather than focusing on Alex's future at post. Nevertheless, Riley wasn't going to be taken in by any subterfuge on Watson's part.

"Alden, it appears to the Secretary, and to us, the team is at odds within itself," Watson continued.

"I quite agree," Van Camp blurted out, although no one had asked his opinion. "Our interagency efforts have been thrown eschew by Boyd, the very man who was responsible for the Ambassador's protection in the first place. It appears he has failed."

Riley contained an emerging anger within himself, knowing Watson didn't like to be interrupted, not to mention that his comment had been directed at Chandler, not Van Camp. Riley saw Watson look briefly at Van Camp, then return his gaze to Chandler, as if Van Camp was an irritating gnat to be ignored.

"You're correct about our internal conflict, Archibald," Chandler replied. "There's one constant obstacle to our joint efforts, and that obstacle is Alex Boyd. He was negligent in providing suitable security for the Ambassador, and since the kidnapping, he's been on a one-man crusade rather than working within the team."

Watson looked over at Riley and motioned him to speak his mind.

"You say Alex was negligent in providing security to the Ambassador," Riley began.

"Yes, he most certainly was."

"I understand from Alex, he repeatedly warned the Ambassador, and you, about maintaining police coverage 24/7. Is that correct?"

"Well, yes, he may have mentioned it on rare occasions," Chandler rebutted. "But, of course, he would say that. That's always the view of Diplomatic Security. Maximum security all the time, regardless of threat."

Chandler crossed his arms in defiance and leaned back in his chair.

"Interesting phrase: 'regardless of threat,'" Riley stayed on point. "You mean, regardless of the very real threat posed by the New Red Brigade? Or do you specifically mean regardless of the track record the New Red Brigade has for kidnapping VIPs in Italy?"

Riley thought Chandler was ever so minimally squirming in his chair by sensing he'd made an error in his own argument.

"Don't try twisting my words, Riley," Chandler's voice rose in self-defense as he leaned forward. "We still don't know exactly how the Ambassador and his wife were kidnapped, but clearly his protection was not sufficient. More to the point, now we've had to deal with Boyd ignoring my commands, and engaging in activities that have placed the Ambassador's life at ultimate risk."

"Exactly," Van Camp said, trying to assert his role as head of the task force. "We officially decided that if the FBI wasn't allowed to make the raid at the farmhouse, then we would leave it up to the Italians, regardless of whether the raid was a good idea or not. Boyd took it upon himself to jump into the middle of it, seriously endangering the Ambassador."

Riley looked over at Watson, who motioned with his hand for

Riley to continue.

"Let's be clear. Let's stick to the facts," Riley said. "When the *Polizia di Stato* offered to have the FBI *observe* the raid, you turned them down, presumably upon advice from the FBI. Did you not?"

Chandler nodded reluctantly.

"According to your own Embassy's reporting to Washington, you allowed two Americans, a DS Agent from the task force and an Embassy CIA officer, already in Bologna to be imbedded with the cops and monitor the raid."

"Precisely. That's why Boyd's presence was unnecessary," Chandler smugly replied.

"But you didn't *forbid* anyone from being present at the raid itself. In fact, it was the police who specifically *invited* Alex to observe because they trusted him and had worked with him during their exercise in Abruzzi. So, what's the difference between two American officers observing, and a third one, Alex by invitation, to do what you'd *already agreed to do?*"

Riley, of course, knew Alex had become an active participant in the raid, and indeed, had been shot, but the DCM didn't know that detail nor did Riley intend to mention it.

"It's not for the *Police da State* to decide who in the Embassy can be present," Van Camp interjected.

"First, Van Camp," Riley snapped back at him disdainfully, "You've been here a week. At least get the name of the national police correct. It's P*olizia di Stato*... and I don't even speak Italian."

Watson grinned slightly.

"Secondly, it's for the *Italians* to decide who can be present. They wanted Alex there. It's their country; it was their raid. I'll grant you, perhaps Alex should have told you about the offer, but that's not very important now.

"Chandler, you should be thrilled that Alex has such powerful contacts who personally asked him to observe the raid." By using the DCM's last name, he intentionally signaled a lack of respect for him.

"Let's leave the security issue aside for a moment and focus on getting the Ambassador back," Riley continued. "Alex is simply your best resource for liaison with the police, who have rejected FBI intervention. They clearly value Alex's contribution."

"I don't accept that we ignore his responsibility for the Ambassador's security. His actions, or rather, lack of action, is central to this entire mess," Chandler blustered.

"He has a point," Assistant Secretary Watson said.

"All right, then," Riley conceded. Reaching into his coat pocket, he retrieved the two papers taken from his briefcase earlier. Watson watched him, apparently curious as to what Riley had in his hand, or "up his sleeve."

"Do you recognize these reports, Chandler?" Riley asked handing them over. "My apologies to you, Archibald, but I only brought one copy of each."

Watson nodded, and said nothing. Riley ignored Van Camp completely.

"Take note, Chandler, these are two memos Alex wrote to the Ambassador, through you, and dated thirty and sixty days ago respectively. They call for maintaining the Ambassador's police protective team seven days a week. In the body of the memo, he justified his position by including the serious potential threat from the New Red Brigade. He also objected to your repeated questioning of the need for such protection. Your initials are on both memos, as are the Ambassador's initials obviously indicating that you had read them. I find it especially useful to read, first, your cryptic hand-written note in the margin that says:

'Nevertheless, we need to keep reviewing this in the future.'

And secondly, the Ambassador's note: 'I agree with Alden, let's keep looking at this matter.'

"So, if we're going to examine responsibility for the Ambassador's protection, then let's start with your lack of support for it."

Chandler blinked rapidly and ran his tongue over dry lips. He appeared shaken by the memos, obviously not having anticipated the Ambassador would send them back to Alex with their notes. Alex had sent copies to Riley in the classified pouch to Washington the week prior.

"Naturally, we needed to constantly review his protection," Chandler back peddled. "Possibly even increase it. I repeat, it was Boyd's responsibility to get the level of protection correct. Evidently, he didn't do so."

"Don't give me that bullshit, Chandler. It's clear *you* and Ambassador Scarmatti wanted less protection, not more. Make no mistake about it, eventually there will be an Accountability Review Board which will note the same thing I'm raising now."

"Yes, you and Boyd do have experience with review boards, don't you?" Chandler snarked.

"I can't believe you want to go there with this argument," Riley rebutted. "If you're referring to the Accountability Review Board's findings in Islamabad two years ago, and their views on Winston Hargrove's performance, then you're damn right I have experience with Boards! Your friend deserved what he got, but let's not digress from the crisis at hand."

"You seem to have missed a crucial point," Van Camp spoke to Riley. "Regarding the work of the task force and the return of the Ambassador, Boyd has become an irritant."

"An irritant to whom?" Riley asked.

"Why to the FBI, of course. We have far more at stake in our relationship with the FBI than we have in supporting the actions of one security officer," Van Camp said. "The FBI expects our support, not our backstabbing."

"One goddamn minute, Van Camp!" Watson said loudly,

forcefully stepping into the discussion. "That view is too cynical even by my standards."

Van Camp's mouth opened in shock.

"Yes, we have a lot at stake with the FBI, or with any agency for that matter," Watson continued, "but the FBI is here to support the State Department and offer the Italians assistance. If we can help the FBI, so much the better. But it's *our* man and his wife who have been kidnapped, not FBI people. I might add," he turned to face Chandler, "all U.S. embassies are supposed to be run by the State Department, not the FBI."

Riley had never seen Watson so angry. Before this trip, he honestly didn't know where Watson stood on the issue of Alex's continued presence at post. Now, it appeared Watson had a fair and open mind, no doubt helped along by the incompetence of Ambassador Charles Van Camp.

As conversation paused, Chandler's secretary knocked on the door to announce Deputy Interior Minister Ferrara and General Ghiberti, head of the *Polizia di Stato,* had just called after hearing that Riley and Watson were in town. They wanted a meeting to talk about the kidnapping. After conferring with Riley and Watson, Chandler told her to call Ferrara back and say he would be bringing them to the Interior Ministry within the hour.

"We want to speak with more people in the Embassy afterward," Riley concluded, "I suggest we reconvene later this afternoon and continue this conversation." All agreed.

"Gentlemen," Chandler stated, I'll have my car pull up in the front of the Embassy in twenty minutes for the trip to the Interior Ministry. I'll meet you in the lobby downstairs."

Once outside Chandler's office, Riley asked Watson if he wanted to meet Alex before they left; he readily agreed, wanting to take full measure of the man himself.

* * *

Alex was talking with Sam Carson when Jim Riley and Watson came down from their meeting. He and Sam both stood while introductions were made. Alex noted Watson looked physically fit with body language that gave him a sense this was a man of action. Nevertheless, he was surprised by the strength of Watson's handshake.

"I've heard a lot about you Mr. Boyd. As you can imagine, both good and bad."

"I have no doubt. What can I do to help you assess the issues at stake?"

"I like your directness. May I call you Alex?"

"Of course, Sir."

"Alex, please tell me about yourself." Watson frequently used this question as a tool to judge a person's presentation skills, organizational ability, and if they could be concise, yet informative.

"Yes, sir. I grew up partially overseas because my father and mother both worked for the CIA. Among other jobs, my father was Station Chief in both Cairo and Paris, where I learned Arabic and French at an early age. After graduating from the University of Virginia with a degree in Economics, I joined the US Navy and became an Intelligence Officer, supporting a Navy SEAL unit on the east coast. After serving four years in the navy, I attended graduate school at the University of Maryland, obtaining a master's degree in Criminology. Then joined Diplomatic Security, serving in Washington, Buenos Aires, Tunis, Islamabad, and now here in Rome. In addition to Arabic and French, I also speak Spanish, Italian, and some Udru."

"Impressive, Alex," Watson grinned. "You're happy working in Diplomatic Security? Don't you want to be a Foreign Service generalist with those language skills?"

"Sir, I'm extremely happy with Diplomatic Security, but in all honesty, I'm less happy with the State Department."

"I understand," Watson nodded.

"Archibald, I want to add that Alex received the Department's Heroism Award for his defense of the Embassy in Islamabad," Riley said. They spoke another ten minutes before wrapping up the conversation.

"Well, we must leave for another meeting now," Watson said. "It was nice to finally meet you, Alex. I expect we'll talk later."

"The same, Sir. I appreciate meeting you in person."

Riley and Watson left the office and joined Chandler in the lobby for the brief car ride to the Interior Ministry.

Chapter 46

THE FINAL DECISION

Returning from the meeting with Ferrara and General Ghiberti, Riley and Watson left Chandler and Van Camp at the front of the Embassy and went for lunch nearby. They needed to refuel before the next round of afternoon meetings began. Besides, the end of the afternoon was decision time regarding whether Alex could remain at post or watch his career crash.

The afternoon meetings all went as expected. Watson and Riley met with FBI Legatt Mark Terranova, but without Reynolds, who told Terranova, in advance, he was too busy to participate. Terranova appeared genuinely apologetic for Reynolds' absence, but parroted the company line about Alex trying to compete with the FBI for police contacts, and felt Alex was too turf oriented. His arguments were received with considerable skepticism by Watson and Riley.

On the other end of the spectrum, extremely positive comments about Alex were received from Ames Burnham in Political, Colonel Jim Watson in the Defense Attaché's Office, as well as from Secret Service Agent Chuck Nelsen.

The only other person who questioned Alex's judgment, other than Chandler and Terranova, was Management Counselor Charlotte Eaton. Watson noted her somewhat lethargic, yet nervous answers to their questions. He knew her well from a prior assignment in Washington's European Bureau, and felt something was bothering her.

Watson then suggested to Riley they speak with Alex's staff. They met individually with Joe, George, Sam, and Master Gunny Clarke. Nancy had previously responded with the highest praise for Alex, so it wasn't necessary to interview her again.

The rest of all conversations went well. Both Watson and Riley were impressed with how often Alex was credited with mentoring his staff, giving them meaningful responsibility, and seeking their views on important matters. As for Alex's specific actions on the kidnapping case, everyone felt he was doing a terrific job, despite being banned from task force operations. The interviews filled up most of the remaining afternoon.

Now, the time had arrived for a final confrontation with the DCM Chandler and visiting Ambassador Van Camp.

Chandler choose one of the Embassy's small conference rooms for the meeting. Riley asked Alex to accompany him and Assistant Secretary Watson to the meeting. When they arrived, Chandler was already seated at the head of the table, with Ambassador Van Camp and Reynolds on either side. Their message of a united front was abundantly clear.

"So glad you could join us, considering your busy schedule," Riley needled Reynolds.

"I had a few minutes available," he replied flatly.

"How do you wish to proceed?" Chandler asked Assistant Secretary Watson.

"I'll ask Diplomatic Security Director Riley to start off." The formality reeked of an inquisition.

"As we told you shortly after arriving," Riley began, "the US Secretary of State is concerned this Embassy appears to be divided in its efforts to rescue the Ambassador and Mrs. Scarmatti from their kidnappers. Unfortunately, that seems to be the case. You three have been critical of Alex's performance, yet everyone else we spoke with praised him, including the Italian Deputy Interior Minister and the National Chief of the *Polizia di Stato*.

"Equally important to our findings," Watson interjected, "the Italians find the task force's approach confrontational."

Reynolds could no longer remain silent.

"Confrontational? Well, maybe so, but if the Italians had allowed us to bring in our Hostage Rescue Team, we might have been able to grab the Ambassador at the farmhouse. As a result, they launched the raid and screwed up." He pointed at Alex. "Your presence there encouraging that raid, may have endangered the Ambassador's life."

"May I speak?" Alex asked Riley who nodded.

"Reynolds, the FBI team was still in Quantico at the time of the raid and couldn't have been there. Also, as we've since discovered, the Ambassador was moved from the farmhouse to another location before the raid even took place. Those are cold, hard facts." Alex stated calmly.

"Should the Italians have waited for your team to arrive, we never would have known about the Lancia used to move the Ambassador and his wife to the south. The Italians developed that information without your assistance. Moreover, the *Polizia di Stato* now has leads of Warfarin purchases, or attempted purchases including video of a likely kidnapper. You realize none of this information resulted from efforts by your task force." Alex slowly folded his arms and calmly stared down Reynolds.

However, Reynolds' bullying style had served him well throughout his career, and he wasn't done yet. He expected to succeed once again.

"Look, Boyd, if you had been cooperating from the start, perhaps the Italians would have been willing to work with the FBI. Instead, you undermined us." He sounded overly heated to the others, on the verge of losing control.

"Interesting point: You said, 'work with the FBI.' Don't you mean work with the Embassy?" Alex asked. "This is not about the FBI, Reynolds. Well, I take that back. Maybe it is for you. But the rest of us only want Tony and Francesca freed. The Italians are working with 'us.' Like it or not, they're working with me, with the CIA, and despite your best efforts to steamroll the Italians, yes, they're working with the task force as well."

"What a bunch of crap, especially coming from someone like you, Boyd, who won't cooperate," Reynolds stated, not letting go of his bully attack.

Watson listened closely to the exchange and had to admit Alex was giving a masterful performance of self-control and logical argument against a self-serving sorry excuse of an FBI agent from the Incident Response Team.

Boyd's argument is impressive, he thought.

"All right, I've personally heard enough about so-called cooperation, Reynolds," Riley declared, raising his voice. Reynolds stared darkly at Riley trying to intimidate him, which was useless. Had he known Riley well enough, he would have known better.

"Since you seem to be big on cooperation, Reynolds, explain to us why the Assistant Legatt, John Cook, met five members of the FBI's Hostage Rescue Team at the Rome airport yesterday, despite the Italian Foreign Minister explicitly telling you they had no permission to enter the country."

Chandler stared hard at Reynolds, looking genuinely shocked.

"Is this true, Reynolds? I didn't know about it," Watson also looked surprised.

"Yes, it is, but only five men, to serve as… advisors, more or less. How did you find out about this?" Reynolds asked. Riley just locked eyes with him, saying nothing.

"But we never received approval from the Italians for that," Chandler protested, raising his voice with concern.

"Exactly my point," Riley said, trying to slam the door shut on Reynolds. "With no approval or coordination from the Italians, or with the Embassy."

"We don't need the Foreign Ministry's blessing," Reynolds spoke again. "We're working with the *Carabinieri,* and *they* want our team here."

"Let me make things perfectly clear to you, Reynolds, especially since you seem to be thickheaded about the meaning of cooperation," Watson sounded fed up; his piercing blue eyes boring into him.

"The Foreign Ministry is charged with leading the Italian government's efforts to find the Scarmattis. *They* are in charge of all policies regarding who may or may not enter Italy. They told this Embassy, and you explicitly, that the FBI Hostage Rescue Team was not wanted and would not be granted access to Italy. For God's sake, man, what don't you understand about that, Reynolds? It's you who has jeopardized our relationship with the Italian government and compromised our ability to work with them to find the Scarmattis."

Alex was shocked, truly shocked. He'd never heard a Foreign Service Officer make such a powerful argument to anyone, much less a senior FBI agent.

"I stand by what I said," Reynolds replied, "we were invited by the *Carabinieri,* and that's what matters to me." He was getting red in the face and clenching his fists on the table.

"You leave me no choice but to have the Secretary speak with the FBI Director about your unprofessional actions," Watson said. Then, addressing Van Camp, he continued, "As for Alex's role in the

Embassy, you are nominally in charge of the task force. Now, I'm not your boss, but I do run Europe for the State Department, and I expect Alex will be included in *all* future task force operations. Is that understood? And that will also be my official recommendation to the Secretary of State. Jim, do you have anything to add?"

"Yes, Archibald, I do. Chandler, we always listen when senior post leadership has a problem with one of our RSOs, and sometimes we remove the RSO, if warranted. But in this case, I won't voluntarily pull Alex out of Rome. If you want to continue making this case to the Secretary, then go ahead, try, but at your own peril, I might caution you. However, when Ambassador Scarmatti returns, he can make up his own mind about who stays at post."

"Very well, then, I guess I'll have to live with his presence here," Chandler said. "I assume Ambassador Van Camp will also allow Boyd to participate in task force matters." Van Camp nodded, still scowling.

"Then, it's settled, gentlemen," Watson said getting up and pushing back his chair.

Turning to Alex, he quietly said, "See me in the hallway."

Watson, Riley and Alex left the conference room together walking ten meters down the corridor before Watson stopped and spoke quietly.

"Alex, there will be long-term repercussions from today's encounter. We'll have bridges to mend with the FBI, but I hope we'll be rewarded by your future conduct. By all accounts from people who matter, you've done an excellent job here; please try to work with Chandler and the task force under these difficult circumstances. Jim and I don't want to regret what we've decided today."

"I appreciate everything you've done, sir, and sincerely thank you for your support," Alex replied. "I'd like to mention one thing. In all my years with the State Department, I've never seen a Foreign Service Officer take such a powerful stand as you just did in the meeting. I'm completely impressed and want you to know that."

Watson smiled and extended his hand to Alex, who firmly grasped it.

"Alex, before I joined the Foreign Service, I was a United States Marine Corps Officer for four years, even saw combat in Vietnam. I'm not sure who you saw today, the diplomat or the Marine. But it was a pleasure to put that jerk Reynolds in his place. Now, I need to speak with Chandler privately before going to the hotel and putting my feet up for a while. Jim, unless you have something else to talk about, I'll see you at breakfast in the morning; I know you have plans for this evening."

"See you then, Archibald."

* * *

Later at dinner that evening before Jim Riley returned to Washington, Carter Ambrose and his wife, Becky, Rachel and Alex took him to Rachel's favorite restaurant, gabbing a table in the corner of the room, far from other diners. After ordering, Carter looked around the table at the friends he most enjoyed. Then, he remembered an important development.

"Alex, you remember the farmhouse kidnappers confessed they moved the Scarmattis after being tipped off about the cops knowing their location from tracing his cell phone signal," he spoke in a voice just above a whisper.

"I definitely recall that," Alex answered. "We figured they had someone on the inside, somewhere."

"Exactly. Well, apparently, they do. Late this afternoon the Italian Intelligence service told me they traced the leak to an employee of the Italian phone company. He has links to people in the New Red Brigade. They've put him under surveillance, both physical and electronic, to determine exactly what he's tapping into. His job's technical, so he has the skills and access to use the phone service to monitor nonsecure Embassy calls."

"But don't you always use secure lines?" Becky Ambrose asked.

Rubbing his hands over his face, Alex took a breath, and said, "We do, except one time. That moron, Van Camp, used a nonsecure phone to call Washington from the task force conference room. During the call he mentioned the breakthrough with the Ambassador's cell phone signal. Obviously, the kidnappers picked up on that vital piece of info."

"That's exactly what I think as well," Carter said. "It was embarrassing to admit to the Italians that the head of State Department's Counter-Terrorism policy office would be so stupid as to use a nonsecure line, but I had no choice. Hey, at least I could say he was State Department."

"Not funny," Riley said. But, in fact, everyone was smiling at Carter's little joke.

"Let me guess," Jim said, "we shouldn't do anything to Van Camp for the moment because the Italians want to find out who the telecom guy is talking to."

"Precisely," Carter responded. "I'll ask that you keep it completely under your hat for a while. You can brief the Secretary of State when you get back to DC, but that's it. No one else in the Embassy, outside of our offices, will know about this development, including Chandler and Reynolds. Especially Reynolds."

"Fine. Now let's enjoy our meal."

Chapter 47

DISCOVERED

Sitting at his office desk the next morning, Alex's thoughts went back to other tough times he'd lived through, like the Embassy attack in Pakistan. He, Rachel, and Riley had come out of that time alive and really bonded over shared memories.

Times are good when one lives to tell such tales, he thought. He and Rachel had become inseparable after Pakistan, and he cherished every second they depended upon one another for support. He loved her so much.

His train of thought was broken when Sam Carson appeared at his doorway.

"Got a minute?"

"For my Chief Whiz Kid? Any time."

"I'm your only Whiz Kid," she said dryly, "and you'll be happy to know I used my secret decoder ring to make a breakthrough in the Ambassador's kidnapping."

Now, she had Alex's full attention.

"Remember when we watched the video tape of Charlotte Eaton

getting into her car to leave the Ambassador's residence?"

"Yeah."

"Remember the sound quality was so bad I turned the volume down while we watched? Well, this morning, I decided to use a new tunable filter I received the other day from Washington. I was able to lose all the unwanted noise on the tape and found something I want you to listen to."

"Let's go," Alex said getting up. They walked down the hall to her office.

"All right, I don't want to prejudice your judgment, so I won't say anything," she said. "I've cued the tape to when Charlotte is leaving the residence's front door. Listen very carefully as you watch."

He saw Charlotte's motor pool car parked under the portico. The passenger side of the vehicle was hidden by the deep roof overhang. Alex watched her walk around the car and this time heard the sound of her footsteps crunching on the gravel. She opened the door of the driver's side, got in, closed it, and seemed to wait. Sam looked at him with a finger to her lips, then pointed at the screen.

Then he heard it: Noise of the front door to the house opening again, and closing a second time, then multiple footsteps on the gravel. He listened closely as he heard two car doors opening, and seconds later, slamming closed, first one and then, another.

"Geez, *two* more people entered Charlotte's car. Can you guess who they were!" Alex caught on quickly. "Sam, you've done it again! The Scarmattis *did* leave with Charlotte. We suspected it all along but couldn't prove it. This absolutely does. You're a genius," he said hugging her hard.

She momentarily blushed, glad he was so happy.

"Now what?"

"I'm going to confront Charlotte. She knew all along, and deliberatively hid it from us. But first, I want Joe and George to hear this." He dialed Joe's extension. Within minutes, both men were in the office listening to the tape and confirming Alex and Sam's view that three people got into the car.

"Joe," Alex said, "I want you to come with me to Charlotte's office. George, stay with Sam and bag the video as evidence for possible criminal charges against Charlotte."

"Do I get a better job title now?" Sam yelled after them as Alex and Joe were leaving.

"You do, indeed.," Alex called back to her. "Official *'Super'* Chief Whiz Kid."

* * *

Ignoring Charlotte Eaton's secretary, they entered Charlotte's office without knocking, and closed the door. She was sitting at her desk looking at spreadsheets. Her hair was somewhat disheveled, and to Alex, she seemed pale, tired, and looking depressed. They sat down in chairs directly in front of her desk. She looked up, but instead of questioning what the hell they were doing just walking into her office, she sighed, and looked resigned to whatever Alex was going to say.

"Charlotte, this is a 'Come-to-Jesus' meeting. We enhanced the audio from the tape of you leaving the Ambassador's residence." A distressed look came over her face.

"It's beyond clear that two people, besides yourself, got into the car before you drove off. Since the servants had the day off, and Alden Chandler had already departed, that only leaves Tony and Francesca as the probable passengers."

Tears filled her eyes quickly and began streaming down first one cheek, then the other. Mascara ran in messy lines from her eyes to her jaw.

"I'm so sorry, Alex. I didn't want to lie, but Alden kept pressuring me to maintain our story that we knew nothing about Tony's trip without protection that day."

Resting her elbows on the desk, she covered her face with both hands. Alex could see she was quietly sobbing, chest and shoulders shaking with each breath. Her breakdown happened so fast, he realized she must have been under tremendous psychological stress for days.

"Tell me all about it, Charlotte. You'll feel better if you do, and it might help us get Tony and Francesca back."

She reached for tissues in her desk, dried her eyes, and blew her nose. Mascara still camouflaged her face in messy streaks.

He debated a moment about first reading her the obligatory Miranda rights. She clearly had obstructed the kidnapping investigation by remaining silent and lying to him, a Federal Agent. Once he reported this to Washington, her career was finished. The State Department might even terminate her employment administratively. Whether criminal charges would be pressed was another matter entirely. As much as he wanted to just get on with the interview without forcing her to reconsider her situation, he felt a Diplomatic Security obligation to do the right thing.

"Charlotte, before you speak, I have to advise you that you have the right to remain silent. If you give up the right to remain silent, anything you say can and will be used against you in a court of law. If you desire an attorney and cannot afford one, an attorney will be provided for you before police questioning." She continued sobbing, but acknowledged what Alex said.

After that, Charlotte spoke for fifteen minutes, relating the entire history of that day and the fact the Ambassador had used the motor pool car on several occasions before that Sunday.

"I told Alden several times we should discuss this with you, but he always said he knew best. He even implied you were open to reevaluating Tony's bodyguard coverage, although, if that was true, I asked, why didn't he just bring you into the picture. I knew it was wrong, Alex. I guess I was afraid Alden would make things hard on me if I didn't cooperate. You know how the system works. He was responsible for selecting me for this assignment in the first place, and he could deep-six me for my next one."

"After dropping you off at your place, did Tony drive off in the motor pool car?" Joe asked. She nodded. "Where were they headed that day?"

"Orvieto. They had gone there previously without the bodyguards."

He pointed to a yellow pad. "Charlotte, I want you to write up a statement, covering all the points we just discussed. Sign it and give it to me in the next hour. Joe will write up his own notes. We'll have to notify Washington immediately."

"I understand, Alex. I'm sorry, truly sorry."

Alex and Joe stood up. "You've had a fine career, Charlotte," Alex said. "You've made major contributions to the country. Perhaps you'll somehow survive this error in judgment."

They left her office and walked up to Chandler's office.

"Do you really think she can survive this?" Joe asked.

"Who knows? This is the State Department. Anything is possible. But, at this point, I really don't give a shit."

Chapter 48

LIES AND MORE LIES

"The DCM doesn't want to be disturbed," Chandler's Secretary told Alex and Joe as they arrived at his office." Alex saw the DCM's door was closed.

"Is anyone with him now?" he asked Liz Waters.

"No, but he's drafting a report to Washington, and doesn't want to be interrupted."

"Sorry, Liz." Without hesitation Alex opened the door and walked in. Chandler looked up from his desk. Joe followed, uncertain how this was going to play out.

"I told Liz I didn't want to be disturbed," Chandler said angrily. "Get out! Now!"

"Would you like me to use a new set of handcuffs on you, or would you prefer the special pair I used on Winston Hargrove in Pakistan?"

Alex knew he was being a wiseass, but at this point he wanted Chandler to shit his pants. Chandler looked totally confused at first. Then, nervously stuttered.

"Wha... wha... what the hell are you talking about, Boyd?"

"I'm talking about conspiracy to hide evidence concerning the kidnapping of Ambassador Scarmatti and his wife and lying to a federal agent."

He sort of made up the charge as he went along, wishing he had stopped in his office to first check the US Criminal Code for correct language. Moreover, he realized Chandler had never given a statement under oath about the kidnapping; nevertheless, he had lied to a federal special agent, himself, who was conducting an official investigation. That was a worth a few years in a federal penitentiary.

"Lying to a federal agent is a felony, Chandler. Charlotte just spilled the beans about your role in the cover-up of the Ambassador using an Embassy car, as well as knowing about the Ambassador's destination that weekend without bodyguards. The police could have used that information from the beginning. You've obstructed the entire investigation."

"I have no idea what you're talking about, Boyd. If Charlotte was hiding information from us, then by all means, pursue it. Are you saying the Ambassador used an embassy car the day he was kidnapped?"

"Bullshit, Chandler. You and Charlotte are in this together. She's already confessed."

"She's lying!" Chandler stood up as he spoke. "Of course, she'll try to spread the blame. But she's in charge of the motor pool and controls the vehicles."

"I'm not buying your story, Chandler. It's inconceivable the Ambassador would go out of town and not tell his DCM where he was going, or how he was getting there. So, here's what we're going to do: Joe and George are going to take a sworn statement from you in a few minutes. I'm going to inform the police about the Scarmatti's use of an Embassy car, and then I'll report this entire matter to Washington."

"Let's get George," Alex said looking at Joe, then he faced Chandler. "They'll be back in fifteen minutes to read you your rights. I wouldn't go anywhere, if I was you."

On the way back to their office, Joe asked Alex, "Aren't you sitting in on the DCM's interview?"

"I'm not for four reasons, Joe. First, I want to take Charlotte to our office, so she can complete her own statement. I'm sure Chandler is calling her right now to get her to retract what she told us. Secondly, if I take Chandler's statement, he'll try to claim it's all about my revenge for banning me from the task force. Thirdly, I believe he'll ask for legal counsel before he makes a statement, so it may not happen in any event. Finally, I want to call the cops and Washington right away with this information."

"Jesus, Alex. You thought all that through just now?"

"Let's just say I've been down this path before. Go find George. I'll get Charlotte."

Charlotte had, indeed, received a call from Chandler before Alex got to her office, yet she was determined to set the record straight. She went with him to the RSO's office, where she sat at Joe's desk and hand wrote her statement.

Alex then called General Ghiberti and gave him the new information describing the Embassy car, as well as Chandler and Eaton's roles in the matter, noting that Orvieto had been the Ambassador's destination. He apologized to Ghiberti on behalf of the Embassy for the cover-up.

Finally, he called the DS Command Center in Washington, and gave them the full scoop. He was about to ask to be patched through to Jim Riley when he realized Riley had just taken off from Fiumicino Airport in Rome, and was currently in the air headed back to DC So, he told the Command Center to pass the info on to Riley when he landed at Dulles.

Before heading to the task force, Alex poked his head into Joe's office, and saw that Charlotte had just finished her statement. He read it with satisfaction, then asked Nancy to join him in witnessing Charlotte's signature after she swore it was true to the best of her knowledge.

"What should I do now, Alex?" Charlotte asked. She looked totally drained.

Alex was torn between showing compassion or telling her to jump off the nearest bridge. He'd had it with State Department officers who avoided security rules and responsibilities, except for ones they made up for themselves on the spot. Then he thought about his own independent streak. Plunging a fountain pen into a suspect's leg wasn't exactly playing by the rules either. Was he any better than Charlotte or Chandler?

Okay, maybe in this case. But, until faced with a situation, who really knows? He thought.

"Charlotte, I can't advise you on what to do. Because of the time zone difference, Washington won't be open for business for another five hours or so. Maybe you can reflect on what you want to tell the European Bureau, and probably the Secretary of State for that matter. I appreciate your cooperation with making this statement, although you could have helped the investigation from the start."

About to leave, Joe and George returned from Chandler's office. As expected, Joe told him Chandler wanted to consult an attorney before making his statement, so the interview would have to wait.

After making a half-dozen copies of Charlotte's statement, Alex walked to the task force conference room. John Reynolds, Ambassador Van Camp, and a few other staffers were there, as were the two Italian cops handling liaison. Rachel, Ames Burnham from Political, and a case officer from Carter Ambrose's office were also present.

He informed the group about Charlotte's confession told them he'd already talked with General Ghiberti and the Diplomatic

Security Command Center. Then he dropped copies of Charlotte's statement on the conference table for all to read. They would note for themselves Chandler's complicity in the cover-up.

He returned to his office without saying another word.

Chapter 49

TRAGEDY STRIKES

After Alex confirmed to General Ghiberti that Orvieto had been the Scarmatti's destination the day they were kidnapped, the police and Carabinieri flooded the area with teams in hopes of developing more information. While law enforcement had known the Scarmattis had purchased ceramics in Orvieto, this new confirmation was like starting over.

They set up new roadblocks to question drivers, put up reward posters in town, and revisited the ceramics shop again listed on the receipt Alex found at the farmhouse where the Ambassador and his wife had originally been held. The owner of the shop remembered the Scarmattis, but said they hadn't returned to pick up their ceramic goods. So, no new leads were developed in the Orvieto area.

That night, in a possibly unrelated break in the case, a *Carabinieri* informant reported that one of his contacts had revealed a possible kidnapper's name—Luigi Colombo. The informant said Colombo, a mechanic, owned a small repair garage in Perugia and lived above the garage.

The *Carabinieri* and police checked their data bases and identified Colombo as a small-time crook, involved in petty thievery and insurance scams; he also had a minor record of left wing activities. The police knew where he lived, and set up a joint surveillance operation with the *Carabinieri*.

By nine o'clock that evening this lead was passed on to the task force. Mike James, the DS Special Agent, was pulling his shift in the conference room and took the information from the *Carabinieri* liaison officer. He immediately called in other senior team members. Within thirty minutes the usual group had assembled.

"So, that's all we have so far?" the somewhat subdued Chandler asked Mike James.

"We need to see this place immediately," Reynolds said to Chandler.

Chandler looked at Mark Terranova and even at Alex, apparently looking for opinions. Alex wondered if Chandler was feeling a little contrite after their confrontation earlier in the day.

"We can ask the *Carabinieri*," Terranova said, without enthusiasm, as he looked over at Alex.

"I doubt they'll let any of us near the garage until they've surveilled it a while," Alex said.

"Hey, this is the first lead we've gotten in the case," Reynolds said, ignoring the fact that Alex and the cops had already raided the farmhouse where the Scarmattis had originally been kept. "We need to get eyes on this target."

Reynolds turned to the police and *Carabinieri* liaison reps.

"Can you guys show us this garage?"

"Not possible at the moment," the *Carabinieri* officer answered. "We can assure you, however, it's under twenty-four-hour surveillance."

"That's not good enough," Reynolds said, raising his voice in typical blowhard style. Then, changed his focus to the *Polizia di Stato* liaison officer. The cop, a big guy and well-muscled, merely crossed his arms defiantly, shaking his head "no."

Reynolds motioned Terranova to follow him into the hallway. "Let's contact General Romano, head of the *Carabinieri*. The source is theirs, not the cops; he might be able to get us a look-see at the garage."

Terranova didn't think this would work but responded: "Okay, John. I'll call him right now." He walked down the hall and called General Romano's cell phone. Meeting Reynolds ten minutes later in the hallway, he reported that General Romano wouldn't allow it now, but said it might be possible in a day or two.

"Shit, let's meet him tomorrow at his office and try to convince him again, in person," Reynolds said angrily, then stomped off to the task force room.

Alex was standing in the doorway when Reynolds walked by and heard him mumbling something about someone being 'fucking useless.'

Did he mean Terranova or Romano? Alex wasn't sure.

* * *

At this same moment, elsewhere, Dr. Gregorio Moretti was leaving his house in the Florence suburbs. Before getting into his Audi, he took off his jacket and placed it on the back seat along with his medical bag. The cop in the surveillance van parked down the street nearly missed this small action. He'd been watching for several days with no results. But, somehow, he sensed the doctor's decision to take off his jacket was different and might mean something. After all, his drive to the hospital took only a few minutes, and the doctor always kept his jacket on. So, what was significant about his action today?

"Viola One to all units. The target is leaving his house. We may be in for a longer drive than usual." The other Florence police units acknowledged his transmission.

Dr. Moretti slowly pulled out onto the street but did not head toward the hospital. After only a short distance, he turned toward the autostrada. Once Moretti got onto the superhighway, he accelerated to one-sixty kilometers-per-hour as he headed south. Luckily for the cops, the other units were using two reasonably powerful motorcycles and a BMW five-series sedan, because the police van fell hopelessly behind. Not able to keep up, the driver decided to fall back and remain in radio communication with the other units.

The ride was smooth for the first twenty miles of high-speed driving, before tragedy struck. While the two motorcycle riders knew it was windy, they couldn't respond rapidly enough at that speed when a strong crosswind whipped over the autostrada. The lead motorcycle wobbled uncontrollably.

Then, he lost control, crashing onto the highway at nearly one hundred forty kilometers per hour. Violently thrown off the bike, he tumbled onto the pavement, sparks from the sliding bike flying everywhere and pieces of broken metal spinning wildly across the road. The officer came to rest in an adjacent field. Though seriously injured, his helmet, heavy leather jacket, and leather pants had saved him from instant death.

The second motorcycle cop, following behind by a quarter mile, saw the accident and pulled over on the roadside to help his fallen colleague. The police BMW sedan, with two officers inside, trailing the bikes by a half mile, raced past the scene still in pursuit of Dr. Moretti, but radioed back to the van to call an ambulance and give assistance at the accident scene. After several minutes of extreme high-speed driving, the BMW had Dr. Moretti's Audi in sight and followed him until he exited the autostrada at Montepulciano. Once the van with two cops arrived at the accident, the second cycle rider radioed the BMW for its location, and took off in pursuit. Within thirty minutes, the motorcycle also exited at Montepulciano, but needed further directions.

"Viola Four to Viola Three, where are you?"

"Viola Three to Viola Four, bypass Pienza and head west a few miles. You'll see us parked on the side of the road."

For the rider, it seemed an eternity, but he finally saw the BMW; its hood raised and one of the plainclothes cops pretending to examine the engine. The bike pulled over in front of the car.

"How is Sergio?" the cop examining the engine asked from under the hood of the BMW.

"He's in bad shape. He regained consciousness while I was there, but probably has a dislocated shoulder, maybe a broken arm and broken leg, maybe some internal injuries as well. An ambulance was on the way when I left him with the guys from the van."

They had all been a team for years and were close friends. If the decision had been theirs, they would have beaten the shit out of the doctor for driving so fast. In their minds, he had been the cause of the accident.

"Where's Moretti?" the bike rider asked.

"In the villa you just passed, but you can't see his car; it's parked behind some trees. We'll stay here. Why don't you drive back about a mile to the café? Have a coffee and watch the road. We'll call you if there is any movement."

Chapter 50

SO CLOSE

D r. Moretti greeted Renzo as he approached the outside of the villa's front door. Moretti recognized him as the young man previously tasked with buying the Warfarin. A second man was standing nearby smoking. Once inside, Moretti saw a third kidnapper lounging in the living room. He presumed the remaining three were in the upstairs bedrooms resting until their night shift.

Moretti took in the surroundings. The living room was large and comfortable-looking, over-stuffed sofas and chairs rested on hardwood floors. A dull old tapestry of a hunting scene hung on the wall over a large fireplace at one end of the room. The window drapes appeared to be made of green silk but were somewhat tattered at their edges. Nevertheless, they were probably expensive when new. The walls were a shrimp-colored plaster. To the left of the living room were stairs that disappeared as they made a right-hand turn upward, presumably leading to the bedrooms on the second floor.

"I need a drink of water before examining the Scarmattis," Moretti said.

He and Renzo walked into the kitchen, which Moretti saw was entirely modern with stainless steel appliances and cook tops. Clearly, Adrianna Esposito, owner of the villa, had put considerable money into refurbishing the kitchen which had originally been her family's home. Although there were other rooms on the ground floor, a dining room and a study, Moretti had no interest in them. He looked at the door leading down to the basement where the Scarmattis were being held.

"How are they feeling, Renzo?"

"They seem lethargic. They are not eating well. And they complain about the stink in the basement all the time."

"That is to be expected. They have been confined nearly two weeks. I'd better see them now."

As Renzo unlocked and opened the door leading into the basement, the smell assaulted their noses. Both he and Moretti put on masks and went down the stairs into a dimly lit cavern.

Ambassador Scarmatti looked up at the sound of the door being unlocked. He and Francesca held hands as much as possible with their free hands, the ones not handcuffed to poles.

"I see from your medical bag you're a doctor," the Ambassador said, his voice raspy from not having spoken in a while. "Are you the one who saw us before?"

"Yes, I am, how are you feeling today?"

In truth, the Ambassador didn't look well. He had a two-week old beard, partly graying now. Moretti wasn't sure, but wondered if some of the Ambassador's hair wasn't turning a little gray as well. Stress could do that; the doctor had no doubt it was happening.

"We're tired. Can we at least have a change of clothes, or maybe see some sunlight?"

"I am sorry. That is not my decision to make," Moretti replied.

"Bastards," Francesca spat the words out with venom.

Moretti looked at her; she was a mess. Her pants and blouse were filthy; maybe with more than dirt, Moretti guessed. Her hair was uncombed, tangled, and oily. Both she and the Ambassador smelled horrendously. The doctor knew that cleanliness would help them stay healthy and decided to talk with di Luca.

"How is your vision, Ambassador?" Moretti asked as he turned his attention back to Scarmatti. "Is your vision still graying out?"

"A little, sometimes."

"What about your sense of touch?"

"I don't know."

Moretti reached into his bag and took out a piece of paper, handing it to him.

"Please take this between your thumb and any finger."

Moretti watched. The Ambassador didn't drop it.

"Now try to hold onto it," he said, as he gently tried pulling it out of Scarmatti's grasp. Scarmatti's fingers held the paper tightly.

"That is good! It seems your previous small stroke has not caused too much harm; it is not in evidence. Have you been taking your normal dosage of Warfarin?"

"Yes, I have."

Moretti checked the Ambassador's pulse, blood pressure, and listened to his heart. Considering the circumstances, he was satisfied.

"I know it's very difficult to be confined, but even with your one hand cuffed to the pole, you both can do some sit-ups, and you can stand and do deep knee bends or stretches. Exercise is even more important for you now because of the stress you are enduring."

Tony Scarmatti thought this doctor was an interesting change from the rest of the kidnapping crew, especially the perpetually angry, enormously muscular guy. They were rough and inconsiderate, but this doctor seemed to show concern for their welfare.

Moretti turned to Francesca and took her pulse. Then he checked her blood pressure and listened to her heart.

"I understand you are not eating well. To me, you look like you have both lost weight. I don't care if you are not hungry. You need to eat to maintain your health. Tell the boys what you want to eat, but I will recommend to them you get more vegetables, and protein, maybe some fish or chicken."

Francesca grabbed Moretti's hand. "Help us get out of here, doctor. Please."

Moretti slipped his hand free from her grasp but knelt and touched her cheek. "You may be here for a while, my dear. But please believe me when I say that you will be released, eventually."

Tears rolled down Francesca's face, but she said nothing.

Moretti stood, looked around, then he and Renzo left the basement. Once upstairs Moretti said, "I meant what I said about feeding them well. They need to be encouraged to eat. Nobody wants them to get sick or die." Renzo nodded.

"I will tell the same thing to Cosimo di Luca. The next time you see me, I'll bring some more Warfarin just in case the kidnapping drags on. Also, try to get them water to bathe and some different clothes; they really do stink. It is unhealthy for them. Listen to me, we may detest the American government, but we don't treat their people like animals."

Moretti walked out of the villa, got in his car, and roared off toward Florence.

The cops in the BMW spotted Moretti leaving. First, they alerted the motorcycle rider and advised him to move closer to the house and keep it under observation. Following Moretti, the cops in the BMW called Florence police headquarters and recommended a full-blown surveillance operation on the villa.

Within an hour, Moretti was back in Florence. Two hours later a team of police surveillance specialists had arrived near the villa outside Pienza and took up positions within a discreet line of sight.

Without knowing, they were incredibly close to their prey.

Chapter 51

FBI DESPERATELY WANTS IN

At midday General Rafael Ghiberti called a meeting to examine new information on the kidnapping investigation. Seated around a small wooden conference table were four key officers of the *Polizia di Stato*: Major Carlo Vicencia, Captain Gina Bianchi, Colonel Vittore Adriani, and Lt. Guido Campanelli, Other support officers took chairs around the fringe of the room.

"Major Vicencia, I see a report that Doctor Moretti left Florence this morning and visited a villa outside of Pienza. What do you make of this?"

Vicencia was a cautious and thorough man as befitted someone graduating near the top of his law school class before joining the police. He was loath to draw conclusions not supported by evidence. Before speaking, he took off his glasses and adjusted his uniform tie.

"Let us examine what we know, and what we don't: First, we know the Ambassador needs Warfarin. Secondly, we know Doctor Moretti wrote at least one new prescription for Warfarin *after* the Ambassador was kidnapped, even though he writes prescriptions for many patients all the time.

"However, if Doctor Moretti *did* write a prescription for the Ambassador, we *don't* know whether he actually *saw* the Ambassador or knew the man was being held against his will, or even if he knew the Ambassador's true identity. Nor do we know if Doctor Moretti *willingly* wrote the prescription that the kidnappers filled. While most doctors insist on examining a patient before writing a prescription, we don't know if this was the case in the Scarmatti kidnapping.

"Furthermore, we are not completely sure whether anyone has actually *given* the Warfarin from Doctor Moretti's prescription to the Ambassador. We can only assume so."

Major Vicencia could see Ghiberti impatiently tapping his fingers on the table, ready to take over the discussion.

"*However,* because Pienza is a little over one hundred kilometers from Florence where Moretti has his practice, and because Moretti had his medical bag with him for the trip, I think the resident of the villa might be a personal friend."

"So, what do you conclude Major?" Ghiberti asked, wanting Vicencia to get to the point.

"We should seriously consider Moretti is involved in supporting the kidnapping, and continue surveillance of the villa in Pienza. It could be where the Scarmattis are being held."

Ghiberti turned to Colonel Adriani. "Do you think the Florence police units handling the surveillance are adequate for the job?"

"I have worked with them before; they are good." He looked over at Lt. Campanelli who agreed. "But they may be stretched to provide twenty-four-hour coverage of the villa near Pienza *and* Doctor Moretti in Florence. I know they are currently running operations against some major crime syndicates, as well, so I recommend we offer to cover the villa ourselves."

"Fine, I'll call the Chief of Police in Florence and make the offer," Ghiberti stated.

"What about the motorcycle officer who was injured this morning? Do we have any news of him?"

"He's in serious, but stable condition," Captain Gina Bianchi replied. "They removed his spleen this morning and set his broken arm and leg, but he may need more operations."

"Thank you, I'll express our gratitude and our condolences. I understand you have information on the owner of the Lancia we've been tracking since it was last seen at the farmhouse."

"Yes, sir," Captain Bianchi responded again. "We believe it belongs to Massimo Esposito, a businessman living in Siena. Esposito is married. They reportedly spend most weekends in the country, but we have not yet confirmed where they go. The police in Siena have Esposito under surveillance now, with two of our liaison officers helping them."

"Major Vicencia, should we inform the American Embassy about Doctor Moretti?" General Ghiberti asked.

"I think not, General. They already want to investigate the garage in Perugia because they know about it."

"More than that," Gina broke in. "The FBI wants to interrogate the mechanic, Luigi Colombo. They are like children in a candy store. Every time they see something, they want to grab it."

"Yes," Ghiberti added, "this man Reynolds from the FBI is especially impulsive. It is a wonder how law enforcement works at all in America with such people."

"I have studied their system," Major Vicencia stated. "I think it works because most criminals are caught by local and state police. The FBI is merely one of America's dozens of federal law enforcement agencies, even though one with a big role to play."

"Well, we have to work with the Embassy on the Scarmatti

kidnapping, but we don't have to tell them everything right now," Ghiberti concluded. "We will hold back the information on both Doctor Moretti and the owner of the Lancia. But we must tell the Foreign Ministry. I'll ask them to keep it close to the vest until the right moment.

* * *

Chandler and Ambassador Van Camp also wanted to speak with the Italian Foreign Minister but were told he would not be available until later that morning. The Minister had actually been putting off their meeting as long as possible, suspecting the Americans would press him on allowing the FBI to see the garage in Perugia.

Moreover, Ghiberti had briefed him on the DCM's role in encouraging the Ambassador to travel without his bodyguards. He found Chandler ignorant for such poor judgment in his position, especially concealing it from everyone since the kidnapping happened. Chandler was the last person the Foreign Minister wanted to meet with and made a mental note to speak with the American Secretary of State about Chandler as soon as possible.

Not able to put off the meeting any longer, and knowing Van Camp didn't speak Italian, the Foreign Minister finally agreed to receive the men but decided to keep the meeting short. He would avoid the use of a translator and only speak English, and he would address the main issue head on early into the confrontational meeting.

"While I understand the FBI wants to see the garage, and no doubt search the premises, I will not allow this until the *Carabinieri* and police agree. Then it can be done, but only under our control and authority. Are you clear on this?"

"Perfectly clear," Van Camp replied. "But we believe that is a mistake, not to pursue this lead aggressively."

"I'm sure you think it is a mistake, but we do not. So far, surveillance has not revealed anything of use. No one of concern has visited the garage, no likely suspects have been seen on the premises, and no additional activity of note has taken place," the Foreign Minister said in exasperation. "It would be foolish to tip our hand that we suspect anything."

"The mechanic, himself, is a likely suspect," Van Camp pressed. "Even if the Scarmattis are not there, he may know where they've been taken."

"Indeed, that is precisely why we have him under surveillance. I am sorry, but you must wait until the Carabinieri and police agree to confront him."

Chandler said little during the extremely brief meeting. Not wanting to agitate the Italians, he wanted Van Camp to feel he was being supportive but found no opening.

"Gentlemen," the Foreign Minister said, rising to conclude the meeting, "I will keep you informed of any progress in the case. Please do not hesitate to call on me again. We all have the Scaramattis' best interest at heart."

* * *

Pressing ahead on all fronts, John Reynolds and Mark Terranova were on their way to talk to General Romano of the *Carabinieri*. A few years earlier, when Romano was still a Colonel, the FBI had sent him to Quantico where he took a multi-month training course for foreign senior police officers at their National Academy. It was an investment well spent by the FBI since it resulted in Romano's complete gratitude and future cooperation.

"So, you say you have excellent relations with General Romano?"

Reynolds asked Terranova for the second time in under an hour. Terranova was looking out the window of the taxi when Reynolds spoke, trying to avoid an in-depth conversation in a public cab.

"Yes, we see each other regularly; he's very supportive of our interests," Terranova replied.

"Then why hasn't he agreed to cooperate on this latest lead?"

"He doesn't have a free hand in the matter. Think of this: if the US Attorney General told the FBI not to do something, then we'd be bound by that order. In this case, General Romano must follow the directives of the Foreign Ministry and Ministry of the Interior."

Reynolds understood completely, but such a situation never stopped the Bureau in the past from doing what it wanted to do, whether domestic surveillance programs, electronic interceptions, or unilateral operations in the counterterrorism field. The golden rule for the Bureau when it got caught doing something illegal or against directives was to just apologize, promise it wouldn't happen again, and ask for a major increase in funding and personnel to provide better oversight. It worked every time. He was frustrated to find the *Carabinieri* didn't operate in this same manner.

They arrived at *Carabinieri* headquarters and were escorted to General Romano's office.

"General, it is good to see you again, even if the circumstances are not ideal," Terranova said.

"As always, it is a pleasure to see you, Mark," Romano replied. "But let's speak in English for the benefit of Mr. Reynolds."

All three shook hands and sat in comfortable chairs around a low coffee table. One of Romano's aides brought in cups of thick, rich expresso and cookies.

"Thank you for seeing us separately from the larger group handling the kidnapping," Reynolds said. Romano nodded. "As you know, we'd like to see this garage in Perugia, perhaps even to enter it surreptitiously with your men to search both the garage and the mechanic's living quarters."

Reynolds reached over and grabbed a cookie from the tray, taking a sip from his espresso, then almost choking because it was so strong.

"I understand, Mr. Reynolds. I would like to do the same. But the Foreign Minister and the Deputy Interior Minister, have made it extremely clear we should handle this as a purely Italian operation, for now."

"Yes, but I thought this was based upon the advice of the *Carabinieri* and the police," Terranova interjected.

"Correct, Mark," Romano said. "But when the lead first arose, I agreed with General Ghiberti we should watch the garage for a short period of time. This means having Italian law enforcement agencies do the surveillance."

Reynolds tried another tack. "Doesn't it seem to you General, that the *Polizia di Stato* is getting all the credit for resolving the kidnapping? They made the raid at the farmhouse, they have the lead in tracking down the Warfarin issue, and they're sharing in the surveillance of the garage in Perugia."

Reynolds almost added that the son of a bitch Alex Boyd was also getting credit for being pro-active. Inwardly, he was seething at the thought.

"I understand how you feel, Mr. Reynolds. Believe me, my men are ready to raid the garage. Our unit, the *Gruppo di Intervento Speciale,* known-widely as GIS, is very capable. We have one section on standby at all times."

"John, the GIS is excellent," Terranova reassured Reynolds. "The group is extremely well trained. Our Hostage Rescue Team has worked with them in the past."

"Exactly my point." Reynolds continued. "As you know, General, we have five of our Hostage Rescue Team members in Rome already, plus another five FBI agents in the Legatt's office. They could complement your GIS in making the raid. I implore you to pressure the Foreign and Interior Ministries to allow us to make a joint raid. Even if we don't find the Ambassador at the garage, we could squeeze the mechanic for information."

"I appreciate your enthusiasm for making a joint operation," General Romano responded. "Maybe in a day or two we can do it. In any event, I will speak to the Foreign Minister today."

Realizing General Romano wasn't going to conduct the raid without higher approval, Reynolds and Terranova thanked him for listening, and departed, still thinking: *There must be a way.*

Chapter 52

ITALIANS MAKE A DECISION

Every country has scandals among high officials. So, when the Italian Interior Minister abruptly resigned over an unrelated, but long running financial scandal, Deputy Interior Minister Umberto Ferrara was promoted to Acting Interior Minister.

Now, in that capacity, he would be introduced by the Foreign Minister who called a meeting of the major Italian law enforcement and intelligence players to discuss progress on the kidnapping. Laura Ricci from the Prime Minister's office was invited to attend. Although the Foreign Minister had briefed her throughout the ordeal, she wanted to hear the latest details for herself.

"I believe we are coming to a critical juncture, and want to ensure we are working in unison," the Foreign Minister said. "I would like Acting Interior Minister Ferrara to start the discussion. I would also like to compliment him on his new status."

"Thank you, but since it is temporary, I can assure you, I won't let it go to my head," Ferrara said with a smile. "First, our backdoor negotiations with the New Red Brigade have not accomplished what we had hoped. The kidnappers were willing to discuss a secret agreement to free the incarcerated terrorists ahead of schedule, but they have demanded the prisoners be released within one year, not five years as we had offered. We are currently at an impasse on this vital point. As for the ransom payment, they have agreed to a substantially reduced amount, which is satisfactory to us."

"Do you think they will give in on the one-year release date?" Laura Ricci asked.

"Perhaps, given enough time, we could come to an agreement on, say, two or three years," the Foreign Minister replied. "The real question is whether we can afford the luxury of a prolonged negotiation."

Ricci nodded her head, scribbled a note, then leaned back in her chair to listen.

"Next, the surveillance of the garage in Perugia has not revealed anything further on the kidnapping." The Foreign Minister said. Then, he addressed the intelligence agency representatives.

"Do you have any further news about the telecom employee who is working inside the New Red Brigade?"

"Nothing positive," the first representative answered. "We can see what conversations he is technically monitoring at the American Embassy and at other sites, and we are intercepting his Internet usage as well. However, we believe he probably only contacts the kidnappers if he has new information to report, which he does not."

The second intelligence man spoke, "As for his physical movements, he has behaved normally. Considering his technical expertise, we feel it more likely he will make contact with the New Red Brigade through electronic communication rather than in a face-to-face meeting."

"Thank you," the Foreign Minister said.

"What about the doctor who wrote the Warfarin prescription?"

Laura Ricci asked.

The Foreign Minister saw General Ghiberti tense for a moment.

He's probably wondering if he, himself, told her about the doctor's visit to the villa outside Pienza, he thought. Then continued speaking to everyone.

"The police have him under surveillance,"

"But nothing further in that regard?" Ricci persisted.

"Nothing to report at this time."

"Moving on, General Romano and I have been visited separately by the Americans," the Foreign Minister informed the group. "The FBI is pressing very hard to look at the garage and the mechanic's apartment above it."

"As you know," General Romano interjected, "contrary to our instructions, the FBI has moved five members of their Hostage Rescue Team into Rome. Thanks to our intelligence service we spotted them at the airport upon their arrival. We believe they do not have weapons with them since they were screened on their outbound flight at the Frankfurt airport. Terranova's deputy actually brought them to *Carabinieri* headquarters and Reynolds requested these five be allowed to join our GIS unit in a raid on the garage, or to enter it surreptitiously and search it."

"You explicitly told them their shooters were not welcome," Ricci sounded indignant, and directed her comment to the Foreign Minister.

"Correct, and they have disobeyed me," he replied. "Nevertheless, they are incapable of doing anything without the *Carabinieri*. We will find a way to even the score later. For now, the question is what should be the next step with regard to the mechanic?"

"I believe it is time to raid the garage and search the mechanic's residence," General Romano stated. "We can bring the FBI along in a secondary role."

"I'd like to hear from General Ghiberti," the Foreign Minister said.

"Our joint surveillance with the *Carabinieri* has revealed nothing so far. The mechanic has conducted himself as a regular citizen, just doing his job. On the one hand, we could watch him a little longer before moving against him. It is possible the *Carabinieri's* source came forward only for the reward, but in any event, we haven't seen anything suspicious yet. Alternatively, if we are proactive and surreptitiously enter the garage and apartment, then we might find something useful."

General Romano added, "We might even find the Ambassador and his wife."

"I'll take this under consideration," the Foreign Minister said. "What do you think Umberto?" he asked his new Acting Interior Minister.

"Let's talk about this later." Ferrara said. The Foreign Minister suspected that Ferrara, who also had been briefed on the doctor's visit to the villa, wanted to discuss the ramifications of raiding one place while the second was still under surveillance.

The Foreign Minister agreed with Ferrara to talk separately, and then he looked at Ricci. "Although I think it unlikely the Ambassador will be at the garage, allowing the FBI to accompany the GIS will remove some pressure on us from the Americans. It will be a show of good faith on our part and could give us leverage in dealing with them at a later time."

After asking for any further thoughts from the assembled group, and receiving none, the Foreign Minister said he would decide about the garage in Perugia later that afternoon.

* * *

In the early evening, around six o'clock, Ghiberti received a secure call from the Foreign Minister informing him that he and Ferrara had decided to let the *Carabinieri* raid the garage the following evening, with the FBI permitted to assist them. The Foreign Minister explained further that he had received a call from the US Secretary of State requesting the raid.

"I am sure that is because Agent Reynolds told the FBI Director that we are 'dragging our feet in pursuing a vital lead.'" General Ghiberti said. "Reynolds called me with the same message."

Clearly Reynolds had asked Washington to intercede at a higher level with support for this action, and got support from Van Camp with the State Department. He really wasn't surprised by this development. It was, after all, the way of the world when big powers had interests to pursue.

At least he had twenty-four hours to decide what to do about the doctor and the villa in Pienza.

* * *

In the late afternoon, Moretti was done for the day at the hospital. He got into his car and drove south on the autostrada once again, unaware that Florence police had been watching him 24/7.

The team was expecting such a move on Moretti's part, so today all units were using souped-up sedans with big engines. At first, they rocketed south on the autostrada, but then, were surprised to notice the doctor getting in the exit lane near Sienna, not further on at Montepulciano. He took the exit and drove into the city center, parking not far from the Palazzo Pubblico and the large Il Campo open area, so beloved by tourists.

"Viola One to all units, target is now on foot, walking through Il Campo."

"Viola Two to Viola One, We see him and are following twenty meters to his left."

"Viola Three to all units, we'll take the right side of Il Campo."

The team had him boxed in and keeping their distance. They followed him across the Campo, then drew closer together when he exited on the far side.

Dr. Moretti walked down Via di Citta toward the Cathedrale di Santa Maria Assunto, until he reached a building with shops on the ground floor and apartments above. Moretti entered and took the stairs up.

"Viola One to all units, is this where I think we are? Remember the briefing? Look for the Siena surveillance team."

Although the cops from Florence didn't know the police team from Siena, they had little trouble spotting them. Once the doctor was out of sight, Viola One walked into an espresso bar across from the apartment building and ordered a coffee and pastry. He watched two women seated at a high-top table near the window, overlooking the street. In their mid-twenties, they were dressed in blue jeans and casual jackets. After a minute he was certain they were from the Siena police surveillance team since they appeared to have little interest in their coffee or talking to one another; one was constantly glancing out of the window.

"Excuse me, ladies," Viola One said after walking to their table. He further noted each woman wearing a discreet earpiece for radio communication. Viola One smiled and subtlety showed his police identification to them. They smiled back.

"Were we that obvious?" the plain-looking brunette asked as she produced her police ID.

"Not at all," Viola One replied. "But we just followed a doctor here from Florence. I think we are working on the same case because I remembered this address from our briefing. Are you watching Massimo Esposito? Am I correct in thinking Esposito owns a blue Lancia?"

"Yes, we are watching him" the second girl replied. "And what case are you working on?" She asked, cautious not to reveal too much.

"Kidnapping of an American," Viola One whispered.

"All right, what we can do for you?" she asked. "And yes, he does own a blue Lancia."

"Are there only two of you?"

"No, there are four others, but they are a few blocks away."

"We are following Doctor Moretti, a prominent physician form Florence," Viola One explained. "We also have a six-man team working him."

"We saw a man enter Esposito's building a minute ago," the brunette stated, "but we didn't know who he was,"

Just then, Moretti and Esposito emerged from the building together and headed back in the direction of the Campo. Viola One had to make a quick decision, so he said to the women,

"We can't have twelve cops tailing them in such confined spaces. I'll have my team return to our cars if you'll help with the joint surveillance."

"You have a deal," the second woman replied.

The policewoman and Viola One radioed the plan to their colleagues. The brunette remained in the espresso bar, Viola One and the other female cop followed Moretti and Esposito back into the Campo, watching them take an outdoor table to enjoy coffee in the dimming late-afternoon light.

Viola One and the female Siena cop did the same thing, but not too close to Moretti and Esposito. The Viola surveillance team members from Florence returned to their vehicles as agreed and monitored Viola One's radio transmissions, while the Siena surveillance cops spread out around the Campo.

After fifteen minutes, Moretti and Esposito stood up and shook hands. Esposito returned to his apartment and Moretti walked to a nearby pharmacy. The female cop and Viola One followed until they reached the pharmacy. He waited down the street and she entered alone behind Moretti. Ten minutes later she rejoined Viola One to say that Moretti had purchased a month's supply of Warfarin. As they were talking, Moretti passed them walking to his parked car. Viola One thanked the Siena cop for her help and parted ways.

Within ten minutes Moretti was back on the highway headed for Pienza with the Viola team in tow. Using his secure mobile, Viola One called Florence police headquarters with news of the Moretti and Esposito meeting, and that Moretti had bought Warfarin. Reaching the villa, they continued to watch.

Doctor Moretti didn't spend a long time there. The Viola team assumed he had only checked on the health of the Scarmattis and delivered the Warfarin. Afterward, he drove back to Florence.

The surprise for the Siena surveillance cops came an hour after Esposito and Moretti parted company at the café when Esposito also drove his blue Lancia to the villa.

The NOCS surveillance team, discreetly spread out some distance around the villa, observed Esposito arrive. When this was reported back to Colonel Adriani, and eventually on to General Ghiberti, they agreed.

"It would seem the doctor and Esposito have just led us to the Scarmattis," Ghiberti said.

* * *

Based upon the latest reports from Siena and the NOCS, General Ghiberti called a snap meeting at the *Questura Centrale*. He felt they were close to ending the kidnapping.

"What do we know about the link between Esposito and the villa? Why was he there at all today, even recognizing he must have brought the Scarmattis there in the first place a week ago?" Ghiberti asked.

"Let me answer that, General," Captain Gina Bianchi said. "We erred in only looking for rural property registered under the name Esposito. Within the last thirty minutes, I decided to check the property records of that specific villa against his wife's maiden name, Mazzoni. It's a match; she inherited the property from her parents. I presume Massimo Esposito was not only curious about how the kidnapping was going, but also has a vested interest in the welfare of his wife's property."

"Vittore," Ghiberti spoke to Colonel Adriani, "The time has come for your men to raid the villa. I know you've been thinking about this."

"I have, General. Our surveillance teams are suggesting the best approach for the assault. Captain Agostino did the planning and discussed it with the other squad leaders."

"Excellent, Vittore. The *Carabinieri*, with the FBI, will be raiding the garage in Perugia tomorrow night. Because we need time to set up near Pienza, I think we should do the raid tomorrow night as well."

"I agree, General, that is what we've been planning," Colonel Adriani replied. "I would like to invite Alex Boyd to come with us."

"He has proven to be a welcome asset," General Ghiberti replied. "Yes, I think we should ask him, but not until tomorrow morning. I have to call the Foreign Minister, Interior Minister Ferrara, and the *Carabinieri* to inform them about our plan. Naturally, the Ministers will have to approve it, but that won't be a problem since they have already approved the *Carabinieri* raid on the garage."

"Please wait here, all of you," Ghiberti said.

He left the small conference room and went to his office to use his secure phone line. The calls to both Ministers were easy; the Foreign Minister said he would call Laura Ricci in the Prime Minister's office late tomorrow afternoon to inform her, not wanting to give the politicians too much advance notice.

But General Romano, the head of the *Carabinieri*, was testy when Ghiberti spoke to him. Ghiberti understood; after all, he had withheld information from the *Carabinieri* about the villa in Pienza. He apologized, lied a little by saying the information only came together at the last minute, and promised to buy him a dinner at the best restaurant in Rome. He then returned to the conference room to inform everyone.

"The raid is on for tomorrow night."

Chapter 53

THE INVITATION

At 9:00 a.m. the next morning, Alex received a call from General Ghiberti asking him to come to the *Questura*. He grabbed a taxi, arriving a few minutes later.

Upon entering, he was met by the beautiful Captain Gina Bianchi who greeted him.

"Good morning, Alex. I'm to escort you to the meeting," she said while extending her hand for him to shake. Always able to appreciate a good-looking woman, he noted she was wearing heels that elevated her to about five-feet seven-inches tall and wore a dark blue business suit. He genuinely appreciated being greeted by her rather than the gnarly officer from last time.

"We have something important to tell you," she said in perfect English as they walked to the General's office. Awaiting him were Ghiberti, Colonel Adriani, and Major Vicencia. Sitting around the General's conference table, Alex noticed a large map of Tuscany along with a second map that Alex couldn't make out since it was upside down.

"Alex, we're certain we've found the location of the Ambassador and his wife," Ghiberti said, pointing to a location on one of the maps. "We'll raid the villa where we believe they are being kept in the early hours of tomorrow morning and would like you to be with us."

Alex's heart picked up its pace as he grinned.

"Of course, I'll join you. Thank you for the offer. I'm truly honored."

"Excellent. We'll pick you up at the Embassy at five o'clock this afternoon. It'll give us time to arrive at the staging area near the villa, give you further briefings, and let you settle in with the rest of your squad."

"It sounds like I'll be part of an entry team again."

"Yes, we assumed it's what you'd want," Ghiberti said. "I might add, you've earned our trust and respect."

"Absolutely, that's what I want. Thank you."

"Please bring whatever equipment you need, such as weapons, clothing, and body armor, or you can use ours like last time."

"I have one request," Alex said. "May I bring one of my deputies? It will be an invaluable opportunity for him, even if he is only allowed to observe."

Ghiberti looked over at Colonel Adriani, the NOCS Commander.

"All right," Adriani said, "but I reserve the right to assign him a noncombat role if I'm not completely comfortable with putting him in a squad." Adriani had met both Joe and George months ago but was careful not to commit at this time. Experienced, he knew some decisions were made in the field, especially if he saw Alex's deputy was not up to the task.

"Good, then I think we should brief you on how we got to this point", General Ghiberti said. "Major Vicencia has asked Captain Bianchi to give the intelligence briefing to you. Captain, you may start."

* * *

354

A while later, Alex returned to the Embassy and stopped at the DCM's office.

"Hi Liz, I need to see Chandler," he said.

"He's with the task force," she replied.

"Okay, thanks, I'll see him there."

"Alex," she said as he turned to go "I heard about the trouble Alden is in, do you think he'll be recalled to Washington?"

"You'll have to ask Assistant Secretary Watson that question, Liz; I really don't know."

He wanted to say Chandler should start looking for another line of work, but Liz was a nice person and didn't want to add to her stress. Giving a wave, he left and headed for the task force. When he walked into the meeting room, he saw the full team already in place, including Rachel, Joe Roberts, and George Cefalu. He and Rachel smiled at each other; Alex nodded to Joe and George.

"So glad you decided to join us, Mr. Boyd," Van Camp curtly stated as Alex took a seat at the table.

You are a sorry excuse for a senior officer, he thought sitting down. When the Washington boys were in town, Van Camp had been humiliated and pushed into the background. Now, in their absence, he was returning to his normal, obnoxious self, pulling rank, as if rank was synonymous with competence.

"I've just returned from General Ghiberti's office," Alex said. "They have the location where the Scarmattis are being held. It's a villa near Pienza which the *Polizia di Stato* will raid tonight."

"Old news, Boyd, we already know," Reynolds said. "The *Carabinieri* told us."

Hmm, should I say anything else, or keep quiet? He thought, *I don't want the FBI to feel invited.*

"In fact," Reynolds continued, "we don't believe the evidence is all that significant."

"And why is that?" Alex asked. The room was quiet, all eyes on the two men.

"Lots of people use Warfarin," Reynolds replied, "so this Dr. Moretti could have prescribed it for anyone. He may or may not have anything to do with the kidnapping."

"Oh, you're probably right, Reynolds," Alex answered flippantly, willing to let the FBI overlook all the connections in the case.

"Don't be a wiseass, Boyd," Chandler said. "You must have something on your mind."

Terranova joined the conversation, "Are there some facts we're not aware of?"

Alex thought for a moment, then decided to lay his cards on the table. He explained the links between Moretti, Esposito, who owned a dark-blue Lancia, the warfarin prescriptions, and the visits to the villa.

"Well, the link to Esposito is new," Terranova said, making Alex conclude he was brighter than Reynolds.

"How long have you known this?" Reynolds asked, clearly upset.

"Just this morning from Ghiberti. That's why they're making the raid tonight. What, the *Carabinieri* didn't mention it to you?"

He looked at the *Carabinieri* liaison officer, who merely shrugged.

"Well," Reynolds said, "if Moretti and Esposito know each other, then it might not be surprising for Moretti to visit his villa."

Alex waited a few moments for others in the room to judge which of them was making more sense. The room remained silent; no one wanted to join the debate.

"Don't you think it's far from coincidental Moretti would pick up a Warfarin prescription in Siena on his way to Esposito's villa? If the Warfarin was for Esposito, why not give it to him in Siena when they met?" Alex continued.

"Okay, maybe you have a point," Reynolds relented. "We can follow up with the police tomorrow. As for now, the *Carabinieri's* source has confirmed the owner of the garage in Perugia is one of the kidnap gang. So, we'll go through with the *Carabinieri* plan to raid the garage."

Alex was thrilled. He actually wished success for the *Carabinieri* and FBI to capture one of the kidnappers, he just didn't want the FBI anywhere near the police raid in Pienza.

"Uh, one more thing: General Ghiberti asked me to accompany them on the raid tonight," Alex said. "I'll call you with results, probably sometime around three in the morning."

Alex looked at Rachael, who sighed deeply, frowned, and was no doubt worried. He knew Chandler was in a dilemma since he'd pushed for the FBI to join the *Carabinieri*. He could hardly say no to Alex's participation in a parallel raid with the *Polizia di Stato*. Following a long pause, Chandler spoke.

"Don't you think it would be best to let professionals handle the raid?"

You condescending asshole, he thought. Instead, he said, "That's *exactly* what we'll be doing."

Unexpectedly, from the end of the conference table, Chuck Nelsen with the Secret Service said, "Good luck, Alex."

That was followed quickly by the Defense Attaché, Colonel Watson's comment.

"Good hunting. Can we help?"

"Thank you, but not necessary," Alex replied. "The Italians have it covered."

Alex locked eyes with Rachael across the conference table. She appeared to be holding back emotion; he could see she was taking some deep breaths. For a tough woman, he knew she had unresolved emotional insecurities to deal with and winked at her. After a short delay, she smiled back.

"All right," Chandler said, "we'll have the task force manned throughout the night. I expect both the FBI and you, Boyd, to report your results immediately."

Alex and Reynolds both agreed. On his way out of the conference room, several Embassy employees came up to shake Alex's hand and to wish him success. Mark Terranova was among them.

Chapter 54

GETTING DUCKS IN A ROW

Joe and George followed Alex to his office, enthusiastically volunteering to go on the raid as they walked beside him.

"First, I appreciate your volunteering. Frankly, I would have been disappointed if you hadn't. Since I've received permission for one of you to go, I can select one, but only one. The other has to remain in the Embassy and handle everything else, like the task force, especially if something goes wrong at the raid," Alex knew he had to choose his next words carefully.

"I have the greatest trust in you, Joe, being able to handle the Embassy." Even with sugarcoated words, Joe, his more senior deputy, looked crestfallen.

"Hear me out. One day you may have to make the same call. You have a lot more experience and rank than George. You've served in two other embassies already. If something happens to me, I have every confidence you can carry on until Diplomatic Security assigns another senior RSO here, or even lets you run the office until the end of your tour."

"But…" Joe started to say. Alex cut him off.

"I know what you're going to say. You're a former Marine officer with combat experience. I appreciate that and, believe me, I would like nothing better than to have you with me in a dangerous situation. But your leadership qualities and experience will be needed back here, regardless of how the raid goes."

Alex turned to George. "In addition to what I just said, I selected you, George, because you're expendable." Alex paused for a moment. "Sorry, just kidding." Joe laughed but George only smirked a little.

"Simply put, both you and Joe can handle the raid, but, George, your Italian language skills are better than Joe's. This will be important in a jam, and, the NOCS are concerned about operating with foreigners who have limited Italian. That's one reason they're not happy with the FBI's Hostage Rescue Team being involved in Perugia. So that's my thinking. Any thoughts?"

"I know you're right, Alex," Joe replied. "It's just hard to stay behind."

"Of course, it is, Joe. We all want to run toward the action. That's why we joined Diplomatic Security. But someone has to help with command and control."

"Command and Control, my ass," Joe smiled. "You're our general, I always thought you'd be best suited for that role."

"Thanks, but I got a personal invitation to join the party, besides, I'm better looking," Alex laughed, "So I get to go."

"Can I bring my own gear?" George asked.

"Yes, bring everything. I am. They're going to pick us up at five o'clock and take us to Pienza. I'm wearing my equipment from here. Look, we still have a few hours, so let's talk after lunch."

* * *

Fifteen minutes later Rachel came down to Alex's office. She looked composed, although concerned. Alex sat at his desk and Rachel sat on the edge, close to him. She brushed her wavy brown hair away from her face.

"Alex, I knew you'd want to go on the next raid. I understand that. It's the right thing to do and it's in your nature to take risks, both physically and professionally."

He started to say something, but she put her fingers on his lips. "I want you to understand, I accept it, but it doesn't make me any less nervous."

Alex stood and embraced her, holding her tightly against him when she stood up.

"I'll be careful, I promise," he said.

She squeezed him tightly, pushing her pelvis against his as she kissed him passionately on the lips.

"Call me the minute it's over," she implored.

"You can count on it."

"I won't say good hunting, like Colonel Watson, because I don't want you to run into anyone violent; I don't want you to be any place dangerous. Just come back safe."

"We'll be in bed together by dawn, I promise."

"We have time before you have to go," she suggested. "Let's have lunch together today, Okay?"

"Sure, I'll come to your office at one o'clock."

"That's a deal. See you then."

Alex watched her walk out of his office. He loved her now more than ever.

Maybe when this kidnapping business is done, he thought, *it will be time for us to get married in Rome.*

With ninety minutes before lunch, he wrote an immediate telegram to Diplomatic Security laying out the new information picked up from the cops and outlining what he knew about tonight's raid. He would call Director Riley after lunch, once Riley had a chance to read his telegram.

The afternoon went quickly as Alex's adrenalin kicked in with the prospect of going into battle again. He called Riley on the secure phone. Riley confirmed that immediately following the receipt of Alex's earlier telegram of yesterday regarding Chandler and Eaton's roles in covering up the Ambassador's use of the Embassy car, there had been explosive arguments in Washington concerning what to do about them. Some believed that if the Ambassador wasn't rescued or able to return to duty, the Embassy would be in a terrible state if they also had to remove Chandler as well.

"Now you know what I face all the time," Riley said as they concluded their chat. "The battle with the Black Dragon Society, behind the scenes, will probably continue until the end of time, but, at least, the Secretary will make a decision once we hear the results of your raid tonight."

"I appreciate the update, Jim. What about the White House? Do any of the staff know about Chandler's role?"

"Not yet, Alex."

"Maybe they should. Scarmatti was a major fundraiser for the President. Surely, somebody would be interested to know that Chandler's irresponsible actions caused a friend of the President to be kidnapped."

"Off the record, I'm considering doing just that. By the way, when we got back from Rome, Watson and I briefed the Secretary about Van Camp and Reynolds. I think Van Camp has just reached the end of his career, but Reynolds is probably untouchable since he doesn't work for us."

"Got it, Jim."

"All right. Great job on your reporting, Alex, and good luck tonight on the raid. I'm envious; wish I could be there."

"I know you do."

"We'll all be in the office until we hear from you this evening. Stay safe."

* * *

Alex and George spent an hour in the weapons room cleaning their SIG Sauer pistols and Uzi submachine guns, both 9mm caliber. They loaded multiple magazines for each weapon, and by 4:00 o'clock changed into assault gear: black cargo pants, black t-shirt, and a black shirt-jacket. Then they swapped dress shoes for black hiking boots. Each placed extra magazines in pockets of their load-bearing vests, worn over their heavier ballistic body armor, but did not put either on until ready for the final assault outside of Pienza. All gear would be carried in canvas holdalls along with their Uzis.

"Are we going to use our own helmets and gas masks, or borrow from the Italians?" George asked.

"I used their stuff last time and it fit fine, so I think we already have enough to carry."

On the way out of the weapons room, each grabbed a black baseball cap with the words, 'Diplomatic Security' stitched on front. They'd have to take it off to wear their helmet, but it was good PR with the Italians until then.

Passing Marine Post One as they left the weapons locker, they spotted Top Clarke who was standing next to the Marine on duty.

"C'mon, Alex, we should be going with you," he pleaded.

"Sorry, Top. You know the answer to that. If I let you come, the Marine Corps would have your ass for leaving the Embassy with weapons. Not to mention repercussions if you came back with holes in you."

"I know, but it just doesn't seem right to be sitting on my ass back here when you guys are taking all the risks and having all the fun," Clarke said.

Alex just smiled. He'd love to take Clarke with him, but the Marines and the State Department would go nuts if he did.

"Good luck, boss," Clarke said.

At the office, Nancy Williams gasped at the sight of them. "Oh my God, you both look like you're right out of a war movie."

"I'll take that as a compliment," Alex said; both men smiling.

"Even in Islamabad, Alex, I never saw you in all your equipment," Nancy said in amazement. "You look incredible."

"I guess that's because in Pakistan the terrorists took us by surprise. This time it's different."

They moved into Alex's office where he briefed George on what happened tactically at the earlier farmhouse raid in Bologna.

Then at a quarter to five, they walked down to the rear Embassy parking lot and saw a dark blue Land Rover from the *Polizia di Stato* waiting. As they approached, the driver, wearing his assault uniform, got out of the vehicle. To Alex's surprise, Captain Gina Bianchi got out of the passenger seat, wearing midnight blue cargo pants with matching shirt. On the back of it was emblazoned, "*Polizia.*" The same word was above her right breast pocket. She wore assault boots; her blond hair pulled back into a ponytail. Even dressed as one of the boys, she looked stunning. Alex introduced George to Gina, and they shook hands.

"I wasn't expecting you to accompany us, Gina," Alex said.

"I'll be there to document any intelligence we find at the villa," she smiled and turned to the driver. "Let's go," she said as he finished loading the holdalls into the SUV.

Alex turned and looked up at Rachel's office, knowing she had a window overlooking the parking lot. Sure enough, she was looking down at them, one hand covering her mouth. Alex waved to her and blew a kiss. Rachel removed her hand from her mouth, smiled, and did the same.

Gina looked up to the window. Alex looked back and forth between the two women as he saw Rachel's eyes shift from him to Gina.

"That's Rachel, my girlfriend," he said gesturing toward the window, then was surprised to see Gina salute Rachel, who smiled and waved back at her.

Alex, George, and Gina climbed into the Land Rover, and the driver turned toward Ciampino Airport to rendezvous with the rest of the team.

Chapter 55

THE PERUGIA GARAGE RAID

The ride to Bologna in the police helicopter was smooth, unlike Alex's previous trip. He watched George trying to make conversation with Capt. Gina Bianchi and found it humorous that he couldn't take his eyes off her during the flight. Too noisy to have a normal conversation, George finally accepted it was best to just enjoy the view—that being Gina, herself.

A few miles from the targeted villa, they landed at a small airport used by the Italian government. Entering a Quonset hut, Alex spied Colonel Adriani talking with several NOCS officers. Adriani broke away from the group to greet Alex and George.

"Alex, you already know my men, but let me introduce George to everyone."

George made the rounds, shaking hands and speaking Italian. One of them asked what he was carrying in the canvas holdall, so George pulled out his load-bearing vest and body armor. Then he took out the Uzi, withdrew the magazine and pulled the slide back, ensuring the weapon was empty. It was now 100 percent safe since the UZI fired from the open-bolt position, and the magazine had been removed. He handed it to one of the NOCS. Then withdrew his Sig-Sauer pistol, again removed the magazine, cleared the weapon, and handed it to another NOCS for his inspection.

'Boys with toys,' Alex thought. Adriani assessed George's actions carefully, then, after a minute, said to Alex, "I approve of George. I can see he thinks of safety and is comfortable with weapons. You have made a good choice asking him to join us."

Pleased that George passed muster, Alex turned to the task at hand: the all-important briefing on how the assault would be conducted. The next hour covered individual and squad assignments. He and George would be attached to the squad entering the front door, but unlike the last raid, he wouldn't be part of the initial entry squad. Rather, Adriani wanted them to follow his NOCS men through the door. Alex guessed Adriani was trying to protect them from injury. Perhaps, General Ghiberti said something about Alex's injury last time. He was fine with his assignment, glad to be there even in a supporting role.

After the one-hour briefing, the men lounged around, some checking weapons for a second or third time. Others smoking, some eating snacks. Gina was inspecting a digital camera and video recorder, no doubt for when the villa was secure. She and another officer had a stack of plastic evidence bags as well.

"Alex and George, come with me, please," Adriani said. They followed him into a separate room. Like Bologna, there were banks of video monitors set up around a central console. Camera feeds were coming in from Lt. Campanelli's surveillance teams, and later, when dark, Alex knew the cameras would switch to infrared. Two officers sat at a side desk listening to long-range acoustic sensors.

"We can monitor conversations on the outside of the villa, and some of the internal ones but not much," Adriani explained in

Italian. "On the board to your right are photos taken by our police aircraft; in this case, it doesn't show anything special."

After returning to the main room, Alex looked at his watch.

"Colonel, exactly when do we leave for the villa?"

"The plan is at two a.m."

"Not later?" Alex asked, knowing some SWAT teams preferred to raid when targets were more likely to be deeply asleep, or drowsy if on guard duty.

"I know, it seems early," Adrinai answered. "But the *Carabinieri* are making their raid at 1:30 a.m. So, we want to roughly coordinate our time."

"Okay, I'll nap in the corner," Alex said. He sat next to some of the NOCS who were already lying down. George couldn't think of a better idea and followed Alex's lead.

* * *

Just after 1:00 a.m., in Perugia, Bill Gordon, the FBI's senior agent with the five-man Hostage Rescue team, sat in a crowded Command and Control van along with his *Carabinieri* counterpart, Colonel Guilio Olivetti. An agreement had been reached for the Hostage Rescue Team members who had come in from Germany to be present and borrow weapons from the *Carabinieri*. John Reynolds, and Joe Terranova were also there with everyone waiting for the 1:30 a.m. time when the raid would begin.

The GIS team was already moving rapidly toward the garage in Perugia, while Colonel Olivetti was monitoring their radio conversations. Gordon and Reynolds, not understanding Italian, were relying on information being interpreted by Terranova.

"Unit one to Command Center (CC), we are approaching the garage doors."

"Unit two, also approaching from the opposite side."

"What did they say?" Gordon asked Terranova.

"Have they seen anything yet?" Reynolds asked.

"They're just approaching the target," Terranova replied blandly, trying to temper their enthusiasm.

Colonel Olivetti had put up with their unnecessary chatter for the last thirty minutes. Reynolds or Gordon continually asking what was happening every time one of his GIS teams communicated was annoying. Their constant interruptions were disruptive, and Terranova's translating was the only thing that made him allow it —for now.

The plan was simple: One unit would break through the double garage doors, while the second unit would demolish the adjacent single door that led up the stairs to the mechanic's apartment. Then, four-man GIS teams would lead the way at each entry point, followed by two or three FBI agents, then more GIS members.

All personnel were wearing typical camouflage fatigues and body armor. The GIS personnel carried Beretta submachine guns in addition to their pistols. Since Perugia had been a joint surveillance operation with the *Polizia di Stato* from the beginning, the police were deployed in plainclothes around the neighborhood and were operating strictly in surveillance roles. Once the raid started, they would block off the surrounding streets to traffic.

At last, all watches read 1:30 a.m. The raid was on.

"All right, on the count of three, hit the doors with the sledgehammers," the GIS team leader said. "One, two, THREE." Big, burly GIS officers swung the heavy hammers into the locks of both the garage doors and pedestrian door. The locks were smashed and both GIS teams rushed in.

"They've just entered the premises," Terranova explained to Gordon and Reynolds.

GIS and FBI agents fanned throughout the garage, but nothing important was there. Two cars were scattered in pieces along with tools lying everywhere. That was it.

The team that rushed upstairs to the apartment, smashed a second door at the top and spread out into each room. Within seconds they found the mechanic, Luigi Colombo, wearing only boxer shorts, sitting on the edge of his bed, dialing his mobile phone. He was violently thrown back and spun around onto his stomach. A GIS officer put him in handcuffs while another seized his mobile. They searched his bedroom and found a loaded small caliber 7.65mm handgun in his nightstand. There was nothing illegal about that, but they bagged it as evidence in case it subsequently matched a weapon used in another crime.

Once the apartment was clear of any potential threats, the FBI wanted to systematically search every inch of it. But the senior *Carabinieri* officer told them to stand down, explaining in broken English, that to preserve the chain of evidence, and be available to appear in an Italian court, the *Carabinieri* needed to be the only ones handling the evidence, not the FBI, who would fly back to America long before the mechanic was put on trial, if it came to that.

Downstairs in the garage, the *Carabinieri* were examining every cupboard, every tool chest, and inch of walls. Then, just as Colonel Olivetti, Terranova, Reynolds, and Gordon entered the garage, they found something.

"Colonel," one of the men called out. "I've found a fake panel over here."

The entire team moved closer to see. Moving a heavy workbench covering a section of the wall, he pried opened some panels to reveal a large secret walk-in closet. Aiming his flashlight, the closet was illuminated with a pale-yellow glow, revealing a small arsenal of weapons. There were several shotguns, at least three assault rifles, and on the shelves, a half-dozen pistols plus ammunition.

"I knew it," Reynolds said to Colonel Olivetti. "The mechanic is probably linked to the kidnap team."

Terranova interpreted, but Olivetti withheld comment. Both knew it was possible the mechanic was a member of the New Red Brigade, but also equally possible he was merely a small-time arms dealer providing illegal weapons to a variety of criminals. It was even plausible he had nothing to do with the kidnapping. The *Carabinieri's* source may have provided the tipoff merely to settle a grudge against the mechanic or to gain a reward.

The *Carabinieri* continued to search both the garage and apartment, but nothing further was found.

Thirty minutes later, Colonel Olivetti returned to the Command and Control van to call the Foreign Ministry task force on a secure phone and report results. The mechanic would be taken to Rome and interrogated at length.

The Foreign Ministry relayed the information to the Embassy, then called Captain Bianchi in Pienza with an update. She would wait to report this to Colonel Adriani. His own raid at the villa was about to begin.

Chapter 56

THE PIENZA RAID

As the mechanic's garage raid ended, Alex, George, and the NOCS team boarded a grey truck with ordinary commercial emblems printed on its side panels. The deceptive use of an ordinary commercial vehicle would mask their approach. Inside the back of Alex's truck were two rows of wooden benches where eight men, plus Captain Agostino, sat.

This group had the call sign Charlie One and would enter through the villa's front door. A second team, call sign David Two, would enter through the rear door leading into the kitchen. As they drove to the drop off point, Alex assumed the Italians had modified the engine or muffler because once they began moving the engine noise was minimal.

It wasn't long before the van stopped and let them out on the reverse slope of the hill from the villa, three-hundred meters away. The teams formed up and walked up to the crest of the hill. Alex felt the humidity in the air and smelled the aromas that dominate a rural area composed of farms and vineyards. Glancing at the sky, he was glad the moon was obscured by clouds since their final approach would be relatively long. He was even happier it wasn't pouring rain like the last raid.

At the top of the hill, they all dropped to the ground so no one was silhouetted against the sky. Then everyone began crawling over the crest and down the slope. Alex could see the rear of the villa in the distance, surrounded by Italian Cyprus trees. A few of the NOCS were using infrared devices to monitor the villa and surrounding area. After waiting in place for five minutes, Captain Agostino, team leader, gave the signal over the radio to proceed.

Alex, George and the rest of Charlie One crawled into the vineyard, hiding their approach to the villa. Alex's earpiece carried continual reports from the NOCS surveillance teams who had been in place for days. Though dark, he couldn't spot any location where they *were hiding.*

These guys are pretty good, he thought.

"Surveillance One to all units, the rear is clear of tangos."

"Surveillance Two to all units, we have two, repeat two tangos sitting in chairs outside the front door. Both are armed with shotguns or rifles."

Alex knew his team would be making its way around the villa and need to take out these two guys before entering the front door. Silently killing sentries in wartime wasn't a problem, but the NOCS were police, and these sentries weren't soldiers.

Wonder how they'll deal with it.

Alex estimated the distance from the crest of the hill to the villa at about two-hundred meters, with the vineyard covering more than two-thirds of that area. They continued crawling; the vineyard ground was a combination of rocks and dirt.

By the time Alex and the team reached the end of the vineyard closest to the villa, he was covered in dirt; his black pants and shirt were torn around the knees and elbows from crawling over rocks. Everyone lay on the ground, now watching and listening. No activity outside the rear of the villa, but a light shone from the kitchen and he thought he saw movement behind the curtains.

"Surveillance One to all units, one tango on infrared in the kitchen. He moves around but remains in the room," the radioman reported.

"Surveillance Two to all units, two tangos in front of the villa still sitting in chairs, awake and talking. I also have infrared images of two tangos in the living room. Cannot see if they are armed. Lights are dim in the living room and drapes are drawn."

Alex heard Captain Agostino reply with his call sign, "Alfa One, copy. Charlie One and David Two, prepare to go on my signal."

Everyone put on their gas masks. Both Alex and George pulled the bolts back on their Uzis and flipped safety switches on.

"David Two, hold until Charlie one is in front and I order you to move. Acknowledge!"

"David Two, acknowledge."

"Charlie one, are you Ready?" Agostino asked over the radio.

"Affirmative," replied a sergeant in charge of Alex's team.

"Charlie one, standby... Go! Go! Go!" Agostino commanded in a calm voice.

The NOCS in Charlie One including Alex and George, stood and jogged silently to the side of the house, then stacked against its wall as the lead man reached the front corner. He peaked around the edge wearing night vision goggles and leaned back toward the rest of the team to give hand signals. Alex felt tension throughout his body, yet controlled the fear. His pulse rate had increased and he was dripping sweat. Despite the adrenaline, his hands were rock solid, no shaking at all. He looked at George, who gave Alex a thumbs-up. Alex returned the sign.

Turning frontward, he saw two NOCS break away and head

toward the sentries around the corner. Seconds later Alex heard groans coming from their direction. Then the sergeant in front of Alex motioned for the stack to move out. He turned the corner, walking quickly toward the front door; the two sentries were lying unconscious and motionless on the ground with NOCS quickly tying their feet together and hands behind their backs with flex-cuffs. The last thing was placing duct tape across the mouths of the unconscious sentries. Over the radio he heard Alfa One tell David Two to proceed to the back door of the kitchen.

Instead of carrying the heavy sledgehammer over the long distance to the house, two NOCS moved swiftly to the front door and attached a relatively lightweight wooden explosive frame-charge against the double doors. Alex heard Alpha One tell David Two to do the same thing at the back door.

"Charlie One to Alfa One, ready."

A moment later: "David Two to Alfa One, ready." A pause, then Captain Agostino's transmission: "Stand by, Stand by... Alfa One to Charlie One and David Two, blow the doors!"

Alex's team flattened themselves against the front wall as seconds later the NOCS set off both charges. Powerful blasts shattered the peaceful night. Flames devoured the front and back doors. Smoke filled the air, as debris rained down on the circular driveway in front. Alex flipped his safety off the Uzi; his weapon was ready to kill.

May the gods of war be with us, he thought.

Chapter 57
A FIGHT FOR LIFE

The shattered front doors lay in pieces. One of the NOCS threw a flash-bang into the living room exploding with loud concussions, illuminating the room. Brilliant flashing, disorienting lights, smoke and tear gas filled the space.

Alex and George waited against the outside wall until the first four NOCS troopers entered. Then, as instructed, followed while the final two NOCS troopers in Charlie One took up defensive positions to guard the front of the villa.

Two NOCS were already subduing the suspects on the sofas. Alex paused thinking he recognized them from the train station in Florence months ago talking to the girl. As he stared, George slipped by him. A brief moment later, Alex's attention was back on the rest of the room. NOCS had spread out to search the dining room and study, but no other suspects were found.

A microsecond after the blast from Charlie One had hit the front door, David Two's explosive charges on the rear kitchen door blew it out of its frame, sending the door across the kitchen in fragments.

Then a flash-bang from David Two stunned the guard standing in front of the door leading to the basement.

The kidnapper wildly fired one pistol shot into the void where the door had been, but a burst of submachine gun fire from a NOCS trooper cut him down instantly. The six members of David Two quickly moved into the kitchen. Using radio communication to avoid any friendly fire incident with Charlie One, two members of David Two swept the maid's quarters, a utility room, and a large walk-in pantry while the other two troopers of David Two went down into the basement.

Less than thirty seconds had passed, and the ground floor was secure. The two Charlie One NOCS members who had cleared the dining room and study now proceeded up the stairs to clear the second floor. Alex and George took up positions at the base of the stairs, waiting to follow, if needed.

Advancing up the stairs, the NOCS had to make a sharp right turn and Alex and George lost sight of them at that point. Five seconds passed. They heard a burst of submachine gun fire coming from above, followed by a second burst from a different weapon. There was another exchange of fire. As Alex started to move up the stairs to lend support, the two NOCS troopers came tumbling down, crashing into him and sending him flying back onto the hardwood floor.

"Grenade! Yelled one, just as Alex saw it bounce onto the landing where the stairs made the right turn. Still lying on the floor, Alex reached up and dragged the nearest NOCS further down the stairs.

The grenade exploded with a massively loud thunderclap. Alex lay on the floor, ears ringing, but otherwise unharmed. He turned to George, who initially had taken refuge around the corner. George was talking to him, but he could barely make out any words. The two NOCS who had been closer to the grenade, were on the floor; neither bleeding, but trying slowly to stand up, with marginal success.

Alex figured the grenade was a concussion type, rather than shrapnel; otherwise the injuries would have been horrendous. Getting to his feet, he helped the two NOCS troopers move away from the stairs, propping their backs against a wall so they faced the living room. He made another quick exam of the troopers while George covered the stairs with his Uzi. Alex found no external injuries and both NOCS seemed to be coming around. His own hearing was starting to return because he heard George say:

"I'm going upstairs."

"I'm with you, George," Alex yelled. George led the way. Getting to the top step, he kneeled and poked his head around the corner for a fraction of a second before pulling back.

"I just see a dead guy that the NOCS greased lying on the floor at the end of the hall. There's a submachine gun next to him and a long corridor with doors on both sides; probably leading to the bedrooms."

As he took a second look, a loud burst of gunfire came from the end of the hall. George was low enough that bullets hit the wall over his head, sending plaster down on them. They lay flat on the stairs. George inched forward to the top again, pushed the barrel of his Uzi around the corner and let loose with a five-round burst, then a second three-round burst, but this time he looked where he was shooting.

"I got him. He's down at the end of the hall."

"Let's clear the floor," Alex ordered.

George nodded and slowly they stood up together. Alex saw two dead kidnappers lying on the floor at the far end, just as two men stepped out from bedrooms on opposite sides, fifteen meters away. Both Alex and George opened up with their Uzis, as both of the men did the same thing with pistols.

Alex shot one assailant with a five-round burst. He staggered backwards, crashing through a window and dropped with half his body now hanging outside. The second target, engaged by George, had dropped to the floor and looked dead, blood oozing from chest wounds. Alex glanced at George, then realized he was slumped on the floor, unconscious.

He noticed a bullet sticking out of George's Kevlar helmet, dead center in the front. Still checking him, a NOCS officers came up the stairs and called out.

"Alex, are you okay?"

"Yes, I need you to clear some bedrooms," Alex yelled back.

Two NOCS moved past Alex. Gently, Alex removed George's helmet and gas mask, and saw his head was fine. The helmet had saved his life. He simply had been knocked clean out from the impact of the bullet, probably sustained a mild concussion. Alex placed the helmet under George's head for support as he started to regain consciousness. Alex then took off his own helmet and mask.

"What happened?" George asked groggily.

"Your helmet stopped a bullet. You'll be fine, but you're going to have a monster of a headache. Don't try to get up; I've got some more rooms to clear."

Alex stood, saw the two NOCS were checking bedrooms at the far end of the corridor, by the dead kidnappers, and chose a closer bedroom to clear.

Slowly opening the first door, Alex stood to the side minimizing himself as a target. Light from the hallway assisted his vision to see anybody inside. He could just make out a bed with ornate headboard, two nightstands, antique lamps with fringed shades, and a large armoire. He entered, cleared the room, then went across the corridor to another bedroom.

Pushing open the door, he saw the same bedroom setup, but as he stepped through the door, it was violently smashed against him. Alex stumbled to the side. In a second, a giant man was upon him.

He ripped the Uzi out of Alex's hands, throwing it on the floor. Alex judged that this man was about six-and-a-half-feet tall and maybe two-hundred-seventy pounds. Even worse, the guy, wearing only boxer shorts, was solid muscle with a massive upper body.

The giant lunged at Alex's gut with a long, thick serrated knife. Alex nimbly stepped back into the room, momentarily out of reach. But there was no more room to back up. The man lunged again, thrusting the knife at Alex's chest; Alex turned sideways and grabbed his wrist, violently twisting it inward toward the giant. The man screamed; the knife fell to the floor.

Smashing him with a left hook to his jaw, Alex realized it had almost no effect. He followed with a solid right fist into the man's solar plexus, but only heard a muted grunt. The he broke the giant's nose with a solid strike upward with the palm heel of his left hand. But, seeming unfazed, the man grabbed Alex in a front choke hold.

Both of his massive hands were squeezing Alex's larynx. Alex tried bringing both his own hands down hard on his opponent's wrists to break the hold, but the man was enormously powerful, stronger than anyone he had ever faced. The technique didn't work. Now the pressure and pain on Alex's throat was excruciating. He tried grabbing his pistol, but it was strapped too low on his right leg; he couldn't reach it. Now, lifted up and dangling in the air, Alex used his right leg to kick the guy in the balls; he kicked him once, twice, and finally on the third kick, the giant let him go and bent over to hold his nuts.

Alex staggered back, coughing, desperately trying to catch his breath, but had no time to wait. He gave the muscular giant a powerful side-kick to his right knee and the man collapsed on the floor. As Alex drew his own pistol, two NOCS troopers came through the door. With great difficulty, and after repeated blows to the giant's back and head, they wrestled the man face down onto the floor, and wrenched his arms behind his back, putting flex-cuffs on his wrists.

Alex picked up his Uzi and sat on the bed to breathe for a few seconds. One of the NOCS from downstairs yelled his name. He wearily got up and went out to the hallway, helped George get to his feet, and they both stumbled down the stairs.

Chapter 58

TO THE RESCUE

Stepping past a dead kidnapper sprawled on the kitchen floor with multiple gunshots to his chest, Alex was certain it was the guy on the video tape who tried to buy Warfarin at one of the pharmacies.

"Alex! We found the Ambassador and his wife in the basement!"

Moving swiftly downstairs to the basement, he found the NOCS had already unlocked the Scarmattis' handcuffs and were sitting them up on the mattresses, backs against the wall.

Seeing Alex, Francesca began to cry, hiding her face.

"Francesca, are you okay?" Alex asked as he knelt down on one knee, concern showing deeply on his face.

"Exhausted, weak, dirty, but thank God, you're here," she cried. "I'm so sorry for how I smell," she cried.

You're alive! You and Tony are safe," Alex said. "That's all that matters."

Tony Scarmatti was slumped against the wall. He managed a weak smile at Alex, but didn't seem fully alert, and had nothing to say. Francesca noticed Alex staring at her husband.

"I think he's had another small stroke."

"Another stroke? You mean he's had one since you were kidnapped?"

All she could do was nod, tears running down her face. Alex bent down on one knee again and placed his hand on Tony's shoulder.

"You're going home now, Tony. The nightmare is over."

The Ambassador nodded, as if to say 'yes', but didn't speak. Alex took deep breaths of his own while watching the older man try to understand he was being rescued. Francesca wanted to try standing and Alex helped her up. She wobbled a bit but wanted to hug him and George. Alex held onto her to keep her from collapsing.

"We've called in the medical helicopter for the Ambassador, Alex," Captain Agostino said, joining the group.

Within minutes paramedics appeared carrying a stretcher down the stairs. They quickly started an IV and hooked the Ambassador up to fluids. Then, hoisted him on top of the stretcher and carried him up the stairs. Another group of paramedics attended to Francesca, who wasn't strong enough to walk or even stand any longer. She was carried out of the basement on a second stretcher.

"Can we go with them?" Alex asked Agostino.

"Sorry, no room in the chopper. But you can use another one and follow behind. If you're ready, let's go."

Leaving the farmhouse, they passed Captain Bianchi and her team of intelligence officers coming in to collect evidence. Alex and Gina smiled in passing. George beamed as they passed while he headed toward a Land Rover waiting in front.

Captain Agostino gave instructions and the driver quickly took them to the landing zone. The medical helicopter with the Scarmattis had already taken off; Alex and George boarded the second chopper. Alex turned to Agostino, who was staying behind.

"Which hospital are the Scarmattis being taken to?"

"Policlinico Umberto Primo, in Rome," Agostino yelled against the noise of the rotors.

Before lifting off, Alex called the task force and passed on the news of the successful raid, telling them where the Scarmattis were being taken. He spoke to Rachel briefly, then to Joe Roberts.

"Joe, call the DS Command Center and let them know what happened. Then ask to be patched through to Director Riley personally. He'll be expecting the call. Tell him I'll call him later from the hospital."

Then with engines at full throttle, the pilot lifted off for Rome.

* * *

The ambulance with the Scarmattis was well on its way to the hospital when Alex and George landed at Ciampino airport in Rome. Captain Agostino had arranged for a police vehicle and escort officer to speed Alex and George directly to the hospital. They stored their Uzis, load-bearing vests, and body armor into the trunk of the police car but kept their pistols as a precaution against any more trouble.

Driving in from the airport, the escort officer, a police lieutenant, told Alex and George about the Policlinic Umberto Primo being the largest public hospital in Italy and the teaching hospital for Sapienza University. Furthermore, it had an excellent stroke unit which could also treat other neurological problems. Alex had never been to the Policlinic but recognized the area as being near the Termini train station. He and Rachel had departed from there, once, on the way to Florence.

At the hospital, the driver stayed with the car, and the escort officer walked with them into the emergency room. Following a brief chat with the admitting staff, Alex and George followed the escort officer down the corridor and around the corner where Alex saw Rachel, Ames Burnham, and Betty Fisher, the Embassy nurse, sitting on a bench in the hallway.

Rachel spotted him and immediately ran into his arms. She cried as they held a long embrace. Wiping her eyes, she stepped back and inspected him for damage.

"I don't see any bullet holes this time," Rachel smiled, still concerned.

"Nope, they never laid a glove on me." He gave her another long kiss.

"Where are Tony and Francesca?" Alex asked.

"The doctors are examining them in another room," Rachel said, "but, I'm worried. Tony wasn't fully conscious, and he didn't look alert. I think something is wrong."

"I know. He looked awful before he was put into the helicopter. Francesca said he'd had a stroke, maybe more than one during the ordeal."

"How are you and George?' Ames and Betty said as they joined them.

"We're fine," Alex replied

Betty looked at George's forehead, now sporting a large purple bruise.

"Oh my God, what happened? Let me take a look." She touched his forehead and George flinched.

"What happened?"

"I got shot in the head."

"What?" Betty yelled loudly.

"Don't worry," Alex told her. "The bullet passed right through his skull, but nothing's there, so no damage."

Ames and Rachel laughed, but Betty didn't think it was funny, even though George was smiling.

"Come with me, George," Betty ordered.

She led him down the corridor to a doctor's station. Alex was bushed, so he sat down with Rachel and Ames, resting his head against the wall. He tried closing his eyes. Adrenalin levels, spiked during the raid, were now crashing and he needed sleep.

As they continued asking questions, he could barely stay awake. Eventually, they left him alone. An hour later George returned with Betty pushing him in a wheelchair.

"He'll be fine," Betty said. "But because of the blunt force trauma, they want him to spend twenty-four hours in the hospital under observation after they do a CAT scan to see if there's any internal bleeding. Just precautionary, but necessary."

"Screw that," George said, "they obviously don't appreciate I'm a New Yorker and tougher than they think."

"George," Alex said as he yawned, "I'm sure they'll know you're a New Yorker in no time. Just follow the doctor's orders. Besides, you're single and I heard the Italian nurses are really hot-looking here."

George paused. "Yeah, really? Maybe I will spend the day here."

A tall doctor in his mid-forties walked toward them and everyone stopped to listen.

"The admitting desk told me you're with the American Embassy. Correct?" he asked. "Do you all speak Italian?"

"Yes, we all speak Italian, Doctor," Betty answered in Italian, "but maybe we all don't understand enough 'medical' Italian."

"All right then," he said, switching into English. "We've just taken ultrasounds and a CAT scan of Ambassador Scarmatti's brain and carotid artery. We'll do an MRI exam later. Of course, we did the usual lab work on both he and his wife.

"The Ambassador had a small stroke, maybe two strokes. But we believe both were minor. This occurs more often than you might think in the general population. I understand from his wife that he's on Warfarin and didn't get enough of it in captivity. We are thinning his blood now with medication. We won't sedate him because I don't want him unconscious. In any case, hopefully that won't be needed. But I want him to rest for a few hours, then, we'll evaluate him again."

"Doctor, he appeared unable to speak when he was rescued," Alex said.

"I'm not surprised. Once we stabilized him and began giving him fluids, his speech was slow, but he was already beginning to make sense. Again, I believe his stroke or strokes were mild. The IV we have him on, plus the medications, should help him a lot. But we'll know more in a few hours. Had he remained in captivity much longer, I wouldn't be so optimistic about his recovery."

"How long will he be resting?" Rachel asked.

"Until noon, at least." Alex looked at his watch, another six hours from now.

"What about his wife? How is she doing?

"She is stressed, undernourished, and exhausted, but otherwise all right. She's resting and we're also giving her IV fluids for hydration."

"Will we be able to see them at noon?" Ames Burnham asked.

"I believe so," the doctor replied. "We're moving them to a private room upstairs. There is a waiting area next to that room. Do you wish to go there?"

"Yes, thank you" Alex replied.

"Come with me. I have to make sure everything has been setup."

The group followed the doctor into the elevator, and they rode up a few floors. Upon exiting, Alex saw two armed policemen with submachine guns guarding the foyer. Since both he and George were still dressed in their filthy black ninja attire, and had pistols strapped to their legs, the cops reacted by pointing their weapons at the group. The doctor interceded, explaining the situation.

For a brief moment, it appeared the cops might not let them pass, but then Alex saw Captain Paolo Capelli walking down the corridor toward them. Now dressed in civilian clothes with his arm in a sling, he was the NOCS officer who'd been wounded in the first raid at the farmhouse. He greeted Alex warmly with a one-armed embrace.

"Alex, how are you? I see you're still playing in the dirt." He turned to face George. "George, this time you also got to play. But what happened to your head? It's purple."

"I caught a bullet," he said with a smile.

"Actually, I heard that from Colonel Adriani," Capelli replied. "But as I recall, you're a New Yorker, so I have to ask: did the bullet survive the impact?"

Everyone laughed. Even the doctor smiled, no doubt understanding the humor from a memorable experience treating New Yorkers as an intern at New York-Presbyterian Hospital.

Then Capelli spoke to the cops and told them Alex and George had participated in the raid that freed the Ambassador. Furthermore, they were granted free access to the floor. With that, the cops lowered their weapons and the doctor led the way into the waiting room.

"The Scarmattis are just across the hall." He pointed to the first room on the left. There were two more heavily armed cops standing on either side of the doorway.

"Alex, George, if you don't mind," Captain Capelli said, "I think it best to put your guns over here." He pointed to a desk that had been set up in the waiting room. "I will be here until two o'clock this afternoon, then another NOCS officer will replace me. I don't want some police officer to accidentally confuse you with the New Red Brigade."

Although Alex would have preferred to keep his pistol, Capelli's logic made sense. They surrendered their weapons.

Rachel walked over to the Scarmatti's door and looked through the glass window. They were peacefully lying on adjoining beds; each had IV lines running into their arms and oxygen masks on their faces. Their chests were wired up to a machine as well. It looked like any hospital room in the States, monitors beeping, machines measuring their pulse and blood pressure, and God knows what else. When she turned backed to face Alex, he saw there were tears in her eyes. Alex met her halfway back to the waiting room and hugged her tightly.

"If you need anything," The doctor said, "you can speak to the nurses or doctors at the central monitoring station." He pointed to the area that appeared identical to those back home. "Although, I suggest you can rest more comfortably at your apartments and return at noon."

Alex looked at the others in the group, but the answer was easy to guess.

"No thank you, doctor. We'll wait here." They settled into the sofas and chairs.

Chapter 59

NEW ARRESTS

Alex called the DS Command Center in Washington on his mobile, giving them an update on the raid and the Ambassador's condition.

After Riley heard a blow-by-blow account of the raid, he told Alex that following his earlier report from the helicopter landing zone, he had briefed the Secretary of State, who briefed the President. Both were relieved the Ambassador had been rescued.

"In the future, they want to hear your first person account of the rescue, but for now they're just concerned with the Ambassador's medical condition," Riley said. Alex suggested the Director of Medical Services at the State Department speak with the Italian doctor directly for a more informed status report. Riley said he'd arrange it.

As a final thought, Alex asked, "Has the Secretary decided what to do with Chandler?"

"I think he wants to remove him from post, but it depends on whether Scarmatti is well enough to stay on the job. As you know, Scarmatti's predecessor became ill and left early. So, having continuity is important." Alex thanked him as they ended the call.

Leaning back in his chair, he tried to close his eyes, but Rachel wanted to talk.

"You never mentioned you were shot at, or that you killed someone."

He opened one eye and looked at her. She seemed more than concerned, more like *'royally pissed-off'* and realized she'd listened to his conversation with Riley.

"Well, yes, Honeybunch. But he only fired a few shots at me. *And, he missed!*" ending on an upbeat note, he smiled.

She stared at him five full seconds, then slowly smiled and shook her head.

"Please just tell me next time when something dangerous happens to you. I can handle it now. Is there anything else I should know?"

"Yeah, you heard me tell Riley that I subdued another guy in one of the bedrooms?"

"I did, what about it?"

"Well, he was an enormous, muscular bodybuilder-type with gigantic hands, who was only wearing underpants; he almost choked me out. I had to kick him in the nuts three times to get free."

She started laughing and even snorted once or twice.

"What bullshit! Don't tell me anything more. You and your fantasy fights."

She laughed and snorted again, squeezing his arm. He smiled back.

Alex must have dozed for two hours when voices in the waiting room woke him up. Slowly, he opened his eyes and saw Alden Chandler talking with Ames Burnham. Carter Ambrose and Ambassador Van Camp were standing with them.

Not giving a shit about Chandler and Van Camp, Alex just stayed where he was and listened. Burnham was giving them a report on the Scarmattis' conditions. When Burnham was done, Chandler and Van Camp departed. Carter walked over to talk.

"I gather you had a busy night," Carter said, sitting down next to Alex.

"Everyone has to have a bit of fun sometimes," Alex replied with a deadpan expression, his arms crossed in a relaxed pose.

"Joe Roberts told me you were in a shootout."

"Yep."

"That's it, yep? Is this your Clint Eastwood impression?"

"Nope. Actually, I'm just tired."

"Let me buy you some coffee in the hospital cafeteria. I'm not being generous, just need to know what happened at the villa."

"Okay, why didn't you say so? It's my pleasure." He turned to George.

"Come join us, Carter's buying us coffee. Rachel, do you want some free coffee?

"No thanks, I'll wait here with Betty."

Alex spent the next hour in a secluded corner of the cafeteria while he and George brought Carter up to speed.

"By the way, remember the mole, the Italian phone company employee?" Carter said, "I received a report about him being surveilled physically and electronically. Pretty clever guy. But they finally picked him up early this morning for his part in monitoring nonsecure Embassy calls. He may be a little fish but could possibly tell us more in the future."

When they finally finished and Carter was about to leave, he said to Alex,

"Oh, I got a call from your Dad. You know we worked together in the Agency. We still see each other when he visits Italy with your Mom. He heard about the rescue on the news and wants you to call him.

* * *

Back in the waiting room, Alex dialed his father's phone number in Virginia.

"Hey Dad, its Alex. How are you? Carter said you tried to call me."

"Yeah, the national news is full of stories about the Ambassador and his wife being rescued by the cops. I assume you're on top of this."

"Very on top, actually part of it," Alex replied.

"You were? I didn't know."

"Dad! You mean Carter didn't tell you when you spoke to him?"

"Okay, well, maybe he did say something."

"Yeah, that's more like it. Anyway, our raid went well."

"Your raid? You planned it?"

"Actually, got invited to go along."

Rachel was listening and admired Alex's modesty, but felt his father should be aware of his bravery.

"Alex, can I have the phone, please." He handed it over.

"Hi Jack, its Rachel. Let me tell you what Alex did last night." She told him most of the story but after five minutes, Alex got back on the line and finished the call, promising to speak again soon.

"Rachel, you forgot to tell him about me kicking the big guy in the nuts,"

"I didn't forget," She laughed. "I just thought that story was as ridiculous as that other one you told me about stabbing a guy in the leg with your fountain pen."

"Geez, nothing gets by you, Honey Bunch," Alex smiled. He looked at his watch. It was only ten o'clock in the morning and would be another two hours before they could see the Ambassador.

Rachel knew it was going to be an extraordinarily busy press day for her, so decided to go home, take a shower, fix her hair, and freshen her makeup. Alex, George, and Ames Burnham stayed at the hospital with Betty Fisher, who appeared delighted to be talking with the other nurses and doctors about the Italian medical system.

An hour later, Joe Roberts joined them and gave Alex the scoop on the FBI's raid in Perugia. Apparently the *Carabinieri* weren't certain if the mechanic was a member of the New Red Brigade, but speculated he had sold them some weapons just to make a few bucks.

* * *

Meanwhile, at Cosimo di Luca's apartment in the south of Rome, he hadn't slept since receiving a phone call from one of his New Red Brigade followers at three in the morning. The man had been expected to arrive at the villa in Pienza at half-past-two for his shift watching the Scarmattis but had been stopped by cops on the road.

Not being able to extricate himself from the roadblock for another thirty minutes, he spun a story of having attended a bachelor party in town. He called because he wanted di Luca to know he wasn't at the villa.

Di Luca then called his men at the villa to warn them but couldn't get through since the phone lines to the villa were already under police control and the kidnapper's mobiles seized. Figuring something had gone totally wrong with his operation, he called all his other associates, including Dr. Moretti and Massimo Esposito, to caution them to look for surveillance. But above all, to deny anything if questioned.

Once the early morning television news channels were up and running, Cosimo remained glued to the TV set. Distraught, he found it was unbelievably true. His entire operation was an abject failure.

By seven o'clock, his wife, Antonietta, and their children, had woken up and were listening to the news with him. She was unaware of her husband's role in the kidnapping.

"What a fascinating story," she said, fixing two cups of cappuccino in the kitchen for them and breakfast for the kids.

"Yes, it is," Cosimo replied, sounding and feeling like a zombie.

"Don't you think you should find out which hospital the American Ambassador has been taken to, perhaps try to interview some of the doctors or staff?"

"Maybe, Antonietta, but I'm not feeling very well today."

Cosimo realized the police had somehow gotten into his inner circle. Mistakes had been made. His success in kidnapping the Ambassador would become legend, but the New Red Brigade would merely be a footnote in history, not a force to be reckoned with.

By eight o'clock, the rescue news stories were becoming repetitive. Antonietta received a call from a colleague at Sapienza University to say the university staff at the policlinic next door reported the police and paparazzi were present in force because the Ambassador was there. When Antonietta told Cosimo, she was surprised he showed little interest.

At nine o'clock, she left to teach two classes at the university, while Cosimo moped around the apartment, uncertain what to do. He paced back and forth, endlessly smoking, trying to imagine how it had all gone wrong, and what would happen to him now.

Shortly before noon a squad from the *Polizia di Stato* broke through his front door and arrested him. He offered no resistance. Cosimo was glad Antonietta wasn't there to witness his humiliation.

Chapter 60

AFTERMATH

Just before noon, Rachel returned to the hospital looking radiant. Alex thought she was stunning: brown, wavy hair flowing loosely; makeup, minimally applied, accentuating her natural beauty. Even her scars from Islamabad, added to her a look of character. She was dressed in a dark blue pin-stripe pants suit with pale blue blouse. In patent leather heels, she was taller than everyone else except Alex, Carter Ambrose, and the Ambassador's doctor.

"There's a huge media circus waiting downstairs," she said. "I guess we'll need to decide if we should release a statement in the lobby."

"You won't have a choice because the hospital will certainly say something," Alex said. She nodded. Once Rachel located the chief doctor, he confirmed the hospital had already discussed how to handle a press conference. They agreed on a joint statement in front of the large gathering of press in the lobby.

"I have good news for you," the doctor said. "The Scarmattis have awoken ahead of schedule about forty-five minutes ago. We've examined them both. The Ambassador seems to be doing extremely well, even speaking normally. I told him we'll keep him in the hospital a few days to run tests and for observation to which he's agreed. Mrs. Scarmatti is, also, doing well and will stay. The Ambassador has asked for a phone to call the Secretary of State."

"You're joking, Burnham replied. "I didn't even know he had the number."

"The mind works in unexplained ways when you've had a stroke," the doctor explained. "Sometimes recent information is forgotten, while older information can be recalled," he shrugged. "In any event, you can see that a nurse is watching through the window at his doorway. She'll signal when he's off the phone. Then he wants to see all of you. I would prefer you keep your visit brief." The doctor left, and the group talked another ten minutes.

Finally, the nurse signaled them to enter the room. Even though Alex had seen them at the villa, he was struck by how frail the Scaramttis looked. Rachel rushed over to Francesca's bed and embraced her. Despite tubes and wires attached to the Ambassador's arms and chest, he extended his arms and shook everyone's hand in turn.

"I just spoke with the Secretary. He's told me what's been happening since our kidnapping; Riley and Watson gave him a full briefing. Alex, I'm deeply sorry for the trouble my stupidity caused. I should have listened to you from the beginning.

"Thank you, Tony," Alex said, not wanting the Ambassador to use too much energy.

"The Secretary also told me about the two raids to rescue me, and what you and George did. I wasn't aware of the first attempt. But the noise from the second one, I will always remember. Alex, George, thank you, I mean it. Later, I'll thank the police personally. I understand they had men injured in the raids. Until I can meet them, Alex, please express my sincere gratitude."

The hospital phone next to the Ambassador's bed rang. George being closest, picked it up. Alex saw his eyes grow wide and his jaw drop open. Then he handed the phone to the Ambassador.

"Sir, the President is on the line for you."

"Let's step outside," Burnham said to the group.

"No, I'd like you to stay," the Ambassador said. After ten seconds listening, Scarmatti said, "Yes, Mr. President. I'm feeling fine; just a little tired."

The group could only hear Scarmatti's side of the conversation.

"Yes, Francesca is also doing well, Mr. President. Thank you, I appreciate your concern. The doctors want to keep me here a few days to run more tests, but they think I'll be released with a clean bill of health. I have every confidence in the Italian doctors. The head of the neurology department even studied at Columbia University. Imagine that!"

Everyone smiled.

"That's truly kind of you. I would like to stay in Italy if that's your wish. Then it's a deal, Mr. President. Yes. Uh, huh, I'll pass that on, thank you. No, that won't be necessary. I completely trust the Diplomatic Security Service. In fact, my team here is the best."

Rachel squeezed Alex's hand. Carter patted George on the back and Ames smiled at both Alex and George. Alex only wished Joe, Nancy, and Sam could have been in the room to share this moment.

"And the same to you, Mr. President. Thank you for calling," he hung up and grinned.

"So, Tony, I assume we're staying?" Francesca asked.

"The President said if I can handle it medically, and get cleared by the doctors, then the job is still mine," he replied.

"I think we should let you rest now," Rachel said. "The press is outside and will want a statement. Can I say you intend to remain in Italy, that you're feeling tired, but otherwise fine, and you trust the Italian medical staff completely? Also, I'll express your gratitude to the Italian authorities for rescuing you. Naturally, I'll ask the doctor if he wants to do a joint press statement."

"That will be perfect, Rachel," Ambassador Scarmatti replied. "I couldn't do this job without you. By the way, the Secretary said he's been impressed with how you've handled press coverage during this crisis."

"Thank you very much, Tony" Rachel said, slightly blushing. Alex squeezed her arm and whispered: I love you.

"Oh, one last thing, Ames, I want to you be my new DCM."

"You mean until you return to full duties and Alden is no longer acting in your place," Burnham replied, believing he was clarifying the point.

"No, I mean immediately and until the end of your tour. The Secretary said they'll approve your new position later this week. In all honesty, I could have forgiven Alden for giving me bad advice about dropping police protection on weekends. But then afterwards, to withhold information from Alex that could have been used to find us sooner was unconscionable. I'll tell him, myself that he's through; he's being recalled to Washington. I only wish I had said something to him as soon as I realized how hostile he was towards you, Alex. I'm sorry."

Rachel crushed Alex's hand even tighter. His smile showed satisfaction.

"Ames, you've done a splendid job with your political reporting, your analysis of events, and what's at stake in Italy for America. Your contacts are first class. That's why I want you to be my DCM."

Carter and Rachel both offered congratulations, while Alex reached over and shook Ames' hand.

"One last item I want to mention," Scarmatti said. "It pains me to say, but Washington agrees with me that Charlotte Eaton also needs to be transferred back to D.C. Her complicity in the vehicle cover-up outweighs her considerable value and skills as the Management Counselor.

"Alex and Carter, the President said that if there's anything you need to help the Italians crush the New Red Brigade, just ask Washington. Money, programs, and equipment are yours for the asking."

"I think the RSO office could use a Ferrari, just in case we need to respond quickly somewhere, don't you?" Alex couldn't resist saying.

Everyone laughed, and began preparing to leave the room,

Just then, the Foreign Minister arrived to see the Ambassador. He wanted to join their press conference, but first asked to speak with Ambassador Scarmatti.

Alex and George talked with Captain Capelli, retrieved their pistols, and waited to go to the lobby with the group. Capelli said he would accompany them, then show them to the police car to retrieve their equipment from the raid. The car would take them directly to the Embassy.

As everyone was waiting for the Foreign Minister to leave the Ambassador's room, DCM Alden Chandler, and Van Camp stepped out of the elevator.

"How's the Ambassador?" Chandler asked Burnham.

"Doing remarkably well."

"He can't wait to see you," Alex said with a smile. Rachel and Alex exchanged glances. He knew she was thinking he was going to be a wiseass again. Chandler looked a little nervous, but Van Camp couldn't resist butting in.

"So, it all worked out in the end, thanks to cooperation between the FBI and the State Department."

Carter Ambrose, usually more diplomatic than even the State Department diplomats, moved inches close to Van Camp's face.

"Van Camp, I've listened to your crap for almost two weeks now. You're a total moron."

Since Ambrose was half a head taller and probably eighty pounds heavier than Van Camp, the latter stepped back and seemed to shrink even smaller.

"I've been thinking, Alex," Chandler said, "Perhaps we could put you in for some type of award for your efforts to get the Ambassador back."

Alex looked at Rachel, who was shaking her head and mouthing the word "no." He turned to Chandler and smiled, then paused for effect.

"First Alden, you can call me Mr. Boyd; and second, go fuck yourself."

"Who do you think you..." Chandler started to say, but Carter and Rachel stepped between them.

"I would advise against saying anything further," Rachel cautioned. Alex saw a twinkle in her eye, the one he'd seen just prior to her using martial arts skills attacking someone's private parts. Chandler looked confused, but shut up, as the Foreign Minister emerged from the Scarmattis' room.

"Will you join us in the lobby for the Press Conference?" the doctor asked.

"I would be delighted," the Foreign Minister said.

Chandler started to say something to the Foreign Minister but was totally ignored as the dignitary walked passed without looking at him and headed for the elevator.

With nothing more to say, Chandler and Van Camp went in to see the Ambassador, while the rest of the group took the elevator down to the lobby.

In front of the crowd of reporters, Carter Ambrose excused himself, not wanting the limelight. Alex, George, and Captain Capelli stayed well off to the side of the lobby, as Rachel, the Foreign Minister, the doctor, and Ames Burnham stood before the press at a makeshift podium with several microphones. Handheld cameras were snapping away, temporary strobe lights illuminated the podium, and television cameras recorded the entire show.

Rachel handled all questions directed at her, answering fluently with self-assurance in Italian. After twenty minutes, the press conference came to an end and the powerful lights were dimmed. Most of the press left the hospital. Everyone from the Embassy thanked the doctor for taking such excellent care of the Scarmattis. The Foreign Minister, after shaking Alex's and George's hands, left with his aides. Alex turned to Captain Capelli.

"I guess we can go now."

Burnham had his own car, so he bid them *ciao,* and returned to the Embassy separately. Alex and Rachel held hands and walked outside, with Capelli trailing a step behind.

Stopping at a newspaper kiosk by the front door, Rachel picked up a copy of the *International Herald Tribune* and pointed to the headline.

**'FBI and Carabinieri arrest kidnapper in Perugia;
Leads to rescue of Ambassador.'**

Everyone laughed as Captain Capelli spoke in English. "Thank God for the FBI."

THE END

ACKNOWLEDGMENTS

I want to thank my wife, Irene, for her ceaseless efforts to improve what I wrote. Her proof-reading, story line suggestions, and character critiques all helped to keep the novel focused and real. As a fellow career Foreign Service professional, Irene served with me around the world, sharing the same risks, frustrations, and exciting times.

Two friends need to be mentioned, Charlotte Grove and Larry Richter, who read my earliest manuscript and gave me their opinions on how to improve it.

My editor, Paula Howard, deserves an extraordinary thanks for reviewing my manuscript with a keen, professional eye. An extraordinary writer in her own right, she taught me how to write more effectively in order to capture the imagination of the reader.

Lastly, I want to thank The Villages Creative Writing Group for their weekly critiques of this novel.

ABOUT THE AUTHOR

During Mel Harrison's twenty-eight-year career with the US Department of State, he was presented with the Award for Valor and with the Regional Security Officer of the Year award worldwide. Serving most of his career in the Diplomatic Security Service, Mel was assigned to embassies in Saigon, Quito, Rome, London, Seoul, and Islamabad.

Prior to joining the Foreign Service, he graduated from the University of Maryland with a degree in Economics and completed postgraduate work at The American University. Following graduation, the Department of State assigned him to the NATO Defense College in Rome for political-military studies.

After leaving government service, Mel spent ten years in corporate security and consulting work with assignments often taking him throughout Latin America and the Middle East.

Now, he is writing a series of Alex Boyd thrillers based on his vast experiences in the overseas world of political and government security. Following his first novel, *Death in Pakistan,* he is releasing his second book, *The Ambassador is Missing* on June 1st. He is finishing his third book in the series to be released later this year. A fourth book is waiting in the wings.

All books are available on Amazon.com.

Made in the USA
Middletown, DE
15 June 2020